ADVANCE PRAISE FOR

A BOND OF BRIARS

"*A Bond of Briars* is a captivating fantasy retelling that perfectly honors the original account of Ruth while still creating something all its own. The use of dark magic is unique, with its consequences masterfully illustrated. The story carries a beautiful message of faith, encouraging characters to embrace light over the darkness, even when that darkness might seem alluring on the surface. The character arcs showed beautiful growth and the overarching messages of forgiveness are so important for today's world. Overall, this enchanting and uplifting tale will keep readers engaged down to the last word."

ASHLEY BUSTAMANTE, AUTHOR OF
THE COLOR THEORY TRILOGY

"Full of longing and hope, this story will sweep readers away to a magical world inspired by the book of Ruth and yet utterly unique. *A Bond of Briars* is a beautiful, moving tale of redemption, love, and true freedom."

BECKY DEAN, AUTHOR OF *LOVE & OTHER*
GREAT EXPECTATIONS

"Take a beautifully-conceptualized fantasy world full of gorgeously lush descriptions, mix in a Pride-and-Prejudice-esque romance, and center it all on a brilliant retelling of a well-loved biblical story, and you've got A Bond of Briars, an insatiable read that will keep your blood singing to the very last page!"

CHELSEA BOBULSKI, AUTHOR OF THE ALL I WANT
FOR CHRISTMAS SERIES, AND *THE WOOD*

A BOND OF BRIARS

ALSO BY ERIN PHILLIPS

A Crown of Chains
Polarity

The Indie Author's Book Launch Workbook

TALES FROM EVIRYIA
The Keeper
The Varken

A BOND OF BRIARS

BY ERIN PHILLIPS

For my husband, Jeremy,
who always loves me at my worst
and sticks by me in the storms.
Thank you for loving me like Jesus
through every moment.

And for those still searching to be fully loved.

GLOSSARY

Banntrach (bon-tre) = widow
> *plural* Banntraichean (bon-tre-ken)

Cairlich (care-lik)
> Cairlichen (care-li-ken) = people or things of Cairlich

Cairline (care-line) = a woman bonded to a spirit that lends her magic by bartering with blood
> *plural* cairlinen (care-line-n)

Càirdeas (car-giss) = affinity for a certain type of dèiligidh

Cridhe (cri-de) = heart

Croìthe (cree-heh)
> Croìthen (cree-hen) = people or things of Croìthe

Dèidh Seo (gee sho) = hereafter

Dèiligidh (die-li-gee) = deal, spell
> *plural* dèiligeadh (die-li-gee-d)
> dèiligeadh ris an diabhal = *literally* deal with the devil

Fuilneadh (fuel-ned) = a blood donor
> *plural* Fuilneaden (fuel-ne-den)

Mallachd (mal-ic) = curse

Mionn (me-on) = blood oath

Rìgh (ry) = the title for the ruler of Croìthe

Sgaoileadh (skil-lag) = someone who buys a cairline's bond from her spirit

Slàinte (slon-che) = health

Teasairginn (te-sar-gin) = a Croìthen tradition that can be evoked when a widow remarries

Thig dhòmhsa (hig dom-sa) = phrase used to summon a spirit; *literally* come to me

Author's Note: Much, but not all, of the language was derived from Old Scots Gaelic.

No *CAIRLINE* HAS THE POWER to bring someone back from the darkness.

We can make hearts love, fruit ripen, and the dead talk, but we can't bring anyone back to life. Sometimes we can keep death at bay when illness takes hold, or make *dèiligeadh*—spells and curses—but once the great darkness has taken someone, there is nothing we can do to bring them to the light again.

And as a cairline, bonded to a powerful spirit that gives me my magic, I sometimes feel as if I have already been claimed by the darkness as well. Even though my lungs breathe, my heart beats, I smell, taste, move, I feel less myself and more the spirit to which I am bonded.

Perhaps it's because the red markings that wrap around my wrists are as thin as ribbon, showing how weak my power is. If the markings were larger, like my mother's—how they dance in spikes and swirls from her fingertips all the way up to her shoulders—maybe I would feel more in control. Maybe if I had more power, I would be able to stop death itself.

Although, that is only a half-truth.

There is always a deal that can be made with a spirit.

But we cairlinen, or our clients for whom we barter, must be willing to pay the price.

So maybe it is possible to bring someone back from the darkness, but the cost would no doubt be too much for anyone to ever make the sacrifice.

It was certainly too much for me.

ONE

"CAITRIN?"

I know she's disappointed before I turn to face her, if only because she's been nothing but disappointed with me since I was a child. And recent events have probably only solidified her opinions of me.

Maybe that's why I'm really leaving the grove.

Nessa Malloch, the most powerful cairline for miles, stands tall in the doorway to my bedroom with her head cocked to the side, feigning concern as her perfume of copper, smoke, and blackberries fills the room.

She never wanted me to marry Tate in the first place and predicted he would get me killed one day by dragging me back to Croìthe with him. When he died, she assumed I would return to her. She never imagined that his death would mean losing me once and for all.

But I have been eager to be free of her for years, and Tate was supposed to be my escape from Ma, my ticket out of the grove to anywhere. Even to Croìthe. While it is the neighboring country to my home here in Cairlich, our nations have been all but enemies ever since the island first divided over magic centuries ago. But I'd chance a thousand cairline-burning radicals over a mother who sees her daughter as little more than wasted potential and bonded blood.

So even though Tate isn't here to take me away from the grove, he is still the way I am getting out.

I take a cotton, yellow dress from the old dresser and refold it hastily. "Ma, Mrs. Raeburn wants to bury her sons in their homeland. I can't very well let her go alone." I place the dress with my other clothes in the carpet bag that sits on the bed and clasp the latch closed. The room feels naked without the curtains covering the single window, and the furniture stripped and empty. It's all been packed away in a small chest for travel along with what other few belongings I own.

"Their *homeland* is Croìthe," Ma says, her words cold and stiff.

I roll my eyes. As I turn to my sewing machine on a small table, she moves toward me, and I instinctively pull back from her. When our eyes meet, I school my features into something confident and stubborn, a mirror image of her own face.

We have the same fair skin, heavy bottom lip, and wavy ginger hair a shade lighter than the color of cinnamon. Ma's clients would call me her younger sister, and she never corrected them. In her eyes, a sister was less trouble than a weak daughter. She thought she could do better than her own mother, eager to prove herself by giving birth to me, as if it would soothe her past sorrows. But I'd proven long ago that I wouldn't enhance her ego, only fracture her perfect persona.

"They kill people like us, wee hen." She tries to soften her expression as she reaches out to stroke my hair back behind my ear. I resist the fear she provokes, a lump caught in my throat as my mind threatens to recall the stories of the Sealg Dorcha, when cairlinen were hunted and burned in Croìthe.

I grab the heavy metal body of the sewing machine and heave it up against my chest, forcing my thoughts back to the present. The floorboards squeak under the weight. Either my disregard of her warning or the sudden movement causes her to pull her hand back.

After I carefully place the machine into a wooden box, I nestle the pedal, thread, and other notions beside it. "They don't kill cairlinen anymore, Ma. Anyone caught doin' magic is merely exiled now." Although sometimes a nearby cliff is the swiftest exit, but Tate had assured me that was very uncommon. I sigh, and face her straight on, my hands braced on my waist. "I'm a grown woman—"

"Eighteen is hardly—"

"—and Mrs. Raeburn is my mother-in-law, and she's a poor widow with no sons to care for her now."

Ma snorts, crossing her arms over her chest. "Meara Raeburn probably doesn't even want you goin' with her. She hates our kind." Her eyes narrow as a smirk appears on her lips. "She tells me what an abomination I am every time I make her a dèiligidh so she can talk to her pathetic dead husband's spirit. That hypocrite is only leavin' because she ran out of money."

I begin searching the room to see if I've missed anything, plainly ignoring her but not because I don't believe her. Meara has made it very clear that, even though she has been a benefactor of my mother's magic on a bi-weekly basis for five months now, she is not tainted by darkness like us cairlinen. But I imagine that's just what most Croìthen are like: self-righteous hypocrites. In my experience, that is much more straightforward to navigate than whatever manipulative affection Ma offers me.

I'll take an honest hypocrite over a lying witch any day.

"Stay here with me. I can help you grow your bond, give you purpose, make you useful."

I spin to face her as my eyes widen and my chest grows hot and heavy. "I have skill, Ma, just not the kind you care about. Or would you rather us both be naked than wear the clothes I've made for us? Or perhaps use all of Mrs. Raeburn's money to supply your closet?"

"Now you are just bein' dafty, wee hen." With gritted teeth, she grabs my wrist, holding it up in front of my face so that the black sleeve of my mourning dress falls to my elbow and reveals the thin, red ribbon of skin there. "You waste the power I've given you."

I wince, pressing my lips together as I suck in a breath. Perhaps I only summon Keres once a week—and make a deal with her less than half the time—because I am careful with my blood. Ma would have me making a dèiligidh every other day, like she does, but I prefer not to *waste* my blood for a little coin.

"Do you know how many spirits wanted to bond with you, the daughter of Nessa Malloch, the *only* cairline alive who can perform *dèidh seo* dèiligeadh strong enough to communicate with the dead?" Ma squeezes my wrist. "This was a gift, and you are not goin' to run away and leave me with nothin' in return."

I wrench my arm from her and push her away from me in one movement.

She trips backward in a daze.

Before all my courage melts, I square my shoulders, holding her gaze. "I didn't think daughters had to repay their mothers for *gifts*. Perhaps you should have made a contract with your expectations before my birth." My words sting my own heart, but as her eyes harden, I worry she isn't nearly as hurt by the truth as I am. I pick up the sewing box to give the adrenaline pulsing through my veins something to do. "I am your daughter, not your property. So if I want to go to Croìthe with my widowed mother-in-law, you're not goin' to stop me."

I walk past her, my brow furrowed. We only have a few things left to load onto the wagon; hopefully we can leave sooner than planned.

"Well, a daughter is supposed to love her ma," Ma whispers under her breath, but not so quietly that I don't hear. I stop dead in my tracks, my bottom lip quivering. If arguing is the only way to keep me here, she'll do it. "You owe me at least that."

"You don't know what love is, Ma," I say without turning to face her. "Because I tried to love you, until I learned that you weren't worth the trouble."

Her words bite back cold. "That makes two of us, wee hen."

TWO

THE GROVE IS AN ENCHANTING mess of dirt paths, ancient oak trees whose branches stretch up like fingers, and rings of fat penny bun mushrooms, with my mother's cottage and garden in the heart of the thicket. While a few other Cairlichen live in houses here and there throughout the grove, they do so only with Ma's permission.

The grove has been my whole world for almost my entire life, save for the summer I apprenticed under a seamstress in a nearby village. Ma tired of me clumsily stitching together clothing for my rag dolls and hoped some training would keep me out of her way.

Nestled on a hill in the low marshes of Cairlich, a short walk from the grove, is a small village with a tavern and several little shops, including a dressmaker.

The seamstress, Sophie Balfour, was a kind, elderly cairline, who used her bond very rarely, and only then to strengthen tired bones, she said. Instead, she found more joy in making things with her hands, rather than her blood, and it was a skill that was useful to others as well. So rather than bartering dèiligeadh for blood, she traded garments for gold.

However, Ma did not agree with Ms. Balfour, and as soon as I shared my desire to work as a dressmaker, I was forbidden from going to the village ever again. Of course, my mother would bring fabric for me to transform into clothing for the two of us, and sometimes Ms. Balfour would tuck a candy or sketch in the folds, but I never saw her again after that summer.

I figured she must have passed away when Ma started traveling to Boìrnam for cloth, but she never brought me with her. And while Ma never brought back more material than what was needed, I learned how to barter a bit of blood to make the fabric multiply or transform.

So this is the first time I've ever visited Boìrnam, and it's nothing like I could have imagined.

The town itself is larger than the entire grove and stuffed tight with cobblestone roads and buildings three or four stories tall. The trees that are scattered all over Cairlich grow thin on the outskirts of the city, or maybe they were cut down and used to build all of the shops and taverns. The babbling brook that runs through the grove broadens into a rushing river, and a wide wooden bridge stretches across it, leading from the wilds into civilization.

And there are so many people. Many more than there ever were in the grove or the little village with Ms. Balfour's shop.

Thankfully, Meara and Orla are much less shocked by the town, having both lived there before moving to the grove, searching for the famous Nessa Malloch. Orla is my sister-in-law and a widow like me, having married Meara's elder son, Ivor, who passed away days before Tate. But I'm glad to see that being near her family again has put her in good spirits.

I stay close to our Clydesdale horse, Ailbert, who pulls a little wagon carrying all of our belongings and my mother-in-law. Meara sits on the bench, her face set and somber just as it has been since the funeral. Her ashy blonde hair—which looks like it had once been as vibrant as buttercup blooms—is pulled into a tight bun at the nape of her neck, as it has been for as long as I've known her. With her arms crossed over her chest and her shoulders squeezed together, she stares directly ahead, dark circles under her eyes.

We follow behind Orla, who leads our way with a skip in her step, her sunshine-blonde hair bouncing in the cool breeze that whips through the narrow town roads. All three of us are dressed in black gowns for mourning, but only mine and Orla's are new and were made in haste. Meara threw away any colors she owned after Ivor died, returning to the mourning clothes she had worn before my marriage to Tate.

"Ma! Pa!" Orla shouts before dashing down the road ahead of us and into the arms of an older man with a round belly and round glasses. A woman drops the dirty rug she had been beating to join in the embrace. Orla's father kisses the top of her head and then pulls back, beaming before a look of sorrow crosses his face, and then he looks over at us.

"Meara, good to see you again, although my condolences," Orla's father, Mr. Turnloch, greets, extending a large hand to Meara.

She doesn't take it, and merely nods her head. "I'm just focused on getting home," she says, straightening her posture and refusing to meet his gaze.

"And you must be handsome Tate's new wife," Mrs. Turnloch says with a warm smile to break the awkward lull. She has dimples just like Orla, and both parents lack red bands of bonding around their wrists, just like her.

My stomach twists. "Yes, I'm Caitrin." I manage a polite smile in return, uncertain of what else to say, since Tate is no longer handsome, but dead, and I'm no longer a newlywed bride, but a widow. Plus, the oval talisman I hid among his ashes would dare me to believe I wasn't *Tate's wife* as much as he was *Caitrin's husband*.

"Orla!" a young boy shouts, running out from the door and wrapping his arms around Orla's middle. He barely reaches her shoulders in height, with a crop of curly blond hair. "I knew you would come back home!"

Orla tries to smile, casting a hesitant glance toward me, like I'm forcing her to come to Cròithe with us.

"Camden, bring their horse and things around back to the stables, alright, laddie? Then you can scrub up and help me with dinner," Mrs. Turnloch says, pulling the boy away from Orla and moving him to face Ailbert and the wagon.

"I'm goin', I'm goin'…" Camden says half-heartedly, swatting at Mrs. Turnloch's hands, then smiling with bright white teeth at Orla.

"You must be tired. Let's get you all settled," Mr. Turnloch says, gesturing toward the door. My eyes catch the wooden sign that sticks out over the stoop, swinging in the wind: Turnloch Bed and Breakfast.

This is where the Raeburns stayed when they first came from Cròithe. It's where Orla met and married Ivor. And where Angus Raeburn, Meara's husband, died from the same disease that took their sons.

A chill runs down my arms as I follow the others inside.

"We're only staying the night," Meara announces casually as she pulls the shawl from her shoulders.

Orla's eyes gloss over with tears when her parents cast a confused glance in her direction.

"At least, *I* am only staying tonight," Meara corrects. "These two young women, no doubt, will be able to start over plenty well here in Boìrnam."

"Mrs. Raeburn…" I start, but perhaps now isn't the time to argue. Not when Orla is looking at me with those large, pleading eyes.

"Let me show you to your rooms, and we can hear all about your plans over dinner," Mrs. Turnloch says, the cheer in her voice cracking as she forces a smile and gestures toward the staircase.

"What plans?" Meara mutters as she pushes past me. "I'm just waiting to die, too, at this point."

THREE

After cleaning up from our travel, Meara and I join Orla's family and the other guests for dinner. The smell of roasting meat and seasoned vegetables drifts from the kitchen and wafts out the open windows. The walls are painted ivy green with dark brown wooden paneling. A quaint chandelier hangs from the ceiling, which is barely tall enough to hold the fixture above our heads. The grand table stretches down the entire length of the dining room, with enough seats for at least twenty to sit comfortably. And it's almost full tonight.

Most of the guests have come from the villages scattered across Cairlich, with a handful of sailors from the ports, all in town for business, leisure, or to visit relatives. And then there are a few withdrawn from the others who sit at the foot of the table, although they don't appear to be traveling together. They hunch over their plates, making little conversation and looking over at each other and the rest of us like they're doing something criminal. Or perhaps their paranoid glances remind me of the inquisitors I'd seen in the village, hunting for a cairline who had been driven insane by the spirit bonded to her.

I shudder at the memory and how my mother laughed at the news. She mocked the woman, but behind her words was a warning: the same could happen to you.

"So you'll be off in the mornin' to Croìthe?" Mr. Turnloch wipes his mouth and mustache with a napkin, smiling lightly at me and Meara before taking another bite.

"Bright and early," Meara responds, stabbing one of the small, salty potatoes with her fork.

"Our guests down at the end there are from Croìthe," Mrs. Turnloch informs us, then lowers her voice after her husband clears his throat. "A couple of them came on the caravan that travels over the border. Perhaps you can find passage with them."

Orla is silent, all of the joy at seeing her family drained away almost as quickly as it had arisen. I'm sure all this talk of us leaving so soon doesn't help, and her resolve has cracked.

Meara grunts. "I think we'll be fine with our own wagon. Who would hurt an old woman?"

"Perhaps," Mr. Turnloch starts, and his wife puts a hand on his arm, shaking her head. Mr. Turnloch swallows the rest of his comments, and Mrs. Turnloch exits to the kitchen.

The couple had been arguing in hushed tones when I came downstairs to fetch some water for Meara. Orla should take their advice. She has a good life here and no reason to follow Meara to the ends of the earth. Not like me.

"Do you often get guests from Croìthe?" I ask out of curiosity and a desire to keep the conversation light.

"Oh yes, some of our best customers! You can't do magic in Croìthe, you know, so they have to come over the border for it. Good business for the cairlinen in town, I hear," Mr. Turnloch says casually as his wife re-enters with two steaming hot raspberry pies.

"A special treat! Made by my bonny baker-of-a-daughter here," Mrs. Turnloch announces, setting the pies down on the table. As she cuts slices and Camden serves them to the guests, delight ripples down the table. Even the Croìthen come out of their shells a bit as the tart smell fills the room.

"If only Orla was stayin'," Camden says, finally jumping up into his seat to dig into the pie. "We could open a bakery right here in the inn!"

"You just want to have cookies and sweets every day," Orla says with a twinkle in her eye.

My posture straightens. "Why *don't* you open a bakery here in Boìrnam?" I ask, continuing quickly before anyone, especially Orla, can argue with me. "We could all make a good life here, couldn't we, Meara?"

Meara is silent for a moment, but there is a lift to her eyebrows as if she is actually considering my proposal. Maybe I can keep my promise to Tate without having to follow Meara all the way to Croìthe. The Turnlochs keep their mouths shut tight, watching my mother-in-law expectantly, hopefully.

Meara takes a bite of the pie, chews, then swallows. "I can't deny it's a good fit," she finally says. "I don't know why any cairline would want to move to Croìthe in the first place."

"A cairline in Croìthe?" one of the guests at the foot of the table, a woman with black hair braided over her shoulder, speaks up. I can't tell if she's pleasantly surprised or shockingly offended. "Why would a cairline move to Croìthe?"

"Well, it's not like they're executed anymore," the Croìthen gentleman next to her argues.

"No, but how would one even hope to be accepted in Croìthen society? Why would someone move to a country where they aren't welcome?"

Moving to Croìthe is certainly not what I want, but my excuse of being a good daughter-in-law suddenly feels flimsy. "Surely you all would accept a cairline to live among you," I say, putting on my friendliest smile.

The Croìthen look away from me.

Meara huffs. "They come here for magic, just like we did," she explains, not bothering to lower her voice. "But they'd sooner be executed themselves than admit it back home."

"Well, things can change." This conundrum would be simple if Croìthen weren't so double-minded.

"But some things won't," an elderly Croìthen woman responds. Her voice is somber and her eyes darken as she meets my gaze. "Those of us who cross the border for magic are in the minority, but even we aren't ignorant of the risks we take in doing so."

"Risks? From your own people?"

The woman's eyes narrow. "Trifling with darkness is always a risk."

The condemnation in her tone, and the ignorance of her words, hang over the room for a moment. I tighten my grip on the fork. Is that what they think I'm doing when I barter with Keres for a favor? Then they are fools as well as hypocrites, for bartering with a spirit is not a trifle or dangerous.

"Well, then I think we should probably just stay in Boìrnam. Why take the risk?" I declare, refusing to look back at the Croìthen.

Orla's gaze bounces from her family to me to Meara. "You really think so?"

"Of course! Mrs. Raeburn and I can help you with the bakery, and I'm sure—"

"Yes, I think you girls should stay." Meara raises her head high, looking pointedly at Orla across from her, and then at me sitting at her side. Once she is certain she has our attention, she scoops more pie onto her fork. "It's pointless for you both to follow me. What have I or Croìthe to offer you? Surely no husbands or prospects of any kind. Certainly not like you have in Cairlich." She takes a bite of the pie as her words sink in.

"But you'll still go to Croìthe," I clarify hesitantly, all excitement draining from me.

"Of course! I must bury my family, and it's best to be home to wait out the rest of my days, long and sad they likely will be." She smiles at me as if I am a child. "No need for you to endure that as well."

I'm speechless, but I know Orla is waiting for me to accept Meara's offer, releasing us from the bonds of family duty. But I can't.

If this mionn is broken, cairline, I expect the payment you withheld from me tonight.

I manage a soft smile for Orla, but I can't meet her gaze.

"Do you mean it, Mrs. Raeburn?" Orla asks.

Meara nods, her movement solid and precise.

A squeal of glee erupts from Orla as she springs up from her chair to throw her arms around her mother. Mr. Turnloch stands, a bright smile on his face as he bows slightly to Meara in thanks, then turns to the table. "I think this news deserves a glass of sparklin' cider to celebrate!" That receives an encouraging applause from the guests.

I lean toward Meara, keeping my voice low so my words are covered by the noise. "Can I speak to you in the hall for a moment?"

She raises an eyebrow, but she isn't surprised by my request. With a sigh, she drops her napkin on the table and rises. I follow her out of the dining room, our exit hardly noticed with all of the excitement.

FOUR

"PLEASE, JUST THINK ABOUT YOURSELF, Caitrin." Meara turns to face me, her hands on her hips and her head held high, trying to make herself appear taller although she only rises to my shoulders. The light in the hallway is dim, just a sliver of the glow sneaking through the crack between the double doors. Excited voices, dreaming up a bakery for the inn, buzzes from the dining room. "I know what you are going to say, but if you come to Croìthe it will only be a burden for both of us."

"But I made a promise to Tate." It's the same thing I have been telling her for days, ever since she announced she was leaving the grove. And I can't change my story now. "And I don't have family or a trade here like Orla. I would be of much better use to you, I think."

"No trade?" Meara gestures to my dress. "You have plenty of skill. I'm sure there is a dressmaker who would hire you."

A dressmaker in Boìrnam? All of the finest ladies in Cairlich have their gowns made in Boìrnam, where there are balls and parties and festivals all year round. All the glitz and glamour I never experienced in the grove. The thought is like a dream, pulling me away from reality.

"Caitrin, you must see reason." Meara places her hands on my shoulders, and my glassy eyes refocus on her. "What is the point in coming to Croìthe? To care for an old widow? It's not as if I can bear another son to be your husband, or that you would want to wait for him to be grown enough to marry!"

I shrug off her hands, rolling my eyes. "Now *you're* being ridiculous, Mrs. Raeburn."

"I am not. I am being quite serious, Caitrin." Her face is cold and set. Even the silky wrinkles around her eyes look like stone. "Athair has not been gracious to me, never once, and I have no love left in my heart after He has taken away not only my beloved, but my sons as well. If you come with me, you will only grow bitter toward me for doing so. So don't. Let us part as friends, and you will no doubt find some happiness."

I want to consider her words. I want her offer to be real. But I don't have a choice. If I turn back now, there will be a cost greater than whatever awaits me in Croìthe.

But Meara can never know. Not any of it.

"You're wrong." I try to muster up not only the right words, but courage and conviction to go along with them. "I'm not goin' to abandon you, Mrs. Raeburn, and if you are goin' to Croìthe or across the sea or back to the grove, I'll be going right along with you. If you want to lay down and die, I'll lay down right beside you. And may Athair—" Or Keres, for that matter. "—strike me down if I break the promise I made to Tate."

She stands silent for a moment. Even with my grand speech, it all feels like a lie, lacking the truth. Yes, I will do all of those things. But not for her. To save myself.

"Why swear it to my god? You don't even believe in Athair. Do you not have devils of your own that you worship?"

One final challenge.

I take a deep breath, resisting the urge to defend myself and my magic. She doesn't want to understand cairlinen, but she does want to use us. I find some comfort in her hypocrisy. "I may not believe in him, but you surely do," I tell her, and she shifts her weight as her eyes leave mine. "Please, don't ask me to stay again."

She raises her head to look at me, resolved. "Alright. Fine. You can come with me to Soarsa. I suppose I will need some help." We both relax instinctively.

While her words raise a thousand questions in my mind, the first one to spill out is, "Soarsa?"

Meara smiles weakly. "Yes. That's the town where the Raeburn Estate is, if it still stands. And that is where my family will be buried."

FIVE

I DON'T KNOW WHAT TO expect when we arrive in Soarsa, but I'm almost too afraid to ask Meara. The journey is tiring enough for both of us that we don't bother with much conversation. But my mind is full of questions, processing not only the uncertainty of what awaits me, but grief mixed with guilt seeps through the cracks.

Yes, I lost my husband, but I don't think I ever let myself really love him. Just in case the spell wore off. I don't even know what the spell did exactly, but I had learned with that one dèiligidh to be more specific when bartering in the future.

Matters of the heart are fickle, Ma always told me. *To make a* cridhe *dèiligidh, to change someone's feelings and thoughts, is a delicate matter, for human hearts are delicate. One twist and they may shatter or turn into stone.*

I wonder if that was how her own heart became so cold.

In any case, I lost a dear friend, since I couldn't claim him to have been more with a clear conscience. The end came so abruptly that I hadn't been prepared for the violence of it. Or the feverish demands Tate would make to ease his fears and pain. Or how I would agree without a single thought to the consequences.

And now I'm a cairline in Croìthe. An outcast for certain,

regardless of whether or not I am discovered doing magic. And if the wrong person catches me bartering, I'll be exiled by law, and I don't think Meara would come with me.

What would happen then? If I part from her, but not of my own free will?

I know Keres never settles when she can have more. And in the years I've been bonded to her, she's never shown an ounce of pity. That's why I always made small deals with her. Until the night Tate died.

What conversations Meara and I do have while traveling concern keeping my bond hidden. I cannot bear to wear long sleeves while the summer heat lingers, so we agree that I should at least wear gloves, which is socially acceptable enough to not raise questions. Hopefully. I don't own any gloves of silk or lace, just a pair of leather gloves, the fingertips worn away from gardening.

Meara agreed they would do until I am able to make or buy a better pair.

Thankfully, the bands at my wrists are so thin that all it takes is a little glove to cover them. Ma was ashamed of my lack of power, but perhaps it will be a blessing given this twist in my story.

The countryside changes slowly as we climb higher from the swamps and thickets of Cairlich into the rocky hills of Croìthe, where the fields are meticulously cared for so they will thrive in harsher weather. Although we pass several small towns, Meara insists that we save what little money we have left for necessities rather than the comfort of a roof and bed.

I don't argue with her if only to keep her happy, but

sleeping under the wagon on the rocky ground does nothing to improve her mood. When I attempt to persuade her to spend a bit on a tavern room the following night, her resolve doesn't change.

"No one is going to rob an old, bitter banntrach," she says as she unrolls a blanket beneath the wagon. At least we find a willow tree just off the main road that offers more shelter and privacy than we had last night.

"What about a young one?" I counter-argue.

She shrugs. "Just show them your wrists, and I'm sure they will run screaming."

And they might run back with pitchforks and torches.

"If you are so concerned, why don't you make one of your little—" She wiggles her fingers, searching for the word. "—a talisman! To protect yourself."

I wouldn't dare contact Keres in the open like this, or with Meara spying on me.

My wrists sting at the thought, and I hiss at the sensation. I've heard of spirits begging for blood when it's been a long time between barters. And I haven't contacted Keres since the night Tate died. Still, Keres must wait until we've arrived at the Raeburn Estate. I won't risk contacting her in the wild Croìthen countryside.

Two more nights sleeping under the wagon, and then we veer off the main road, passing a quaint wooden sign that says Soarsa.

"We're almost there, Ailbert," I say, patting the horse's gray nose as I lead him forward, my heart pounding faster with each step. Walking is helping my nerves a little bit, and my backside hurts from sitting on the stiff wooden bench for so long.

"We'll have to pass through the town square," Meara says from the wagon, her posture stick-straight. It sounds more like a warning than a simple direction. She tugs at her black shawl, pulling it up over her head and throwing the ends over her shoulders. "Hopefully no one will be in the mood for gossip today."

"You think someone will recognize you?"

Meara chuckles bitterly. "I don't know which is better," she says. "To be newcomers, whom they know nothing about so they can create whatever stories about us that they wish, or to be Meara Raeburn, who ran away with her family to Cairlich only to return years later a widow with a cairline in tow."

"Or maybe we can just be ghosts. Pass through and no one will notice us."

Meara laughs, amused at my optimism. "We are dressed from head to toe in black mourning clothes with a tired horse, a half-filled wagon, and the stench of Cairlich following us. They won't think we're ghosts," she says, shaking her head as her tone grows dark. "They'll say we're demons."

SIX

UNLIKE IN BOÌRNAM, ONLY A dozen or so buildings make up Soarsa's town square, with varying heights and sizes, but they are all constructed with the same warm stone walls and wooden trusses. A large lake borders the southern rim, covered in floating flowers with long trailing stems that create a tattered blanket over the surface of the water. The lake looks dangerously close to the foundations of some of the buildings, as if it is attempting to slowly swallow up the town square.

When the dirt road transforms into carefully crafted cobblestone, Meara makes me sit with her on the bench, snapping the reins in hopes that Ailbert will quicken his steps. As we pass the first two buildings that edge the wide road, I'm hit with the warm smell of fresh bread. It reminds me of Orla's kitchen, with a fresh pie baking.

Maybe she would have liked it here after all. I almost smile.

The square isn't bustling, but several people are coming and going from the different shops and establishments. My eyes scan over the signs as Meara keeps her focus fixed, ignoring her surroundings. A post office, a town hall, a tavern, a butcher, a general store, a bakery…and then my heart fills with light.

A large window features a pretty, pastel green gown of ribbons and lace, and a painted sign above it reads Hew's

Textiles and Tailoring.

"Meara, wait here!" I nearly shout, climbing down before Ailbert comes to a full stop.

"Caitrin! Get back here!" Meara hisses behind me, but she doesn't dare raise her voice.

I don't have any money to spare. Not yet. But maybe they need another dressmaker or someone to do small repairs. Anything. I'd do anything to have a bit of my old life here.

I reach for the handle of the door just as it swings open and step back instinctively.

A young woman with straight, brown hair and pale, freckled skin steps up. Her eyes are dark and wide as she almost runs into me, folding a garment bag over her arm as the door closes behind her. Her pink dress is plain but made of quality cotton, with a white apron tied around her waist. Silver snips hang on a ribbon around her neck.

"Can I help you?" she asks gently, her eyes quickly searching me like she is looking for weapons. I feel her gaze slip over my gloved hands, and I resist hiding them behind my back.

"Do you work here?"

"Where are you coming from?" she counters. "Abercorn? Or..." Her eyes meet mine for a second, then dart to behind me, where no doubt Meara is glaring from the wagon.

I swallow. "My mother-in-law is just returning to town, but I'm trained as a seamstress if—"

"New in town?" The gruff voice, oozing with charm, comes from my right. As I turn to see who it is, my hand is snatched up and lips press against my glove-covered knuckles.

My heart skips a beat before a rush of anxiety ties knots in my stomach.

The young man is tall and thin, with a freshly shaved face that might look youthful if it wasn't for the piercing glint in his blue eyes. His blond hair is cut long, swirled and styled on the top of his head. He wears a neatly tailored green jacket with a simple shirt and tall boots.

"Yes, just lookin' for work." I pull my hand away and drop my arms to my sides, hoping the folds of my skirt hide my wrists, just in case the gloves aren't sufficient.

"Well, let me be the first to welcome you to Soarsa," he says, giving me a flourished bow. "I'm Knox Baines, at your service, and this is my sister…" He gestures to a girl on his right.

"Paisley Baines." The petite girl has bouncy, honey-colored hair and Knox's blue eyes, but she is less entertained by the mystery of a newcomer in town. She puffs out her chest—or maybe it's the large bow over the bust of her green dress that makes her look haughty—and looks at me like she's waiting for me to curtsy. "And that's Shona." Eager to fill the silence, she points to the dressmaker, her eyes wide as she studies me. Shona stiffens like she had wanted to disappear rather than be introduced.

"I'm Caitrin Raeburn—"

"Raeburn! Well, won't Father be amused." Knox laughs, smirking as he elbows his sister. She bats away his arm.

"Raeburn? I thought they moved to Cairlich." Just as the word leaves Shona's mouth, she freezes, and her gaze flicks to my wrists again.

"So you married one of the Raeburn boys, have you? Which one?" Knox pesters with questions, but it only takes one look at the wagon for him to see there are no men traveling with me. His eyebrow lifts. "Just you and the old woman then?"

"Unfortunately."

The three of them share a glance, but the paranoia and assumptions are clear when they hesitantly look back at me. The hair raises on my arms, ready for an attack.

"Are you a cairline then?" Paisley crosses her arms and steps closer to me. She quirks her eyebrow, her unblinking stare reminds me of a cat preparing to pounce.

A pair of women walking toward the general store glance over as Paisley's voice echoes through the square.

I stiffen. "Not everyone in Cairlich is bonded."

"I didn't ask about *everyone in Cairlich*. I asked about you." Paisley squints her eyes, refusing to blink. "You know what we do with cairlinen here in Cròithe, don't you, Caitrin?"

"You won't have any trouble from me." I force a smile. "I'm just here to help Mrs. Raeburn settle back down on her family estate."

Shona nearly gasps at my answer, as if it was an admission of guilt, and she steps away from me. A group of men exit from the post office, laughing jovially together. Paisley snorts, turning away from me and hurrying to join them.

A fresh smirk crosses Knox's lips as he steps up to whisper, that dangerous glint returning to his eyes. "I don't mind trouble...if it's the right kind."

"Caitrin! We still have a couple of miles to go, you know!" Meara shouts from just behind me, and I nearly jump out of my skin with relief. She places a firm hand on my arm, pulling me back a step, and grimaces as she scans over Knox and Shona with recognition. "I see Lewis Baines hasn't managed to raise a son with manners."

"Who needs manners when you have an empire to run?" Knox straightens his posture so he stands a foot taller than Meara. "My family didn't run off to marry hackit cairlinen because of a little drought, after all." He shifts his weight, folding his arms over his chest, and I almost snarl at the insult. "And that wee empire, including the Raeburn fields, well, they have been more prosperous than ever in your absence."

"I'm glad to hear it will be in such good condition when it returns to my family name."

"You expect someone to evoke a *teasairginn* for your family?" Knox asks, his eyes flickering to me as he laughs at the thought. "That tradition is for loyal Croìthen who don't run away from their country. Not to mention, it's illegal to marry bonded cairlinen." He winks at me, and I scowl instinctively in return.

Meara's hand dashes out, flicking Knox's ear. Knox gasps, his hand flying to cover the side of his head as his mouth hangs open. Shona is frozen, eyes wide and skin white.

"Maybe that will teach you some manners to go along with your empire." Meara snorts. Then, with her head held high, she nods at me in a very genteel manner. "Come along, Caitrin. Raeburn women don't waste time on dafty woppers."

With a sharp turn, she stomps back to Ailbert, and I beam as I follow her.

SEVEN

MEARA DOESN'T SAY ANYTHING AS she guides Ailbert with a firm hand on the reins, driving the wagon down a wide stretch of dirt road, past acres and acres of farmland. I had thought maybe after her encounter with Knox we would have something to bond over, but instead she seems more irritated than ever. I just hope she's not quietly fuming because of me.

The further from town we get, the more I can smell the salt in the air, and, if I listen very carefully, I think I can hear the waves crashing against the cliffs. Soarsa sits at the very edge of Croìthe, high above the sea that separates our island from the mainland. But sight of the cliffs from the main road is hidden by fields and pastures that stretch to the horizon.

When we pass a particular field, with fluffy highland cows grazing about, Meara groans, hot air coming from her nose as she pinches her lips together.

"Is something wrong, Mrs. Raeburn?"

"Those fields there, those cows…" She nods to her left. "Those are Raeburn fields and Raeburn cows. Best cattle in all of Soarsa and the surrounding villages. Not to mention our famous raspberries and rhubarb."

"Those fields belong to us? I mean, to the Raeburn family?"

Meara snickers, shaking her head. "My husband sold them to the Baines when we left. But we'll get them back." Her voice is dark, coated with determination and bitterness.

I don't know how she expects us to be able to buy them from such a wealthy family, especially if they truly are so prosperous. I spot a little calf, his hair stringy and wild, calling for his mother and stomping his hooves. The picture instantly reminds me of Knox.

You expect someone to evoke a teasairginn for your family?

"What's a teasairginn?"

"It's a Croìthen law to protect widows like us without children to carry on our family name," Meara explains coolly. "I'm too old but you…well, a teasairginn is when a single man marries a widow and takes on her family name in exchange for his own, giving up the inheritance for any heirs he may already have to pass it on to any children *she* has with him."

"I don't see how that would help us…or threaten the Baines."

Meara snorts, an amused smile crossing her lips, but she keeps her eyes fixed ahead. "With a teasairginn, the remarried widow can buy back any family land that was sold off, regardless of if the present owner wishes to sell it." Her gaze flicks my way to see if I understand, but as soon as my mouth opens, she sighs. "Although, they shouldn't be threatened. It's forbidden to marry a cairline in Croìthe."

The wagon jolts as we turn from the main road down a wide path that travels into a thicket. Perhaps the path was once better maintained, with oak trees that arch overhead, but the weeds have grown wild, nearly camouflaging the dirt ground completely. The sounds of a distant babbling creek and birds chirping fill the air as an osprey swoops past my view. It's almost like I'm back at the grove.

We may be miles away, but it's the same continent. The same island. Some things don't change, but I hope this place feels more like home than the last.

"This will take some work to restore," Meara mutters.

"I'm sure we can manage it."

"These old knees sure won't."

I chuckle, but she doesn't soften. It will cost money to hire someone to do the work, and being hired by the local dressmaker seems out of the question unless I can prove I'm trustworthy. The townsfolk have no proof I'm a cairline...but I also have no way to prove to them otherwise.

My palms start to sweat, and I pull off the gloves, irritated with the dilemma.

I look down at my wrists, which burn for me to use my power. I could start small, nothing that would cause any harm. Surely there are people here like those in Boìrnam, like Meara, who may outwardly reject magic, but secretly desire a talisman to cure aching bones or protect their flowerbeds from critters. I have always managed to barter with Keres for little favors.

Not that I've ever bartered a dèiligidh for someone else, only ever for myself, but I've heard Nessa talk business enough times to know how it's done.

Meara curses under her breath, and I look up to see the thicket has grown thin. Blocking our path is a tired iron fence, with a gate broken on its hinges and sitting half open. On the other side of the gate, the path circles around a stone fountain, which has dried up completely. What was once a quaint garden has erupted into a jungle of weeds and overgrown hedges that have conquered every inch of the grounds, swarming around the house's foundation.

My eyes widen as I lean forward, taking in the estate itself.

The manor looks like a tomb. Withered wisteria creeps out from dark, empty windows of shattered glass like black veins against cracked, grey stone skin. One of the grand double doors lays discarded atop the crumbling stairs that lead up to the entrance. There is a hole in the shingled roof, where it looks like a chimney must have caved in.

"Boggin' looters. Have they no honor in this town anymore?" Meara continues muttering as she climbs down from the wagon to force open the gate with one strong shove. Weak knees indeed.

I jump down to guide Ailbert by hand through the gate, still processing that this rubble is my new home. "How long has it been since you left? Maybe it has just decayed with time."

"Oh yes! Time has smashed the windows and torn off the doors!" Throwing her hands in the air, she lets out the rage that I assume she has been holding in for years. "I would suspect it was the birds and mice that ran off with my fine porcelain and silverware as well? And Athair himself reached down and struck the entire thing with lightning!" she shouts up at the sky. "Curse me all you want, Athair! I'll curse you right back! Until you put me in the ground just like you have everyone else I love!"

Then she collapses on the ground, her shawl catching on a thorny bush and tearing as she falls. But she doesn't notice as her wails are reduced to a quiet sob.

I'm frozen, clutching Ailbert's harness and holding his large, soft head close to me. Thankfully, he doesn't spook at her tantrum, but I am paralyzed. I don't know the right thing to do to comfort her, or maybe she would rather be given some privacy to mourn.

Then I notice she is moving her hands slowly through the weeds, ripping them from the ground and then discarding them.

Perhaps she is finally doing what she's been threatening to do for weeks: dig her own grave.

"Caitrin!"

I flinch at the sound of my name and how firmly she says it.

"Bring my family."

Without hesitation, I move to the back of the wagon and lift the crate holding three urns. The wood is worn, with sharp edges that threaten to bury splinters into my hands. I hurry to her, careful not to disrupt the urns or startle Meara with my swift obedience, and sit the crate on the ground, dusting my palms on my skirt.

"Maybe there is a shovel or…" a more appropriate burial site? Perhaps a family cemetery somewhere on the grounds.

"Leave me!" She growls. Her hands are stained by the moist dirt, which she has piled on her lap. "This is my family. It's my duty."

I go to my knees across from her, with the shallow hole between us. I reach out to help her dig. "Tate was my husband. I should at least—"

"Husband," Meara scoffs, stilling her hands and shaking her head. Then she looks up at me, her eyes red, her gaze hardened. "I've allowed you to come with me to ease your guilt, but you are not my family, and he was not your husband."

My breath is caught in my lungs. Guilt? What does she know? My lips part, but nothing comes out.

"You know the truth as well as I: Athair killed my family just for trying to survive. He cursed our land and withheld the rain for too long, and when we moved to Cairlich, he took Angus. And then Ivor married Orla, a Cairlichen, and Tate...Tate died because he married *you*. A cairline. An abomination." She looks away from me to resume her digging with more fervor. I pull my hands to my lap, every muscle in my body tense. "He punished them with death and me with living. I don't know what gives him the right!" She raises her voice, as if that will make her god hear her better. "What kind of god tests his people like that? Suffer and do not sin! Do nothing to save yourself from struggle! It's sadistic!"

"So my children aren't making up stories, I see."

Meara and I both jump at the deep, male voice, and my heart restarts with a fury. Meara twists around, the dirt falling from her lap back into the hole, to spot a man standing beside Ailbert, patting the horse's nose. Behind our wagon stand two brilliant white horses. One of the saddles is empty, but the other carries Knox and Paisley, who watch from afar with smug smiles.

The man, who I presume is their father, is tall and round, dressed in a tailored, black suit with a watch chain hanging from his breast pocket. Hidden behind a salt-and-pepper beard that matches his coifed hair is a sly smirk.

Meara hurries to her feet as recognition dawns on her, and her cheeks warm pink, although her body is as stern and proper as ever. She doesn't even bother dusting off her skirt.

I stand more slowly, uncertain if this man is a threat or not. Judging by his relations though, I don't expect his visit to be one of pleasantries.

His eyes move to my wrists with amusement, and I flinch, realizing I'm not wearing my gloves. Quickly, I tuck my hands behind my back.

"Lewis Baines." Meara sighs dramatically. "I hope you're coming to deliver your condolences."

"Oh, of course!" He smiles widely, placing a hand on his heart and bowing slightly. "So sorry for your loss, Meara."

"Meara! I am not the woman who left Soarsa all those years ago, Lewis." Meara raises her head and takes a slow breath. "Meara is gone. You can tell the gossipers in town that she is dead like the rest of my family."

Mr. Baines gives an amused chuckle. "If Meara is dead then who are you?" His eyes sparkle, brimming with suggestions.

"Muireall. Meara is gone. I will go by Muireall now."

I look to Meara. Is she being serious? And yet the name came to her so easily, as if she had been planning to change it for longer than a few moments.

"Of course. A bitter name suits a banntrach like yourself."

Though Meara—Muireall is certainly more than a foot shorter than Mr. Baines, the way her gaze narrows as she looks at him down her nose adds inches to her height.

Mr. Baines steps closer as he slips his hands into his pockets casually. "When my children told me you had returned with a cairline in tow, I thought surely they were making up stories!"

"They are known to lie on occasion," Muireall says.

Mr. Baines' eyebrows bounce with contempt, but he restrains a retort. "Well, glad to know you have returned to your…home safely. I don't expect you returned having doubled your fortune?"

"Did you not see the piles of gold in our wagon?"

He ignores her comment and looks up at the manor, glee covering his expression. "Well, I bought those fields with more than a pretty penny. Not sure what you wasted it away on in Cairlich."

"Trying to save my family from dying, for one," Muireall says coldly, crossing her arms over her chest.

Nodding, Mr. Baines puts a hand to his mustache for a moment, as his eyebrows raise.

"I can see where Knox gets his manners from…or lack thereof," Muireall presses, her eyes narrow and hard.

"Frankly, Meara—"

"Muireall. But it's Mrs. Raeburn to you."

"—your whole family died the day you abandoned Soarsa. I bought that land not because we were doing well—everyone was struggling, not just your family—but I'd hoped the extra gold would give your family a means to return. Not stay in that hackit land until everything was gone." He takes another step forward. "And if you have half a mind to foolishly try to marry off your little cairline in hopes of evoking a teasairginn, think twice. You won't be reclaiming your fields without a full payment, as tradition demands."

Muireall doesn't flinch. "Oh, I haven't forgotten, Lewis."

"It's Mr. Baines," he corrects, with a nod of his head, shifting his attention to me. "And you should watch yourself, cairline. No one is going to come after you, unless you're caught creating dèiligeadh. I suggest you keep that darkness in the dark. Because if it's brought to the light, well..." He chuckles. "We Croìthen protect our own, at any cost."

"Take your mirth and your charity and get off my property, Lewis," Muireall snaps, and I'd almost believe she was defending me if she hadn't so fervently disowned me just before our uninvited guest showed up.

"Of course," Mr. Baines agrees, retreating back down the overgrown path with long strides and an arrogant smile.

Muireall spins towards me. Now it's not only her eyes that are red but her entire face. She won't meet my gaze, looking past me at the manor. And then she grabs the crate as if it weighs nothing and stomps away. However, instead of going to the manor entrance, she rounds the corner, making for the back garden.

EIGHT

Behind the crumbling manor is a small pond in the center of a sprawling garden with a little stone wall bordering the edge of the estate property. To the right sits a small barnyard I assume had once housed chickens but is now vacant and decaying. I hope it will be good enough for Ailbert until we can fix it up. I unharness him from the wagon and guide him to the pen as I look over the rest of the grounds.

There is a little gazebo next to the pond that looks like it had once been perfectly white, ideal for afternoon tea or parties, but it has since chipped and rotted. I'm almost surprised it is still half-standing, with withered wisteria climbing up the columns to the collapsed dome roof. On the far side of the pond is a cluster of trees, nestled up against the short wall; through the leaves and branches, I can just barely make out the farmlands that had once belonged to the Raeburns.

Muireall is stomping her way through the garden, in between the overgrown hedges, untamed topiaries, and flowering bushes that surround the pond. I look ahead of her trail, spotting stone through the flora, and my eyes light up. A cottage. A little garden cottage! Hopefully it is in better condition than the manor.

I remove the reins from Ailbert and set him free to rest in the small pen after making sure the fence is secure enough. Although, he is probably too exhausted to wander away. Taking what is left of his feed from the wagon, I set the bag just inside the dingy barn.

Once I'm confident he is properly cared for, I grab our two bags from the wagon and make my way to the cottage. It's more of a challenge than I had expected, with all of the thorny branches grabbing at my dress and hair and the sudden movement of critters against my boots. I hold my skirt wrapped around my legs to keep it from catching.

Task one: clear a path to the cottage. Surely there is something around here I can use to dig up these weeds and cut down these thorns. Maybe in the barn.

"Bowfin birds! Get out of here!" Muireall shouts from the cottage as a couple of robins come flying out of the open door, tweeting as they escape. The cottage is built from a collage of mismatching stones, with a brick chimney and brown shingles that look relatively undamaged. Especially when compared to the manor. Ivy has climbed all the way up and into the chimney.

The green paint is peeling off the shutters on the windows, with wisteria dripping around the frames. A wild rose bush is nestled right up against the cottage, so one could reach through the window and pluck a blossom without stepping a foot outside.

Muireall comes out of the front door, coughing as she shakes out a rug. Dust poofs into the air, surrounding her and drifting out over the pond. "Well, come help me clean up this place a bit!"

I jump over the last few bushes to the door and follow her inside.

"This was the guest cottage. I suppose the looters didn't notice it as worth anything," Muireall says as she lays the rug on the ground and pulls a dusty sheet from a small sofa that faces a fireplace on our left. Opposite the sitting area is a small kitchen, all squeezed up against one wall with cabinets, a counter, and an old rusty stove and sink. A little round table with two chairs fills the remaining space.

Muireall flings open the cabinet doors, inspecting the contents. Mice seem to have gotten any food that was left, but a simple dish set looks undisturbed. She starts stacking the plates and cups on the counter. "These will all need to be washed."

There is a small archway that leads to a narrow hallway with two doors at each end and one in the middle. The first door reveals a coat and linen closet that is mostly bare. The second door, to my relief, is a tiny washroom. Wisteria climbs in through the open window shutters, sinking down into the stout bathtub and filling it. The tub is cozy for certain, and stained with mildew, but at least it looks like it will work after a good cleaning. A little toilet and sink are shoved next to it.

Behind the last door, at the end of the short hallway, is a small bedroom with one bed, a sitting chair, and a dresser. Ivy has overtaken the chair, wrapping around the bedframe, and draping down to the wooden floorboards. The bed is covered with a sheet, which I pull off and wind into a wad, revealing a pretty, yellow quilt of eyelet lace and embroidered flowers with a matching pillow. The crate of urns is shoved in the corner.

I guess I'll be sleeping on the sofa then.

Leaving her bag on the bed, it takes only a few steps to be back in the main living space, where Muireall has rolled up the black sleeves of her mourning dress and emptied most of the cabinets. I set my carpet bag on the sofa and take a deep breath. The musty scent of dust coats my lungs.

"Would you like me to—" I cough to clear my throat.

"Of course, of course," Muireall says, slouching into one of the wooden dining chairs. She rests her forehead in her hands, then wipes her hands over her face. "It'll take a lot to get this entire estate back in order."

"I'm sure we'll manage with a bit of time and some hard work," I say, trying my best to be optimistic, although I feel completely overwhelmed when I glance out the window toward the garden and manor.

"And money," Muireall says, her voice dry. She shifts her head slightly to the side, studying me for a moment. "But you can probably help with that, can't you?"

"I can try, although…" I hold up my wrists, reminding her of my bands. "I'm not sure who will hire me once Mr. Baines spreads the word."

Standing, she takes my wrists firmly in her hands. "No, exactly." Her brown eyes dark and set. "You can just *make* us some money, can't you? A nice little dèiligidh to get us on our feet."

Slowly, I start to pull my hands from her, but she moves her grip to my fingertips. "It's not that simple. If I had a job, maybe I could create a favor to get a raise or…" My words trail off, hoping she doesn't realize my inexperience when it comes to dèiligeadh. "But maybe I could make one to increase our favor in town? So that people don't mind that I'm bonded?" Of course, that kind of dèiligidh would no doubt be rather costly.

Muireall releases me, turning away with a wave of her hand. "I doubt you are powerful enough to change their minds on that, lass," she says with a snort. "Croìthen have stubborn hearts."

"So I've noticed, Muireall." Her new name is bitter on my tongue, sour and wrong.

She raises an eyebrow. "Yes, well. We'll think of something." Muireall glances back to my wrists, then meets my gaze once again. "I don't suppose you could help me contact my husband, could you?" It's not a question of willingness, but of ability. And I'm not nearly powerful enough to contact the dead. I hope I will never be that strong.

The sacrifices my mother made to gain that kind of power...

"I think we both need some rest."

She notes my deflection with a 'hmm'.

"After we get cleaned up and this place put in order, I'm sure we'll be able to come up with some solutions."

"Solutions for a curse?" Muireall asks despondently.

"We're not cursed," I say with a smile, hoping to lighten the mood.

She laughs and rolls her eyes. "You're a cairline, and my husband and both my sons are dead. We're *both* cursed, Caitrin, there is no denying it; just not in the same way."

NINE

TAP. TAP. TAP.

I flinch at the soft sound, refusing to open my eyes as I curl up tighter under the quilt. My head is foggy and my shoulders ache from the scrunched-up position I slept in. But I'm not ready to wake up quite yet.

Tap. Tap. Tap.

I peel open one dreary eye to catch the blurry sight of the morning sun peeking in through the shutters. The tapping is probably just a woodpecker or a squirrel. I wiggle to roll over and face away from the light, and something brushes against my nose. I sniff against the tickling sensation. And then it comes again.

Tap. Tap. Tap.

Something flutters against my eyelids. I open one eye as I swipe my hand toward whatever is bothering my slumber and come face to face with another set of tiny eyes.

With a yelp, I fall backward and straight onto the floor with a *thump!* The brown moth takes flight, drifting drunkenly toward the crack of sunlight.

"Meara? Everything sunshine-y in there?" says a woman's muffled voice from the front door, followed by the now-familiar, insistent knocking.

I stand quickly, taking one step toward the door before freezing as the image of my current appearance pops into my mind: a young woman with knotted bed head hair and dark circles under her eyes wearing only a chemise.

Blushing at the almost-embarrassment, I call out "one moment!" and turn to face the sitting room, searching for something to improve my current state.

"Meara? Is that you?"

Pulling open my carpet bag, I fetch out my yellow dress and pull it over my head quickly before running my hands through my hair. My fingers don't make it through all the knots, so I tie a linen handkerchief around my head instead. With one huff of a breath to calm myself, I put on my best, most hospitable "please don't chase me out of town" smile, and reach for the handle.

It's only then that I see my bare wrists and panic seizes my heart, squeezing my lungs so that I can't breathe.

I turn to grab my gloves, but the door swings open all on its own.

Spinning to face the intruder, I tuck my hands behind my back and shrink away.

"Meara?—Oh!" Two elderly women stand at the door. While they differ almost entirely in appearance, they each have a basket looped over an arm with brown aprons tied over their plaid dresses.

"Mrs. Raeburn—she goes by Muireall now—she's still asleep, I believe." My heart is still hammering in my chest. Perhaps I should wake up Muireall. Or maybe she is already awake and I just haven't noticed. I've only just woken up myself. I glance over my shoulder at the darkened hallway.

"Oh! Then you must be Caitrin, her daughter-in-law?"

I snap my attention back to the women, eyes wide, worried about what else they've heard. "Yes, that's me."

"What a bonny lass you are!" one woman says as she extends her hand with a warm smile on her face. She is short and plump, as if inches of her height migrated to give her body more softness over the years. Her white hair is pulled to the side in a thick braid, with loose curls that lay against her fair skin, which winkles around her eyes, cheeks, and neck. "I'm Vaila, sweetheart."

I stare at her hand, not wanting to be rude but not wanting to expose my bond either. It would be nice to have a couple people who didn't judge me so quickly for something so little.

Instead, I offer the widest, toothiest grin I can and bend my knees in a slight curtsy. "Pleased to meet you."

"Such a lady," the other woman comments. The opposite of her companion, she is tall and lithe, standing with stiff proper posture. Her gray hair is curly and fluffy, like a cloud that crowns her head, with sparkling hazel eyes that are bright against her honey-brown skin. Rather than offering her hand, she simply nods her head. "And I'm Yvaine."

"We were just making our way to the fields and thought you and Meara would want to join us," Vaila says, glancing toward Yvaine with the first hint of discomfort.

"The fields?" I twist my fingers together behind my back, wishing Muireall would hear us chatting and rise from her bed already.

"Yes! Oh, she must not know, I suppose, being new to town

and all." Vaila's voice is warm and full of excitement.

Yvaine clears her throat in preparation of a thorough explanation. "Tradition is that widows may glean from the fields, to gather the leftovers for ourselves. Of course, not many of the landowners around here care much for such sacrificial kindness anymore, not that it would be particularly safe for a bonny lass such as yourself if they did."

"Although they seem happy to let the produce sit there and decay!" Vaila interjects with a strong finger pointed in the air.

"Well, yes, some of the fruits may have rot or worms." Yvaine scrunches up her face in a very animated fashion as if I am a child she is telling a fairy tale to. I giggle, amused by her effort. "But you learn how to cut out the bad and keep the good with time. Fortunately for the four of us, the Lockharts are just as generous as ever! We are allowed to take anything that is unharvested. Bas-kets!"

Yvaine gestures to Vaila, who picks up two extra baskets and holds them out to me. "Come join us!"

I smile appreciatively, clenching my hands against my back and glancing toward to the hallway. "I shouldn't accept until I've spoken to Muireall about it."

"Oh!" Vaila pulls the baskets back to herself, the three baskets cumbersome in her arms. "Well, if you decide you want to join us, I'm sure Muireall remembers the way. Ask Brodie when you get there and he will tell you what field we are in."

"The orchard maybe. Some apples have probably fallen by now," Yvaine suggests.

Vaila brightens at the idea. "Maybe the orchard!" Then, she drops the two extra baskets on the stoop. Or maybe she had intended to set them down. "If you decide to join us. Figured you might need a sturdy basket or two."

"Thank you again," I say, bowing my head. Although, was I thanking them again or for the first time?

"Of course, darling."

As I look up, the two women wave politely, then turn arm in arm to help each other navigate the overgrowth. I close the door carefully and then press my back against it for a moment. They don't seem too bad? Certainly kind, and if they are suspicious about my origins, they hid it well.

Snatching my gloves from the kitchen counter, I go to Muireall's bedroom, knocking softly on the door before pushing it open. "Mrs. Raeburn?" I whisper.

She groans and turns away from me in the bed, causing a great deal of squeaking. "I'm still sleeping," she mumbles. "There's nothing for me to do here but sleep anyway. Sleep then die."

I bite my lip. She's in a foul mood this morning. "Well, we can also harvest some produce from a nearby field. Yvaine and Vaila just came by to invite us—"

With another groan, she looks over her shoulder at me. Her ashy hair is a frizzy mess, and her face is pale, making her wrinkles seem even more pronounced than usual. "They still do that around here?"

I shrug. "I guess so."

"Hmm…well, if Yvaine and Vaila will be there, it must be safe." She flops back down onto her pillow. "Just don't get us banned from gleaning."

And then she snores, already asleep again. Or maybe it's a

show to get me to leave. Either way, I close the door.

Maybe a bit of a walk and some productive labor would do me good. It sure beats waiting on Muireall hand and foot when she's grumpy.

I splash my face with water, then brush my hair and pull it back with a ribbon. After I lace up my boots and put on an old apron, I pick up the two baskets left at the door.

Which way? Muireall didn't give me directions.

I doubt she will help me in her current state, but I'm not completely resourceless.

Setting the baskets down again, I grab the small knife I have hidden in my boot. It's a primitive-looking thing with a crude, narrow blade, and leather straps wrapped and tied for a handle. It's too bright to summon Keres for a real dèiligidh, but hopefully she is listening since it's still early morning.

I part the weeds and kneel at the edge of the pond. "*Thig dhòmhsa*," I whisper as I prick the tip of my pointer finger, letting a drop of my blood fall into the water. "Just tell me which way the women went."

The droplet causes a tiny ripple in the water, and I watch it for a sign, but the ripple seems untainted by magic.

"Keres…" I hiss, clenching my jaw as a dark urge fills me, and I know the price she wants. With a sigh, I relent, and give her two more droplets of blood. The ripples begin to bounce across the surface of the water with a red tint, creating a wave that splashes against the western edge of the pond. "Thank you."

Standing, I shove the knife back into its hiding place and tug on my gloves. I wince at the slight pressure against the small wound, but it will heal by the time I reach the fields.

Keres had better not be playing a trick on me. I gave her more than enough of my blood for some simple guidance. It was hardly magic at all.

TEN

ONCE I REACH THE MAIN road, I turn left in the opposite direction of the town square. The walk gives me time to really wake up, even though a slight throbbing in my head refuses to go away. If Yvaine and Vaila are right, I should be able to gather enough for Muireall and myself to get by for a few days while we figure out how to make some money.

While I have no idea how we will *ever* get enough to restore the estate, we can certainly improve our situation at the cottage. I would love to at least have a proper sleeping arrangement. Maybe Muireall will let me convert the sitting room into a private space for myself.

Off to my left, a crab apple orchard stretches out in neat rows, their fluffy leaves packed full of small, red fruit. What a sight it must be in the spring when the trees bloom. The orchard goes on for what seems like miles, rolling across the uneven ground into the horizon. A sweet scent mixes with the salty sea breeze that carries from the cliffs, just out of sight on my right, behind an enormous cornfield.

I skip a step forward, beaming with pride. I can take care of myself. If Muireall wants to stay in bed and waste away, that is her choice, but I plan on making something of myself here. Somehow.

Rather than climbing over the simple wooden fence and taking a shortcut through the orchard, I stay on the main road. I want to do things as properly as possible, to make the best impression. The wide, gravel path that leads into the Lockhart Estate is trimmed with the curtains of willow trees and the blooming of white gladiolus and dahlia flowers. It feels natural, and yet well-maintained at the same time. Sunlight peeks through the willow leaves dancing in the wind.

I can almost imagine taking a carriage down this path and arriving at a grand palace for a masquerade. Of course, in my current state, I'm more likely to be a servant at a ball than an attendee, but that makes the dream of looking like a princess and fitting in with society here all the more desirable.

Wishful thinking, but I don't banish the thought.

After all, isn't that what cairlinen do? We make wishes come true.

Quickening my pace, a large fountain comes into view, and the gravel path curves around it, then off to the side, no doubt to a stable elegantly tucked out of sight. And my vision is filled with the Lockhart Mansion.

Or maybe they call it the Lockhart Castle.

It is no doubt the biggest building I've ever laid eyes on, and it's hard to imagine what one would do with so much space. White-washed stone walls climb up three stories, with a huge double-wide door at the front. Large, arching windows line the first floor, and the roof is steep, topped with chimneys and spiked snow brackets. It looks like it was designed with great detail and maintained with as much care.

The curtain in one of the second-floor windows moves,

drawing my attention immediately. In the window is a woman with dark brown hair, piled in curls on top of her head, wearing a pale gown. She stares back at me from the shadows, and, instinctively, I bow my head.

When I look back up, the light fabric of the curtain is swaying, covering the window once more. Was she waiting for me, or drawn by my uninvited appearance? Is the woman still watching me?

I'd better hurry before someone withdraws the invitation to glean.

A gardener is tending a flowerbed of begonias and heathers, but not another soul is in sight. Fields stretch out to my right, and a horse pasture sits to my left, with the apple orchard just beyond. There must be a magnificent garden around back, and I can't even imagine what the inside…

I'm not here to gawk.

Tearing my gaze from the mansion, I walk toward the gardener. "Excuse me? I'm looking for someone named Brodie?" I say, trying to be as polite and cordial as possible.

The servant doesn't look my way, keeping his head buried in the plants, but points with his spade toward the stable tucked on the other side of the wall of willow trees.

"Thank you." Without bothering him further, I pick up my skirt and hurry toward the stable.

Stepping through the large, open double doors, the salty smell of Soarsa is overwhelmed by that of hay and leather. The stable alone must be large enough for over a dozen horses. It's wide and well insulated, painted completely white with not a single nail loose. Atop a tall ladder sits a loft overlooking the stalls. Everything is in such perfect order.

I tug at my gloves, making sure my bands are sufficiently covered, and cling to an optimistic attitude.

"Ah! There you are, miss." A young man pokes his head out of one of the stables with a smile, then ducks back out of sight. "I heard you might be coming around here."

"From Yvaine and Vaila?" I clarify hopefully.

"Aye!" he shouts, and then emerges from a stable with a beautiful black stallion in tow.

I take a step back. While Ailbert is sturdy and strong, even he would be dwarfed by this creature.

"Don't be too scared! He's only feisty when there's a bonny wee filly to impress," the man says, patting the horse's neck firmly. He can't be older than seventeen, or at least he has a very youthful face and a noticeable lack of facial hair. He is stocky with arms strong enough to handle even this giant stallion, although he barely reaches my nose in height.

"Are you Brodie?"

"That's me! Here to help banntraichean like yourself."

"Banntraichean!" I almost laugh at the archaic word. Or maybe at it's being used to describe myself. "I may be a widow, but Yvaine and Vaila, they are banntraichean. I think someone should have to be at least…fifty to be called a banntrach."

"So when you're no longer young enough to marry again, you say?" He ties the stallion to a hitching post and then retrieves a blanket, situating it on the horse.

My mouth gapes open. "I didn't mean to imply—that is, older women can certainly…"

"Ah, it's only a little tease, miss…" He gestures for me to

fill in the gap with a proper introduction.

"Caitrin Raeburn." I push a loose curl behind my ear. "Mrs. Raeburn is my mother-in-law, you see."

"So you're the Cairlichen everyone is talking about." He speaks so casually, as if we are making nothing but small talk. There are no curious glances at my wrists or even a suspicious lilt to his voice.

"Yes, that's right."

The young man turns his back to me, and I prepare for the rejection, for the warnings, for the condemnation. My spine straightens, my muscles stiffen. He grabs something and turns to face me, that same pleasant smile on his face, slightly strained from the weight of the saddle in his hands. "Quite a change of scenery, ain't it?"

"A little…" My brow furrows for a moment before I lick my lips. "So Yvaine and Vaila said that I could come and glean? Is that for anyone? Even if…I mean…I'm not *from here*."

Brodie chuckles lightheartedly, his smile growing wider. "Of course! The Lockharts are very determined to keep up the old traditions."

"That is very charitable of them, but I don't want to impose if the tradition doesn't extend to…" I swallow back the words *cairlinen* and *Cairlichen*. "…foreigners."

"To foreigners especially!" Brodie exclaims. With a heaving grunt, he lifts the saddle onto the beast's back and begins securing it around his belly. "You are welcome to anything left on the ground, whether dug up from the soil and left behind or fallen too early. Take what you need. Yvaine and Vaila can show you how it's done."

"And where are they now?"

"The orchard last time I saw them!" He awkwardly squats beside the horse, who stomps his foot impatiently. "Whoa there! I'm still down here, sir!" Brodie tells the stallion. "You can cut through the pasture that way, Miss Raeburn!" Brodie points out the other side of the barn without looking up at me, focused on his task.

"Thank you." I hastily curtsy, not wanting to neglect my manners. Hurrying through the stable, I take a path that cuts the pasture in two, leading straight to the apple orchard. I feel a bit foolish running around someone else's property alone, just taking whatever I find left behind.

I certainly don't want to be caught and accused of stealing.

"Caitrin! Well look there, Vaila, she did decide to join us."

Once I reach the far side of the pasture, I find the two women sitting under a tree, enjoying the late morning sun. Their baskets are already full of apples.

"You two work quickly, I see!" I'd only just met them an hour earlier, and yet the sight of them puts me at ease immediately. It almost feels like magic. If we weren't in Croìthe, I'd guess that they had calming talismans on them somewhere.

"Well, we didn't have to walk all the way like you did, by the look of that dirt on your hem." Yvaine winks at me playfully. "Brodie gives us a ride three times a week. I doubt we could make the journey and still have the energy to gather food otherwise!"

I smile, tempted to sink down on the ground beside them for a nap. But I have work to do. There will be plenty of time to rest when I'm back at the cottage.

"Yes, it's very kind of Lord Lockhart to lend us Brodie." Vaila's eyes are closed, the sunlight falling over her face. "And he would've given you and Meara a ride as well—" she peels open one eye, making sure it's only me present, then closes it again. "—if she'd joined you."

"I'll definitely take that offer next time. And she goes by Muireall now."

"What a strange bird she is," Vaila says, shaking her head. "But I'll try to remember if she ever comes out of that cottage again."

I look down at my empty baskets, feeling rather lost in comparison to their full ones. And Muireall and I need more than apples ideally. "So how does this work?"

"That's what we are here for," Yvaine says, grunting as she sits up and uses the tree to stand upright. "Come along."

Vaila stays on the ground, leaning back contently, waving for me to follow Yvaine.

Yvaine leads me into the orchard a few rows in deep concentration, her head turning side to side, systematically scanning every square inch of the ground. "We've cleared just a bit of this-ah! There we go!" She hops forward a step and bends to pick up a small red apple from the grass. With a proud smile, she holds it up for me to see. "Found it on the ground, so I can take it. And so can you."

She tosses it to me, and I clumsily catch it, my thumbing into a large, brown squishy spot. My nose scrunches up, and I drop the apple into one of my baskets if only to stop holding onto it.

"That will clean out easily. But it does mean you need twice as many apples for one pie," Yvaine says, nodding her head like a dutiful teacher. Then she points up into the branches of the tree. "But that shiny, red one there, that one we must leave to be harvested and sold."

"It's that simple?"

"That simple!" Yvaine raises her head with a twinkle in her eyes.

She's the kind of mother-in-law I wish I had. Surely, a *mionn* that bound me to her would be no burden at all. Maybe she can give Muireall some pointers.

"I think I can manage that."

"You certainly can," Yvaine says, patting my shoulder. "And Brodie can help you too, once he returns from taking us home, that is."

She walks past me, heading back to Vaila, who has now stood, cradling her basket in her arms like it's a babe.

I spin, following a couple steps after her. "You're leavin'?" My limbs stiffen. I haven't had time to gather anything! I can't leave with them yet, but staying here alone seems equally unfavorable. And yet as I remain frozen, I realize that soon I will be very much alone. Maybe it's for the best. After all, as kind as these elderly women are, their warmth will surely vanish if they discover my secret.

Best to not get too close to either of them.

The thought does little to comfort me.

"You'll be perfectly fine, dear. The Lockhart Estate is the safest place for a young woman like yourself," Vaila calls back to me.

"We'll join you again in two days. Bright and early," Yvaine adds cheerfully, before taking up her own basket.

With an encouraging wave, they start off for the stable, leaving me alone with two baskets and one half-rotten apple.

ELEVEN

I don't know how much time passes as I fill my basket. Thankfully, the wind whistling through the orchard and the chatter of birds calm any nerves, and a simple contentment settles over me as I search for fallen apples. Once this basket is full, then I can try to find what other fields are in season for harvesting. And should Brodie or the Lockharts change their minds about me, hopefully I will be able to escape with at least the apples.

Looking down at the basket, I count eight. I found more than eight but had decided that only these eight were salvageable. Although I think my standards may be dropping the more I search. At first, one blemish was all I would allow, but now half the apple could be mushy and brown and I'd still take it.

My stomach grumbles as a warm breeze rushes over me, rustling the tree leaves and shaking a shiny red apple, hanging on a low branch. It looks utterly perfect and delicious. And as I watch it sway, I start to imagine it snapping off and falling right into my hands. The perfect noontime snack. Or lunch, in my case.

Walking over to the apple, I don't take my eyes off it, almost salivating at the thought of biting into it. Perfect,

unbruised, and whole. I won't take it right from the tree—
that's forbidden—but if I just happen to be standing nearby
when it dropped all on its own, that would certainly be
permissible.

"Usually banntraichean struggle to pick up apples from the
grass, much less reach up into the branches themselves."

My eyes go wide, realizing I had stretched out my hand,
and draw it to my chest quickly. Will I be kicked out for *almost*
breaking the rules? "I wasn't going to—" I spin, dropping both
baskets to the ground as my heart races, eager to defend myself.

I swallow my words at the sight of the stranger. He's taller
than me, but not by too much, with dark brown hair that is a
little wild and a little long, covering his ears and falling over his
forehead. A bit of scruff edges his jaw. He is dressed simply in
a linen shirt, the sleeves rolled up and a few buttons undone at
the neck, with a tailored woolen grey vest, and durable, brown
farmer's breeches. His hands are tucked into the back pockets.

But it's the curiosity in his green eyes and the hesitant yet
wistful smirk on his lips that make my mouth go dry. I flush
with embarrassment, my gaze dropping to my gloved hands.
Then I spot the basket which has tipped and spilled the apples
at my feet, fresh bruises on the skin.

Only half of the halves are probably usable now.

Any surprise, embarrassment, or fear inside melts into
something new: irritation.

I take a deep breath, reminding myself that this is charity,
and this man may very well be the manager of the orchard, or
maybe even the Lord's own family. A spoiled brat here to taunt
the unfortunate, like Knox and Paisley Baines.

With my head held high, I look up at him and boldly hold his gaze.

"Brodie said you're Meara Raeburn's daughter-in-law?"

A sliver of anxiety returns, but I keep it at bay by focusing on exuding confidence. "Yes. I'm Caitrin, but Mrs. Raeburn's husband and sons died in Cairlich. That's why she moved back. And she goes by Muireall now." I don't know if I should curtsy or something, so I force my hands to rest against my sides and stand tall, proud. I have nothing to be ashamed of, after all.

"Right, from Cairlich." His eyes drift toward my hands, but they don't linger once he sees my gloves. He shifts his weight, rubbing his neck as he looks away for a moment. "Sorry about your husband."

I smile apologetically, and then realize that's the wrong way for a mourning widow to respond, although I don't think I could fake tears. "I'll pass on your condolences to Mrs. Raeburn." That also seems like the wrong thing to say. He squints and his lips part, but he doesn't respond. I should just change the subject. "I wasn't going to take it, by the way. The apple. I know I'm not supposed to."

He walks toward me, closing the polite distance between us. "I'm not here to kick you out over an apple," he says with a chuckle. "Brodie told my mother you were in our orchard alone, and she wanted to make sure no one was bothering you out here."

"*Your* orchard?" I swallow and curtsy, hoping to make a good impression before he makes up his mind about me. "Um, thank you for your charity, sir."

Twisting his head to the side, he almost laughs, but he restrains himself. "Callen, actually."

"What?" My brow furrows in confusion.

His smile droops to one side, stretching out his hand to me. "My name's Callen." I hesitantly offer my hand, uncertain if he will shake it or kiss it. His grasp is firm and confident, almost as if I were some wealthy equal. "Lord—not sir—Callen Lockhart, although I don't care much for formalities."

I try not to act too surprised, or worried, as I pull my hand away from him. His smile falters. "Well, thank you for your charity," I say, not meeting his gaze again. Chewing my lip to keep myself from saying anything embarrassing, I spot the apples and baskets on the ground. "I should really..." Crouching low, I start to gather the apples back into the basket, doing my best not to grimace at their increasingly damaged state.

His hand meets mine as I reach for the fruit, and I spy a sliver of red at my wrist. I grab the apple quickly and hide it and my hand in the basket, looking up to see Callen bent down beside me. His gaze flickers up to mine, then he grabs another apple and stands, examining it. I hurriedly collect the remaining fruit into my basket and rise, waiting to receive the last one from him.

"This hardly seems of Lockhart quality," he says, before chucking the apple past me. I glance over my shoulder and watch the brownish-red ball disappear into the distance, my heart nearly sinking at the sight.

Then a hand reaches past my head, and I stiffen at our close proximity. I'm too frozen to step away from him, and I flush as he leans forward, his gaze fixed behind me, but I can feel his breath on my cheek. I look down at the curve of his collarbone and the collar of his shirt. A hint of hazelnut mixes with the fresh air.

I blink, and a red apple fills my vision.

The apple from the tree. Freshly plucked.

"Here," he says. I glance up to see an almost boyish grin cross his face. I hesitate, my brow furrowing in confusion, but I can't resist a small smile. "I'm sure we can find a dozen or so perfect Lockhart crab apples for you to take back to Mrs. Raeburn." He gestures to my basket full of rotting fruit. "Your mother-in-law would certainly have my head if I sent you home with that scrabby scran."

I know the rules; Yvaine and Vaila had explained them to me very well. I shake my head. "Oh no. This is fine. We can't really afford to pay for—"

"I don't intend for you to pay." He is so sincere that I almost believe him. "You were told that we give banntraichean food for free, weren't you? Perhaps I should give Brodie clearer instructions."

"Yes, I was told...charity for widows...but..." But if Ma taught me anything, it's that there is a cost for everything. Maybe it won't be money or even something required immediately. It might be a favor in the future, something you never even agreed to. A good cairline knows to never make a deal without knowing the cost first.

If this mionn is broken, cairline, I expect the payment you withheld from me tonight.

I've already made that mistake once. Twice would no

doubt be deadly.

"Your family is *very* generous." I don't mean to be patronizing, but his frown makes me nervous. Or maybe I just miss his smile. I clear my throat. "But I don't want to impose on you any further than I clearly already have."

"It's no imposition at all. Plus, even if Mrs. Raeburn wouldn't scold me for such poor-quality fruit, my own mother certainly would."

I force a polite grin, certain the growing knot of tension in my stomach must be obvious as his eyes narrow slightly.

"I'm sorry. Is there a reason you don't want fresher apples?"

"It's not a matter of want. I *really* have nothing to offer you for them, and I'd rather not accept a favor I cannot return." I hope that he doesn't take my rejection poorly and refuse to let me have even the half-rotten apples. Then I will have wasted my morning with nothing to show for it. What will Muireall say to that, if I return empty-handed? "But I really am thankful for the charity you do for us widows. Even a wee bit makes a difference."

He shakes his head, the wistful grin returning. "You don't have to be polite."

"Neither do you." I hold his gaze, keeping my expression sober.

He seems to respect my forwardness, straightening and twisting his head, a sparkle in his eyes at my response. "I'm guessing you haven't heard much about the Lockhart family around town yet, have you?"

At the irony of his statement, I can't help but laugh. The

sound vibrating through me feels good, untying a few of the knots inside my chest. "And you seem to not have heard any of the rumors about Muireall and me." His smile wavers, and I choke back my playfulness. Now he knows there are rumors to hear.

Good green earth, why do I have to always say too much?

"What are they saying about you?" he asks, more as a challenge than an interrogation. He reaches up to the tree beside him, plucking a leaf from the branch and twirling, waiting for my answer.

But I know better and keep my mouth shut.

"Surely it can't be worse than what they say about my family, if that's any comfort." He laughs, but his mouth is pulled into a grimace despite his attempt at humor, and he rolls his eyes, trying to make light of the accusations. "Last time I went in town, they were checking my wrists for—"

He cuts himself off, his eyes wide and instinctively glancing at my own hands. I want to run as his face drains of color; my own must be as bright as the apples. Neither of us seem to know what to say, and my gaze drops from his. My heart begins to race, and my free hand fidgets with my apron. A shaky breath is released from my lips.

"Um...I didn't mean that as..." Callen shakes his head as he braces his hands on his hips.

"No, you're right," I say, clearing my throat. "They really hate cairlinen here, don't they?" I force a chuckle, but it's weak.

"People always find something to hate," he says quietly. I glance up at him. Callen has tucked his hands into his back pockets again, his face stern as he gazes off into the distance to his right. "I think it's more that they need something to justify their hate than anything else."

A breeze rustles the curls against his forehead, and he slips deeper into thought, or perhaps into memories. I don't want to say the wrong thing, so I don't speak, but neither do I look away.

"Have you eaten lunch yet?" He asks, breaking the silence. "We always have plenty. Brodie said you walked the whole way here and you haven't taken a break all morning."

I'm completely caught off-guard, the heat of the day catching up to me. I look down at the seven half-rotten apples in my basket to avoid his gaze. "I really should get home to Muireall."

"Of course." He sounds disappointed. No, probably relieved. "Brodie will give you a ride—"

"Oh, it's not far! I can walk just fine," I tell him, starting for the barn.

Callen laughs, the sound comforting and full of life. "I know you *can*, of course. But it's the least I can do for startling you and taking up so much of your time." He falls in step beside me. Our arms brush, and then he puts more proper distance between us.

I keep my hands clutched around the handle of the apple basket, with the empty one slung around my elbow, bouncing against my side. "You don't owe me anythin'."

"The feeling is mutual."

Once he knows for certain that I'm a cairline, he won't be so generous. I shouldn't get too comfortable with his polite manners when they are sure to disappear eventually. And even if he doesn't reject me outright, the only positive way a cairlinen can hope to be viewed with in Croìthe is as a curiosity. Otherwise, I am destined to be an outcast. So I just nod, keeping my attention fixed ahead, making straight for the path through the pasture.

"I suppose there is one favor you could do for me," he says, slowing to a stop. I pause, and while I don't turn to face him, I listen intently. I knew it. "Allow Brodie to escort you home."

"I already told you—" Thunder echoes in the distance, and he doesn't argue with me. But his smile grows, knowing I can't reject an offer to outrun the storm. "Then we're even." I smirk, continuing toward the barn with more determination.

"Actually," he teases, hurrying to keep pace with me. I glance to the side to see a twinkle of mischief in his green eyes. "I think I'll owe *you* a favor in return."

I almost hit him with my basket, but the mere urge to be so playful is a reminder to restrain myself.

It's only a matter of time before his curiosity wanes.

TWELVE

Only when we arrive at the cottage and I turn to grab my baskets do I find that they have been filled to the brim with bright, healthy apples. And there are two more crates filled with vegetables in the wagon. Straining to carry the baskets myself, I spot Brodie lifting up a crate. "Those aren't for us," I tell him, but it would appear that Callen has ignored my rejection of his charity.

"Callen was very clear. He said to remind you that 'he owes you a favor'," he says, working his way around the pond. An almost-path has been created simply from all the stomping to and fro, but he still has to move gingerly to avoid the rosebush's thorns.

"I doubt his parents would approve of so much generosity. It's unnecessary," I say, but I can't deny that it would be nice to have more than apples to eat. My eyes slip to the cottage, where the door and shutters are still completely shut. It's past noon. Could Muireall really still be in bed?

"No, no. His father died years ago, so it's just Callen and his mother now. And he's the lord of the province, so he can very well do whatever he likes." Brodie's voice drops to a mutter. "Although I'm sure town would rather just forget he has any authority."

"Are they tired of payin' their taxes?"

Brodie pauses just as he reaches the door, considering if he should answer my question frankly. Instead, he shifts the weight of the crate over one arm precariously and awkwardly reaches for the door handle. "Something like that."

I hurry to open the door for him. Brodie thanks me and sets the crate inside. I apologize for the mess, but he doesn't seem to notice, hurrying to fetch the remaining crate while I fling open the window shutters to let in some light. Should I awake Muireall?

"This is all of it. I'll see you the day after tomorrow!" With a wave he is off, back to the Lockhart Estate.

I suppose I'm going back with Vaila and Yvaine in two days. Although, as I turn to process the bounty before me, I'm not sure we'll need more food by then. And I wonder when Callen will come calling for some kind of payment. Surely his comment about owing me anything was nothing more than a tease. Perhaps he's waiting for a more discreet time to ask me to barter a dèiligidh for him. If there is strife between his family and the rest of Soarsa, maybe he wants my help with some kind of revenge.

My blood runs cold. I've never made a mhallachd dèiligidh. I've never had need for a curse. If magic could be dark, then that was dark magic. Even in Cairlich you could get in trouble if you were caught having bartered any kind of curse—not that the threat stopped people from making them. It never stopped my mother.

Piling the vegetables on the kitchen counter, I distract myself by rinsing off the dirt from the produce, the water cool and refreshing on my hands. My stomach twists when I finish scrubbing the last radish clean. There isn't a single blemish in the bunch: not a tiny rotted hole in a potato or a wilted leaf of cabbage. Either his crops are doing abnormally well this year, or he intentionally gave me the best of the best.

This isn't mere charity. This is bargaining.

I'll need to strengthen my bond in case the dèiligidh he asks for is more than I've done before.

Perhaps if I wasn't already indebted to him, I could have charged him for such a service. It would have certainly helped our money problem. Now, instead, I will have to freely give my blood for his dèiligidh.

Foolish cairline.

"What is all this?" Muireall's voice booms out over me as if she has already found a reason to be upset this morning. When I turn, she is still disheveled but dressed for the day, wearing a black skirt with a black blouse buttoned up to her neck. Her faded hair hangs loose over her shoulders, rather than her usual style. I've never seen her so unkempt.

"It's from the Lockhart farm." I step aside so she can see everything laid out.

Muireall's eyebrow quirks at the name with a grunt. "I guess I wouldn't have assumed the Baines would have even let you on the property." She passes me, picking up a carrot and looking it over. "They're getting lazy with harvesting over there, aren't they? I suppose that's to be expected. Tuethal Lockhart always was too good for Soarsa."

"Callen is the lord now," I inform her, and my mind is filled with the twinkle in his green eyes and the curls of his brown hair.

"Callen! And the town has accepted that?" Muireall chuckles as if I am telling a joke, trading the carrot for a turnip.

"And I didn't glean all of this. He said it's a gift."

Muireall turns toward me, a startled look filled with shameful assumptions in her eyes. "Why would he give *you* a gift? What did you give him in return?"

"Nothing! I tried to turn it away, but he insisted."

She crosses her arms with a sigh. "I didn't mean to upset you, dear. But if you understood his family's reputation… His mother wasn't always a *lady*, Caitrin. Castles and jewels don't turn a donkey into a mare."

I gawk at her words but push away the urge to gossip. "He didn't ask for *anythin'* and I promised him nothin'!" Muireall is unimpressed by my exclamation. "It's probably just his condolences for your losses. But I'll send it away if you'd prefer."

She chuckles darkly, looking over the produce. "They always did think they were better than the rest of us, keeping the old traditions like they do."

"At least we have plenty to eat."

"Lots of vegetable stew, I reckon," Muireall mutters, picking up an apple, then turning to me. "We should get a couple of hens! Some eggs would be good. Maybe a goat as well, if you think you can manage them all."

"If *I* can manage them all?"

She nods, as if we have just made some kind of agreement. I open my mouth to argue further, but she cuts me off, pacing to the sitting room. "Surely someone in this godforsaken town will hire someone like you. Or maybe you can find something valuable left in the manor to sell." Muireall takes a big bite of the apple, facing me with an expectant smile, challenging me to deny her requests.

I shake my head, dumbfounded by her demands for goats and chickens, on top of her desire to restore the cottage and estate and tame the grounds. Does she really expect me to do it all by myself? "Muireall, that is—"

"The least you can do? You say you want to be a good daughter-in-law, so why are you complaining? I'm not asking for much, Caitrin." She takes a step towards me, her grip tight on the fresh apple, her gaze softening. "Maybe if you would let me talk to my husband…"

Folding my arms over my chest, I look away defiantly. An uncomfortable silence settles between us.

"I'm taking a bath," Muireall announces abruptly, disappearing into the hallway. The door slams shut behind her, echoing throughout the small cottage.

THIRTEEN

I TAKE MY FURY OUT on the weeds covering the path and then make a simple vegetable stew for dinner. In the back of my mind—as I cut carrots and potatoes, and pluck thyme and rosemary from the garden—I hope that Muireall will see the soup as a peace offering. Instead, she doesn't even acknowledge my existence, much less join me at the table.

With one sniff of the broth, she groans and stomps with her bowlful back to her bedroom. So I take my rage out on eating every last drop of savory stew, the salt and steam burning my tongue, until there is none left if she comes for a second helping.

After all, I am the one who worked all day long while she rested. And maybe I wouldn't be so upset if she had uttered even a simple word of thanks.

When the sun rises, so do I, eager to be out of the cottage before Muireall awakes. I know I probably have hours, but even just sharing the roof with her feels burdensome.

I only packed four dresses, including my black mourning gown, which I won't wear again unless Muireall asks me to. Additionally, I have a greyish-purple dress with little white blossoms I embroidered along the collar and hem, my yellow dress with puffed sleeves which is my best-made and most elegant out of the four, and a simple olive-green dress, fit for a long day of hard work, like today.

I braid back my hair and tie an apron around my waist. Grabbing an empty crate, I stomp up to the decrepit manor to search for anything we can sell.

Maybe I can scavenge enough to not only buy a few necessities for the cottage but some fabric for myself as well. No doubt, Muireall would think such expense a waste, but I need more to fill my days than gleaning and cleaning. If I bring my sewing things to the manor, Muireall probably won't even suspect I'm doing anything but her bidding.

The dew on the flowers and shrubs outside the cottage fills the air with a sweet smell of morning as the timid sunlight drifts through the dreary fog hovering over the grounds. It's serene, like a dream, and my agitation shifts into mere diligence.

While there are several entrances into the manor, the large patio doors are glass and have been completely shattered. Even in my boots, I don't like the thought of trekking over the shards. Instead, I enter through the scullery, pushing aside the ivy curtain that hangs over the open doorway.

Inside, it's dark and musky. A broken vase lays at my feet, with flowers that have long wilted, sitting dusty and dry against the faded, wooden floorboards. Cabinets are pulled open or have been completely removed, and all of the knobs are missing. Someone stole the cabinet knobs?

Hopefully the looters left something of value somewhere in this giant house.

I shuffle through the little cupboard room, glancing into the cabinets to double-check that they are empty.

A mouse scurries under my feet and then out of sight. I suck in a breath, steeling my resolve.

"Mice are better than rats," I whisper to console myself.

Entering the kitchen, the rust, dust, and decay consume every inch. Wooden spoons and spatulas with nibble marks are discarded on the stone floor. The large brick oven is crumbling and dark. It's easy to imagine hissing or whistling coming from the gaping mouth that had once warmed food. I set the crate on the large, wooden island counter, surveying the space.

Of course, nothing of note will be out in the open. With a deep breath, I reach up to a closed cabinet above the rusted double-wide sink. I pull open the doors and step far back in the same movement, just in case some kind of rodent jumps out at me.

Instead, the silvery strings of a web that houses a large, black spider stare back at me. My blood runs cold, imagining the spider scurrying from its perch and crawling after me. Onto my boots, up my legs. With a shriek, I slap the cupboard door closed, my heart racing.

Even though the windows let in plenty of morning light, I've lost my nerve with all of the dark corners and recesses.

Besides, if there is anything of value left in the manor, I don't think I'll find it in the kitchen.

Leaving the crate behind, I exit through a swinging door that squeaks noisily on its hinges and enter the dining room. My eyes light up with surprise and intrigue. While most of the room has been stripped bare—there are shadow stains where mirrors or maybe paintings used to hang, and the porcelain cabinet is empty—the long table and all of its finely crafted chairs are mostly undisturbed.

Laying over the table, covered in a film of dust, is a large tablecloth of fine, sky blue linen. I wipe off the dust as best I can, but it clings to the fabric like it has been painted in place. It will take some effort to clean. Pinching the cloth, it slips like silk between my fingers, thick enough for a gown. With clever cutting, I can avoid the stains and holes. Perhaps I could make something impressive enough that the seamstress in town will look past my less-desirable qualities.

I pull the fabric from the table in one swift motion and roll it up into a wad. Setting the roll on the bare tabletop, I survey the space. It will work perfectly for a sewing room, especially when the sun is high, shining its light through the giant windows that run along the length of the room facing the garden.

Already satisfied with my findings, I move through the double doors and across the hall into what I assume was once a ballroom. The space is wide open with a tall, domed ceiling of glass, most of which lays shattered on the marble tiles. The walls are lined with a handful of sunken sofa chairs and rotten benches, and a giant chandelier lays broken in the center of the space, the crystals smashed and its golden arms bent awkwardly. Laying in the mess of shards is a small, dead robin. Maybe some of the crystal is salvageable.

My steps echo around me as I make my way to the center of the room.

"So you're the cairline everyone's talkin' about."

I spin to find a woman not much older than myself with tawny brown skin and curly dark hair framing her sincere face.

She wears a deep purple dress with long sleeves, laced up the sides over a brown chemise. Her arms are folded over her chest, and her is head held high as she holds my gaze with large eyes that seem to see right through me.

"There's no use denyin' it. I can see your bondin' bands well enough." Her tone is casual, the familiar Cairlichen accent comforting, but she stands with stone coldness.

My breathing hitches and I straighten my posture, resisting the urge to hide my hands. Maybe this is an opportunity to follow in my mother's trade. "Yes. I'm bonded. And…and for a few coppers, I can make you a favor…"

She almost laughs at that, the first emotion her face has shown: contempt. "I don't need the kind of favors cairlinen offer anymore."

"Anymore?" I raise an eyebrow. "I come from a line of strong cairlinen. I'm certain there is somethin'—"

"I want nothin' from you." She takes a step forward. "I just wanted to see if the rumors were true."

I place my hands on my waist with a huff. "Well, here I am! Soarsa's first resident cairline."

She smirks. "Not the first, lass." She wets her lips but decides against whatever she was going to say next.

"What do you mean?" My curiosity overcomes my desire to appear confident. "Who are you?"

Her smirk dims, twisting into something less amused. Maybe it's not contempt. Maybe it's something more like sorrow. "Una McDow, the Cairlichen goat-girl who lives on the cliffs." Then she snorts. "And no, I'm not bonded." She pushes up one of her sleeves just enough to show her wrists, where instead of the red swirls of a cairline, I spot, for only a split second, what looks like white scars. "But that doesn't mean they like havin' me here. So don't expect to find friends easily in town."

She's not a cairline, but she is from my country. Perhaps I won't be accepted in town, but surely another Cairlichen...

"And I'm not interested in being friends with a cairline who barters with spirits," Una says, holding her head high.

I shift my weight and cross my arms over my chest. "What is it you want then?"

"Why did you run away from Cairlich?" She takes a step toward me, lifting her eyebrow.

"I didn't run away from anythin'. I came here with my mother-in-law, that's all."

"Ah. Well, then I suppose there was no point in comin' to meet you."

"Why? Who did you think you'd find?"

Una looks me over, her expression melting as a hidden hurt reveals itself in her furrowed brow and dark eyes. "Perhaps a cairline lookin' to escape the darkness that enslaves her, lookin' for a spell to break her bond." While Una doesn't say it, she might as well have: *dèiligeadh ris an diabhal.*

I want to scoff at her accusation, but something deep inside me twists with intrigue at her offer. There is a part of me that hopes she will explain what she means, and another that is pridefully afraid of what she knows. My wrists sting like briar thorns biting my skin; Keres wants me to do something, but I don't know what. "If you really are from Cairlich, you would know the bond can't be broken. And I'm not interested in sellin' myself, if that's what you're offerin'."

"Of course not." Without a farewell, or even a nod, Una turns and walks out of the ballroom.

And my veins are on fire with a need to hide, or chase after her, and yet the fire turns to ice, keeping me frozen and stiff as a board.

When the air grows still, and I'm certain she is gone for good, my muscles find movement again. Like I've woken from a daze, and I'm quick to exit the ballroom into the foyer, just to make sure I'm truly alone again. But Una's words linger in the breeze that carries through the manor.

I find a few items made of fine metals or laden with gemstones, but I don't have the motivation to search the house thoroughly. My mind is too preoccupied with questions.

Maybe Muireall will know more about Una or the first cairline to live in Soarsa.

Or maybe it's best to leave Muireall alone for the day.

When I return to the cottage, the sound of splashing water echoes from the washroom, so I quietly grab a couple apples and my sewing box, and head back to the dining room of the manor. I busy myself by cleaning up the table so I can cut and sew, and then set to work washing the fabric with water from the pump.

I see Muireall move past the kitchen window at one point, but she doesn't seem to notice me outside. After hanging the fabric to dry, I make another pot of soup for dinner. I don't even tell Muireall that it's ready, gulping down my bowl as the sun sets outside.

Then I take my pocketknife and head for the thicket

between the manor and the road.

FOURTEEN

THE SUN HAS HIDDEN ITSELF completely away and the pitch
black of night engulfs me. The sky is freckled with stars, the
moon hidden by shadow. Wedging a tall, white candlestick into
the stump of a fallen tree, I strike a match and light it.
Surrounded by such utter darkness, the flame looks small and
weak.

With a prick of my knife, I let a drop of my blood fall into
the fire. "Thig dhòmhsa."

Come to me…

The flame flickers, and then it is snuffed out instantly,
although the air is perfectly still. The smoke from the blackened
wick gathers up, rising steadily until it surrounds me. I hold my
breath for only a moment to keep from coughing before the
swirling smoke pulls together into the shadow of a spirit. Wisps
of black reach out like hair, or maybe fingers, from the form
with a hiss.

"This place…" Keres growls with the voice of some
creature not quite human and only vaguely female. Her tone,
hollow like a whisper, is full of contempt. She shifts around the
clearing in the thicket, but her attention stays fixed on me.
"You should have called for me sooner, so I could have
cautioned you from coming here."

She drifts close, and goosebumps rise on my arms as her wispy fingers reach out toward me. But I have nothing to fear. Even if she is upset with me, *the cairline is the master of the bond.* That's what Ma always told me.

"Well, I have need of you now." I cross my arms and raise an eyebrow.

Something like a laugh comes from Keres. "A curse for this cursed land, I hope. It's dangerous for us here, little cairline."

"Dangerous for me, but you're safe in the spirit world," I say dismissively. She shifts, a shiver running through her as she grows slightly smaller, almost my size. She doesn't challenge my statement. "And not a curse, but…information."

"Dèidh seo dèiligidh?"

I stiffen. "No. Not the future. The past."

"Either way. The truth on such things is no small dèiligidh."

I bite my lip, my knife still clutched in my right hand. I have seen Ma barter with bone dust and bird feathers, but the blood was always done in the secret of darkest night. And I've only ever known Keres to be greedy.

"I want to know about the first cairline here in Soarsa. Is she *still* here?"

Keres hisses, floating away from me. "You do not want to know of that."

I step toward her boldly. "Yes, I do. I want to know what happened to her."

"I'll tell you for free, little cairline." Keres's words drip and echo around me like acid, biting my temples with a sudden, sharp pain. I wince but wait patiently for her to explain. "That cairline is nothing but an empty shell now. Useless and marred. An outcast."

"You mean she can't do magic?"

Keres laughs, and the pain eases as her shape grows larger again. "Not a drop."

"What happened to her spirit?"

"It sold her off like a slave to some human master."

"A *sgaoileadh*," I whisper, remembering the stories my mother told me as a child, warnings of what I might become if my bond is weak. Her words were always full of hatred and anger when recounting the stories of her youth, of her own mother, enslaved and broken, but there was fear in her eyes.

If a cairline's bond is too weak, if her connection with the spirit is dead, the spirit might devour every drop of her blood, driving her mad and breaking the bond. The only alternative was a sgaoileadh, a human slave master who pays the payment of blood on the cairline's behalf. The threat of a sgaoileadh was what had motivated me to stay in contact with Keres all these years, just enough to keep her happy, to keep our bond alive.

My mind spins. "A Croìthen sgaoileadh?"

Keres stills, the light of the stars blacked out by her smoke. She won't tell me more, even if I spill blood for answers.

It's better to let it go for now and move on to my other business with Keres. "I also want a talisman, for my mother-in-law."

A reddish-orange glow appears from deep within Keres, embers through smoke. "Is it her greed for money or her insufferable behavior? We both know you can't handle contacting the dead yet."

Yet. I stand taller, attempting to gain her respect. "We both know I've a *càirdeas* for cridhe." My gut pinches and twists, but I force a smile. I should be proud of my affinity for favors of the heart, not burdened by shame of how I have used it.

"Tell me what you desire and what you will trade for it then." The wisps of Keres's form start to surround me, drawing me closer to her.

"I want to improve her disposition so that she might be a wee bit more appreciative of me, and maybe help out a bit."

I pull out from my pocket the cleaned bones of the robin, with his shiny brown and red feathers, along with a sharp shard of crystal from the chandelier and a few hairs I had gathered from Muireall's brush. Keres surveys the items, lifting them out of my palm with her wisps, weighing their value in the air.

"You never are happy with other people. No one is good enough for Caitrin."

I gasp at her accusation, my brow furrowing. "Actually, Keres, it's that I'm never good enough for anyone else."

"Hmm…" Keres muses. "Well, you are still not quite wicked enough for me, either."

Shifting my weight, I hold out my hand, palm up. "A handful should be enough." Keres seems to light up with glee at my offer. "It doesn't need to last long—just a bit of time to ease her out of her grief."

Keres nods, her wisps spreading over my palm, seeping into my pores, seeping into my veins. And then, she takes my blood, tainting her shadowy fingers red. "Careful, little cairline. Grief can last a lifetime." Keres cuts off the flow. My whole hand feels numb, as if pricked by a thousand needles, and I pull it to my chest.

The red wisps wrap around the bird bones, crystal, and hairs, which float in the air. Then, with the force of a hurricane, she crushes them all together, tighter and tighter. "And it usually does, for those who are capable of truly loving." The ground trembles under my feet as the ball of crushed items and blood glows bright red, like molten hot metal. "Which is probably why you moved on from your own husband so quickly."

I look away from her shapeless form, grimacing and wrapping my arms around my middle. I don't want to say anything, don't want to even acknowledge her words, but I can't bear the silence. "Just hurry up."

The trembling ceases, and I reach out my hand as the ball cools to a dark black marble and drops into my palm. In the darkness of night, I can still see the inner glow of magic.

"Pleasure doing business with you, little cairline."

A gust of wind rushes through the thicket, taking Keres with it and chilling me to the bone.

The talisman in my hand, however, is warm and comforting in the wake of Keres's departure. I feel a little faint, as I usually do after bartering with her, but it should help me to sleep better tonight, at least.

In the morning, I'll slip the talisman into Muireall's pocket, or maybe her pillowcase. The change should be quick, and, even if the new mood doesn't stick, I'm looking forward to getting some sort of support from her after all the hard work I've done.

I clutch my skirt and turn to head back to the cottage, but instead of the empty, blackened thicket, I find a man standing in the shadows, staring at me with wide eyes.

FIFTEEN

Tucking the talisman in my skirt pocket, I clutch the knife tighter. My stomach turns to stone as I hold my breath, ready to defend myself. But the stranger is just as still as I am, and his features become clearer in the starlight: a crop of wild hair, a strong figure, and a shirt sloppily tucked into breeches.

Callen Lockhart.

"What are you doin' here?" I narrow my gaze, allowing my tone to be harsh and displeasing, but sweat gathers under my arms, even in the midnight chill.

Callen's mouth falls open, his eyes glancing at the nothing behind me.

I suck in a breath through my nose. What did he see? To be a cairline is one thing, but to be caught doing magic is far worse.

"Just taking a walk." Everything about him is stiff, from his words to his posture, like he anticipates an attack at any moment. "I forgot these woods aren't vacant anymore; they have been for so many years."

"Hmm. I'd think you'd have plenty of your own land to stroll about in the middle of the night." I cross my arms, raising my head.

The glint of my blade in the moonlight catches his eye.

"And what do you need that for?" He must have seen Keres, or he saw something at the very least. But his suspicions only prove how ill-informed he is about how our magic works.

Still, I'll admit to nothing. "A lass needs to be able to protect herself."

"And what's it you're protecting yourself from?" Callen takes a hesitant step toward me. Even in the dark I see his eyes shift, waiting for something to jump out and grab him.

I shrug, a grin tugging on my lips. "Strange men stalkin' me in the dead of night maybe?"

His mouth twist to the side, almost a smile, but his brow remains furrowed, his eyes darting around, refusing to meet my gaze. "I didn't mean to…scare you." He walks towards me, each step testing to see if I'll spook and run, or maybe worried that I'll try to stab him.

Uncrossing my arms so the knife hangs at my side, I step forward to meet him half-way. "I don't think I'm the one who's afraid."

Callen tenses, his jaw tightening as his eyes snap to mine. My grin falters. "So what are you doing out at night like this?" He tucks his hands into his pockets.

I bend down to sheath the knife back in my boot. "Just takin' a walk."

"Is it true that cairlinen can only do magic at nighttime?" he asks, his voice quiet with concern. When I glance up at him, there isn't fear in his eyes, but the sparkle of curiosity.

I straighten, trying to decide if I should be honest or playful in my answer. Either one sounds dangerous. But I suppose I take too long to answer.

"It's good to be cautious," he says, looking away as he bounces on his feet. "I wouldn't trust a Croìthen either. I've seen my kinsmen make up wild slander just for fun. I can't imagine what they'll do if…" His eyes are drawn to my wrists and he leans away from me, ever so slightly.

My bonding bands, as thin as they are—although perhaps a hair wider due to another dèiligidh made—are on full display. He knows for sure what I am now. My mouth falls open, but no words spill out, just deep breaths.

Callen presses his lips into a firm line and his gaze slowly pulls up to meet mine. Even in the dim light, his eyes gleam rich green, filled with mystery. If I wasn't so worried about what he will say or do next, I might get lost in them.

A roll of thunder shakes us both from our thoughts, and we look upward to signs of rain. It comes only moments after the flash of lightning strikes the sky, first in drizzles, then with a steadiness that beckons a storm.

"Please stay off our property unless invited from now on," I tell him. After all, he is trespassing.

He chuckles nervously as the rain begins to soak us through. "Only if you'll be sure to return to my own. For Mrs. Raeburn's sake."

I don't know how to respond to his hospitality, contrasting my own hostility. Without another word, he takes off through the trees toward his estate.

I don't move for a moment; I'll be drenched soon enough anyway and running won't improve my condition. I can only hope Muireall will be asleep in bed when I return, so I won't have to lie about where I've been, or who I've been with.

I soak in the hot water until it grows tepid, and then I sink down into the tub to guard my skin from the chill of the night air. The talisman sits next to the sink faucet, ready to be hidden amongst Muireall's things, but my mind turns with the events of the past days, weeks, months.

I'm pulled back to the week before I met Tate, a month before we'd marry, half-a-year before now. It was the first powerful dèiligidh I had ever bargained. I gave Keres my favorite dress as an offering, and she took more than enough of my blood. All I wanted was to escape the pressure Ma placed on me, to experience what it was like to really be loved and wanted. The magic had worked better than I expected, better than I had wanted. And then I realized why Ma always told me to be specific when bartering; spirits have a humor of their own when given too much freedom.

The night before our wedding, I gave Keres an offering of pearls. It was a necklace Nessa had been given by a wealthy client, and she it passed along to me—she prefers gemstones and jewels. That night was the first time I'd ever made a dèiligidh that affected my own heart, and it didn't stick then.

Will it stick with Muireall?

I comfort myself with the notion that even just a few days of pleasantry from her will be enough. If she returns to her old self, it is a simple spell to recreate when she becomes too burdensome again.

No one is good enough for Caitrin.

Keres's accusation still stings, how she would taunt me with my own insecurities. Perhaps if I was good enough for someone, I wouldn't need magic to make anyone love me.

As it is, magic is the only way to get results, and it is easier to control the outcome when bartering with a spirit than when dealing with fickle humans. Humans break promises and change expectations; magic is consistent.

I drain the bath and dry myself, dressing in my soft, worn chemise for sleeping. It's the dead of night, and Muireall's snoring fills the hallway. Carefully, I open her door a crack. My mother-in-law lies almost peacefully in her bed, her mouth open with one hand dangling off the side of the bed. Sound asleep. Knowing her patterns well enough, I grab the dress I assume she will wear the next day and bring it to the sitting room.

In the light of a single candle, I conceal the talisman in the folds of the skirt hem; she won't even notice it's there. Better than a pocket, and I can easily rip it out and move it the following night.

Replacing the dress where I found it in her room, I collapse on the sofa, struggling to get comfortable as my feet hang over the armrest into thin air. The quilt, thankfully, is large enough to swallow me whole. As exhausted as I am, I can't seem to keep my eyes closed, staring blankly at the ceiling as my mind continues to spin with regrets and second-guessing.

And suspicion.

Did Callen see Keres? Does he know what I was doing?

He knows for certain what I am now.

Generosity and kindness are easily imitated, and such easy

actions hold no deep truth. I won't be surprised when he demands a favor in return for his charity and silence.

Or maybe he'll go to the town and expose me, have me exiled from Soarsa.

And then Keres will come to collect.

SIXTEEN

BRODIE ARRIVES BRIGHT AND EARLY with Vaila and Yvaine, and they act just as they had days before. At least Callen hasn't shared my secrets yet, however many of them he has gathered by now. Regardless, we have enough food for a few more days, so I decline to harvest with them.

My heart races at the thought of seeing Callen again, of having him ask too many questions, of lying to him and having him know the truth anyway. I'm not just a bonded cairline; I'm actively breaking Croìthen law. I can handle being an outcast in Soarsa, but being cast out will cost me too much.

Muireall sleeps in, as usual, and I take the morning to work on the tablecloth dress. My workroom in the manor has started to feel a little bit more like home, even with all of the crawling creatures and dusty decay. My hands work with a mind of their own—cutting, pinning, stitching—while I listen to the song of the birds that fly throughout the manor.

It's not until well past noon when I'm threading a needle for finishings that my stomach starts grumbling. I look toward the cottage and see Muireall crouching in the overgrowth with a spade and a floppy hat shielding her face.

Leaving the dress behind, I exit the manor through the patio doors, which I had swept clear the day before. With a bright smile, I approach Muireall. "Good morning, Mrs. Raeburn. Beautiful day outside, isn't it, with the warm sunshine?"

"The cottage is a little stuffy, so some fresh air was due. And I might as well get rid of some of this muck while I'm out here." She tosses a handful of weeds into a small pile she's been accumulating. "But I'm getting hungry, and all we have is vegetables. I could go for some meat, or even just eggs."

I want to say her mood has changed, although the change is not as drastic as I was hoping.

You can't change who people are deep down inside, Nessa told me once about cridhe magic. It had been a small comfort during my time with Tate, but now it feels foreboding.

"Well, I have some things I can try to sell in town. Maybe it will be enough to get us a couple hens."

Muireall looks up at me, her eyes glassy, her wrinkles softened, and her usual grimace gone. "You found something valuable in there, then?"

"Some trinkets from the manor, and I'm finishin' up a dress to sell as well. Maybe that seamstress will hire out some mendin' to me if she truly can't stand to have me workin' in her shop."

Muireall grunts, resisting some negative reaction, and looks back to her weeding. "Sell what you found and we'll manage for now. I'll do my best to clear a real path here today, but we can fix up the hen house next. Fresh eggs every morning—what a treat that would be! And maybe some baking too. I miss the smell of fresh bread."

We. It is the one word that makes me know the talisman is

working as I'd hoped. "I'll see what I can do when I get back from town. Who do you think I can sell to? Is there a general store or—"

"Should be someone who will buy whatever you have, maybe a peddler in town. Peddlers are always working their way along the cliffside towns."

And now she's being helpful. Thank you, Keres. "I'll go finish up the dress then and be on my way!"

"And be sure to eat something before you go," Muireall calls after me absent-mindedly. She digs with her spade into the weeds. "Apples and carrots certainly fill a stomach, if nothing else."

A smile creeps up on my face as I look back at her, hunched on the ground, digging up roots to prevent regrowth. "I will, Muireall."

SEVENTEEN

AFTER I CAREFULLY FOLD THE freshly-finished tablecloth dress and nest it in my carpet bag along with the trinkets, I saddle up Ailbert and head to town with renewed confidence. Ailbert seems to appreciate the opportunity to stretch his legs, too, as he prances down the road. A few wagons pass, and I make sure to wave, but the most I receive in return from the drivers is a discreet nod.

The cobblestone street lined with quaint buildings and businesses which make up the town square is nearly empty when I arrive. A woman sits on a bench outside the post office, reading a letter while her two small children play with pebbles. An elderly couple chats with a man in a fine suit as the three exit the office of a Dr. Kilpatrick. And a carriage drawn by two horses sits outside the town hall, its driver lounging in the sun.

Outside the butcher's shop—which has a hastily painted *closed* sign on the door—is an unattended peddler's stall. I suppose Muireall will have to wait a little longer for meat. However, the general store door stands wide open, ready for customers. Perhaps they will have some eggs, at the very least.

But first, I need money.

With my head held high, I dismount Ailbert and tie him to a hitching post where a trough of water sits. Grabbing my carpet bag, I tug at my gloves to make sure they sufficiently cover my wrists, then enter Hew's Textiles and Tailoring.

Bolts of fabric in varying colors and textures line the far wall, with spools of ribbon and thread, and jars of buttons displayed on the shelves. My eyes scan the options, drawn toward a pink fabric with a puckering texture and then a deep purple linen, as design ideas spark and morph in my mind.

"Can I help you?" the woman behind the counter asks, her voice shaking, forcing out the words. Shona. I recognize her from my first day in town, with her brunette hair and petite frame. Her eyes go wide, and I can tell she hopes I will respond with a quick "no" and leave before I curse her or the shop.

I swallow, making my way to the counter slowly so as not to spook her with my mere presence. I set my bag on the counter. She hugs herself, pulling back from me, her eyes darting to the bag and then back up at me quickly.

"I brought somethin' for you..." I start, hoping to ease her fears as I pull out the dress. She gasps, taking a step away from me. Does she think I'm going to perform a spell, or that the dress is cursed? I plaster on a smile with more determination. "This is a dress I made—it's brand new, never worn, not once—and I was hopin' you might sell it for me. Or maybe inspect it—"

She doesn't make a move to even touch the dress. "We don't sell second-hand clothing. We're a tailoring and dressmaker's shop, you see."

I feel hot under her paranoid stare. "Of course! But it's not second-hand. It's brand new—"

"My apologies but the smell..." Shona swallows, her brow

creasing with worry as she avoids meeting my gaze. I'd hoped the lavender water I washed the fabric in would disguise the mustiness. Apparently not. "It can't be new. The fabric certainly isn't, at least."

My chest burns with embarrassment. "Right. Sorry to waste your time." I straighten and grab my bag, throwing the dress over my arm as my cheeks flush red. I turn away, nearly set on stomping all the way back to the cottage.

"Wait!" The woman shouts, and I stop dead in my tracks. My heart skips a beat as hope and anxiety collide. "You're not going to curse me or anything, right?"

Of course I won't curse her. But a favor to make her more tolerant of me might be of use. But I'd need something of hers for such a spell, and I doubt she will let me get within a foot of her, much less take a strand of her hair. She's watching me like a scared field mouse, ready to scurry away and hide.

"No. I would never," I say politely, looking back at her with a flat smile. I can tell by her stillness and her unblinking eyes that she doesn't believe me. "You're just runnin' your business. Thank you for your time."

Exiting quickly to the town square, the peddler has returned to his stall, opening it up to reveal a collection of jewelry, glass bottles, mirrors, and other trinkets. The thought of heading straight to the cottage seems foolish, and if I've already endured humiliation once, what is one more time?

There is always a chance he'll buy from me, especially if he is just passing through and doesn't care for local gossip.

"Morning, lass! What can I do you for?" he asks me. His brown, bald head is shiny in the noonday sun, with soft wrinkles accentuating his face, but his warm smile makes him look a dozen years younger.

I open up my bag with a smile and extend it toward him. "Want some new things for your stall? I'm lookin' for a buyer, or perhaps a trade if you've sugar or buildin' supplies hidden in your wagon somewhere?" He takes the bag from me gingerly, searching through it. Then I raise up the dress to display it properly. "I have this too. Brand new, never worn. Made it myself."

Glancing at the dress quickly with an approving nod, he closes the bag to examine it. I bite back a comment that the bag isn't for sale, because I'd certainly part with it for a good deal.

"I'll give you fifty silvers for the dress, bag and all. I don't have much in the way of what you're looking for, but take a look around, and I'll give you a discount if you find anything of use. Does that work for you, lass?" His smile takes up half of his face, so eager to show me kindness.

"Perfect," I say with a laugh. A trade is a trade after all.

He is quick to give me the coins and then gives me space to browse his wares. Looking over his stall, I grab a bundle of buttons I could easily find a use for, and he sells them to me for two silvers. I nod my thanks and step away, leaving him to his business.

Facing the town square again, I tuck the buttons in my pocket and set my sights on the general store. I can see through the windows that it has several customers already inside, a group of young ladies by the looks of it. Still, I have forty-eight silvers, enough for some eggs, flour, and sugar to do some proper baking. I wouldn't mind being able to do more with those apples than eat them raw.

Stepping into the general store, I quickly survey my surroundings. Wooden shelves fill the space, with a long counter on one side where a middle-aged man stands, reading a book and waiting for customers. He glances up when I enter but barely registers my presence before returning to his book. He isn't interested in helping me, but I prefer that over an interest in kicking me out.

The shelves are filled with jars of jam, bags of beans and grains, and boxes of nuts and candies. At the counter are crates with large stamps that read eggs. I move toward the bags first, searching for sugar and flour.

A gaggle of giggles erupts from the other side of the shelf. I try to ignore them, but the hair on my arms stand on end as whispers reach my ears.

"That's her?"

"Yep. My pa saw her arms plain as day." Paisley Knox. I cringe and hurriedly grab the bags. "She's bonded."

Gasps.

"You think she'll curse us?"

"I'd be more worried about her begging for your table scraps or trying to seduce your beau."

"I'd like to see her try," a male voice responds.

One of the girls feigns a cry. "Don't even joke like that, Knox."

My cheeks grow warm and sweat gathers on my brow as I carry the bags to the counter. They can stare all they want, but hopefully they won't follow me.

"Eight silvers, miss." The cashier looks up again, but this time he seems to truly see me. And recognizes me. Standing slowly, he doesn't blink, doesn't look away, as the color drains from his face.

I hurriedly count out the coins and drop them onto the counter before he has a mind to decline me the sale. A silver rolls onto the floor, and I bend to pick it up when a hand meets my own. I pull back quickly.

Knox rises, the silver coin pinched between his fingers, a toothy smile plastered on his face. "Well, if it isn't Soarsa's new cairline," he says, bowing to me with an exaggerated flourish.

"How are you finding our town, cairline?" Paisley asks, appearing at his side.

"My name is Caitrin, and I actually have errands to run so…" I toss another silver to the cashier, who fumbles to catch it as he pulls from his daze, then hide the rest of the coins in my pocket. Grabbing the flour and sugar, I head for the door, but Knox catches my shoulder, his fingers slipping down to my elbow. I wrench myself away, dropping the flour in the process.

The bag hits the floor and explodes all over the hem of my dress. Three more girls come out from hiding behind the shelves as the whole group laughs at my predicament. Four silvers wasted. At least I still have the sugar.

Sucking in a breath and stealing myself against their mocking, I ignore the mess and exit the shop.

Unfortunately, they aren't polite enough to let me go.

"We're just trying to be nice, Caitrin," Paisley says as she and her posse follow behind me. "Or is everyone in Cairlich as rude as they are rotten?"

I keep my head high, refusing to turn toward them, refusing to be provoked. "Pardon me if I seem rude, but I must be gettin' back——"

"Of course! Your errands. Let us accompany you." Paisley loops her arm through mine, and I stiffen as I face her, eager to pull away but worried about dropping the sugar as well. "I hear you're spending a lot of time at the Lockhart's. If you truly don't mean to curse any of us, surely you would try to fit in instead of running away, wouldn't you?"

"Oh, I'm sure this little cairline feels right at home with banntraichean and bastards," Knox says, stepping up beside me, his arm brushing against mine. I pull away, further into Paisley's faux-friendly embrace, and then try to make myself smaller so I'm not touching either of them as their three giggly friends surround us.

"They are certainly much less suffocatin' than present company," I say through gritted teeth. I slip my arm from Paisley and take two big steps and turn to face them. "What is it you want? A spell? Maybe a little talisman to make your hair as curly as a pig's tail?"

Paisley folds her arms over her chest with a huff, and her friends follow her example. Knox takes a step toward me, but I don't back away. Reaching out, he slips a finger against my cheek, and I return his amused stare with one that is cold and unintimidated. "You won't last longer than a week, I'd wager, before you get caught and sent back to Cairlich."

I don't flinch, straining every muscle to keep still and not let them know how hard my heart is beating. A pig snort of a laugh escapes Paisley. "Or tossed straight off a cliff."

EIGHTEEN

"Why don't you leave the lass alone?"

I nearly jump as Callen steps between me and Knox. He doesn't look at me, but my breathing hitches at the sight of him. And then my thoughts start to race, recalling our encounter from the night before.

Will Callen turn me in?

A horse snorts off to the side, where Brodie's wagon sits, filled with produce. Brodie eyes us as he grabs a crate of apples, and the group of girls scoot out of the general store doorway so he can enter. He clears his throat, catching Callen's attention for a moment, but doesn't say anything.

"We were just giving her a warm Croìthen welcome," Knox says with a snort, then he narrows his eyes. "Well, not as warm as your *father* might have given her…"

"And what's that supposed to mean, Knox?" Callen's arms tense at his sides as his hands clench into fists. I take a half-step back, certain a fight is going to break out at any moment, and I don't want to get caught in the middle.

Paisley chuckles at the question. "Oh, Callen. You're old enough to know that your mother and your father didn't marry for *love*."

"That's exactly what happened, and I won't have you

besmirching his name saying otherwise," Callen responds coldly, his chest rising slowly with control. He's like a cat, waiting to pounce. "Unlike *some* people in this town, my father never held someone's past against them." Spinning on his heels, Callen starts for the wagon, but he halts when Knox opens his big mouth to retort.

"Your mother's prostitution wasn't in her past when your father met her."

The girls gasp at the scandal, but they aren't surprised by the statement, merely that Knox has said it so bluntly. My eyes, however, go wide. Lady Lockhart? A prostitute? And Callen doesn't even deny it. I feel a pinch of guilt for being so startled by the revelation.

"It is now," Callen says through clenched teeth as he looks over his shoulder with dark eyes.

"Tell me, Caitrin," Knox says, putting an arm around my shoulders, and I shrink into myself, too shocked to pull away for the moment. His mouth presses close to my ear as if he is going to whisper, but his words are plenty loud for everyone to hear. "What's the difference between paying for someone's bed and paying for someone's blood?"

I shove him away, glaring at his insinuation, heat searing across my skin.

Callen narrows his eyes, stepping up beside me. Our arms brush, and I hug the sugar bag tighter. "You should leave her alone, Knox."

There is a gleam in Knox's eyes. "It doesn't matter how rich you are, Callen, or how many titles you steal. If your 'father' knew you were hitching up with cairlinen to dèiligeadh ris an diabhal, he'd die all over again, don't you think?"

Knox turns to his sister to laugh, but Callen lands a punch hard on Knox's cheek. Callen's knuckles slip over Knox's nose with a crack, sending blood flying all over Paisley's pink dress. She squeals, stepping back and stiffening like a marionette doll. Her friends gasp, jumping away from her. I don't know whether to be horrified or impressed by Callen's attack.

Knox raises a hand to his bloodied nose in shock, still half-bent from the blow.

"Oh, just get out of here, Callen!" Paisley shouts, her eyes darting around the street as her voice quiets. "I don't care who the *rìgh* says is Lord of Soarsa, you know everyone wants you to just stay out of our business."

"I'd gladly stay out of it if you would allow me the pleasure," Callen snaps back.

Knox starts to straighten, his entire face scrunched up with rage. "My father is going to—"

"What?" Callen asks, taking a step forward, and Knox can't help but move away from him. "There's nothing your father can do to me, no matter how many letters he writes to the rìgh or how many rumors he starts in town."

Paisley's eyes dart to me, sparking with something mischievous. "We'll see about that." Taking her brother's arm, she pulls him away from us and down the street, the gaggle of girls following behind, looking back at us and whispering to each other.

The bag of sugar is clutched tightly against my chest, so tight I'm sure my skirt is now covered in not only flour but sugar dust as well.

Callen and I stand next to each other in silence, watching them go. I can hear each of his breaths, deep, as if he just ran all the way from the estate to stand up to these bullies. I chance a glance toward him. His face is as hard as stone, glaring after the twins, even when they disappear into the carriage and the driver hurriedly gets the horses moving.

Uncertain of how to break the awkwardness of our situation, I decide to simply say nothing at all. Better to get away before Callen starts asking me questions about the night before. I still don't know how much he saw, how much he knows.

I start for Ailbert with my lone bag of sugar, the silvers clinking in my pocket. Even though the Baines are gone, I can't face the cashier again after the mess I made inside.

"Caitrin!" Callen calls after me.

I halt my steps and turn reluctantly.

"You didn't come to glean this morning with Vaila and Yvaine." The furrow of his brow and the parting of his lips make me uncertain if he is glad or disappointed.

I hesitate, second guessing my answer. "Are you sure I am still welcome? I seem to be causin' quite a bit of trouble in this town."

His expression softens, but the smile he gives me is forced and flat. "Of course. The Lockhart family will always care for Soarsa's banntraichean. Even the troublemaking ones." His smile becomes lopsided as his eyes light up for a moment. I hold his gaze just long enough to see his smile slip.

Brodie exits the grocery store and Callen's attention is pulled away. He rolls up his sleeves over strong arms, his knuckles still bloody from his blow to Knox's nose, and heaves out a crate.

He must have felt me watching, because he looks my way and my cheeks warm. Something runs through me, from my heart to my toes, as I turn to Ailbert, grip the saddle and pull myself up. I have to resist pushing the old horse to gallop all the way home, the desire to run away from this town as fast as possible pulsing through my veins.

NINETEEN

WHEN I ARRIVE BACK AT the cottage, Muireall has completely cleared a path through the garden to the cottage door, leaving a giant pile of weeds and branches for me to deal with. But I don't mind. At least she is helping.

I, on the other hand, was not as successful as her with my time. I can only hope the talisman will keep her disappointment at bay.

Entering the cottage, I find her sprawled out on the couch, dozing off after her morning of hard work. I don't know how long it has been since she has done that much manual labor. Hopefully it won't cause her too much pain later.

I can fill her a hot bath with some lavender from the garden. That is certain to be nice. And maybe keep her attitude pleasant when the talisman wears off. With enough time, I'll figure out how to make her happy. Or, at least, happy with me.

"Muireall?" I whisper as I set the bag of sugar on the counter. Walking up behind the sofa, I peer over it to try and guess just how asleep she is. There is the slight smell of odor rising from her; I'm surprised she didn't change. My nose wrinkles at the thought of her lounging on my quilt. But then I spot papers scattered across her lap, one in her hand, and a few on the floor.

Moving around the sofa, I reach gingerly for one of the papers.

My dear Meara—

Knock! Knock!

Muireall jolts awake, frantically looks around and then at me. "Well, get the door!" she shouts, grabbing the papers with haste and quickly folding them together. Tucking the papers in her pocket, she starts racking her fingers through her hair, trying to tame the fly-aways back into her bun.

"Right," I say, hoping she didn't notice me snooping.

"Caitrin? Did you not make it to town?" She glances down at my flour-dusted skirt.

I smile sheepishly. "I did, and I sold a dress and some trinkets." I pull out the coins from my pocket and quickly hand them over. As soon as the coins slip from my hands, I wish I had kept some for myself; she wouldn't have known. I can only hope she is impressed with the sum. "But I only managed to get the one bag of sugar."

"It's certainly more than we had—which was nothing!" Muireall smiles briefly as she tucks the coins in her pocket. "Why only the sugar? Not even flour too?"

"It's, um…" The words get stuck in my throat as my stomach twists with embarrassment. I close my eyes, freezing to collect myself. "I did get flour, but I dropped it—"

"I'll just have to find the energy to go to town myself." She grimaces. "I fancied baking a pie today, but I guess it will have to wait. I'll need some butter and—"

Knock, knock, knock!

Muireall snaps back to the present with a shock. "Well, get

the door!"

I nod and open the door. Greeting me is a middle-aged woman with blonde hair pulled into a braid and a dutiful smile. She holds out a pie to me. "Just a bit of comfort food for your mourning," she says, bowing her head to me as I take it from her.

"Elspeth? Elspeth Dougal?" Muireall steps beside me and folds her arms over her chest.

"It's Elspeth Kilpatrick now, Mrs. Raeburn." Elspeth bobs with a slight curtsy. "Wiley Kilpatrick, my husband, is the head doctor now too."

"Married to a doctor? Well, you certainly aren't the little farmgirl flirt covered in mud that I remember, now, are you?"

Elspeth straightens, her smile unwavering, unwilling to let Muireall upset her manners. "Dr. Kilpatrick wanted me to check on you two, what with that dastardly disease spreading."

"An illness?" I ask before Muireall can loosen any more stinging words.

Elspeth nods curtly. "Nothing too serious yet, but he worries it's contagious. Has the butcher and his family in quarantine until it gets sorted." Her eyes shift from Muireall to me, and her smile slumps. "He thinks it may be foreign."

"Neither of us are sick at all! And we haven't been in years," Muireall says, stepping in front of me with her hands on her hips, trying to stand taller to meet Elspeth's height.

"We don't get many contagious diseases in Cairlich," I say, but Muireall pinches my side, reminding me that is only because of dèiligeadh that Cairlichen stay healthy so easily. "But what are the symptoms? I can let you know if I've heard of anything like it." I resist offering to make a talisman for the infected, knowing my kindness would be twisted as malice.

Elspeth is unimpressed. "Well, he had a hot fever at first, but now his body has swelled up all over, like spider bites everywhere, but my husband hasn't found any wounds indicating it's an infection from an insect or animal. He's calling it the Dhubd Blath."

The Black Bloat. My nose wrinkles at the image the name creates. But it doesn't escape me that they used the old tongue for the name, like they believe it is a curse. Magic. I stiffen, eager to prove otherwise. "It could be from some kind of poisoning."

Muireall's elbow bumps against my ribs, as if I have incriminated myself by the suggestion.

Elspeth's gaze dips to my gloved hands, her eyebrows pinching together. "I should really be getting back. Although, I'll let my husband know that you both are in good health."

"And let him know my daughter-in-law wouldn't hurt a fly, much less bother with cursing someone she doesn't even know!" Muireall snaps before stomping away from the door.

I wince, but my heart swells at Muireall's defense. "And thank you for the pie!"

Elspeth only glances me over, her lip curling before she turns away.

Closing the door behind me, I set the pie on the table. "Am I wrong to doubt this pie was brought out of kindness?" I ask with a slight laugh in an attempt to ease the tension in the air.

Muireall huffs over to the sink, then faces me with a dark look in her eyes. Is the talisman wearing off already? "Oh yes, kindness indeed. One silly pie and an arsenal of accusations."

"I suppose as a man of science, the doctor would want to discover the illness' origin."

"A man of science, ha!" Muireall grabs her shawl from the dining chair and throws it around her shoulders. "He's just trying to figure out if it's a curse. Didn't you catch that?"

"It's not so surprising. If we were in Cairlich—"

"But we're in Croìthe, Caitrin." Muireall's usual annoyance seems replaced with a motherly gentleness, a warmth in her glassy eyes. And then I remember the talisman in her skirt hem, and the warmth turns to ice before it reaches my heart. "She was here to see if the rumors were true, to see if *we* brought that disease to Soarsa."

"She can see we're perfectly healthy."

"If you cursed the town, then of course you'd protect yourself and your family." Muireall grabs an apple. She stares at it like it's something to devour, or maybe use as a weapon.

Family. The word echoes in my mind, like a warm blanket on a rainy day, and I don't even mind that her pessimism is unchanged.

"They'll blame you for every cursed thing that goes wrong in this town now, you know? And whatever they blame you for, they will hold me responsible for as well." Turning, she places the apple on the counter, grabs a knife, and begins chopping. "So we'd better start praying this Dhubd Blath clears up quickly. I might have come back home to die, but I was aiming for something peaceful and quiet, not an execution."

TWENTY

"Cut out the bad and keep the good," Vaila says, dropping the bruised potato into my basket with a smile. The morning sun is warm, but a gentle breeze brushes over us, carrying with it the scents of the farm—freshly-tilled soil and dew—which have become familiar and welcoming.

After a couple weeks of gleaning alongside the banntraichean, all worries of being chased off the Lockhart Estate have finally subsided. And while Callen always sends me home with more food than necessary, the lighthearted company of Vaila and Yvaine can only be found in these fields.

"Works for people and potatoes," I mutter, digging through the dirt with my gloved hands. Cutting out the bad is exactly what my talisman has done to Muireall. She has gone to town several times and kept the cottage fairly tidy in my absence. Plus, her apple pies far exceed Elspeth Kilpatrick's.

The elderly widows taught me how to scavenge what was left by the tillers in the turnip field, and the method is the same for potatoes. The sun is rising higher in the sky, and I'm thankful for the wide brimmed straw hat I had found in the manor, which shields me from the heat. Plus, my olive green dress is made from the lightest linen, keeping me cool.

"So, you *also* quarter people and just keep the good parts?

I thought it was just me," Vaila says with feigned surprised, but the gruesome nature of her joke almost makes me choke on a chuckle.

Yvaine throws a rotted potato at the stout woman, hitting her squarely in the chest. Vaila gasps at the attack. "Now you've gone and shocked the girl into nearly choking to death!"

"No, no, I'm fine," I say, recovering from my laughing-turned-coughing attack. "Does that work well for you, Vaila? I suppose half a corpse is better than a complete insufferable fool." Yvaine groans at my response, and my grin grows too wide for my face.

Vaila beams. "See, she can be a good craic too, Yvaine."

"They'll think we're mad banntraichean indeed if the farmhands hear you two cackling on." Yvaine rolls her eyes, making a show of checking to see if anyone is close by.

"If I'm being serious, with people you either have to forgive their flaws or not accept them at all. What a very lonely life that would be." Vaila grabs a potato from the dirt, giving it a firm squeeze before dropping it in her basket. My brow furrows as her words weigh me down more than the basket full of vegetables in my hands.

"Aye," Yvaine chimes in. "You can't force anyone to change, and we all have room to grow. It's too easy to get caught up in accusing others when we each have plenty of rot to clean up in ourselves."

Except I can force people to change. And I have. A stone settles in my stomach. "Good thing I've found two perfect banntraichean to be my friends here then," I say kindly, clearing my throat. "I wouldn't change a single thing about either of you."

Yvaine and Vaila look at each other then burst out laughing. They are laughing so loudly, I'm certain every farmhand across the entire estate can hear them.

"Oh, what is it now?" Flustered, I stand up straight, leaving my basket on the ground and putting my hands on my hips. A breeze brushes my braid against my back, sending wisps of loose hair over my face.

"Perfect? My girl, you just haven't learned our flaws yet," Vaila says with a wink. I'm certain their flaws will not compare to Ma's or my own. I don't see the brandings of a bond on their arms, after all. "I hope you'll still accept us when you do!"

"She has certainly learned at least *one* of your flaws, Vaila," Yvaine says, crossing her arms with a raised eyebrow. "What with that nonsensical morbid joke you made moments ago."

Vaila wiggles her head proudly at Yvaine's accusation, and the motion shakes from her head to her shoulders to her hips to her toes. "And now she has learned one of yours: a self-righteous *lack* of humor!"

"I can enjoy a *good* joke!" Yvaine protests, grabbing a turnip from her basket and tossing it at Vaila, who blocks the attack with the brim of her bonnet.

"Well, you certainly *look* quite dafty, Yvaine," Vaila challenges, squealing as Yvaine proceeds to chuck all of her preciously gathered vegetables at Vaila, one after another, with the gusto of a bandit.

Watching them makes an uncontrollable giggle burst from me, and the desire to join them wells up in my heart. Despite the insults and potato-turnip war that has ensued, there is a joy between them. True friendship. Acceptance.

Does it include me? My heart fills with hope, with want, but my wrists sting, reminding me that I don't belong here.

"Ladies, should I call for some reinforcements? Or perhaps a mediator?" Callen's voice startles me, and I nearly trip over myself as I stifle my laughter. I turn toward him and back away in one movement, my heart skipping a beat.

"No need for any help here!" Vaila shouts, grabbing a potato and chucking it at Yvaine, who dodges the throw with a sidestep. "I can defend myself just fine!"

"If you insist." Callen tucks his hands into his pants pockets and glances over at me, his green eyes searching for something in my blank expression. His lips part, but he decides against saying anything, and he smiles apologetically. My own lips tug to mirror his.

Just as he turns his head, Vaila sneaks behind him, and a potato lands hard on his stomach. He doubles over in shock.

"Defend yourself then! Don't hide behind Lord Lockhart!" Yvaine shouts, preparing another toss.

Callen ducks closer to me, leaving Vaila completely unprotected.

"Surrender!" Yvaine shouts, to which Vaila responds by sticking out her tongue like a child.

I pick up my basket and straighten my hat nervously. Or should I keep looking for potatoes? My basket is full enough, although Yvaine and Vaila have ruined half their own by this point. Perhaps I should help them. I nearly start forward—it's only a shadow of a movement—when Callen takes a breath to speak, causing my muscles to stiffen.

"I actually came to invite you up to the house for lunch," Callen says, watching the two women, but there is an edge to his voice. Is he hoping I will decline?

I smile weakly and shake my head. "I don't want to impose."

"Impose, my buttons! Yes, she will certainly join you for lunch!" Vaila declares, and I realize the war has ended in a truce. Yvaine and Vaila share a look, then smile at me and Callen. A mischievous twinkle remains in their eyes from their friendly dispute, or perhaps it's something else.

"We all will." The words spill out of my mouth before I realize how rude it sounds. I can't very well invite someone to a table, to a home, that isn't my own. I turn sharply toward Callen, certain the panic is marked in my eyes just as it is pumping in my chest. "If the offer is extended to all us banntraichean that is."

"Oh, Caitrin. You are hardly old enough to be called a banntrach," Vaila says with a snort, stooping to gather turnips and potatoes back into her basket. "A bonny lass like you is plenty young to marry again." She nods her head twice toward Callen.

I suck in a breath, cringing as my knuckles press against my lips. My chest tightens as my body grows ten times hotter, and, for whatever reason, I nervously glance at Callen to see his reaction.

"I always love having the banntraichean at my table," Callen says graciously, holding in a laugh. His mouth goes straight for a moment, then he licks his lips. "May I escort you?" He extends an arm to me, and words are caught in my throat.

My heart pounds as the urge to run away seizes me, colliding with the desire to accept his offer. Yvaine's meddling tease aside, I resist believing he is only being polite. After all, Elspeth's pie wasn't mere kindness. I shouldn't let my guard down too easily.

"We'll join you once we've cleaned up here," Yvaine says, shooing me away with her hands.

I carefully wrap my hand around his bicep, trying not to think about how strong and firm his arm is, gripping my basket with my other hand even more tightly.

"Ah yes, the casualties of war!" Vaila triumphantly tosses a turnip into her basket.

Yvaine gives me a wink as she picks up an overly bruised potato from the dirt. "We'll be right behind you, Caitrin."

We walk in silence across the field with the grand mansion looming ahead of us, slowly growing larger and closer.

Once we are out of earshot of Vaila and Yvaine, I do my best to slyly start my inquisition. "So, that night in the thicket…"

"I didn't mean to trespass, honestly! And I haven't invaded your property since. We just have a big harvest coming up— the entire lot is going to the Kaledon markets—and sometimes a walk helps me to clear my hear so I can actually get some sleep."

"Sometimes," I repeat with a snicker. "I suppose stumblin' upon me didn't help, did it?"

Callen chuckles, his face growing red.

My eyes widen, worried that my wording gave him the

wrong impression. "I mean, you probably don't usually run into knife-wielding cairlinen during your late-night walks."

"Uh, no. Not usually," he concedes, clearing his throat. "So...were you, uh...how did you meet Tate?"

I know what he was going to ask me, but his diversion isn't an easier topic. With a huff, my eyebrows bounce up and down. "Well, he moved to the grove," I begin, annoyed to have to talk about Tate at all, knowing my answer will only make him distrust me more. Or perhaps, it will embolden him to ask me the questions he really wants answered. "With Mrs. Raeburn, and Ivor and his wife, Orla, because Muireall wanted to talk to her *late* husband. And my ma, she's really good at—" I'm not ashamed of my heritage, but something causes me to choose my words carefully. "—facilitatin' that kind of communication."

Callen almost freezes. He pulls slightly away from me, tripping in the process. "You mean, cairlinen have spells that..."

"We can do all sorts of things." I slip my hand from his arm, gripping the heavy basket with both hands.

"Here! I should have offered—" Callen reaches for the basket.

My expression hardens, wishing I had stayed behind with Yvaine and Vaila. "I've got it," I say firmly, forcing a smile. "I can take care of myself."

His cheeks flush as he nods and doesn't offer his arm or further assistance, simply responding with, "of course."

"So, Callen Lockhart. Is it a spell you want from me?"

Callen shakes his head, grimacing like the question is

hurtful. "No, I don't want anything from you."

I snort and roll my eyes. "You don't want anythin' from a dirty cairline."

"I didn't say that."

"Well, this is a lot of charity for someone who can't pay for it. Nothin' in this world is ever really free."

"I've been blessed, so it's only right to pass it along," Callen answers. I sigh at his politeness, wishing he would just be honest instead of making me spell it out. "And I don't think that just because you're a cairline that—"

"You're losin' money, and rich people hate losin' money. I know that at least." He doesn't argue. "So what's it you're gainin'? It's worth losin' somethin' if you gain somethin', right?" I stop dead in my tracks and turn to face him, demanding an answer. He looks over at me, rotating only slightly, as if he knows what I will ask. "So what's it you're gainin' from me?"

His brow furrows as he holds my gaze for a moment. Then he turns to fully face me. "Nothing."

While I know he's lying, his words sting. As if I have nothing to offer. "It's never nothin'. And I saw what happened in town, just like you saw what I was doing in the woods. You know, I could help you…" I step toward him, closing the gap between us, holding his gaze. He takes a step away, his brow still furrowed, but his eyes don't move from mine. "You want revenge? You want them to leave you alone? You want *real* power over this whole town? What do you really want? I can give it to you."

Callen shakes his head, his expression softening. "I don't

need anything from you." His eyes are truthful, sincere, matching his words.

It sends a chill through my heart, like lightning in the night sky. My lips part, but nothing comes out at first. But then my head clears. He's just lying. "Everyone wants something," I whisper, refusing to give in to his charms. I continue toward the house, and moments later, Callen swipes the basket from my hands. "Hey! I said—"

"You don't need help," he finishes for me. "I understand, but I was raised to be a gentleman and to not let a lass struggle, even if she can manage it." I try to grab at the basket, but he pulls it out of reach. "You know what I want? To show you some kindness without you accusing me. Everyone deserves some kindness."

"Even Knox and Paisley Baines?" I ask, taunting him, unable to deny that my arms appreciate the reprieve. "Kindness like a broken nose?"

Callen doesn't respond, knowing I've found a flaw in his excuses.

"Kindness is a farce," I mutter, crossing my arms. We don't speak again until we reach the mansion.

TWENTY-ONE

I GLANCE DOWN AT MY green dress, the fabric limp with sweat and the hem crusted with dirt. As I fold my arms over my stomach, my cheeks redden further at the sight of my gloves. How can I eat with my gloves on? It is not only improper but unhygienic after all the digging around I've been doing all day.

This was certainly a bad idea. And after how rude I was to Callen, even if my words were truthful, I wouldn't be surprised if he withdrew his offer and sent me home.

"Have a seat," Callen says, handing my basket to a maid before pulling out a chair just next to the top of a long table. The table is set with the best glasses, fine napkins, a large bouquet of dahlias, and enough seats for a couple dozen guests. We climbed a few dozen stairs from the fields up to the patio that sits just outside the mansion, the balcony providing a brilliant view of the horizon.

"The others will be along shortly."

"Others?" I ask, stepping forward, but not taking a seat.

Callen chances a glance at me, but his eyes quickly shift away again. "The rest of my employees. We eat lunch all together every workday."

I'm joining lunch with his staff? "Are you hiring me?"

Callen groans and shakes his head. "I wish you'd just

believe me when I say I'm not trying to trick you. You're invited as my guest."

"Our guest."

A woman emerges from the open doors, covered by curtains, that lead into the mansion. She is tall, regal even, with elegantly arranged dark brown hair, framing her face with curls. Her cheeks are rosy against pale skin like she hasn't seen the sun in years. Her expression is set but soft, betraying her age, with piercing blue eyes. She studies me for a moment, taking in my appearance with care rather than judgement.

"You must be Caitrin Raeburn," she says, not moving from the shade of the doorway. Her voice has a slight accent, causing her words to sound soft and smooth.

I bow my head with a slight curtsy. "Yes, ma'am."

Her eyes narrow slightly, an almost smile on her lips. "I'm Lady Ardala Lockhart, Callen's mother. I've given very specific instructions to my son and his staff that you are not to be scorned or condemned as long as you are on the Lockhart Estate. So please don't feel uneasy, whatever your history in Cairlich. You are a Raeburn, and a Cròithen now, and you will be treated as such, not as a foreigner."

Her speech isn't rehearsed, and, as formal as her words are, I can tell they come from her heart. I glance at her bare hands, almost expecting to see red bands, but her arms are unmarked.

"Of course, Mother," Callen says before I can thank her for her hospitality. It strikes me that her words might be more of a reminder to him than an offering to me.

"Thank you, Lady Lockhart." I curtsy again, and when I

rise, she has disappeared into the house. I steal a glance at Callen, then finally take the chair. "So *she's* why you're being so nice to me." I smirk, but the revelation leaves me feeling small and silly, nothing more than a pawn in their games. "Can you at least explain why she's taken an interest in me?"

Callen stands to the side of my chair, awaiting the other guests, and neither of us looking at the other. "She's not from Croìthe originally, either. She came from across the sea with my father after a battle on the mainland." His words are cold and to the point, although we both remember the insults spoken in town.

"Your father was in the military?" I ask, fiddling with the various forks and spoons and knives that are set in front of me. There are too many of them for a simple lunch. I bite my lip, hoping my inexperience with fine things isn't too obvious.

"Yes. He was a close friend of the rìgh."

Even I know the weight of being close to the Croìthen rìgh, the most powerful man in the country. After all, it was a rìgh who first ordered cairlinen to be punished for their bonds.

Callen shifts his weight. "What does your father do?"

"I don't know. I never met him." My fingers drift over the silver wear, and I sink against the chair.

"Did he die?" Callen's words are low, heavy. Safe.

I shrug, my head shaking slightly as I stare at the subtle floral pattern embroidered on the tablecloth. We sit still in the silence, but I don't know what he's waiting for me to say. Or maybe he is at a loss for words, my own heritage more scandalous than his. A nervous laugh escapes me. "I asked Ma about him when I was younger, but she said there wasn't any point in telling me stories about him. Any questions after that were answered with silence." I look over at Callen, forcing a flat smile onto my lips and apathy into my words.

But he isn't looking at me. He seems lost in his own thoughts, staring blankly at the table.

"I'm starving!" Vaila breathes heavily as she emerges at the top of the stairs. She and Yvaine each cling to one of Brodie's arms, his forehead dotted with drops of sweat from the weight of the two women, but his smile is warm and unbothered despite his strained muscles.

Vaila rushes to take the closest chair as more farmhands appear coming up behind them, their pace slowed down by the banntraichean. Yvaine, however, looks pointedly at me, then to Callen, and decidedly takes the seat next to me. She gives me a kind smile, reaching out to squeeze my gloved hand, as if encouraging me to remove them.

Once everyone is seated, a wet cloth is placed in front of me, and I pick it up awkwardly as the others wipe the dirt from their hands.

"You'll have to take off your gloves, dear," Yvaine says, but I don't think she knows what she is asking me to do.

Sweat gathers on my temples and palms. I eye those at the table with suspicion as they begin to chatter amongst themselves. Only a couple glance back at me with curiosity.

Callen trades his cloth for a plate of food after he has cleaned his hands. "You don't need to be afraid, Caitrin," he whispers. Maybe he means to be comforting, but it only makes me more convinced I should stand up and leave immediately. He leans forward to capture my fully attention. "My mother meant what she said, and no one here would risk her wrath. Believe me." With his signature lopsided grin, he bites the small, boiled potato from his fork.

My heart begins to pound as I tuck my hands and the wet cloth into my lap. The desire to rip off the gloves and wipe the grime from my pores grows stronger, battling the pounding inside my chest. My heart is beating so loudly it fills my ears.

"This is utterly delicious! Caitrin, have you tried the roast yet?" Vaila calls to me from down the table, but she doesn't pause for me to answer. "Truly, you are a most generous host, Lord Lockhart."

Callen scrunches up his nose as he cuts into the meat. "You know I despise it when you call me Lord Lockhart, Banntrach McDow."

"Well, I think it's time you took ownership of the title. Your father was very generous, too, just like you!" Yvaine reaches across me to pinch Callen's cheek, and he graciously allows her, giving me a look of helplessness that eases my nerves.

As Yvaine returns to her food, I slip my hands out of my gloves. The cool air hits my skin, and I sigh with relief, wiping at my hands with the cloth. But I don't quite relax. I could pull the gloves back on to eat. They may have heard rumors that I'm a cairline, but they don't *know*. If I put my hands above the table, they will all *know*.

It's easy to combat the gossip the Baines family spreads as nothing more than rumors, but with an audience of over twenty, the knowledge of my bond wouldn't be mere gossip. It would be fact. What would the town do to me then?

"Your father hosted a ball every season, if I remember

rightly!" Vaila says, and the memory sends a wave of nostalgic smiles down the table.

"I reckon we are due for another ball. It's been years since we had a proper good gathering in Soarsa," Brodie pipes in.

Callen's face hardens at the idea, but he isn't forward enough to interrupt the conversation, so he focuses on the plate in front of him.

"You have to go all the way to Abercorn for a merry ol' time these days! And they're nothing like the parties Lord Lockhart used to throw," one of the farmhands adds, and everyone starts complaining and complimenting all at once.

In the midst of the excitement, I find my courage. Leaving my gloves on my lap, I pick up the fork, strike a buttery potato, and shove it in my mouth. Tucking my wrists behind the table, I chew slowly, looking around to make sure no one has seen. Luckily, talk of a ball has enchanted them.

But when I glance toward Callen, his eyes shift away, as if he was watching me the whole time. His mouth is a firm line, almost a smile, almost a look of torture. I don't know if it's the prospect of inviting all of Soarsa to the Lockhart Estate or my presence at his table.

"We must show Caitrin a proper good Croìthen time, Callen," Yvaine speaks up as I am timidly slicing away a chunk of meat.

The table goes quiet, and it's no surprise. Everyone looks my way right when the red ribbons encircling my wrists are on full display. I suck in a breath, determined not to let them see me squirm. Squaring my shoulders, I jab the slice of roast into my mouth, pretending that I'm not bothered by their stares.

I immediately cut a carrot, adding it to the roast, and giving them all a good look at my wrists. Breathing slowly through my nose, I swallow and force away the fear. Lady Lockhart said no one would scorn or condemn me. And as the table stays silent, I believe her: no one will judge me *out loud*. But they will judge me in their hearts.

I can only hope they fear me as well.

In my head, the words sound like Ma's voice.

"Absolutely," Callen says, raising his water glass. "I believe you are right, my wise banntraichean."

"Truly?" Brodie exclaims, followed by cheers and applause as Callen nods, reluctantly agreeing to their demands like a hostage held at knife point.

My stomach twists as Callen picks up my free hand, and I instinctively drop the knife to the table.

His hands are warm and firm, and while my red markings are clearly shown, he doesn't even glance at my wrist. His eyes are firmly on my own, almost straining to not look away. "I would be honored to have you present at Lockhart's first ball since my father's death, Caitrin Raeburn."

I truly have no idea what world the Lockharts live in, but it is certainly not Croìthe, or even Soarsa for that matter.

His glace flicks upward, to something behind me, and he releases my hand, returning to his meal as if he has accomplished his duty well. Turning, I spot Lady Ardala Lockhart, staring from behind the curtain of a second story window. She returns my gaze, but she does not smile.

She simply stares back at me, almost like she is looking in a mirror.

TWENTY-TWO

BRODIE, VAILA, AND YVAINE HAVE not stopped talking about the ball, with the banntraichean mostly reminiscing about their younger days. Brodie, on the other hand, seems keen on dancing with one girl in particular, but he is careful not to let any details slip about who she is.

Their excitement is contagious, and I listen attentively, not knowing what to add. I've never been to a social event, much less a ball. Even my own wedding was a small party with only immediate family and a few others who lived in the grove. The anticipation and dreams of what it might be like also summon a singular fear: I have nothing to wear. Of course, I've dreamed of making myself a sparkling gown of lace and satin fit for a princess, but given our impoverished state at present, such wishes are devastatingly impossible.

When we arrive at the cottage, Yvaine hands me my basket, and I am instantly suspicious. It's lighter than it should be, lacking the pile of potatoes and turnips I had gathered. Instead, the basket contains a thick fold of beautiful, pale blue fabric with stripes of embroidery. Two spools of thread and new needles are nestled next to it, with another bundle of cream cloth and lace trim peeking out from underneath.

My heart skips a beat. It's not the lace and satin I'd

imagined, but it is certainly better than anything else in my wardrobe. Certainly far more expensive than we can afford.

Brodie rounds the wagon, making way for the cottage door with an overflowing crate of vegetables.

I hurry after him.

"This is too much," I say, opening the door ahead of him. "I can't accept all of this without payin' somethin'." I glance around, but I don't know where Muireall keeps the coins stashed. Surely there must be a few silvers left that I can give Brodie for the material, but even just by looking in the basket, I can tell that the lace alone is far outside of my budget.

"You know he would have my head if I took any payment," Brodie says. "And it's a gift! You're not supposed to pay for it." He sets the crate down on the counter. "Plus, I don't mind going into town now and then instead of staying at the estate."

"*You* picked out this fabric?"

Brodie shrugs, but his cheeks bloom pink. "I may have had some help."

"How did he even know I sew?" The questions begin to unravel out of me, and I block his exit, intending to not let him leave until he answers all of them. "Maybe he wants me to make something for his mother, but I need measurements for that—"

Brodie breaks out laughing, shaking his head as he takes the basket from me and sets it on the table. "It's a gift. Do with it what you will."

"A gift? I hope it's money." Muireall grunts as she appears in the living room.

It's then that I realize I forgot to move the talisman last

night, and the night before. I cringe at the thought of the *old* Muireall returning, but hopefully I can correct my mistake once she goes to sleep.

Brodie bows politely. "No, ma'am. It's cloth," he answers with a smile.

Muireall raises an eyebrow, unimpressed. Then she spots the crate on the counter. "At least I don't have to worry about getting gout with all these vegetables."

Brodie's smile falters as his brow furrows, uncertain if she is mocking the generosity or not. "Well, I'd better get the other banntraichean home as well." He makes a move for the door. "And I'll leave a bag of feed for you horse by his pen."

I grab the basket, shoving it into his chest. "Don't forget this!"

"Oh, don't be dafty, Caitrin." Muireall takes the basket, looking through the contents as if searching for hidden gems, disrupting the perfectly folded fabric. I flinch, wanting to snatch it away from her, but manners keep me grounded.

Brodie waits on the stoop, shifting uncomfortably, like he anticipates Muireall will thank him. I know she won't if she's moody. "Tell Callen, and Lady Lockhart, thank you for us, Brodie." I try to sound grateful, but it comes out more as defeated.

He nods with a warm grin, and I close the door behind him.

"I bet a dress out of this will sell very well in town."

I turn slowly to face Muireall. Of course she would want to sell it instead of allowing me a new dress. Although, maybe the fabric is too fine for the life I lead. I would definitely worry about the embroidery getting caught on the sharp ends and splinters of the cottage.

Muireall shoves the basket back into my arms and flings open the door.

I have to move quickly to get out of her way. "Where are you goin'?"

"*We're* going."

Brodie's wagon disappears around the manor. That's when I hear gentle clucking, and I spot three hens sharing the pen with Ailbert. The hen house is hardly suitable for them yet, but I suppose Muireall didn't want to wait any longer.

"You were able to find some hens to purchase?"

"Might not have if I had done the laundry *before* I left."

I follow her around the pond, my chest growing heavy, like my lungs are filled with stones. Clinging the basket to my stomach, we walk toward a clothing line on the far side of the pond. Two of her mourning dresses hang on the line, drying.

Goosebumps raise on my arms.

"Caitrin." She points to the ground. "Why was *that* in my skirt hem?"

The shiny black marble, the talisman, stares up from a patch of dirt next to the wash bucket.

A lie comes to me quickly and easily. "Maybe whoever made your dresses wanted to weigh down the hem—"

Her palm lands hard against my cheek, and the slap forces my face to the side. "How *dare* you make a dèiligidh to use against me!" she growls.

My skin stings, and I can't get a full breath, stunned by her outburst.

"You think I don't know a talisman when I see one!"

My mind races, trying to push past the panic and pain and invent a reason she will believe, or at least a reason she might forgive.

With a kick into the dirt, Muireall sends the talisman spinning into the air, and then it lands with a *plunk* in the pond. "After all I've done, *this* is the thanks I get."

Forget trying to acquire her forgiveness. Perhaps I should make her beg for mine. I drop the basket to the ground. "All *you've* done?" I snap, clenching my fists. She stiffens as I step toward her. "It's only because of *me*, because of *that* talisman, that you were finally useful at all!"

Muireall rolls her eyes, but her confidence is betrayed when she steps back away from me. "I'm grieving—"

"Grievin'? How long are you going to use that as an excuse to be rude and make demands of me?"

"Until I die!" she answers, her gaze cold and hard. Impenetrable. "Leave if you don't like the way I am. I didn't ask you to come with me to Croìthe!"

"Without me, you wouldn't have any food or money or…chickens!"

"Maybe I would have been better off then!" She takes a deep breath, her eyes glossing over. "I don't *care* about me, Caitrin. My life's over."

"But it doesn't have to be!" I try to soften my words, to pull out the Muireall who had been baking pies and withholding sarcastic jabs, to bring back Meara. "I know you have lost so much, but think about how good you've felt—"

"I don't want the company of some cairline who will curse

me just because she's tired of an old banntrach's sorrows."

"It wasn't a curse; it was a favor!" My self-control bucks against my frustration, which is barely contained as I grit my teeth, wishing she would just listen.

"If that's what you call a favor, Caitrin..." Muireall steps right up into my face, and I straighten so she has to look up to make eye contact. "Then keep your charity to yourself from now on."

The words ring in my ears. Tears well up, making my vision blurry and threatening to spill.

Shoving past my shoulder, she stomps back to the cottage. I don't watch her go. Instead, I grab the basket and head for the manor, the tears running hot down my cheeks. If she doesn't want my help, then she will stop getting it.

TWENTY-THREE

MY STOMACH STAYS IN KNOTS for hours after my fight with Muireall, and the manor feels more like a refuge than ever. The spiders in darkened ceiling corners and the scurry of mice from the baseboards are somehow comforting company. I can't go far from Muireall lest I break my mionn, but I certainly don't have to stay under the same roof as her.

Perhaps it's time to stop believing Muireall will ever be kind in return, to give up hope that she will be the mother I've craved.

I don't need her anyway. I don't need anyone.

The beautiful basket of fabric and notions is the perfect distraction. I swallow my pride, and any lingering thoughts about returning the gift, and roll out fresh paper to start working. The determination to use every last scrap of cloth and inch of trim just to spite Muireall, so there is none left for her to sell, fills me like a fire.

I consider taking off my boots, longing for the comfort of bare feet, but Sophie Balfour's warnings from my youth echo back to me. One story in particular, of a tailor she knew who worked barefoot…that is until the day he dropped his tailoring sheers and they fell straight down, impaling the top of his foot and crushing into the wooden floor below.

I'm not sure if her story was true or not, or if the leather of my boots would be enough to repel the sharp, heavy tool, but I don't want to risk any distractions, especially one so disastrous.

I use the last light of the sun to cut each gore of the skirt and curve of the bodice, my sheers heavy and steady. When night falls, I light candles so that I can keep working until the dress is done. Adjusting the pattern from the tablecloth dress to save time, I sew with meticulous fury and determination.

The fierce desire to finish this dress by the morning—to flaunt it in Muireall's face that this gift is for *me*, not for her to sell—motivates me to push through even the loneliest hours of the night.

I carefully pleat the fabric at the waist and make sure the puff of the sleeves falls just right, with delicate bows at the shoulders and cream lace trimming every edge. After lining the dress with care, I cover the peddler's buttons with fabric scraps to use at the center front closure.

It's certainly the most expensive dress I've ever made, ever owned. I put it on to check the final fit, and even though the skirt only falls to my mid-calf, perfect for a cool summer's afternoon, I feel like a princess.

I feel as if this manor could one day be restored, be mine.

It could be a home.

Surely, I can figure out a way to live in the manor, even with the bugs and rodents. They may be better tempered company than Muireall anyway. At the very least, they don't badger me with chores and callous comments.

The morning sunlight fills the dining room as I step up to

the half-shattered mirror I brought from the powder room. My eyes are red with dark circles underneath them. I look weak, tired. Running my fingers through my hair, I grab a discarded length of wide ribbon from the table and use it to tie up half of my hair.

That's a little better.

Some breakfast will do the rest.

When I approach the cottage, I'm prepared to step lightly so as to not awaken Muireall just yet, but I'm surprised to hear the whistling of the teapot as I open the door.

If I had heard that whistle one moment sooner, I would have turned away, but it's too late now. Holding my head high and planting a smug smile on my face, I enter the cottage and grab an apple from the crate, which Muireall has moved to the ground. I ignore the fact that critters will get to it more easily there. It's not my problem now.

I'll glean some food for myself tomorrow at the Lockhart's farm.

"Are you ready to apolo—" Muireall starts as she spins toward me, kettle in hand. Then she sees my dress and her eyes harden, scanning over the garment. "I thought we'd agreed to sell it."

"*We* agreed to nothin'. And it was a gift to me, so I decided to keep it for myself." I take a bite of the apple—sweet and crunchy and perfectly ripe—and go to the sofa, gathering up my things from the armchair to bring to the manor. Surely there is a sofa or bed there that isn't musty and molded. At least I have all day to clean up a space for myself.

"We need the money, Caitrin, and food and a dozen other

things more important than a"—she raises her voice an octave higher, mocking me—"*bonny wee dress*. What are you going to do with it? Attend afternoon tea? Be courted?" Muireall huffs with annoyance.

With my arms full, I face her, maintaining complete composure. "You said you don't want my favors, so I'm stayin' out of your way from now on."

I head for the door, and Muireall sets the kettle down, hurrying to follow me. "Caitrin, you will go change out of that—oh!"

I stop abruptly as I spot our guest, and Muireall nearly slams into my back.

Callen Lockhart stands just outside the open door, seemingly hesitant to move forward or maybe considering turning around all together.

Did he hear our entire spat? He must have, with how Muireall tends to ramble on, loud as a billy goat. And what a sight I must be, with my arms full of clothes and underthings and a half-eaten apple.

"Callen Lockhart?" Muireall guesses.

He smiles reluctantly, closing the distance between us and handing a brown paper bag to Muireall. "My mother said it was rude to give Caitrin cloth for a dress but nothing new for yourself."

I remain frozen, too startled by his appearance here at this very moment. Then his eyes move to my shoulders and the bows of my dress.

My new dress. Made from the fabric he gave me just yesterday.

My cheeks redden.

Muireall takes the bag, peeking inside. "These are all colors. I'm still mourning," she mutters, but it's not with her usual grit; her tone is almost apologetic. "Come back inside and change, Caitrin. Before you embarrass me further," Muireall whispers into my ear.

I turn slightly toward her, my eyes fixed on Callen and the mystery of his visit for a moment longer. Then I meet her gaze and whisper back, "You've embarrassed yourself plenty so far."

She pinches my side hard, and I jump away from her. Callen catches my arm, as if I had tripped instead of trying to escape.

But I can't go far. Oh no, that stupid mionn keeps me from truly escaping Muireall.

Why did I let Tate convince me to create it in the first place? I shake away the thought, not wanting to admit the answer.

"Nice to see you again, Callen." I start down the path, leaving Muireall huffing. Maybe Callen will be able to put some sense into her. She seemed shocked enough by his presence to at least be cordial.

Once inside the manor, I drop the things on the dining table and let out a long sigh, bracing myself on a chair back for a moment.

But I can't stop for longer than a moment. I need to keep busy, or the questions and concerns lurking in the corners of my mind will consume me. With a deep breath to regain focus, I look around, wondering if I should pull a sofa in here since this is the cleanest room at the moment.

"The dress...I mean you look..." Callen's fumbling words make my heart skip a beat, and I turn slowly, trying not to appear shocked that he followed me. He is smiling, but it's full of pity, or perhaps an attempt at encouragement.

I look down, running my fingers over the embroidered fabric that covers my stomach. "I worked all night to finish it." Meeting his gaze, I clear my throat. "Muireall threatened to sell it, so I had to work quick to keep it for myself."

His eyes widen slightly. "Sell the fabric or the dress you made with it?"

I shrug. Maybe it's rude that I made the dress for myself more out of spite than gratefulness, so I edge away from the full truth. "I've been wearing the same things since we left the grove, so it's nice to have something new."

"I'm glad the fabric suits your tastes." He clears his throat, pacing and looking around the room. His eyes glide over my workstation, my shattered mirror, the broken doors and cobwebs of the manor.

With a nod, I force a smile, but there is an emptiness, an awareness of just how beneath his station I am. My fingers entwine, trying to release the restless energy coursing through me. "Callen, what are you doing here?"

Shaking his head, Callen faces me. "Dropping off the clothes from my mother for Mrs. Raeburn, like I said." He knows that's not what I mean, but maybe ours is a relationship of only half-truths.

"Well, thank you. Job well done. Mission accomplished."

He laughs, shoving his hands in his pockets. His cheeks flush with color, but I don't know why *he* would be embarrassed. It makes me want to disappear so he won't be so uncomfortable. When I don't respond, he steps toward me, eager to offer an explanation I didn't ask for. "It was Brodie's idea, by the way. After I saw the dress you sold in town—the peddler said you made it—well, Brodie thought maybe you would appreciate some new fabric. And he may have a slight crush on Shona, so...I probably shouldn't have said that."

"I do appreciate it." The admission almost feels like giving something up. "But why? Why are you *here now*?"

Callen's face tightens, like he's holding in a smile. "I just... The dress turned out beautifully. You..." Then his shoulders slump, and he stares down at his boots. "It's beautiful."

Beautiful. With that one word, the joy I felt this morning when I first put on the dress returns. And while I try to remind myself that he said the *dress* is beautiful, it is hard to separate myself from it. A small spark within me hopes that he wasn't just talking about the dress.

We stand in silence for a moment as he refuses to look at me, but I can't look away. My gaze slides from his curly hair to the bob of his Adam's apple as he swallows. A fluttering in my chest tells me to stop staring, or perhaps move closer to him.

Without warning, his gaze meets mine, and a shiver of excitement races from my head to my heart to my toes. I clear my throat, folding my arms as I look away. Straightening, he backs toward the broken doors of the dining room. "I'll see you tomorrow." Then he disappears as if escaping temptation.

I busy myself with turning the crumbling mansion into a home so I don't have to think about why I can't stop smiling.

TWENTY-FOUR

I SPEND THE REST OF the day cleaning up the manor to make a suitable living space for myself. I clean cobwebs off of a chaise lounge I find in the musty study, where half the books have been eaten away, and wash dusty linens from an upstairs bedroom. It isn't glamorous, but it will do until I can make some money. I don't even know how much it will cost to replace all the broken glass alone, but I have to start somewhere.

When night falls, I sneak out to the woods and call on Keres. Bargaining with my black mourning gown, we create a dèiligidh to keep the creatures away from me. At least I won't have to worry about spiders climbing in my hair or mice nibbling on my toes while I sleep. She's pleased to see me so soon and only asks for two drops of my blood along with the dress. As I slip the talisman—a jet stone pendant shaped like a moth—onto a chain to wear around my neck, I notice the ribbons around my wrist have grown wider than my thumb.

My heart beams, wondering if Ma would be proud, but seconds later, my stomach twists. Do Croìthen know that the stronger our bond becomes, the more power we possess, the wider our bond markings grow? Will anyone notice mine are wider? Is that evidence enough to prove I've broken the law?

I push away the worries as best I can and climb into my new bed. I should have slept soundly, basking in how well I am providing for myself, but elusive fear fills my veins, making the slightest noise cause panic and the shadows of night dance like ghosts around the dining room.

Pulling the quilt over my head, I try to shut everything out. While I manage to fall asleep, my dreams are filled with memories I'd rather forget.

The first dress I made for myself burning, creating my first dèiligidh.

Tate arriving in the Grove with Muireall, unable to keep his eyes off of me.

The drowning knowledge that he might not truly love me.

Keres's wispy form filling the bedroom while Tate lies dying before me.

A mionn that enslaves me to Muireall just to appease a dying man.

TWENTY-FIVE

THE SUN AWAKENS ME AT dawn, its light unhindered, filling the dining room. The cheerful chirping of birds echoes throughout the manor. I groan and twist on the chaise lounge, exhausted but not eager to return to sleep and nightmare memories. Although, I should probably find something to make curtains from so that I'm not woken so early every morning. I stretch, clutching my fists against my neck and then spreading my arms out wide. My muscles welcome the pull and I smile as the sunlight washes over me, the fears of the night chased away by the gentle brightness.

After brushing my hair, I braid it into two strands that I twist and pin over my head. Luckily, the cracked sink in the downstairs washroom still runs with water, and I wash away the grime and oil that has built up over my body. Feeling refreshed, I pull on my worn purple dress, skipping back to the dining room as the hope of a new day takes hold.

And the hope that I might not have to talk to, or even see, Muireall today.

In the washroom closet, I locate some sheets that may work for curtains, amused when whatever creature is hiding there scurries into the darkest corner, obeying my dèiligidh. Cleaning up the manor will be much more comfortable now that I don't have to worry about tiny, unwelcome guests attacking me.

I check on the hens, a wary eye on the darkened cottage, but find that no eggs have been laid yet. I can hardly judge them for it though; the hen house is in desperate need of repairs. My stomach growls, and I have my fill of water to try and appease it, reminding myself that it's harvest day, and I won't be hungry for much longer.

Rather than waiting at the manor, I meet Brodie at the road. However, Vaila and Yvaine aren't accompanying him as usual, and my heart dims. Brodie explains that they are taking an extra day off to make stew for the families that have fallen ill, and that they may join me later. Of course, I'll still be able to harvest, but it won't be quite as fun without them. If I wasn't so desperate for my own store of food separate from Muireall, I might have declined going to the farm at all today.

I climb up next to Brodie, doing my best to not be discouraged by the turn of events.

"Chin up, Miss Caitrin," he says, the usual sparkle in his voice as he smiles widely. "I know your friends are excellent company, but I don't think you'll be too lonely today."

"Are there other banntraichean gleaning today?" I try not to sound too intimidated by the prospect.

"Maybe!" he exclaims just to keep himself from saying something else.

I squint and quirk a brow. "Brodie, is Callen up to somethin' again?"

"No one's up to anything, Miss Caitrin." He's a bad liar. Glancing over at me with a gleam in his eyes, he chuckles to himself and refuses to say anything else.

The sun rises quickly as he drives us to the estate; I can already tell today will be hotter than usual. I wish I had brought my hat to keep the heat from my face and wonder if the spike in temperature is the true reason my elderly friends stayed home. Swallowing hard, I remove my gloves, hoping Brodie doesn't notice any difference on my wrists. But it's probably better to suffer silent judgement than sweaty palms today.

When we arrive at the grand estate, Callen is waiting, checking over some crates that have been filled with a variety of vegetables and fruits. He starts toward us as Brodie pulls the wagon to a stop, then halts, rambling off instructions to a farmhand and then letting out a deep breath. His head tilts upward, and I follow his gaze to the upper windows of the mansion.

Lady Lockhart stands at the window, peering past white curtains, looking down at us. She smiles warmly at me and nods. I bow my head in return, and then the curtain falls in front of her, hiding her from my view.

"Caitrin." Callen's voice startles me as he reaches toward me like a true gentleman. My heart starts to beat faster as I place my hand in his own, the red band wrapping around my skin so boldly on display. His grip is gentle enough that I could pull away without much resistance, but firm enough to keep me steady as I step down from the wagon. "Your hair looks nice like that."

My eyes glance up to meet his own, a cautious smile on his lips. He must be straining not to stare at my wrists. "Thank you." Taking my hand from his, I brush my fingers up my neck to the braids, feeling exposed. "It looks like it will be a warm day, so I'd better get to work."

I start for the fields, but Callen's fingers brush against my arm. "Caitrin, I'm sorry but…." He straightens his posture as I face him hesitantly. Perhaps I am not invited to harvest since Vaila and Yvaine aren't here with me. Or maybe since I am alone, I require one of his farmhands to chaperone me. After all, why would a Croìthen trust a cairline?

"I've already had food gathered for you today." He gestures to the crates, and I face him fully. "It's a little hot to be out in the fields, even for my own workers."

"But those look ready to be taken to market. Aren't banntraichean supposed to get just the leftovers?" I raise an eyebrow, challenging his intentions. I'm not going to be tricked into a deal I didn't barter. "I can gather myself; I don't mind the heat. Unless I'm not trusted…"

I wait for him to deny my assumption, but he fidgets uncomfortably. Well, at least I won't have to swelter away under the sun.

"At least let me pay. I can make a gown for your mother for the ball, perhaps, or…" I swallow, fidgeting with the pendant around my neck. I may not be very powerful in my bond with Keres, but it is strong enough to grant him a wish. And yet I can't say the words, knowing he will reject them.

He runs his hands through his hair. "It's a gift."

"Eventually you're going to have to tell me the *real* reason you're giving me so many gifts." Although my words challenge him and I drill him with a stare, daring him to lie to me one more time, my heart sighs with surrender. "I don't see Vaila and Yvaine going home with overflowing crates, after all."

Perhaps I should barter a dèiligidh that will make him be completely honest with me for once.

"Believe me, the banntraichean are cared for whether or not they come to the fields." Callen mirrors me, folding his arms over his chest and standing taller. He must be as frustrated with me as I am with him.

Flustered for a moment, Brodie grabs a package wrapped in ribbon from behind him. I brace myself, ready to reject whatever it is.

"This is fabric that my mother picked for a gown for the ball," Callen says awkwardly, gesturing for Brodie to hand me the bundle. So I am finally right on two accounts: one, the surprise was indeed fabric, and two, Callen is finally asking me to do something in exchange for his 'gifts'. What I don't expect, is the sting this realization brings with it. Nothing is ever free.

I carefully accept the package for a closer look. "Oh!" I say despite myself, my heart welling up as I take in the beauty of the fabrics. On the top is a bundle of embroidered flowers, strung together like trim, along with silk ribbon. Underneath the trims are folds and folds of soft, champagne-colored netting and light pink silk. The materials look much more expensive than I believe Shona's little textile shop carries. "I'll need measurements as well, of course."

"I, uh…" Callen glances at Brodie who shrugs with confusion. "I figured you'd get those on your own. Do you require assistance?"

I laugh, shaking my head at the ignorance of the men. "If I'm to make a gown for Lady Lockhart, I'll need her measurements. I don't need help, but I'll need to see her."

Callen seems at a loss for words.

"I believe the fabric's for you to make a gown for *yourself*," Brodie clarifies carefully. "Since you're to be the Lord's guest."

Callen clears his throat, and my smile evaporates as my gut feels punched a second time. Nothing is ever free, and I've already accepted too much.

I shove the bundle back into Brodie's arms, but my eyes are fixed on Callen, drilling him with a hard stare. "Do you intend on showing me off like a pet?"

Brodie stiffens beside me, and Callen sucks in a breath.

I step up to him, inches away so that he cannot help but look me in the eyes. My heart begins to race, frustrated. Or perhaps it is the heat. "I want to work hard for what I earn. And I could! If you would let me! I'm not some doll who needs to be pampered."

"Caitrin, you misunderstand. I know that you could—" Callen's eyes are full of worry and yearning, and my fury almost melts into something else, but I hold fast to my frustration.

"Be honest. Why are you doing this? What's the point? Why me?" The last question catches me by surprise, and I bury any hope that wells up at the anticipation of an answer.

Callen glances toward Brodie and steps back. "My mother insists."

"Your mother insists," I scoff, throwing my arms out. It sounds more like an excuse than an explanation. "Then your ma should be down here givin' me these things."

"The people here in Soarsa have not been kind to her, as

you have witnessed yourself. She had a difficult life before my father wed her and brought her here. And even now the people have not forgotten her past. Just as they may never forget where you came from, or what you've done." He nods to my wrists, and I strain not to squirm under his scrutiny. "She could not bear the thought of you being treated as she is and wanted to make sure our family at least shows you kindness."

While I feel touched by his explanation, it is accompanied by a sinking disappointment I hadn't expected.

He doesn't want to give me anything; it's only the wishes of an old, lonely widow, perhaps trying to pay penance for her past or correct the wrongs committed against her. I nod slowly. "I see."

Of course. It's not really charity. It's not really *free*. By being generous and gracious towards me, they get to feel superior to those who treat them poorly. Really, it's rather selfish. I want to rise up with pride, but instead my spirit is flattened.

Keres is right.

No one will love me without a dèiligidh to trick them into doing so.

"Well, I guess I'll get out of your way so you can return to more important things." I turn to climb back into the wagon, but Callen catches my wrist.

"Actually…" His thumb rubs over my soft under skin, over the ribbon of red there. My heart skips a beat, my skin tingling under his touch, and my breathing hitches at the sensation. I face him once again. A curl of hair falls over his forehead, brushing against a drop of sweat on his brow. Then he glances up at me, holding my gaze in a way that feels intimate, intrusive.

I force myself not to be mystified by his stare. "What else do you want? Did I not grovel and thank you enough?" His eyes darken and he releases my wrist. The fight drains out of me all at once. Two slow breaths fill my lungs as shame sinks its teeth into me. I wet my lips. "I mean…"

Brodie pats Callen's shoulder and then leads the horse and wagon to the stables.

"There was something I wanted to ask you," Callen admits, daring to glance up at me as he shoves his hands into his back pockets. I guess whatever he sees on my face makes him braver. But I feel weakened. Callen bites his lip, holding back a tentative smile. "If you want, you could say I need a favor. Although Brodie would probably say my dancing is more akin to a curse."

"Dancing?" My heart wells up at the image the word creates, my breathing shallow. I barely hear the word 'favor'.

Callen rubs the back of his neck, a hint of panic flashing across his face as he tries to maintain his nonchalant confidence. "There's a ball coming up, or so you might have heard, and I'm quite out of practice."

"I don't know any Croìthen dancing. Or any dances at all! Ma never…well, I've never really danced with a partner before."

"Not even at your wedding?"

The question catches me off guard, and while my mouth falls open, I stop the dark secret threatening to break free through my lips. "No," I respond, shoving the truth down and away from my mind. "But, in teaching me you'll surely remember all the better yourself! And keep me from looking like a fool."

Callen smirks, but his brow is furrowed, as if his face is at war with itself. "So you'll do me this favor?" He extends a hand to me, with a slight bow.

I place my hand in his own, then turn our hands to shake on an agreement. "Yes, although it may be more helpful for me than you in the end." I step up to him again, the heat in the air spiking, and I don't resist the playfulness that arises in my chest. "Are you sure you're not scared to dance with a cairline?"

His grin falters, falling into something more sincere. "No, I'm not scared of you. But perhaps I should be." I laugh gently at his jest, and he almost relaxes. Almost. I seal the agreement with a firm shake, and then pull my hand away from his. But I wish I hadn't.

TWENTY-SIX

THE GAZEBO SITS AT THE edge of a creek that wanders through the apple orchid and the Raeburn thicket, transforming into a river near the edge of the property and rushing toward the large lake surrounding the town square. Bright pink begonias bloom and blossom around the white pavilion, with ivy climbing up the columns and a weeping willow swaying overhead. It's beautiful and quiet, with only the sound of a babbling brook and the content chatter of a kingfisher nesting in the tree.

I follow Callen up the three wooden steps out of the burning sun and into the shelter of the gazebo. In the shade, it doesn't feel quite so warm, and the breeze that brushes over the creek keeps the air cool.

Then Callen turns toward me. That same curl of his wild hair springs over his forehead, pointing to his sparkling green eyes and wistful lips.

I'm struck with just how alone we are.

And how intimate dancing can be.

Tate didn't like to dance. Or maybe he just didn't like dancing with me, except on our wedding day, and that was a mess. We were both drunk on the faux joy I had bartered and created for each of us the night before, thinking it might keep us happy all our days.

It didn't.

All joy is fabricated in one way or another, and all love comes at a cost.

"So, where do we start?" I ask, shoving the memories back into the recesses of my mind and locking them in a box there.

"Well, do you know the waltz?"

"I don't think I know any formal dances, much less by name." I twist my fingers together, my nerves building and buzzing in my chest. Maybe this was a mistake.

"It's like a box step, but it's only three counts instead of four." He forces a smile, but his lips are pressed together too tightly. While he has invited me to dance, his hands are tucked securely in his pockets.

I cock my head to the side, almost laughing. "Maybe you should *show* me?" I force my arms to my sides, waiting for him to make the first move.

Instead of offering me his hands, his feet begin to step, three steps at a time, like an awkward, dancing stick. Or perhaps he is afraid of touching me for such a prolonged amount of time. Croìthen have no idea how our magic works; maybe he believes I can curse him simply with a touch.

"Callen..." I shake my head, smiling at the feeling of his name on my lips, and lean back against one of the columns that holds up the domed gazebo roof. Callen stops abruptly, looking up at me, his face flushed with heat. "You seem to be dancing quite proficiently all on your own. Am I just here to watch?" I stifle a giggle.

"Right, of course." Letting out a deep sigh, he unbuttons

the cuffs of his shirt, rolling up his sleeves as if preparing for hard work, accentuating his biceps.

Then he reaches for me, palm up.

I swallow. Hopefully, I'm not about to make an utter fool of myself. Pushing off the column, I put my hand in his, and he gives me a slight tug causing me to trip closer to him.

"Sorry," he mumbles. There is still a polite distance between us, but we feel infinitely closer skin to skin. He guides my free hand up to his shoulder, and then, with an embarrassed grunt, his hand glides around my waist to my back. Through the fabric of my dress, I feel the pressure of his fingers, as if he wants to pull me closer but refrains. Or maybe that's what I want.

I shake my head free of the notion.

His gaze is glued to our feet and I look down as well, but his touch is hard to ignore.

"So as I step back, you step forward—same foot! Yes, like that."

I follow his instructions, like a pupil with a teacher, vulnerable and ignorant, at the mercy of his command. Should he teach me something incorrect, I won't have any way to know better.

It makes me uncomfortable, so uncomfortable that I almost pull away.

Forgetting myself for a moment, my foot collides with his, and our heads bump together. "Oof!" Callen laughs nervously as he glances up without raising his head. I glimpse a smile on his lips, genuine but cautious. We're as close as we were at the front of the house, except I'm not yelling at him this time.

Somehow, it's more intense, my senses heightened, noticing his every touch, every breath, every blink.

"You're getting the hang of it," he says. "Although, I don't think staring at the floor is how two people are meant to dance." He looks back down as we continue to move through the simple steps again.

"I'm just followin' the example of my teacher," I say defensively, pulling back slightly, but his hand on my back keeps me from pulling away.

Callen laughs. "My apologies." He straightens, and I wish I hadn't said anything at all. As awkward as it was with both of us looking at our feet, it'll be worse if we have to look at each other's faces. Worse, because already my heart has begun racing, like it's afraid of something. But I'm not afraid of Callen.

And that simple acknowledgement scares me more than anything.

"You have more practice than me. I'm still warmin' up." I school my features and focus on our dancing, watching my feet follow his, trying to anticipate his next move, eager to prove that looking down is the only reason I'm successfully dancing at all.

I kick his shin, moving too quickly.

"Ow!" Callen releases me, bending to rub his leg. "Trying to wound me, now?"

"I didn't mean to! I'm so sorry," I say, holding my hands up helplessly as my stomach turns with embarrassment.

"No harm done," he says, a twinkle in his green eyes. "This time"—he holds out his hands, inviting me back into his embrace to continue dancing— "let me lead, and you won't have to worry about injuring me further."

I prefer to be independent, in charge of myself. "Sure," I mutter, looking back to my feet as we take the first steps, but then he stops, pulling me to a halt along with him. "What?" I snap looking up at him.

"If you keep your eyes on me, instead of my feet, you won't be so obsessed with knowing what's next. Just trust me. I won't let you go waltzing off into the creek," he says casually, pleased with his humor, but my chest tightens at the words.

Just trust me.

He makes it sound so easy; he clearly doesn't realize just how dangerous trust can be.

But I don't want him to think I'm too stubborn, so I straighten my posture, boldly meeting his gaze. My confidence wanes as soon as we take the first step, and my grip on his shoulder tightens. His grin tugs to one side, and my own smile falters.

"See?"

"I'm a quick learner." I can't let him take too much credit.

Then he steps slightly to the side, and my arrogance slips as I struggle to keep up. I start to glance back down, no longer able to anticipate his steps as the dance begins to spin.

"Trust me," he whispers into my ear, sending sparks down to my toes.

Perhaps out of stubborn pride, and not wanting to trip all over him, I force myself to keep my eyes up, returning his challenging stare. But it's almost more challenging to not get lost in his green eyes than it is to follow his steps.

"If you relaxed, maybe you'd actual enjoy dancing," he suggests, his posture rigid and proper.

"You're one to talk. You're stiff as an oak, with your precise and perfect steps…that's hardly relaxed either."

"I suppose you're right," he admits, but my victory is short lived. He lifts our hands with a gentle push on my waist, sending me into a quick twirl. The dress flutters around my feet like the rippling tide before his arms capture me again. "How is that for loosening up a bit?"

I want to glare at him, but the thrill of the movement has my heart yearning for it again. "Do you want me to trust you just so you can trick me?" I challenge, but it comes out less playful than I intended. Before I can stop my heart from wondering, I ask him, "Do you think you can trust *me*?"

He should say no.

He saw me in the woods.

TWENTY-SEVEN

"WELL, YOU'RE THE FIRST CAIRLINE I've ever met." He doesn't need to say more to me to understand that my bonding bands give him pause. But he continues, and I stiffen, ready for future explanation. "But you're not just a cairline. You're far more than a cairline. You're Caitrin. And…" he hesitates, his gaze holding mine, stealing my breath. But then he breaks away, his eyes wide, banishing the rest of his words. "Unlike those scoundrels in town, you've no interest in the private affairs of my family, and you don't seem intent on taking advantage of my fortune."

I laugh, trying to ease the tension built up in my chest. "You don't know that! Perhaps I'm a gold-diggin' cairline, come to take all your apples and potatoes."

"I believe that would make you a potato-digger, which doesn't have the same threatening ring to it, you have to admit." He winks at me, then he spins me out again. My feet know what to do this time; I twirl out and then back into his arms. I can't help but laugh, the tension in my body loosening with the movement. "And I've known a potato-digger or two. They're easier to spot than you might think."

I raise an eyebrow. "What are the signs, then?"

"One, they always giggle far too much, even when you're

not trying to be funny! And you are far too honest to coddle my ego like that."

"I can't argue with that, I suppose."

"Two, potato-diggers are very materialistic. One gift is never enough, and it can't be too small either. I can barely give you one gift without you complaining it's too much!"

"And three?"

"And three!" He snorts, looking away from me to consider his third point, but a memory steals his humor in an instant. "And three, they never miss an opportunity to call you and your mother names behind your back."

My amusement dims to an ache. "I'm sorry. You don't deserve that."

"Deserving or not," he admits, the sorrow slipping away. "At least now I know the signs, so you see"—he spins me out again, lightening the mood instantly—"I'm not worried about you being a potato-digger one bit."

"Well, I'd think my bond would be enough to put me on your distrust list, along with that potato-digger." I laugh lightly, more at myself than anything, and refuse to meet his gaze, staring over his shoulder instead.

"I probably shouldn't get too comfortable with a woman who dèiligeadh ris an diabhal." While his tone is playful, there is underlying judgement, mocking me with the condemning phrase.

I huff, wishing his words didn't get under my skin so quickly. "We don't sacrifice babies to demons or anything like that. I know that's what the Croìthen say about us."

"Any sort of blood offering seems..." He hesitates, but his

hesitation alone tells me what he thinks. "It seems strange to me."

"Life from life, is what we say." Pride wells up in my chest as we continue to spin in the steps of the waltz. Perhaps I can enlighten him that my bond is something to be respected, not feared, not judged. Now *I* am the teacher. "How can you ask for somethin' if you aren't willin' to give anythin' yourself?"

"And how is your…"

"Her name is Keres."

"How is she able to make dèiligeadh that have such power?" His eyes are filled with genuine curiosity, and something else. Something soft and kind.

"The spirits are from a different realm than us. They have power over things we don't."

"Power over life?"

"I suppose."

"Power over *your* life?" As his tone hardens, I recognize what I thought was tenderness in his eyes is actually pity.

I stiffen, and our steps falter. "What are you implyin'?"

"Creating dèiligeadh branded your body." His eyes glance down at my arms, and I pull out of his grasp, bringing our dancing to a complete stop.

"These markings aren't brandings like on cattle to be sold. They're a symbol."

"A symbol of what?"

"Of the strength of my bond. Of my power." I stand tall and resolute, refusing to feel ashamed of my magic.

"A symbol of your bondage to a spirit." His eyes darken, searching mine to uncover the secret to convincing me he's right.

"My *bond with* a spirit. She gives me power to make life better for myself, and for others."

His muscles tense, but he is trying not to let his frustration show. "In exchange for your blood."

"Life. From. Life." Each word bites at the air, not surrendering a single syllable.

The phrase echoes between us, and a silence settles in. I've certainly soured whatever mood had been between us, and Callen seems unable to say anything in return. Without the moving of our feet against the worn, wooden floorboards or our words filling the air, the sounds of the farm flood my ears. The bubbling of the creek mixes with the chirping of birds. Laughter echoes from the storage barns.

Callen flexes his fingers at his sides, then balls his hands into fists, then flexes again. Perhaps I pushed him too much. My heart thumps as if being hit by a falling tree over and over again. What if he refuses to continue to let me glean? No one will hire me in Soarsa if not even the town outcast can tolerate me.

I can make him understand. I can ease his concerns. "It's not quite so gruesome as you all seem to think it is." I try to keep my voice sweet and convincing, rather than argumentative. "And even in Cairlich, cairlinen aren't permitted to create mallachd: curses, dèiligeadh that cause harm." I smile, hoping he will realize that, while I may be a cairline, I am not uncivilized. None of my people are. Well, most aren't.

"How could a spell *not* cause harm?"

I press my lips together and restrain myself from lashing out. Instead, I pull the chain around my neck away from my décolletage, showing off the moth-shaped pendant there. "This talisman was made from a dèiligidh." Callen's gaze darts to the pendant. The realization that he had been inches away from it while we were dancing dawns on him, and I can tell he wants to shrink away. "It's nothin' dangerous, and I didn't have to dance naked in the moonlight or sacrifice some livin' creature to create it. It was a simple exchange."

He raises an eyebrow. "So what did you exchange?"

"An old dress," I say, still uncertain if I will tell him of the two drops of blood. They are hardly worth mentioning.

Callen twists his head to the side. "An old dress? One you found in the Raeburn Manor?"

"No, my mournin' gown. It was made in a hurry and hardly useful to me anymore." I let the talisman drop back against my bosom.

"I'm sorry. That must have been difficult." He shakes his head.

"It was nothing."

"Nothing?"

I don't need to explain myself. I won't.

And manners keep him from asking too many questions about my marriage. But he doesn't stop asking questions. "What does a demon—"

"Spirit."

"—need with a gown anyway?"

"Whatever is accepted to make the dèiligidh is melded into a talisman."

Callen nods at my necklace. "And what does that talisman do?"

"It keeps the bugs and critters away from me in the manor." I almost roll my eyes, embarrassed that I used my magic for something so trite.

"Really? That's it?" He seems just as amused, a smile returning to his face.

My smile softens. "That's it."

"But I thought…spirits required blood."

I laugh nervously, and relent, holding up my right hand, knowing each finger looks similar enough. "I'm a seamstress who pricks her fingertips daily. The tiny scar of a prick to give a drop or two of blood for a dèiligidh looks the same as when I stab myself by accident with a needle. It's no huge sacrifice."

He is quiet for a moment, considering my words. I don't know why a drop of blood should be such a big deal. Better to be given freely than by force or accident.

Then he reaches out, presses his palm to mine and threads our fingers together. My breathing hitches as he steps close, and I instinctively step away, but my back presses against one of the columns of the gazebo.

"And what if you didn't have a need for spells that keep critters away?" There is an intensity in his eyes, drawing me to him. He lowers our hands, and his reaches out to tuck an escaped ginger curl behind my ear. "What if you had a home that was safe, and warm, and whole?" His fingertips are like butterfly wings against my cheeks, trailing along my jawline. My eyes dip to his lips. "Caitrin…" I look back up, his face full of concern and his eyes searching my own. "If you had no need for magic, would you break your bond?"

And the momentary enchantment is broken. I stiffen and clear my throat, then slip away from him. He doesn't know what he is talking about—there is no way to break a bond; at least, no dignified way—but his question prickles nonetheless.

"I should be gettin' back home." The word 'home' almost sticks in my throat as I say it. Turning, I start to descend the few stairs of the gazebo.

"Will you have enough time to make a gown?" Callen shouts after me.

I glance over my shoulder to smile, straining to be polite. "Three days is plenty time. I don't have anythin' better to do."

His lopsided grin starts to appear, strained with embarrassment, like he's chased me away. But I'm not running away from anything. Am I?

"Well…." He hesitates, and I spot that look in his eyes again: pity. I can't be wasting my time dancing when there is work to do. "I hope you'll tolerate another dance with me at the ball."

My smile falters, and I don't know how to respond. Even after all that, he still wants to pretend that he will dance with me in public? I can only hope his mother had the good sense to purchase silk gloves for me as well. Their employees may know better than to speak their condemnations aloud, but if I've learned anything for certain since moving here, it is that their other guests, the townsfolk of Soarsa, will not be quite so restrained.

TWENTY-EIGHT

BACK AT THE MANOR, I try to clear my head, but Callen seems to have taken up residence in my thoughts. And it's his irritating words that linger the most vibrantly.

If you had no need for magic, would you break your bond?

Why does it matter so much to him? It doesn't matter to me who his mother is or that he's a lord. Why should those things matter when he is kind and respectful, when his hands are firm and comforting, when his lopsided grin makes his green eyes sparkle?

I drop the fabric on the dining room table and shake my head. None of those things matter to me, either. I'm not some lovesick girl, easily won by gifts and grand gestures. I'm a cairline, a seamstress. I can take care of myself, and I have work to do.

The idea of cutting into such beautiful cloth is too overwhelming and intimidating for the time being. And there were no gloves included to cover my bonding bands. I could make gloves, but it is perhaps the most tedious task a seamstress can undertake, with the tiny seams and curves. Surely there will be a pair at one of the shops in town that will complement the fabric. I just need the funds to acquire them.

The study has a large fireplace, towering bookshelves, and

a spacious desk, but it is stripped bare apart from the deteriorating books and heavy furniture. The drawing room is much the same, with sunken sofas and arm chairs, broken frames barely containing torn canvas, and the shattered remains of a vase.

Opening the doors on a side table, a mouse jumps out. With a swallowed scream, I fall backward against the floorboards, and the rodent scurries away from me obediently. It takes me a moment to recover enough to reach into the darkness of the table. And there, tucked in the back of the cabinet, covered in a film of dust, is an ornate, egg-shaped box.

Taking out the object, I can see that the box alone will be worth something once I've cleaned and polished it. It's embellished with trumpets, music notes, and stars. Tipping up the lid reveals a small, mirrored surface with tiny painted sunflowers. The contents of the container, if there are any, are covered by a metal plate, cut with intricate swirls, and a little key sticking out of a hole.

Twisting the key doesn't unlock a secret compartment; rather, it winds up something within, and when I release the key, a gentle melody swirls up in tiny tinkering notes. I bounce with delight at my good fortune, knowing this must be worth quite a bit. Closing the lid, I tuck the music box into the pocket of my apron. A few more little treasures like this and I'll not only be able to buy gloves but start saving up for repairs too.

Two hours later, and I have a handful of pleasant trinkets like the music box gathered from the first-floor rooms. I wipe the dust from my hands, arms, and face, and remove my dirty apron. Good enough for a little trip to town. Fetching Ailbert reminds me that the hens need their own little home repairs. Another item on my ever-growing to-do list. I saddle up Ailbert and pull on my work gloves.

The ride to town is short, but with the setting sun, I hope some shops stay open in the evening. Thankfully, even though the grocery has closed, *Hew's Textiles and Apparel* still appears to be open, and the peddler still has his stall set up in front of the butcher's shop.

The peddler gladly takes my trinkets, having remembered me from his last stop in Soarsa. He trades the items for a small hammer, a pouch of nails, and a simple pair of screw-on earrings, sparkling with quartz set in rose-gold for the ball, and gives me fifteen silvers for the rest. I hope it's enough for silk gloves.

As I start across the town square, the postmaster exits his shop, whispering to another gentleman who follows him out and locks up the door for the evening. He glances my way anxiously, but I smile in return, hoping to ease any concerns. Three carriages and a wagon pull into the street, parking in front of the town hall. The postmaster goes to meet them. Lewis Baines steps out and shakes the gentleman's hand.

He looks over at me with a cold determination, and I disappear into the shop.

A little bell rings above the door as I enter to find two ladies at the counter already. I recognize one as Elspeth Kilpatrick, but her friend is a stranger to me. Shona looks up, her eyes wide, and I slip toward the wall of fabrics, hidden by shelves, before the other women can spot me.

I try to browse, but I can't help but overhear their

conversation.

"Oh yes, he's quite ill, and Wiley doesn't think it's fatal, but he's also never seen anything quite like it," Elspeth says, eager to share the gossip despite the nature of the news. "He thinks it's something foreign, maybe from Cairlich—"

"Foreign like…like a curse? Oh, Elsie! Do you think Meara and that cairline brought a curse from Cairlich with them?"

"Would you like this blouse wrapped up?" Shona asks. I peer through a shelf of notions to see her standing behind the counter, slouching with a long face.

"Yes, yes," Elspeth responds with a wave of her hand, annoyed with the interruption. "I suppose Meara could be cursed, although she looked *quite* healthy when I saw her. But you know both of her sons and her husband died over there. Did you hear she wants to be called Muireall now? Maybe she is cursed, but it's only the men around her who are affected." Clearly, these women have no idea how dèiligeadh work.

"Oh, I hadn't heard. How strange! So, you think she cursed the butcher?" the friend asks, gleefully shocked at the theory. "And if that's the case, Callen Lockhart won't be far behind, now will he?"

Now it's Elspeth's turn to gasp. "What do you mean, Rowan?"

"Well, Meara's daughter-in-law is over at the Lockhart Estate almost every day, the rumors say. I suppose it's not too surprising considering his father married a harlot; why shouldn't Callen marry a cairline? Perhaps it's a family tradition to dirty one's bloodline." Rowan grins deviously with a shrug. "Do you think she has put a spell over him?"

"All done! Here you go, ma'am," Shona says loudly, shoving a paper bag tied with ribbon toward Elspeth. "I'm closing up soon, so…"

Elspeth grabs the package without another word to Shona, continuing to chatter and gossip in whispers with Rowan as they exit. I stay hidden until they are gone, watching them through the display window of the shop as they head toward the Town Hall, where a group of wagons, carriages, and horses have gathered. The windows are lit up for an evening meeting, it would seem.

"So, what do you want this time?" Shona calls from the other side of the shop, and I spin around. She is forcing a smile, but her eyes are wide with panic. "I really am locking up now." She grabs a ring of keys from the wall, but she doesn't move from behind her counter of protection to escort me out.

Straightening and doing my best to not appear threatening, I clasp my hands in front of me. "I am just lookin' for some gloves for the ball this weekend," I tell her, fishing the coins from my pocket. "I have fifteen silvers…I hope that is enough."

Her lips twist to the side, eying the money in my open palm and weighing her options. Then she nods. "Ten will suffice. What are you looking for exactly?"

Hurrying to the counter, but not too quickly, I set the coins in front of her, determined to show her that I am an honorable and worthy customer. Maybe once she sees I'm not trying to trick her, she'll be more open to my potential as a valuable employee as well. "Long and silk, maybe in a light pink or cream?"

Shona turns to a set of narrow boxes on a shelf behind her, checking tiny, handwritten labels on the edges of each one. She grabs three and sets them on the counter. Without any fanfare, she removes the lids to display the options. "Any of these?"

The first pair is bright white, with buttons at the wrist and rather simple, but made of fine silk. But too white. The second pair are velvet, a soft pink color that perhaps is the same shade as some of the embroidered flowers, but if it's not, they will clash. The third pair, however, is a warm cream color, the same shade as my skin and the netting back at the manor. The buttons are rose gold, and the perfect complement to my new earrings.

"These ones, please! And thank you so much. They are perfect!" I point to the cream pair, waiting patiently for her to box them up properly for me. Or maybe she won't. Perhaps I am assuming too much.

Shona slips on the lid, her hand hovering over the slim box as if still deciding if she will sell them to me or not. She glances up at me and swallows, but as our eyes meet, her gaze softens with the shadow of a smile. With a sigh of surrender, she takes out a little, brown paper bag from under the counter and places the glove box inside. With a scrap of ribbon, she ties the twin handles of the bag together and hands it to me.

"What Elspeth and Rowan were talking about…" she says, her voice quiet. I hold my breath, preparing to defend myself. "The Lockharts really are lovely people. I hope their words won't make you think otherwise." Shona adds a small smile, but it doesn't reach her eyes.

"No, of course not. They've only been kind to me. And

thank you for the gloves!" I turn to hurry out of the store.

Just before I exit, she calls cautiously after me, "I look forward to seeing your gown at the ball!"

Beaming, I nod eagerly. "And I yours!"

TWENTY-NINE

I SPEND TWO DAYS SPLIT between three tasks.

First, I tackle the manor kitchen, doing my best to clean away the dust and dirt, and clear out the cobwebs and nests. Despite the talisman, I still shriek when a particularly large, hairy spider climbs out of a shadowy corner or an entire family of mice emerge from a hole in a cupboard. At least chasing the critters out of the manor makes the hard work of scrubbing much more tolerable in comparison.

Second, I manage to use broken bits from the manor to properly fix up the pen and hen house. I clean out the barn of old muck, so that Ailbert can be more comfortable, before bathing and grooming him. The next morning, the hens all laid two eggs each, a reward for my hard work.

The third task has been the gown. I haven't ever really made a ballgown, or anything luxurious, and I worry my taste won't match the extravagance of the event. Or that I will be *too* extravagant. I make guesses based on the fabric choices Lady Ardala provided and fill in the gaps with my own preferences.

Muireall hasn't come into the manor once. Although, when she goes outside to check on the hens—I make sure to leave eggs for her—I see her trying to get a glimpse into my room. That's what I've settled on calling it: my room. It's easier than saying dining-workshop-bedroom-room.

Her judgmental stares are enough to remind me of what I've avoided by moving out of the cottage. Maybe Keres is right: no one is good enough for me. I did try my hardest to be a good daughter-in-law, and she couldn't bear to reciprocate my kindness. Why waste the effort on someone incapable of giving anything back?

The morning sun has risen high enough to light my room well, and with a filling breakfast of fresh eggs scrambled with potatoes and turnips in my belly, I set to work on the finishing touches of the gown. Without a dress form to assist in my work, I fashion a makeshift contraption out of several hangers and a round basket I found. Tying the items together, I hang them on a stick that is braced on top of the open, double doors that lead to the ballroom.

The dress doesn't hang perfectly—far from it—but it will do so I can set the hem and lining, and make sure the trimmings are draped just right. I stitch, one hand holding the needle and the other keeping the fabric steady, with pins pressed between my lips.

I recall a story my seamstress teacher, Sophie Balfour, had told me once, smirking at the thought and feeling a little rebellious.

She had said there was once a seamstress working on a gown, with pins clenched between her lips. She was so deep in concentration that the world slipped away as she stitched, and she didn't even hear a troublesome young boy enter her workshop. When he shouted right into her ear, intending to scare her, she sucked in a breath to scream and swallowed the pins!

I had asked if the seamstress died, but Ms. Balfour wouldn't tell me; she simply said I shouldn't put pins between my lips unless I want to find out. Another one of her cautionary stories to discourage bad habits.

But surely this habit isn't quite so bad.

"What a mansion you are living in." Muireall's voice fills the space.

With the story of the pin-swallower fresh on my mind, I spit the pins out of my mouth and across the floor. My breathing is labored, either from the danger of swallowing pins or the surprise of Muireall's visit.

I stand from my stool, leaving the needle and thread to dangle from the hem, and turn to face Muireall with a huff. "It's nothing extravagant, but I make it work." I know if I say anything more of my small improvements on the space, she will claim the manor is as much hers as it is mine. More so hers than mine.

"Well, *that* certainly looks quite extravagant," Muireall says, nodding at the dress with a frown as she crosses her arms. "Were you planning on telling me you were going to attend the Lockhart ball un-escorted? As a single woman, that is quite improper, you know."

Going unescorted was hardly noteworthy when the entire town was gossiping about my bond. But I hold my head high, not stooping to a petty retort. "There are, of course, societal exceptions for banntraichean, like myself."

"Oh, of course. You. A banntrach," Muireall snickers. Smoothing the stomach of her dress, she glances around the room, her cynical gaiety fading as she takes in the broken state of the dining room. "Well, I was hoping you were attending, in any case. I suppose being an unaccompanied young woman isn't the most scandalous thing about you."

Although her tone is casual and her statement true, her wording stings. I frown, my muscles tensing as I strain to control myself. She wanders over to the table, picking up the silk, cream gloves I had purchased. "Where did you get the money for these?" she asks, raising an eyebrow as if to accuse me, but I can tell she is surprised, no matter how I acquired them.

With restraint, I stomp over to her and snatch the gloves away. "I don't want them dirtied," I mutter, checking them for grime. "Why does it matter to you if I'm goin' or not?" The sooner she leaves, the sooner I can continue my work in solitude.

"Ah, yes." Muireall begins to stroll around the room, studying my chaise lounge bed, and the table covered in pencils and pins, sheers and fabric scraps, keeping her hands to herself. Her critical gaze is dirty enough as it is. "Being introduced to Soarsa society for the first time is quite an important affair, and I want you to make the best impression you can."

I fold my arms over my chest, shifting my weight with a sigh. I don't know what advice she could possibly offer me when she stays holed up in that cottage, crying and complaining.

"As you know very well by this point, truly restoring my family estate will take some effort, and a lot of money." She runs her fingers over the makeshift curtains I fashioned from threadbare sheets, spotted with holes from mice and moths. "After all, while the bones of the house remain in good condition, updating the appearance is the true challenge." She turns to face me. "So we'll need to find you a new husband."

Her declaration causes my jaw to hang wide open. While I try to form words, blinking wildly, the only sound I make is a nervous laugh. Finally, I swallow, and find some control. "My husband, your *son*, has been buried barely four months. It's hardly appropriate for me to be seekin' suitors so soon." And who in Soarsa would be willing to marry a cairline anyway?

She bats her hand in the air. "Details. Besides, *I'm* the one grieving his death, so I think I can decide when it is an appropriate time." I grimace, my hands balling into fists. "And, with the right suitor, we could even evoke a teasairginn, reclaim the Raeburn fields, keep it all in the family name, as it should be."

"I am not some cow you can sell for money," I spit at her. "If I marry again, it'll be for love."

Muireall laughs again, a full belly laugh that causes her to double over, bracing herself against the table. "Like how you married my son 'for love'?" She looks up at me, her face hard and calloused despite her outburst.

"I did...love him." I hope she takes my hesitation for sorrow.

She shakes her head slowly as she stands straight again. "That wasn't love, Caitrin."

I suck in a breath through my nose, clamping my lips shut as my heart picks up speed. Does she know? But how could she possibly know? Not even Tate knew, for all his confusion and frustrations in the end. Even then, he had no idea.

"That was infatuation. But, of course..." Muireall brightens with a spark of inspiration. "I suppose you could do something to make the whole predicament easier on yourself. Just a little blood, a little dèiligidh..."

"I told you, I'm not strong enough to contact the dead."

"Not the dead. But I hear there is magic that can change hearts." She drills me with a glare, her brittle lips pressed together. "Isn't that what you tried to do to me?"

So maybe she doesn't know.

I don't know.

I don't know what she knows, but I'm trapped by her stare. By her judgement.

Even without a bond, she still has power over me.

Perhaps it's the mionn.

"I have work to do." I turn, tense and heart racing, and go back to the gown. "I only have a little bit of time to finish and get ready."

Muireall doesn't say another word, but she smiles bitterly as she exits.

I stitch with furious stabs. How dare she assume I will marry just so she can have money to spend? Perhaps if she was a mother-in-law worthy of such a sacrifice, if she was someone who was capable of loving and being loved...but as it is, she is just a bitter, old hag with a grudge against the entire world.

I owe her nothing. The debt I owed Tate, I've already paid. I'm paying it now—a penance for the pain I caused her and her family, whether she knows it or not.

I thrust the needle through the hem, and it burrows into

the tip of my finger. I wince, pulling away quickly so as to not stain the fabric. Blood begins to bloom on my fingertip like a droplet of rain from a cloud.

One drop of blood. That was all my guilt cost. And now I will never escape her.

THIRTY

GETTING DRESSED FOR A BALL seems like the kind of thing a girl should do with her mother or sister or friends, laughter and joyful expectations about the evening buzzing around the bustle. I, however, get ready alone in the upstairs bedroom in complete silence, as if preparing for a battle.

I don't know if makeup is fashionable in Soarsa, so I keep it simple, which is easy considering I have only a few items to use. I darken my lashes with a brush of kohl and blend rouge onto my lips to deepen their color. After pinning back my ginger curls, with spiraling tendrils falling around my face, I add the earrings from the peddler—the perfect complement to my ensemble, not too flashy or too plain.

I stare at my reflection in the vanity mirror. My appearance is wild, like my magic, and I can only hope that I won't stand out too much.

After dressing down to my underthings, I tug on a pair of lightweight stockings and worn heeled shoes I found in the back of a drawer. I would prefer to wear my boots, which are far more comfortable, but I worry that my feet will be seen when dancing, and I won't risk the embarrassment. No doubt, I will have plenty of other things to be embarrassed about tonight. A little discomfort is easy to endure to lessen my list of worries.

Putting on the gown is a slightly more difficult challenge, as I cut and boned the bodice like a corset. I pull on the dress, with the back in the front, feeling exposed and vulnerable as I lace two sets of cords through the rivets. One set starts at the top, the other at the bottom, and they meet at my waist. Spinning the gown around, I clumsily adjust the lacing best I can, looking over my shoulder in the mirror to check my work.

I wrap the cords at each side around my hands—two ends in each hand—and tug. The laces obey me, straightening and closing up over my upper-back and hips, but not tightening too much. I adjust my bosom, making sure my chest is comfortable and situated properly. Then, with a deep breath to gather my strength, I grip the cords firmly and pull up and out, my elbows braced on my sides. The pressure builds against my waist, and, as if I were a marionette doll coming to life, my posture straightens. I take a deep breath, then pull once more, just to make sure the dress is secure, before knotting the cords all together. The tails trail down over the back of my skirt, getting lost in the folds.

And gloves are the final touch to my ensemble.

Spinning to face the mirror, I examine the fit of the dress, hoping for the best. While I had tried it on several times, checking the fit and making adjustments, this is the first time I'm truly *seeing* it.

The style of the dress itself is simple enough with a bustier-style bodice that sculpts my figure elegantly and a gored skirt that gathers at my hips and falls in folds to my feet. The champagne netting covers the pink silk, with extra netting on the lining for a makeshift petticoat to give the skirt more fullness. The embroidered flowers, which are in an array of rich pinks, purples, and reds with green vine-like-leaves that connect them, lay arranged over the straps and bodice and trail down the skirt. It reminds me of the house and cottage, growing wild from my waist, evasively covering the rest of the dress over time.

The entire gown feels like a spark of inspiration brought to life.

Standing before me isn't the cairline from Cairlich whose husband died and whose mother-in-law loathes her, a girl lost in a foreign land, an outcast with no prospects. Instead, I see a princess. Royalty of the rarest kind.

My chest wells up in awe and pride at how my hard work has paid off, and I resolve not to let anyone make me feel inferior tonight.

A bell rings, a broken, empty chime that echoes through the manor and into the bedroom. Out the window, the sun is tucking itself behind the trees, the last strays of golden glow fading into orange, pink, violet.

As if by instinct, I grab my pocketknife, contained in the leather sheath, and tuck it in my pocket. I shouldn't need it tonight—maybe it's foolish to bring it at all—but the thought of being surrounded by townsfolk who despise me seems reason enough to have a little protection. Just in case.

Gathering up my skirt, I hurry through the manor, careful not to trip in the unfamiliarity of my shoes or the volumes of my gown. The stairs give me the most challenge as the netting catches on the broken banister twice during my descent. Luckily, nothing tears, and I reach the front door unscathed.

On the stoop stands Brodie, dressed in a grey suit jacket and trousers with a brown vest over a cream linen shirt and a simple green cravat around his neck. Behind him waits a white, covered carriage. Silky, black stallions are tethered in the front, creating a striking image of luxury and wealth. As I emerge from the deteriorating manor, I feel like I am stepping out of a harsh reality and into an impossible dream.

"You look stunning, Miss Caitrin! Truly transformed," Brodie says with a kind smile, offering his hand to help me climb into the carriage.

"Thank you, Brodie. You're quite handsome yourself. Will a certain young woman you're hopin' to impress be at the ball tonight?" I ask as I situate myself on the cushioned bench.

Brodie blushes red from his ears all the way down to his cravat. "Oh…uh…did Callen…? Anyway… Don't want to be late!" With an uncontrollable grin, he closes the door and climbs up to drive the carriage.

I almost laugh to myself, and the worries of the night ahead slip away.

Leaning against the window, I watch as the thicket drifts by and the main road comes into view, lined with rolling hills of farmland and crowned by the stars as they come out of hiding. They twinkle, ever so slightly, ever so bravely, as the sky darkens like a curtain of velvet. I try to pick out the constellations as the carriage travels toward the Lockhart estate. Finally, we turn and line up behind a dozen other carriages, slowly approaching the mansion one by one.

I sink back into the shadows of the carriage as my heart begins to race. I don't know the first thing about attending a ball! Do I need to do something specific when I arrive? Or go someplace first to prove I was invited? I wish Muireall was here with me.

The realization is almost revolting, but it's true. Certainly, even with her cynical attitude, she would instruct me in what is proper to do. I'll have to rely on my wits and common sense instead.

Our carriage pulls to a stop, and the door is opened by a footman. I don't recognize him, but he presses his lips into a firm, forced smile at the sight of me. "Ah. Miss Raeburn." He bows slightly with a sigh and gestures for me to exit, offering his hand but not meeting my eyes.

I don't accept it out of stubborn pride alone, taking much care to step out of the carriage without tripping. It's only by some miracle that I land on both feet without stumbling or stepping on my skirt.

The castle is lit up brilliantly, with a candle in every window, and lanterns scattered around the entrance so that it's almost as bright as day. However, the light fades when set against the night sky, where the stars have finally appeared in all their glory, the moon waxing as it awakens from its slumber, refreshed. Their light gives me the strength to walk forward and follow the couple in front of me, who enter the mansion gleefully.

I've never been inside the Lockhart mansion. I walk slowly, taking in the grand foyer, decorated with marble statues and wall fountains on either side of the entrance. Several doors branch off from the foyer, all of them open and as wide as carriages.

People flood around me, adventuring into the various rooms or straight ahead, further into the mansion. To my left is a drawing room, furnished with richly upholstered sofas and exquisitely carved tables, and then a grand dining room, with a long table covered in platters piled with treats. Guests mill around the table, filling up small plates and chatting contentedly with each other. Servants scurry to and from the kitchen through a swinging door, keeping the refreshments filled and the room tidy.

To my right, there is a billiards room with a bar, where several gentlemen lounge, secluded from the more lively guests. Next to it is a large library, furnished with comfortable sitting areas and grand paintings. Guests who are already tired relax on the sofas, reading contently or gossiping quietly amongst themselves. I suspect that Vaila and Yvaine will make their way to this room, huddled around the tea table, playing cards and matchmaking.

That is, if they haven't retired from the party altogether yet. But hopefully, my banntraichean friends are here somewhere.

Pressing forward, I exit the foyer and enter the ballroom, which seems to spill beyond the walls through tall, glass doors onto the patio where I had eaten lunch with Callen and his employees.

Stepping to the side, I press my back against the wall, trying to remain unnoticed until I get my bearings. A giant chandelier glitters above the center of the room and mirrored staircases curve up to a balcony that rims the grand room, leading to corridors and the rest of the castle. Between the top of the two staircases, a string quartet plays, the music drifting joyfully down to the energetic dancers below. I scan the crowd—it's more people than I even knew lived in Soarsa and the surrounding villages!—to see if I recognize anyone, hoping above all to see my elderly friends.

Instead, I spot the troublesome twins, Knox and Paisley Baines, snickering as they sip from goblets. Knox meets my gaze, and I grimace, straightening my posture. I refuse to be intimidated by him.

He nods to me, raising the glass in a mocking toast. I roll my eyes. It might be a good idea to get lost somewhere else, somewhere the Baines twins can't see me. Applause breaks out as the swirling dance ends. It was *not* a simple waltz, I note bitterly. I move from my spot against the wall toward a darkened alcove nestled behind one of the twisting staircases, weaving through the guests as they find new partners for the next dance.

Fingers brush against my hand, then they grip and spin me around.

Knox Baines.

"What do you want?" I do my best to keep my voice low and polite as I rip my hand from his.

"I just thought you might indulge me in a dance," he says with a devilish smirk, one that might charm other ladies, but it makes me snarl.

I raise an eyebrow. "You want to dance with *me?*"

"No, he doesn't," Mr. Baines steps from behind me, and I nearly jump to move away from his low, gravelly voice. "I did not expect you to be in attendance, Miss Raeburn."

I strain to keep my face neutral. "The Lockharts are very hospitable."

He snorts, a smile forming under his bushy mustache. "Far *too* hospitable, if you ask around town. The rìgh had his reasons, I assume, to turn a blind eye to Ardala's past, but you...I doubt the rìgh would be so forgiving."

"I can make sure you don't cause trouble for Callen." Knox reaches for my hand again, slipping his other around my waist.

I step backward, resisting the urge to push him and cause a scene. "I'll wait for a better partner."

Mr. Baines pulls Lewis away into the crowd with a firm hand on his elbow. "I told you——"

"I'm not going to *marry* her, father. Just a bit of fun." Knox looks back at me with a wink, and I roll my eyes in disgust.

"We'll lose everything if you have *too much fun*. And it won't go away with money this time..."

The music swells, covering up their scheming, announcing the next dance is about to begin.

A body collides with mine, and I stumble as the dancers skip and swirl far too close. "Look out!" Someone shrieks before they are swept away by their partner and I step back.

"It's been a while since we had some good fun in Soarsa." The voice is sweet and soft and vaguely familiar. I look beside me to see none other than Shona Hew. She wears a blush pink ballgown, with precise pin-tucks, fabric flowers, and pearls embellishing the design.

"Callen told me you made your gown, just as I hoped you might," she says, analyzing my work but not meeting my eyes.

Her fingers brush against the flowers trimming my shoulders, then press against my side, pressuring me to turn. "Can I see the back?" I oblige, turning slowly until we face each other fully. "This is excellent work."

"Thank you," I say, wondering if I have Callen to thank for her change of heart. Or perhaps Brodie's frequent visits.

Shona's eyes flicker to my gloves. Clearing her throat, she smiles and finally meets my gaze. She looks younger when she is smiling, porcelain skin with pink cheeks and dark eyes that are somehow as bright as the twinkling stars. Her brown hair is swept back into an elegant bun, with pearls and flowers pinned on one side.

"Perhaps I do have use for you in my shop." Her smile falters. "In the back, of course," she mutters, looking away.

I don't blame her for her caution, my heart leaping with hope at her words. "Absolutely!" I agree quickly. "I'd appreciate any kind of work."

"I'll have to check with my brother, Tavish, first of course." She glances to the dancers, her lips twitching; she probably wishes she was dancing among them. Where is Brodie?

I stretch up on my tiptoes, eager to win her favor further, scanning the heads for one that bobs in and out of view, shorter than the rest but a man all the same. Then my eyes land on the wall by the entrance, the same wall I had found brief refuge in. I reach up slightly, trying to catch his attention without Shona noticing. Brodie is watching the dancers furiously, his hands wringing the edges of his jacket, wrinkling it with his nerves.

A pair of dancers whirl past me, and the eyes of the woman catch mine. I turn, staring back at her. She's unfamiliar, like most of the guests, but she seems to know who I am. Her gaze is suspicious, her eyes narrow, although her lips part slightly in curiosity, or perhaps disgust.

Past the swarm of dancers, there is a whole gaggle of girls glaring at me—some of the them I recognize from my run in with Paisley—although they turn away sharply when they notice I see them.

Let them stare.

I'm more free than any of them will ever be, bound by their self-righteous judgement.

"Miss Hew?" Brodie's voice is soft and questioning. He extends a hand to Shona with a bow. "Would you honor me with the next dance?"

Shona beams, although I'm not certain it's Brodie's attention that excites her as much as the prospect at having any dance partner. "I'd be delighted." She gives him her hand and he kisses her knuckles gently. Her cheeks grow even more pink, and Brodie is as red as a tomato. She doesn't seem to mind, and they stand together silently, arm in arm, anxiously awaiting the song to end and the next dance to begin.

I slip away from them. Hopefully, Shona will not forget her offer to me in the morning. The opportunity to make some real money, to have some real independence, is the best news I could have hoped to receive this evening.

THIRTY-ONE

THE BRIGHT STACCATO MUSIC ENDS when I reach the edge of the ballroom, where the doors are wide open leading out onto the patio. The night breeze rushes over me, carrying with it a hint of earth and dew. The coolness soothes my skin in contrast to how warm it is inside, with so many bodies pressed tightly together. I let out a sigh of satisfaction, looking down at the gown that has brought me so much favor.

And I didn't even need a dèiligidh to change Shona's mind. Just a kind word from Callen.

He said he wanted to dance with me tonight.

My fingers twitch at the thought, my breath caught in my chest for a moment, remembering his hand on my waist…and the unpracticed nature of my steps.

"I must make for a poor escort," Callen laughs nervously.

I spin to find him casually walking toward me, his hands tucked into his pants pockets. He is a slightly more put together version of his usual self. His hair is still unruly and wind-tousled, and his worn boots have been polished but not replaced. However, instead of his worn trousers and linen shirts, he wears a crisp, midnight blue jacket. A cream satin sash, trimmed with gold, crosses over his chest, matching his pants and the cravat around his neck. The title of Lord

Lockhart certainly fits him tonight. "I meant to come to you as soon as you arrived, but that's quite a crowd to get through."

"You knew when I'd arrived?"

He looks down, slowing his steps as he nears me. When he looks back up at me, the curls of his hair fall over his forehead, his green eyes deep and earnest. "You're hard to miss." He reaches out for my hand and I give it to him. He presses his lips against my knuckles so gently I almost don't feel it because of my gloves, but the way he holds my gaze is far more intimate than the elegant greeting.

I almost forget to breathe, almost forget everything, when he looks at me like that. Like I'm the only other person in the world, and he prefers it that way.

"You clean up well yourself," I say, desperately trying to sound mature and detached. Still, my heart shrinks when he pulls his hand away and tucks it back in his pocket.

"Caitrin…" Callen chuckles. "I look fine, but you…" He shakes his head, his smile genuine and his eyes playful and bright. "I think the stars are shining brighter to try and compete with you."

I blush, breaking away from his gaze, wishing he wasn't so kind. It makes me feel weak. But I can't help but grin as my heart flutters. "Fine fabrics make for a fine gown, every time." I grab my skirt, swishing it to show it off, trying to deflect his compliment.

He steps closer, his hand drifting down my arm and taking my hand again. "Yes, the dress is lovely but you…" I look up at him and something seizes my heart. My lungs constrict and my stomach turns on itself. Callen bites his lip. "I don't mean to make you uncomfortable. I guess tonight has me feeling more..."

"Poetic?" I offer.

"Sure." He winks at me, as if I can read his mind and know what he was going to say instead. But I don't let myself make any assumptions.

The music from inside swells, drifting out into the night sky, and Callen takes the opportunity to pull me from the railing, spinning me out so the skirt of my gown floats around my ankles. Then he draws me back in to him, one hand on my waist and the other shifting his grip on my hand. "So, will you tolerate another dance with me?"

I try to frown at the suggestion, but I'm unable to wipe the smile off my face. "I might be able to tolerate a *waltz*." I glance inside where couples have paired up in a complicated pattern as the dance begins. They spin and twirl and skip and clap in time with the music, each person in sync with the others. "But I don't think I can manage *that*."

"Well then, Miss Caitrin Raeburn"—Callen steps away from me to give a flourished bow—"will you grace me with a waltz?" He extends his hand out to me.

I roll my eyes at his dramatics, but the joy in my heart at his invitation is so unbridled that I can't resist. "Very well, Lord Lockhart." I place my hand in his, and we step together, resuming our positions for the waltz. Although, I grab my skirt with my free hand to keep it up and out of our feet.

And as the music begins the refrain, Callen steps forward, pulling me into movement with him. Tonight, I don't seem to have a problem holding his gaze. As we step and swirl, looking into each other's eyes under the starlight, it's almost as if we are the only two people in the world. The sounds of the ball, even the music, disappear, replaced with the song of the night. I don't dare speak and break the spell.

But Callen is not as concerned. "I'm glad you came. It must not be easy." He snorts. "I'll admit, if you weren't here, I probably wouldn't have come out for the ball, either. Perhaps just to make appearances with my mother, but nothing more than that."

"We outcasts have to stick together." I square my shoulders and lift my chin. His smile fades ever so slightly, and I wonder what I've said wrong. "Did somethin' happen? Have people been rude?"

"No, no. Not to my face, at least," Callen admits, his gaze drifting from me to our surroundings in thought. "It's a little strange, having everyone be so polite, calling me Lord Lockhart. In town, I'm just Callen, even to those who don't indulge in the gossip. I'm not sure which I prefer, honestly, but I don't mind the Baines feigning respect for once. And as long as they don't disparage my mother when she makes her appearance, it seems tonight will be rather uneventful."

"Uneventful?" I almost laugh. "Callen, this is likely the event of the *year* in Soarsa. I'm not sure uneventful is the right word." He shrugs, unconvinced. "I thought you were feeling poetic?" I tease, and that seems to bring some life back to him.

He squeezes my hand gently. "I wish you didn't have to wear these gloves."

"This town isn't ready for a cairline who doesn't hide her markings."

"What if you didn't have to hide them? What if you didn't have them—"

"Callen," I snap, my expression immediately dropping, but I don't pull away from him or stop the dance. "Please don't ruin tonight like that. I told you: it's not possible. A bond is for life."

He presses his lips together, nodding his head. "I'm sorry. I shouldn't have brought it up."

Our steps are slowing. I'm losing him.

"Whatever you've heard, I promise that my bond isn't somethin' to be afraid of." We stop dancing completely. I drop my skirt and move my hand to his shoulder. When he looks up at me, I smile and my fingers brush against his neck. "In fact, it can do a lot of good. I'll prove it to you, if you give me a chance."

I hold his gaze, and, while he doesn't look away, I can tell he is conflicted.

Then he leans toward me. He parts his lips to answer.

And cheers erupt in the ballroom, pulling his attention away from me as the loud voice of a maestro fills the air and echoes out to us. "Please welcome her ladyship, Ardala Lockhart, our gracious hostess!" A polite, hesitant applause ripples through the crowd, followed by whispers and gasps of amazement.

"I'm supposed to escort her out!" Callen sprints for the door, pushing his way through the crowd, whispering apologies as he goes.

Without his embrace, the chill in the air returns. I wrap my arms around myself, missing his warmth. Wishing we had more time together. But I stop myself from hoping for more than compassion, or maybe companionship from him. We're both outcasts in Soarsa, but while a lord might stoop to dance with a cairline, he can't offer me more than kindness. Anything more is outlawed. Whatever magic surrounds us tonight will be gone by the morning, when reality sets in again.

I step back into the ballroom to glimpse Callen leaping up one of the grand staircases and disappearing behind a dark curtain. Moments later, the maestro steps back up the railing of the second-floor balcony.

"Lord Callen Lockhart and his mother, Lady Ardala Lockhart." The maestro bows and backs away as Callen emerges with his mother on his arm, guiding her to the staircase he had just run up. He looks flushed, breathing heavily and forcing a smile.

Lady Ardala, on the other hand, looks like an ethereal queen as she descends, head held high like she is wearing a crown. Her gown is gauzy, the color of lavender flowers, and trimmed with delicate black lace, a striking contrast against her fair skin. Her brown hair is braided up and secured with golden pins. Hanging from her neck is an obsidian gem, set in sparkling gold. It looks eerily familiar.

A chill runs down my back, settling in my stomach.

I press closer to the crowd, unable to look away from the necklace.

"I thought maybe she had died…" a middle-aged woman says.

"Who is Callen smiling at? Is it me?" a young girl, one of Paisley's friends, whisper-squeals.

But when I look up, it's me Callen is staring at. He winks, and a soft smile spreads over my face.

The girl turns, following Callen's gaze, and freezes. The silence of the room grows eerie and awkward. "You're the cairline who is cursing this whole town!" The girl shrieks, and the attention of the crowd shifts from Callen and his mother to me.

I shrink away from their stares, my face growing hot and my stomach tying itself in knots. Surely the Lockharts will regret their kindness to me if I cause a scene now.

"Welcome, and thank you…" Lady Ardala's voice travels over the crowd, capturing their attention once again. She falls quiet, her eyes wide as her chest expands and holds the breath. I force the air out of my lungs, as if willing her to do the same. The heat in the room rises with the silence as my stomach twists and tightens. Ardala glances at Callen and squeezes his arm. She doesn't look away from him.

Callen doesn't miss a beat, continuing her welcome speech. "Thank you for accepting our invitation. It is a great honor to continue my father's tradition of…"

Retreating back onto the patio, I hurry to the balcony and brace my gloved hands on the stone railing. Forcing a few deep breaths, I gaze out over the fields—blue in the moonlight— simply trying to calm my nerves.

Perhaps I should just head home now.

Music resumes, and I glance over my shoulder to see the crowd remains parted as only one couple takes to the floor. Callen and his mother, I assume. And not an eye looking at me. The knots in my stomach begin to slowly unravel as the uncertainty of what I should do looms before me.

I braved their stares for long enough. With all the guests and their gossip, it would be a kindness to leave, rather than add more fuel to the fire with my mere presence. And I've given Callen the dance I promised him. Surely, he will be content to not see me again until I return to glean. When reality returns to both of us.

Decided, I push myself away from the balcony. Hopefully I can find Brodie without causing too much alarm.

Edging behind the crowd, I press against the wall so that they barely notice me. All eyes are on Callen and his mother. They sweep across the floor, Callen poised and Ardala as elegant as a ballerina. Her gaze is gracefully downcast to the side, as if trying to forget the spectators that surround them.

I glance back to the corridor that leads to the front of the house; it's pressed tight with guests, including Brodie and Shona, who stand shoulder to shoulder, beaming. I steel my resolve, knowing I must take Brodie away from her.

"Mother?"

A gasp. Then a scream.

My attention snaps back to the center of the room.

Lady Ardala lays limp in Callen's arms. Collapsed and unconscious, exposing a large black wart creeping out from under her neckline and up to her shoulder.

"It's the Dhubd Blath!" Someone cries, and the room erupts in chaos.

THIRTY-TWO

"GET OUT BEFORE YOU CATCH it!"

People are dashing for the exits, giving a wide berth to the Lockharts. I can barely spot them through the chaos.

If the Dhubd Blath is contagious, then how did Lady Ardala contract it? She hardly leaves the house, from what I know.

Paralyzed by the madness, I watch helplessly as Callen shakes his mother's shoulders, looking around for assistance, then back to his mother. Even from the distance and in the blur of rushing bodies, I can tell Lady Ardala's neck is swelling, her skin taking on a gray pallor.

My wrists begin stinging underneath my gloves.

I should help them. There must be a way.

And maybe this is my chance to repay the Lockharts.

I push my way through the rushing guests. They are like the waves of the ocean, surging and shoving. I could easily be carried away by the crowd if my resolve was weaker. Pushing against the people with more fury, I force my way forward.

Brodie is off to the left, trying to direct guests with the other servants to the exits. His eyes are wide, fearful, lost.

"Go get Dr. Kilpatrick, Brodie!" I shout at him, my face stern and commanding. Even if he heard me, he remains frozen.

"Mother? Mother!" Callen bends over Lady Ardala, his ear to her mouth, his face pale as hers turns purple. When Brodie hears Callen's voice, he moves into action, disappearing into the crowd to find the doctor.

Finally, I break free, like a wave upon the shore, into the center of the ballroom, where only Callen and his mother sit.

Rushing to them, I drop to the floor, my eyes on Lady Ardala. Her throat has swollen so much in just a few minutes that her breaths are coming out more as gasps—desperate, strained, and stilted. The black gem on her necklace taunts me, calls to me. It's not restricting her throat as a choker would, but I have a feeling it's causing her ailment.

A curse.

The sounds of the crowd dull as the realization dawns upon me.

I rip the necklace from her, the teardrop pendant glistening boldly against my cream glove.

Lady Ardala tenses, her eyes bulging as she sucks a full breath into her lungs. Then she relaxes, breathing more easily, as her eyelids flutter closed.

Callen glances over at me, wide eyed but relieved. Then, in a daze, his gaze is drawn down to the necklace in my hand.

"Where did this come from?" I clench my jaw.

Is the Dhubd Blath just a curse, or is the curse an imitation? It's cairlinen like this who bring condemnation to the rest of us. Even in Cairlich, using magic to harm another is considered immoral; the standards don't change in Croìthe, no matter how they despise us. We must be better to change their minds.

Instead, whoever made this curse has declared the Croìthen assumptions true.

I close my hand in a fist over the pendant. It must be destroyed. And then I'll discover who this malicious cairline is and destroy her as well.

Callen shakes his head slowly. "I don't know. I've never seen it before."

I glance around to see that the majority of the guests are gone. Those at the rear of the crowd are pushing forward, glancing back with wide stares, fearful that Lady Ardala will rise and devour them.

"We should get her to her bed to rest," I tell Callen.

"Yes, yes." He moves into action, tearing off his jacket, sweeping his mother up into his arms, and standing.

My hand clenches the necklace in my fist.

I follow Callen through the mansion, wishing I had something more practical to wear as we climb the staircase and trek through long corridors. Callen rattles off orders to several servants, redirecting them from their tasks of cleaning up after the abruptly-ended ball. When we reach Lady Ardala's quarters, a servant pulls the doors open for us, revealing an opulent room of whites and blues.

Callen places his mother gently on the bed as the servant at the door, a middle-aged woman with curly red hair, rushes forward. "Please make sure she is comfortable, Helda."

If I am to destroy the talisman, I will need blood. My gaze snaps to Lady Ardala and the maid arranging her on the bed.

Helda goes to the wardrobe to fetch a nightgown and robe for her mistress. "Can I take a look at her?" I ask Callen.

He nods dismissively with a deep sigh, his shoulders slumped. He wanders to the window with his forehead cradled in his palm.

Cautiously, I go to Lady Ardala's bedside and kneel beside her. I tuck the necklace in my pocket for safe keeping and trade it for the knife, slipping it out of its sheath and hiding it in my lap. Taking a handkerchief from the nightstand, I pull Lady Ardala's hand into my own, the knife hidden by the handkerchief. I poke ever so slight, wincing myself as Lady Ardala shifts with a slight groan, but she doesn't awaken.

Just a few drops should be enough.

I pull the handkerchief away and glance down to see a red blotch no bigger than a rosebud; the wound will clot before anyone is the wiser. I turn my attention to the wart on her neck. Now there are two.

They look unnatural, swelling as if hot tar is trapped under her skin. Even though I suspect it's not contagious, I don't dare touch it.

"Miss?" Helda says from behind me, bringing a nightgown to change Lady Ardala. I stand quickly, clutching the handkerchief and knife into the folds of my gown and head for the hallway.

"Where are you going?" Callen calls after me, and I slow my steps, turning to look at him as I slip the incriminating items into my pocket. He has sobered, his face hard, determined. I don't want to lie to him. He's had enough cruelty for one night. His eyes move to my hand, hidden in my pocket. My fingers close around the necklace.

I back out of the bedroom into the corridor as Helda begins

to help Lady Ardala change, and Callen jogs after to me.

He doesn't stop his advance until he's mere inches from me, my back pressed against the hallway wall. Does he know that I took her blood? Did he see? Does he suspect *I* cursed her? I suck in a breath, bracing myself.

"Where are you going?" He demands, keeping his voice low.

I hold my head high and square my shoulders as I hold up the pendant for him to see. "This is a talisman. A curse." He starts to reach for it, and I snap it away, concealing it in my fist again. "It needs to be destroyed to break the dèiligidh."

He nods, his eyes wandering as he processes my words. "And you can do that."

"Yes."

Callen swallows. He knows I will use magic to do so. I will summon Keres, and on his property no less. But it must be done as soon as possible to give his mother a fighting chance at recovering from the illness.

"If it's destroyed, the curse will leave her body, but it will take time for her to regain her strength. But I can create a new dèiligidh to help her heal more quickly." I've never bargained for a *slàinte* dèiligidh before, a spell to change the physical body, but surely it is simple enough, given the circumstances. I wouldn't be asking Keres to regrow a leg or cure blindness. Healing spells are almost rudimentary.

Callen is silent for a moment. "So a cairline did this."

I shrink at the words as shame grips me.

But I didn't do this to her. "And a cairline can save her," I say, just as much for myself as for him. "I'll be back soon." I move from between him and the wall.

"I'm coming with you."

"You want to…?" My gaze narrows, eying him suspiciously. "You know what I'm goin' to do, don't you, Callen?"

He nods sternly, full of understanding. "She's my mother. I should be there."

It's not a good idea. I've only had an audience once, and look how that turned out. I press my lips together, take another deep breath, then look back up at him. He is resolute, immovable.

Swallowing hard, I nod, but my heart is pounding. "Alright," I consent, against my better judgement.

Keres won't like having an audience, either.

THIRTY-THREE

THE WORLD HAS GROWN COLD and silent. An eerie breeze whistles through the apple orchid. Here, we will have some privacy, away from the prying eyes of servants. The moon's light is obscured by the trees, allowing us to stand in the dark shadows of night.

Callen doesn't say a word as he follows me. He carries a lit lantern in one hand, a candlestick tucked in his pocket at my direction. I am thankful for his compliance; it eases the tension in my bones.

When Callen went to get the items, I kicked off my shoes and yanked off my stockings, needing to feel grounded, the earth between my toes. And it makes walking easier as the hem of my gown drags through the grass and dirt, no doubt blemishing the color.

Finally, we reach a spot I think is hidden enough.

Kneeing in the dirt, I remove my gloves and toss them aside. Then, with my bare hands, I dig a small hole. "The candle. Will you light it?" Callen takes the candle from his pocket, lights the wick with the lantern's flame, and then carefully hands it to me.

I bury it in the ground, making sure the dirt is packed tightly so the stick doesn't fall. A drop of hot wax lands on my hand and I suck in a breath. Despite the pain, there is something warm and comforting about the familiarity of it.

Not bothering to stand, I take the knife from my pocket, careful to keep the necklace and handkerchief concealed for now. I hesitate as I hold the sharp point in front of me. The metal glistens in the starlight that penetrates the leaves and branches of the apple trees. I can feel Callen watching me, his eyes no doubt dark and glistening with judgmental curiosity. But silent. Accepting that this must be done to help his mother.

I close my eyes and let out a breath. Then I press the tip against my finger, anticipating the sharp pinch that follows. A bead of blood blooms and falls into the fire.

"Thig dhòmhsa."

The flame shudders, then is snuffed out in mere seconds. She's angry.

Tendrils of smoke from the tiny wick gather and grow, surrounding us. Callen steps back, the grass crunching under his boots, but I don't look at him. He is nothing more than a spectator, and I have work to do. As the smoke blackens and swirls, I stand, ready to bargain.

Keres takes shape with a hiss, sharp wisps of her form retreating from Callen.

He seems equally shocked, frozen with fear.

And I stand between them.

"What is the meaning of this, Caitrin?" Keres's voice is a hollow echo, coming from all around us, not just her form.

I take out the talisman, showing it to her, proving to Callen that I am in control. "I need to destroy this cursed talisman."

"You have the blood?" she asks.

I nod curtly, wondering if Callen will understand it is his mother's blood on the handkerchief or if he will assume it is mine. Will he be angry if he discovers the truth? Even if he is, it needed to be done. Without Lady Ardala's blood, there is no dèiligidh that can be made to help her. Pulling out the handkerchief, I hold it up so it unfolds, revealing the spot of red.

Keres breathes in deep, inhaling, and I catch a whiff of copper with her smoke. Callen scoffs.

"This is to save your mother, boy," she says haughtily, laughing at his discomfort.

"I want to know the name of the cairline who made it as well," I demand, drawing Keres's attention back to me.

Her wispy form shifts, contemplating my question with piqued interest, drifting close to me. "Do you? Are you certain?" she whispers so quietly that I doubt Callen heard anything. "Ah, little cairline. It is someone far more powerful than you."

I straighten, my eyes narrowing. I won't let her belittle me so easily. "I am growin' more powerful with every dèiligidh. So let's barter."

Keres laughs, floating away from me, her tendrils of smoke growing longer, reaching for Callen, teasing and testing him. He shrinks into himself, trying to shrug off her touch, but Keres is everywhere. He must know that if the curse goes uncured, his mother will only get worse. Surely the rumors of the Dhubd Blath have reached the Lockhart estate.

"You want me to destroy that talisman? And improve her health, I suspect," Keres says.

"You…you can do that?" Callen says, stepping closer to me, closer to Keres.

"I can do many great things, boy," Keres almost seems to flirt, her tendrils swirling over Callen's cheek and down his neck. He doesn't flinch this time, regaining his resolve.

Stepping fully between them, the candle which anchors Keres to the ground at my feet, I place my hands on my waist. "And what will you ask for in return? This gown? I'm sure Callen would sacrifice a few of these beautiful trees."

A snicker, quiet at first until the cackling transforms into a crack of lightning across the sky. "A dress? You always think so small, so simple, little cairline…" She grows until she is no longer a form, just smoke surrounding us. "Life from life."

I take a deep breath, and Callen's fingers brush against my own, startling me. He takes my hand in his, keeping attention fixed on the spirit surrounding us. "We don't have to do this. There must be another option."

"There isn't," Keres and I say as one, and it makes my blood run cold.

I pull my hand from his, step forward and clear my throat. "Life from life," I repeat, and the small knife in my hand feels heavier than it had seconds before.

"How much?" I ask, resisting the worries that claw at my heart. Keres would never demand enough to truly harm me, perhaps weaken me to feed her own pride, but it's a cost I am willing to pay.

A gust of wind strikes the ground, thrusting me backward into Callen's chest. His hands brace me, firm, ready to carry me away from here. I jerk myself from his grasp—this must be done—as Keres holds the pendant and handkerchief in the air. If I am to make the best bargain, I should offer first, instead of waiting for her demands.

"Two handfuls." Tucking the knife in my pocket, I hold out my palms over the candle.

"I want two full arms…from each of you," Keres counters. Callen stiffens behind me at her words. "Then I will destroy this talisman and create a new one that will keep Lady Ardala in good health until this illness has passed from the village."

"And what then? After the illness has passed?" Callen asks, suspicious. Angry. Scared.

I look over my shoulder at him. "The talisman will lose its power. She will be…normal. Completely unaffected by magic."

"And without the new talisman…will the illness return?"

Keres snorts like a frustrated horse.

"We aren't tryin' to trick you, Callen," I say defensively, but he doesn't have my experience. With a sigh of compassion, I stare into his eyes, trying to capture his focus and build up his confidence in me. "I'll make sure of it." I turn back to the spirit, who has gathered herself back into a single, wispy form. "Remove the curse permanently, so that Lady Ardala cannot be infected again, whether by natural infection or by a spell."

"And you will give the payment owed?"

"Yes," I agree. Callen touches my arm, urging me to leave, or perhaps steadying himself.

"An arm and a leg, then, from each," Keres agrees, changing her barter. A stronger dèiligidh means a larger payment.

"Four full limbs is cruel, Keres," I scoff, crossing my arms and trying to remain confident. "How about my full arm and my leg up to my knee, and then just one arm from Callen—"

"I can't do this. I can't...it's an abomination," Callen whispers from behind me, pressing closer.

He doesn't understand, but that doesn't mean I don't pity him. And I won't ask him to deny his conscience. But this is my opportunity to repay him. It's the least I can do.

I face him, and his grip relaxes, falling down my arm until it reaches my hand. I take his fingers in my own to reassure him. "It won't hurt. You may be weak, but this will work."

He shakes his head ever so slightly, worried that Keres will see, tightening his fingers around mine. "Perhaps Doctor Kilpatrick can help her."

Keres laughs. "A human without a bond can do nothing to cure a curse, boy."

"She's right." I smile, a small smile, as Callen stares back at me, pleading. "I will give the full payment for you. For her. It's the least I can do to repay all of your kindness toward me."

"There is nothing to repay." He cups my cheek and pulls me closer, his eyes searching mine. But he won't convince me. Not when the opportunity has finally arisen.

I shrug away from him. "It may seem like nothin' to you, but it has meant a great deal to me." I twist my head toward Keres. "Is that acceptable?"

"Of course! Life is life," Keres says, a sickly sweet happiness in her words. She is always so eager to make a deal.

I give Callen one last smile, but the way his eyes hold mine makes my confidence falter. Fear threatens to creep into my veins, like something is wrong. Like he knows something I don't.

Pulling away from his gaze, I focus on my task. The dèiligidh. The blood. It will be a significant drain, but Keres will only weaken, never wound. That is how the bond works. She sacrifices power, and I sacrifice blood.

I hold out my arms to her. "Just make sure I don't fall, okay?" I ask Callen, trying to sound nonchalant, although my heart has begun racing faster, like it had the first time I ever bartered a dèiligidh.

Callen steps up behind me, his hands on my waist, his lips pressed against my ear. "Caitrin—" He begins, but Keres's tendrils attack my limbs like a swarm of snakes, shocking him into silence. Her wisps sink into my skin and pull. Callen's arms wrap around my middle, holding me steady.

I take a deep breath and close my eyes, sinking back against him. My fingers clench into tight fists as my heart begins to pound louder and louder in my ears, trying to keep up with the blood that drains from my body and into Keres's spirit.

I feel lightheaded. Weak. Floating.

Falling.

Callen holds me against him, his stubble brushing against my neck, his breath hot on my shoulder, like he can't bear to watch but he's afraid of letting me go. I peel my eyes open. The handkerchief is twisted around the pendant as they are melded into a single object, but they are only tinted pink, not red enough to complete the deal. The numbness in my arms is creeping past my shoulders, and I can't feel the left side of my body at all.

Everything is silvery and blurred.

I've never given this much at once. Perhaps it's a larger cost than I realized.

My vision darkens.

Just a little more.

And a shriek fills the air.

"Fool! I need it *all*. This is for you, selfish brat!" Keres's insults pierce my ears.

I'm on the ground, leaning back against Callen's chest. Did I faint? Keres's wisps have retreated, interrupted.

"Callen…" I mutter, struggling to sit up. "I must give the payment."

"You owe me nothing." His voice is tender, a final desperate plea to convince me, as his lips brush against my temple.

"It is to me that her debt is owed, boy," Keres says without missing a beat.

I try to stand, ready to fulfill my part of the deal, but he is stronger than me. Callen tightens his hold around my waist. I breathe in deep; he smells like apples and hazelnut, giving comfort that I didn't know I needed.

"The deal is off!" Callen declares. Then, more to me than to Keres, he adds, "We'll find another way."

"Caitrin, how dare you *waste* my time," Keres hisses. Her smokey tendrils surrounding us, brushing over Callen's arms, under my eyelashes, in-between my lips.

"My mother wouldn't want this. Even if it costs her life, she wouldn't ask this of you, Caitrin. And I won't either."

But the choice is still mine.

I sit up enough to get my bearings, and his grip loosens. "Are you sure?" I ask Callen quietly, my vision blurring again, but this time with tears. Why am I crying? I twist in his embrace to look at him. "She might die if I don't finish this." A tear slips down my check as my hands clutch his vest, wrinkling the lapel. I *need* to finish this. To be free of the debt. To be free. "Please, don't stop me. I know it's scary, but I'm not going to die; I'll only be weak for a little while, I promise. I want to do this for her. For you."

"No." Callen's voice is firm, but his face is soft, compassionate, warm, safe. He shakes his head, his fingers brushing over my cheeks, begging me to believe him. "I don't want this from you."

The surrender feels more akin to failure than relief. But I don't have the strength to fight him right now. And I don't want him to hate me for going against his wishes, regardless of his reasons. "Then the deal is off."

Keres shrieks, swirling around us with a gust of wind. She's angry. More angry than I've ever seen her before. The branches above us shake as her shriek is replaced with a howl, like that of a lone wolf. "Fine!" Keres shouts, her voice booming around us like thunder, so loud it makes my ears pop. "I have enough anyway."

"What?" I gasp, wiping away the tears that cling to my cheeks and turning to the spirit.

"Do you want the talisman or not?" she snaps.

A smile breaks out on my face. "Thank you, Keres!"

"No, I don't want it!" Callen argues.

But he doesn't understand. She demands no more blood

from me to complete the dèiligidh.

Keres disappears in a flash of lightning. And a small, obsidian cube drops to the dirt beside the candle.

Using all the strength I have left, I crawl from Callen and grab the talisman. "Your ma is healed," I say, placing it in his hand and closing his fingers around it.

His eyes are wet, and he is breathing deeply as he stares at me. My fingers slip from his. He says nothing, just staring down, his knuckles white as he grips the talisman tighter. Is he angry with me? Overwhelmed?

"The curse has been cured." I stand, my arms limp at my sides, and my left leg still completely numb. I sway, leaning against a tree to find my balance, acutely aware of his staring. I glance at my arms and notice that my bands have grown again, twice the width they were before. I think of my mother's arms, marked from her fingertips half-way up her biceps in swirling red patterns. I swell with pride, feeling stronger by the moment. "But if you want her to regain her strength quickly, and keep all other illness at bay, place that talisman under her pillow."

I meet his gaze again as he kneels at my feet, a look of desperation, of sorrow. I *need* him to say something. But he is quiet. "Are you angry with me?" I whisper when he doesn't break the silence.

"No," Callen says, shaking his head, his gaze dropping to his fist. Then he stands. "I'm just sorry we have to live in a world with magic at all."

"But my magic saved your mother." My lungs constrict as I choke out the words.

"And magic cursed her." His words are hard, ringing with hurtful truth. He drops the talisman into his pocket and steps closer to me, placing his hands gently on my shoulders. "Caitrin, I need you to promise me something."

I still, my heart pounding in my chest. I can't seem to bring myself to look up at him.

"Promise that you will never use my blood, or my mother's blood, for magic ever again."

My muscles tighten and my gaze hardens into a glare. "I would never use it without your permission."

His lips press together, and I remember the handkerchief. Maybe he is right not to trust me. With a shaky hand, I pick up my knife from the ground. "I can do better than a promise." The strength of moments before drains from me as I consider what I am offering. A mionn. A blood oath.

Just like I gave Tate.

But after a moment of stillness, Callen pushes my hand back to my side. "Your word is good enough." He'll always judge me for what he's seen here tonight.

I look away, exhaustion overwhelming every emotion. "You should get back to your mother."

I'm just sorry we have to live in a world with magic at all.

A world without magic.

Who would I be without my magic?

Powerless.

And yet, even now, after I've just performed such a powerful spell, I don't feel strong.

I feel fragile and ready to break at any moment.

THIRTY-FOUR

THE SWEET SMELL OF CINNAMON apples fills my nose like a dream. Stirring and stretching in my makeshift bed, I peel my eyes open, expecting the scent to disappear as soon as my vision clears.

But it remains, warming the air.

Sitting up, I survey the room. The gown I had slaved over lays rumpled, dirty and discarded on the floor. The curtains have been pulled back so that bright rays of afternoon sun flood into the space.

Clink. Clink.

I twist toward the sound and nearly jump out of my skin, pulling the quilt to keep myself covered.

Muireall sits at the dining table, wearing one of her usual black frocks, a chipped teacup and spoon in her hands. On the table sits a pitcher of water, and bowl with a spoon.

"It must have been *quite* the ball for you to not even stir until past noon," she says, more observing than condemning, as she stands and brings the bowl to me. The smell grows stronger as she hands me a breakfast of syrupy cinnamon apples.

"Thank you," I mutter, rubbing at my eyes with my free hand before attempting to sit up on my bed like a proper lady without spilling. "Have you heard what happened already?"

"Mrs. Kilpatrick stopped by to check on me at the cottage in the middle of the night. She was looking for you, I think, although she didn't say it."

Looking for me? My skin turns clammy as I force a spoonful of apples into my mouth, chewing slowly. The apples almost seem to melt in my mouth, sweet and sticky, as I wait for Muireall to elaborate on what else she has heard.

Taking a seat at the table again, she sighs and grants my wish. "She said Lady Lockhart fell ill with the Dhubd Blath—everyone in attendance saw it—and her husband went quickly to attend to Ardala and assess her infection. Apparently, he was changing one of the warm cloths on her neck and the warts had just disappeared. As if by magic." Muireall raises an eyebrow, anticipating my confession. Her eyes dart to my wrists, clearly noting how my markings have grown.

I have nothing to be ashamed of. "It was a dèiligidh that gave her the cursed condition, so I destroyed the talisman." I sit taller.

"A talisman..." Muireall picks something up from the table, holding it so the sunlight makes it shine. My moth-shaped talisman. "Like this one?"

I forgot to put it back on when I returned last night. A shiver crawls down my spine and I try not to think of what might have crawled on me while I slept. My smile droops. "It just keeps all the creatures living here from bothering me." I take another bite, this one a bit more spiteful.

"Yes, you've been quite busy in this manor, haven't you?" Muireall sets the necklace back down on the table. "I remember you wore a necklace with a black gem at your wedding with my son, didn't you?"

My heart seizes, wanting to burst with the truth but my mind is fearful of the consequences. "Perhaps. I don't remember every detail," I lie.

Muireall snorts. "Of course not. Are weddings so trite to Cairlichen?"

"That's not what I meant," I snap back. Perhaps a bit too defensively.

"But you did wear one. What did it do?"

I force another spoonful in my mouth. It would be impolite to talk while chewing. But Muireall is patient, studying me. By the time I swallow, I've devised my answer. "It was to calm my nerves, if you must know."

"Why were you nervous? My son was completely enamored with you from the moment he laid eyes on you." Her eyes narrow, knowing I won't divulge the truth. A stalemate. "Elspeth also said that the servants saw you and Callen Lockhart sneaking out into the orchid while his mother was laying sick in her bed."

"I thought you didn't indulge in the town gossip."

"Is it gossip if it's the truth?"

"Yes, most certainly, if its main goal is selfish superiority or some other twisted purpose," I scoff, and while I know my words hold wisdom, my heart urges me to defend myself. "The servants had no business betraying their employer's private life, nor did Mrs. Kilpatrick have any reason to tell you of what she heard, true or not. I'm sure her motivation was not one of care for me."

"Regardless, you know the gossip will spread. Is there a reason you wish to deny it?"

I huff, setting the bowl next to me and crossing my arms over my chest. "If you must know—although it is none of your business—Callen went with me to destroy the talisman that cursed his mother. He thought it was his duty."

"Truly, that's all that happened?"

"Yes. He wanted to see if I could break the curse."

Muireall watches me for a moment, then shifts her posture. "You know, Caitrin, Callen Lockhart is *very* wealthy. Wealthy enough to buy back our family fields. So if something…untoward had happened while you two were alone…well, perhaps his…fascination with you can be used for our advantage."

If I had been standing, I would have surely fallen to the floor at her crude assertion. Instead, I slump back against the lounge, my mind going blank. Then a gasping breath of laughter leaves my lips. "I can't believe you would think me—or Callen!—capable of such a thing! I would never…especially not—" I stop stammering; I am being overly defensive. Nothing had happened. Nothing would happen.

"Cairlinen live by different rules than the rest of the world. Your mother never had a husband, and it didn't stop her from having a child."

Heat bubbles up within me, ready to be released in a torrent of curses at her, but I resist. Muireall isn't bothered by raised voices or cutting words. Pushing down the anger, I do my best to mirror Muireall's cool attitude. "Is this about Callen and your fields, or is it about me not giving you a grandchild while Tate was alive?"

"Did you even try?" Her voice breaks, betraying her grief. Sorrow over so many lost things.

I don't answer her question; the truth would only make things worse. Whether she likes it or not, I would never take advantage of anyone. Perhaps if I had been able to trust Tate's feelings for me…but as it was, I felt too guilty about marrying him to add a child to my burden.

"You are so selfish," I mutter under my breath, looking away as I roll my eyes.

"Selfish?" Her bitterness rears its ugly head, and she stands to her feet. "You're one to talk! You didn't even have the courtesy to continue caring for me in the cottage! Why not just move all the way back to the grove if I'm so *selfish*? If you hadn't married my son in the first place, I would be here with *him* and no doubt we would all be happier!"

I rise with control and raise my head high so I look down my nose at her. "I made a promise that I must keep, but caring for you doesn't mean enduring your insufferable attitude."

"Insufferable—!"

"I tried to be a good daughter-in-law, to provide for you and make your life as comfortable as possible, but it's never enough. Nothing is ever enough for you, is it?"

Muireall's jaw stiffens, deep wrinkles cut into her furrowed brow.

"Even if I *was* powerful enough to create a dèidh seo dèiligidh, that wouldn't actually bring your family back from the dead. Now that you've left my ma and her spirit, you're forced to face reality—your husband and sons are *never* coming back—and rather than process the truth and find a way forward, you take out your anger on me. *I* didn't take Tate away from you! Your god did!"

Muireall is still for a long time, holding my gaze as if looking away admits any fault. For a moment, her eyes gloss over, and she swallows back tears. "You are cruel for berating an old banntrach, Caitrin," she finally says, her tone careful to hide how I've hurt her. My heart wells with shame. Even if my words were true, they were spoken in anger.

Muireall stomps over to my gown and grabs it like it's a pile of dirty rags. "Now that you've had your fun, I'll be selling this."

It's not her right to take it, but I've already won one argument and found no satisfaction. The fight drains out of me. "No one will want a dirty gown."

"It wouldn't be dirty if you hadn't blemished your reputation. No one will marry you if the rumor spreads."

I roll my eyes, shaking my head. "No one wants to marry me anyway because I'm a cairline, an abomination. Not even Callen! And why would I want to marry someone who condemns my bond, who condemns everythin' I am?"

"I wish Tate had possessed that kind of wisdom, to see you for who you really are."

Her words punch deep into my gut. Would he have seen me that way if I hadn't made the dèiligidh with Keres? I hadn't earned his love—I had created it. Now that he was dead, and free of the dèiligidh, did he ask his god to curse me for revenge? I hadn't meant to hurt anyone by it. But I guess even the best intentions can come back to haunt you.

THIRTY-FIVE

THE THICK LAYER OF DUST and dirt that covers the manor is almost comforting as I drag a bucket of water and a handful of rags to one of the upstairs bedrooms. It's time I had a real space for myself in the manor.

I spent the past two days recovering physically from the dèiligidh, and today I can't sit still. My mind keeps replaying the events of the ball, obsessing over the details, second guessing every moment. I need to keep myself distracted, keep busy, or I'll go insane trying to decipher how many mistakes I made that night.

Clearing the rugs from the floor, I strip the linens and quilts from the bed and throw them over the banister that overlooks the entryway. A puff of dust floats into the air, shining in the sunlight like tiny gems instead of lifeless particles. The room lays bare without the coverings.

Two large windows let in the daylight, dulled by the dust that hangs on every surface and in every breath. A few panes of glass have shattered completely where the branch of a towering oak tree has grown into the room, hugging close to the wall; perhaps it regrets its decision to move in and is looking for an escape. The mattress is large enough for two people but slumps in the middle as though it's only ever cradled one body, held by a metal frame that squeaks from even the slightest movement.

I set the bucket down, and the water sloshes over the side and onto the hardwood floor. Soaking the rag, I get to work dusting the desk first, occasionally wrapping the cloth around my fingertip so I can clean the sharp corners. The detailed work is relaxing, absorbing all of my focus so I don't have time to think about Muireall or Callen or even my bond.

Just the task at hand.

The breeze through the busted window keeps the room from overheating as I scrub away the layers of dust. My curly strands of hair are made more unruly by the slight sweat on my brow and they spring over my eyes. I bat them away with the back of my hand, standing up straight to stretch my back and release a long breath.

Hopefully I will wear myself out so much that even when I'm done working, I'll be too exhausted to think. Then I'll draw myself a nice hot bath to soak in and let the world melt away.

I dunk the rag back into the water, which quickly turns murky.

"Hello?"

The wind whistles through the manor, carrying the word with it. Or perhaps I hadn't really heard anything to begin with.

"Caitrin?"

I freeze. My name is spoken clearly, almost formally, with an edge of roughness.

Callen.

My heart flips and somersaults into my stomach. I drop the

rag and spin to catch my reflection in the vanity mirror. My hair is knotted and held back loosely with a ribbon, and my yellow dress is covered in streaks of dust and damp from splashes of water. I look a complete mess, although I don't know why I should care.

All he sees when he looks at me are the red markings around my wrists.

Especially after the ball.

"Caitrin? Are you here?"

I swallow and exit the room, holding my head high. I refuse to feel ashamed of saving his mother's life. I did him a favor, no matter how disgusting he thinks I am for doing so.

Looking over the banister that wraps around the second floor, open to the foyer below, I see Callen. He's dressed simply, and sloppily, in just trousers and suspenders over a white shirt with the sleeves rolled up clumsily. He must have either dressed in a hurry, or didn't undress for bed the night before.

"I'm comin'," I say, not quite shouting down at him but allowing my voice to be carried by the echo of the open space. His head snaps up, but I turn away, walking to the stairs.

What could he possibly want from me?

"Yes?" I ask politely when I reach the foyer. My hand lingers on the railing, covered in dust and grime, as I step onto the dull, marble tiles. Then I force myself to look up from my feet to see him walking toward me boldly. My foot starts to back up until I see his face, and I hesitate my retreat.

Callen is smiling weakly, with a flush in his cheeks, but smiling all the same. As if he can't help it. "My mother seems to be all better," he says, his hands hanging limp at his sides. "Whatever you did, it worked."

My eyebrows bounce at his words. *Whatever I did...* "Spirits do not break their promises," I say, lifting my chin proudly.

His smile falters. Just as I expected.

"So why are you here? I would think we're truly even now."

With a heavy sigh, he looks away, shaking his head. I wince, wishing I hadn't been so abrasive. "I came to check on you, to see how you're doing after...everything." He glances back up at me, his gaze holding mine.

"I'm doin' just great. Stronger than ever." I know that my lingering fatigue was a result of the spell—I remember times when my mother would rest for weeks after creating an especially powerful dèiligidh—but my bond is stronger, so it isn't really a lie.

"I'm glad to hear it, especially since Brodie told me he nearly had to carry you inside when he brought you home."

My cheeks grow hot. I didn't remembered Brodie bringing me home at all, but I did remember ripping off that dress, the intense desire to be comfortable and asleep. "It had been quite an excitin' night." I fold my arms over my chest, hugging myself. Best to not waste any more of his time. "Well, now that you've seen I'm fine, you're free to go back to your work. You have a big harvest to prepare for still, don't you?"

"Actually, since I walked here...walking helps to—"

"Clear your head, I remember."

He smiles brightly, a soft, clumsy smile, like it was special to remember such a small thing. "Would you like to join me?

There is a trail that cuts through your thicket straight to the edge of the orchard." He gestures to the door.

I almost smile back; the look on his face is dangerously contagious. While I hold my lips taut, my heart warms under his gaze, and the hope it holds. Maybe by his mother's miraculous healing, he has seen the truth about my bond. "I suppose it would be nice to get out of this stuffy house for a bit." I try to not seem too pleased with his invitation as we walk toward the front entrance. I still haven't figured out how to get the fallen door back onto its hinges.

"At least you have plenty of breezeways." Callen chuckles.

"I'm actually tryin' to figure out how to make it less 'breezy'," I say with a helpless laugh.

As we exit the manor, Callen stops to examine the doors. "Seems a simple enough fix. I'll send Brodie and a few farmhands to fix up the door."

"Oh, no!" Not more favors! I jump between him and the door defensively. "I can do it myself. I just haven't gotten to it yet."

His face fills my vision. It's probably improper for us to be so close. My back presses against the doorframe as my breath catches in my throat. Callen steps back politely after a moment, a twinkle in his eyes. But he doesn't withdraw his offer. And I secretly hope he will follow through on it despite my objection. It is rather unnerving to sleep in a home without a proper door.

We start down an overgrown trail through the thicket. The red caps of mushrooms and tiny buds of yellow, red, and white wildflowers spot the ground. Callen clears his throat. "I asked my mother who the necklace was from. The one with the talisman."

My ears perk up.

"She said it was an anonymous gift. I think she hoped it was a sign of amity from the town. Brodie found the package for her at the front door the morning of the ball."

I nearly gasp. "You think that Brodie—!"

Callen coughs, swallowing air in shock at my accusation. "Oh, no! Absolutely not! He's almost like family, been working on the farm since he was a boy. There's no reason for him to curse my mother. And he's not a cairline."

I furrow my brow. "Given the right trigger—jealousy, betrayal, selfishness—everyone has a motive to hurt anyone." Even I, given the right circumstances, might have a motive to try and kill Lady Ardala. Except Callen saw what I did to save her. That should be proof enough to vindicate myself. "And while a cairline created the curse, it would have easily been bargained for someone else."

Callen shakes his head, his lips bending into a frown. "Whoever did it, it's a cruel trick, giving some random curse to her like that."

"It wasn't random." I put my hand on his arm to get his full attention. His eyes shoot to my hand, and my cheeks warm as I pull it away. "Most dèiligeadh require very specific things to be created, and curses and favors alike require somethin' personal from whoever it is made for. Only a very powerful cairline can create a curse that will affect someone random."

"So you think there is a powerful cairline near Soarsa?" Callen asks, his concern growing.

"That's what Keres said." I press my lips together when I

see him hesitate at the mention of my spirit. "Either way, there is another cairline in Soarsa. And whoever she is, she's dangerous. And she managed to steal somethin' from your mother." The memory of taking Lady Ardala's blood pinches my gut, but I push it away in exchange for the image of the girl I found in the manor and the strange things she had said. "I met someone when I first arrived; she seemed to know more than most Croìthen. Dark hair, bronzed skin…"

"Una?" Callen twists his head, then begins shaking it. "No, she couldn't have done this."

"Yes, that was her name! She said I wasn't the first cairline in Soarsa, and I didn't get a good look at her…she could be bonded."

"No, she isn't," Callen corrects me quickly. Too quickly.

I fold my arms over my chest. "How do you know?" My stomach twists and my resolve loosens. I don't know why my heart is already sinking even before he has spoken.

"She *used* to be a cairline, but she isn't anymore."

THIRTY-SIX

I STEP BACK AS MY breathing hitches. "What do you mean? That she…"

"She broke it, the bond."

I nod once, soberly. "A *sgaoileadh*."

"Sgaoileadh?"

"A human who buys a cairline's bond from a spirit. She didn't *break* the bond; it was sold."

"A slave? But she's free; she's not enslaved to anyone."

"Then she escaped or killed her master because a cairline only breaks her bond by allowing herself to be enslaved to a new master."

"A *new* master?" Poor choice of wording. He'll never forget that I said that.

"A bond can't be broken. Ever. At all. Not even by a sgaoileadh," I say, making my words sharp and pointed. "But the bond can be transferred from a spirit to a human. The cairline gives up her power for a prison." I take a calming breath, shaking my head. "Una must have been really desperate to do something like that."

Callen frowns. "You mean…desperate to be free of the bond?" he says the words as if they should spark something in me, but he still doesn't understand.

"There are only two reasons a cairline would sell her bond." I don't allow him to pull me in with his pity, starting to walk forward again. He follows me eagerly, and I recite the words my mother told me as if we are in a classroom. "First, because she isn't willin' to barter with her spirit. A cairline who starves her spirit is useless. The spirit can either convince the cairline to sell herself or drive the cairline mad."

"Because she wouldn't give the spirit her blood," Callen clarifies. I didn't say it on purpose, knowing he would fixate on that part, especially after the ball.

I continue without acknowledging him. "The second reason would be because she has nothin' but her blood to barter with. We call them *fuilneaden* because they give their blood to be used for another cairline's dèiligeadh—spirits don't like to share—like my grandmother." The resentment in my tone belongs to my mother, not myself, but I feel it all the same. It's a part of my heritage. "My grandmother was a fool who couldn't bargain two pennies for a cup of water with her spirit, and so penniless and homeless, she sold herself to be a fuilneadh.

"The sgaoileadh who bought her was my ma's father, and Ma was raised like a slave in his house. She created her bond after my grandmother's death, usin' her ma's very own bones to summon a strong spirit. My ma was powerful from the very beginnin', because she was always willin' to sacrifice anythin' for the strongest spells." I should be proud, so I hold my head up high, but the words prick at a hidden wound, deep inside.

She had always sacrificed anything. Even her own daughter's blood, if the spirit demanded it.

Bonding with Keres had been a way of freeing myself from my mother. After all, a bond to my own spirit meant that Nessa couldn't barter using my blood anymore. I refused to be her fuilneadh forever.

I swallow, pushing away the pains of the past.

"Whatever her reasons, Una certainly came to Soarsa to escape either her master or punishment for murder," I explain, hoping Callen doesn't notice the slight change in my tone. "No cairline would dare enter Croìthe to take back a fuilneadh."

Callen is silent. I had expected him to retort with a defense of the sgaoileadh, or maybe ask more clarifying but uncomfortable questions. Instead, he is quiet, and only the sounds of earth crunching beneath our boots and the chirping of birds fills the air.

At first, his silence feels victorious. I've finally made him understand, at least a small part, of the truth about cairlinen.

But as the silence stretches on, I start to feel more defeated. Why doesn't he say anything? Maybe I shouldn't have told him about my ma or my grandmother. Perhaps my family history is just as shameful as Ma always said it was. I should have kept it to myself.

Callen stops walking just as a babbling creek comes into view. I turn to face him, eager for him to speak, no matter what he says. Anything but this deafening silence.

"What does a sgaoileadh pay? To buy the bond?"

I open my mouth, but the words don't form naturally. I want to ask why he is so curious, but I'm afraid of the answer.

Perhaps I've told him too much.

But there is no chance he would ever spill even a drop of

his blood for a dèiligidh.

"Their blood, of course." I don't mean to sound condescending, but surely he expected nothing different. His eyes meet mine, and I hold his gaze, making sure he hears me very clearly. "As much blood as the cairline is worth to the spirit."

I nearly jump when his hands take my own. He looks down, and his thumbs graze over my wrists. My breath comes out shallow. I feel exposed. And I see the questions in his gaze, in the way he examines my markings.

Then his green eyes look up and fix on mine, intense with hidden desire. A cool drop of rain falls, landing on my cheek.

I shake my head. "I don't want to break my bond with Keres, Callen." His hands cradle my own, drawing me closer. "I tried to change for Tate, but it didn't stick. And I'm not ashamed…" The words get stuck in my throat. I shouldn't feel guilty. I'm not. My nose tingles with the threat of tears welling up in my eyes, so I glance sideways into the forest. I sniff, forcing the feeling down deep.

"I'm not asking *you* to change," Callen says, a hand slipping up to my cheek, inviting me to look up at him again. "Not who you really are. There are parts of you that don't belong to Keres—you're hardworking, creative, passionate, you know how to dream big but start small, and you're not afraid to get your hands dirty or stand up for yourself. I think you may be the bravest girl I've ever met." The words spill out of his lips effortlessly, enchanting and shrinking the space between us. He brushes a lock of my hair behind my ear. "That's the *real* you. Never change her."

Another drop on my arm.

My hands brace against his chest, part of me wanting to push him away, and the other part...

"Cait, all I want is—"

"I know," I interrupt him. And while I'm not sure what he was going to say, I don't know if I can bear to hear it. Whatever plea or petition he might make, it won't do any good. I'm happy with my bond. I'm proud of my bond. Aren't I? "But what about what I want?"

His brow furrows, confused, maybe frustrated. Heat radiates off his body, one of his hands on my cheek, the other tentatively at my waist. He's so warm in contrast to the sudden chill in the air.

The rain is falling steadily now, and I barely notice until I see the droplets of water sprinkling his face and his unruly hair.

I'm desperate to know what he was going to say.

"What do you want, Caitrin?"

I lean closer to him, fearful of my answer. I need power, independence, things my bond gives me. And yet...perhaps what I want is different than what I think I need. Panic seizes my heart at the thought of voicing it aloud.

"Whatever it is, Cait, I'll give it to you." His eyes are drawn to my lips.

Maybe we want the same thing.

My lips part, but no words come out, only shallow breath. My eyelids flutter as his hand brushes into my hair. The space between us is almost non-existent.

Thunder cracks and the rain falls as the heavens open up.

I can't help but laugh, looking up as water soaks me from

head to toe. Lightning flashes across the sky and dark clouds roll in above us.

"We'd better get back!" Callen says, shouting over the sudden gale that bursts past us.

"You're not fond of being struck by lightnin'?" I take his hand in my own, not ready to let go of his warmth, and we sprint down the trail together.

When we arrive back at the Raeburn manor, laughing and screaming with delight as the thunder and lightning chase us from the thicket, we're far too drenched for decency. I offer Callen an old, musty coat from one of the closets, but he declines, lingering in the doorway for a moment.

"Do you want to wait out the storm?" I ask, more out of hope than to be polite as I drape the coat around myself. Even if he only stays to argue, I'm becoming accustomed to his company, and the storm cut our walk short. I pull the coat more tightly around my shoulders to cover my dress, the soaked fabric clinging to my body. My hair falls down my back in dripping waves, my ribbon having fallen away during our run. Droplets hang from my eyelashes.

Callen looks away, but he is unable to stop smiling. His shirt is nearly see-through, the wet, white fabric sculpted around his torso, framing strong muscles. He runs a hand through his soaked curls. "Probably best to get home and change into a dry set of clothes," he says, shuffling his feet for a moment.

I get the idea he isn't ready to leave yet, either. With a deep breath, I step closer to him. "I wouldn't mind the company." I admit with a shrug. "I have a feelin' you have more to say."

Callen smiles boldly, his cheeks warming as he tightens his hands into fists, restraining himself. He taps his clenched hand against the doorframe, pondering his options. "I think this time, you've left me speechless." And then he steps backward. Away from me. My grin falters. "I'll see you again soon, Caitrin."

The curtain of rain closes around him. With one last wink, he shoves his hands into his pockets and begins to walk contentedly away from the manor as if it were a bright sunny afternoon, not a cloud in the sky.

THIRTY-SEVEN

My dreams are filled with warmth and light, sparkling green eyes and a smile that is only for me.

The next day, when the skies are clear without any threat of rain, I gather all my courage and head for town. My markings have grown too wide to be hidden by my gardening gloves so I dress in my old, green dress, with its long sleeves. Luckily, the final heat of summer has slipped away and the air has begun to cool considerably.

I hope with all my heart that it isn't a busy day at market and that Shona will remember her offer to me at the ball.

And that she hasn't changed her mind.

I need to secure a job, and keep my funds hidden from Muireall. I have to stay with her, but I'm not obligated to finance her every whim. She is cared for well enough already.

With one final breath for courage, I enter the town square, adjusting my wide-brim, straw hat, which I wore more to shield my face from anyone who might recognize me than to protect against the sun.

The main stretch of town is full, with people going in and out of the general store and post office. It's early enough that the bakery is still open, the smell of fresh bread drifting into the open air and tempting me. But I don't have even a penny in my pocket. Not yet.

Despite the bustle of townspeople, there are no merchants selling wares from make-shift stalls today, although several doors and windows—including those of Hew's Textiles and Tailoring—are set open to let in the sunshine and cool breeze. In the window of the shop, Shona is dressing the display with her back to the street. With an extra skip in my step, I hurry to the door and enter before anyone else wandering around town notices me.

Shona grunts, heaving a voluminous gown over the mannequin, which has already been dressed in a petticoat, tempting it to topple to the ground.

"Let me help you!" I rush over to hold the dress form steady. My hat falls back, the tied ribbon under my chin catching it from dropping to the ground.

Shona freezes mid-movement. She stares at me, eyes wide, her mouth open but silent. "Thank you," she finally says, bowing her head and then hastily returning to her work. I help her pull the skirt of the dress over the top of the form, then I kneel to straighten the hem. A spark of anger swells in me as I recognize the tiny stitching.

I glance up as Shona begins to lace the back of the bodice, full recognition settling in over me.

It's my gown from the ball. "Did Muireall sell this to you?" I ask carefully as I stand, unable to pull my eyes from the dress.

I don't know when I would have ever worn such a dress ever again, but I didn't truly expect Muireall would get rid of it. She didn't have a right to sell it and keep the profit all to herself. The fabric had been a gift for me, and it was my hands that labored over the cutting and stitching. My jaw grows rigid and my lips pinch together. I shouldn't have let her take it so easily.

"Yes, she was here yesterday afternoon, first thing when I opened," Shona explains, her voice soft and cautious. She glances over at me for a moment, then hides behind the mannequin, working at the lacing with more focus. "She said you gave it to her to sell."

I guess I did, technically. At least, I didn't stop her from taking it. I relax the tension in my shoulders.

"It's beautiful. I was able to really examine it and you do wonderful work. Careful hands like yours would save me a lot of time." Shona fixes the drape of the skirt, and then steps back to admire it. "And I was able to clean up the skirt from all of the…" She looks over at me, catching my eyes and letting the rest of her words hang between us.

Dirt.

"I didn't curse Lady Ardala."

"Oh! No! Um, of course not!" Shona's politeness is strained, concerned, as she holds her hands up in defense.

I shake my head, forcing a smile as my cheeks warm. "I'm a little on edge, I guess."

"We all are," Shona admits. "You're here about the job, aren't you?"

Here it is. She's changed her mind. I straighten with a deep breath, ready for her rejection. "Yes, if the offer still stands. I can do anythin' you need. Even if it's just cleanin' up around the shop until you feel you can trust me with more."

"Around the shop…" She crosses her arms over her

stomach, biting her lip. Then her eyes snap to the window and the door, and the potential customers mulling around the town square.

"Or in the back! I can do the buttons and trims and hems."

Shona nods, thinking over my suggestion, a small smile crossing her lips. "If you want this job, then…no one can know. You understand, of course." She sighs, twisting her lips as if holding in an apology.

I do understand: I'm here to work, but she can't have my presence hurting her business. "Of course."

"Anyway, I think you might be more comfortable back there. No one goes in the back room except for myself, and my brother when he's in town."

"Your brother?" I vaguely remember her mentioning a brother at the ball.

"Tavish. He lives in Abercorn, not far. He has a little textile shop there with weavers, selling fabric like the ones I have here all over Croìthe." Shona gestures to the bolts of fabric that line the edge of the shop.

"Oh, that's impressive."

"Yes, but um…this way, and I'll get you set up." Shona turns with a wave, making her way around the counter to the back door. I slip off may hat as I follow her. "The Barton twins shot up like wildflower weeds this summer, so all their dresses need ruffles added."

"Well, I didn't expect the horse to…"

Shona and I both whip around at the voice.

Brodie stands in the doorway, awkwardly clutching a bundle of half-eaten rush broom flowers in his fist. He is beet-red, his gaze shifting from me to Shona, then shoving the small bouquet behind his back. Shona giggles, fidgeting with her fingers and glancing over at me nervously.

I feel like I'm interrupting something, except I was here first. "Good to see you, Brodie!"

"Uh, what?!" Brodie says, his gaze breaking away from Shona. Perhaps he had already forgotten I was here. Although, perhaps he would be awkward even if I wasn't here at all.

"Shona is giving me a job," I say, standing tall and confident.

"Oh! That's a most excellent idea!" Brodie says, punching the fistful of flowers out with too much enthusiasm. Tiny petals puff into the air at the sudden motion. "Oh dear."

I turn back to Shona, her cheeks pink. "Adding ruffles, you said?" I ask to capture her attention.

Her eyes go wide. "Oh, um yes! Uh…I have it ready—oh, Brodie, I have to—right this way, Caitrin—Brodie, just a moment!" Shona is like a chicken without its head, one moment starting for the backroom and the next turning to her suitor.

Brodie pulls at the collar of his shirt as if he has never buttoned the top button before today.

I open the door to the backroom, blocking Shona's way for a moment. "It's all back there already?"

Shona nods, biting her lip, completely overwhelmed.

"I'll start cutting those ruffles while you, uh, help this customer." I wink before entering the backroom. "And we can figure out the details of my employment later." Lest she forgets in the excitement that I'm not working for free.

She lets out a long breath to calm herself and then, instead of following me, she hurries back around the counter toward Brodie. "How can I help you today, Brodie?"

The door closes behind me.

The backroom feels much more like home. The shelves that line the left wall are stuffed with boxes and baskets. A bar next to the door is filled with hangers, some empty, others with paper patterns pinned to them, and a few sporting half-finished garments. Two large windows are on the back wall, with thin curtains pulled back and half-opened so the breeze drifts into the room, and the view of the lake is unhindered. Several dress forms with mock-ups sit in the corner.

And in the center of the room is a large table, as big as a bed, covered in soft, white muslin. On top lay six dresses, each with a bolt of fabric—those must be for the ruffles—and a little basket with Shona's shears, snips, rulers, pencils, and a fabric tape measurer sits off to the side. I grab a piece of paper pinned to the first dress.

Add six inches. Leave plenty for the hem and seam allowance to let out again in the spring. Free of charge if Mr. Barton passes.

My heart swells at the note, struck by the Barton's struggle and Shona's charity all at once.

Perhaps Callen isn't the only generous soul in Soarsa.

I set the note down, a surge of energy rushing through my veins as I place one of the pencils behind my ear and grab the fabric tape measurer to calculate how many yards of ruffles I'll need for these hems.

And there is something inside of me that isn't so concerned with how much Shona will pay me for the work.

THIRTY-EIGHT

THINGS ARE FINALLY FALLING INTO place. I have a job—and not a last resort job mucking stalls—a real job, my dream job as a seamstress. I finished the ruffles for the Barton girls in two afternoons flat, and Shona was so impressed that she not only paid me handsomely but also let me take four yards of breezy cotton home to make myself a new dress. She even said if there was no work to be done, I was welcome to use her shop.

Needless to say, I don't sleep a wink that night, and by morning I have a new meadow-green dress, which imitates the latest styles of Kaledon I had seen on the fashion plates in Shona's workroom. The skirt is full and perfect for dancing, falling to my ankles, with long sleeves and a bodice that mimics a bustier. With the scraps, I made a skinny little bow that sits in the center dip of the sweetheart neckline.

Shona demanded I make two more of the same style for her to sell in the shop, and I happily obliged. I used a bit of my wages to buy new fingerless gloves made of brown fishnet lace that reach half-way up my forearms. They are a bit see-through, but they hide my markings enough that I don't have to wear long-sleeves to disguise my arms, giving my skin room to breathe.

And the manor is starting to become home, bit by bit. As

promised, Brodie came with a couple others from the Lockhart farm to rehang all the doors, presenting me with two new keys that fit fresh locks. Muireall stays out of my way except on the rare occasion that she thinks she can get something from me. When I see she has been tending to Ailbert and the hens all on her own, I give her the extra key to the manor, and she takes it without any accusations.

And then there's Vaila and Yvaine, who stop by the shop to say hello to me in the backroom whenever they are in town, even if I have just spent the morning with them gleaning. The mystery of Lady Ardala's curse has faded as my life has become full with friendship and sewing. I haven't had any reason to contact Keres since the ball, but I summon her once just to keep from going mad. She doesn't say a word, merely taking a drop of my blood and disappearing. I guess she doesn't miss me, either.

And then there's Callen...

I breathe out a deep sigh at the thought of him as I walk down the main road, remembering how his curls fall over his green eyes, how the shirt clung to his chest after the rain, how we danced on the balcony under the starlight, even if we did argue half the time. On the days when I don't go to the estate to glean, I'll find him taking a walk through the woods, and I usually invent a reason to join him. He doesn't understand me completely, but he feels safe, like he *wants* to understand. We just come from different worlds.

Like how Tate and I came from different worlds. And look how that turned out.

But there is no magic this time.

None that I know of, at least.

I swallow, a chill running down my arms as alarm bells sound in my mind. I don't know what reason someone would have for placing a love spell over Callen, but is it possible?

Not that he loves me. Not that he even likes me, a cairline, an abomination. At least, he hasn't tried to kiss me again. If he was going to kiss me at all that day in the rain.

I shake my head, refusing to think about it further.

I should get home and finish cleaning up the sunroom. I found a few books in the study that are still readable, and the sunroom will be the perfect place to relax and read after a full day of work.

As I make my way down the wide path that leads to the Raeburn estate, Muireall comes into view, pushing open the gate. "Caitrin?" She is dressed from head to toe in black, per usual. And she is rushing toward me. What does she want this time? "Caitrin!" There is an urgency in Muireall's voice that is rare, and I've only heard it once before.

The night Tate took a turn for the worst.

"What is it? Did something happen?"

She grasps my hand, not as though she needs to hold onto something, but as if she needs to be held. I grip her hands reassuringly, panic rushing through me as she looks at me with wide eyes.

It is almost as if we're back in the grove. Back when she wore colors.

"Vaila is at the cottage with Yvaine. I don't know how they managed to walk all this way, but—"

"Vaila and Yvaine? Muireall, what is going on?"

"Yvaine has the Dhubd Blath." Muireall's expression grows grave as she squeezes my hand with an iron grip of fear. "And they're in my home. They brought the curse here!"

My concern crashes against my condemnation for Muireall's selfishness. "If she's cursed, it won't affect you," I say, releasing her hand and picking up my skirt to hurry.

"Are you certain?" Muireall says as she follows behind me.

I don't answer her, rounding the manor and making for the cottage, where the door has been left open.

Inside, Yvaine lays on the sofa, breathing heavily and sweating, as Vaila presses a damp cloth over her forehead. Large, black welts cover Yvaine's brown cheeks and hands.

"Caitrin!" Vaila breathes a sigh of relief as she says my name. "I heard you helped Lady Ardala, so I thought maybe…"

"Why did you bring her here? Caitrin could've come to you," Muireall asks from the doorway.

Vaila shakes her head. "We had to get out of the house."

I kneel beside the sofa, pulling Yvaine's white braid from over her shoulder, revealing another black welt. No cursed necklace this time. But a talisman must be somewhere on her. "Have you called for Dr. Kilpatrick yet?" If they haven't, I have more time to work. I pull at the laces of Yvaine's boots and tug them off her feet. Shaking each boot, I pray for a pebble to fall out, but nothing.

"No. We came straight here."

I begin grasping at the fabric of her dress, searching the pockets and seams. "When did she get sick?"

"This morning. Or maybe during the night. The warts

came on so suddenly…"

I tug along the hem, both hoping and dreading that this cairline used the same trick I did.

"Find anything?" Vaila asks, but when I look up at her, Muireall is standing just beyond. Even though she can't think I did this, her eyes are dark as she watches me.

"There's nothin' here. It must be hidden in her room." While the talisman isn't on Yvaine currently, it has infected her all the same. And until the talisman is found and destroyed, there is no hope of her recovering.

I look up at Yvaine's face, her eyes closed tightly, her breaths laborious and raspy.

"We should fetch Dr. Kilpatrick. Surely there is a way to keep her comfortable at the very least."

"Which one of us will go?" Vaila asks. It is obvious by how she sits on the stool that she is too tired for a journey into town. And Muireall will no doubt refuse.

I stand slowly, taking my knife from my boot. I'll need some of Vaila's blood to break the curse.

A knock echoes from the open front door and a gruff voice follow. "Ladies?"

We all turn to see none-other than Knox Baines standing at the door. He has a quizzical brow, assessing the room, his eyes jumping from Muireall to Vaila to me—he lingers, a smirk forming on his lips—then his gaze dips to Yvaine. "Another victim." It's a statement, no fear in his voice.

"You should leave before you catch it. But send Dr. Kilpatrick," I say, hoping he might do this small favor.

He chuckles. "I'm not so sure it's contagious. No one at the ball caught it. And Yvaine didn't attend."

I twist my head, narrowing my eyes. Very astute of him to notice. "Why are you here, anyway?"

"One of your hens was found eating all our corn. Came to tell you she'll be our dinner." Knox's eyebrows bounce with amusement. I couldn't care less about a hen at the moment. "What do you need that knife for?" His expression hardens as he squares his jaw and nods to my hands. "Were you about to take her blood?"

"Of course not!" I grip the knife tighter.

Muireall huffs, either knowing my lie or with frustration at Knox. "Yvaine's already cursed, Knox. Do you think Caitrin would do her even more harm?"

"Cursed?" Knox's eyes widen. "You mean…"

"Based on what I've seen…" I half-shake my head, wishing Muireall hadn't said anything at all. But Knox won't easily forget what he's heard, so perhaps it's better to give him the full truth. "I found a talisman on Lady Ardala, so her sickness was a curse at the very least. But I didn't create it! I'm just tryin' to help."

Knox scoffs, scrutinizing each of us suspiciously before responding. "I'll get Dr. Kilpatrick, but…" He takes a step toward me, his eyes narrow, like a cat stalking its prey. Even I know that cairline markings only grow because they are using magic, Miss Raeburn." With lightning speed, he snatches my wrist, yanking the fishnet glove to expose my wrist and holding up my arm. The knife in my hand catches the stray rays of sunlight in the room, and my wide markings are on full display.

"You don't know anythin' about magic," I say through

gritted teeth, staring him down and refusing to look away, or even blink.

"You should leave, Miss Raeburn. Before you cause any more trouble." Knox releases my wrist with a shove. "Before anyone else gets hurt."

I don't back down. "I can help her! You think medicine is any match for magic?"

Vaila stands with a deep breath, calm and composed. "Knox, stop. She won't harm us. Just go get the doctor."

"We can't trust cairlinen. We shouldn't have let her into town. That's when all of this started, wasn't it?"

None of us answer, because we know he's right.

But that still doesn't mean I cursed anyone.

"If she dies, if any of the infected die, we'll know who to hold responsible," Knox says, his eyebrows turned down ferociously.

"Oh, get out of here, Knox," Muireall says sternly, crossing her arms over her chest.

"Just remember, little cairline…"

I flinch at Knox's mocking nickname. It's too familiar.

"Magic is illegal in Croìthe. And it won't go unpunished."

Then he leaves out the front door.

"Knox! Get Dr. Kilpatrick!" Vaila shouts after him.

We all breathe a sigh of relief when he is gone. While his threat remains, it doesn't change what I have to do.

"There is only one way to stop this," I say, breaking the silence. "Once I find the talisman, it must be destroyed. And I can only do that with her blood."

Vaila has an expression of utter resignation, surrender. She walks over to me slowly. "No, dear," she says, smoothing my hair behind my ear. "Athair will watch over her. She will not die unless he allows it."

My entire body stiffens as I clench the knife at my side. "But she will suffer either way."

"Yes." Vaila nods, closing her eyes, holding back tears as her mouth bends into a deep grimace. "She will suffer, and so she needs the comfort of friendship all the more."

I glance toward Yvaine, her chest heaving in short, shallow bursts.

Keres asked for so much last time. What will her price be a second time? I must force a better bargain.

"This isn't your choice to make, Caitrin," Vaila tells me softly.

"But if she dies…"

"Athair is in control," Vaila repeats, her eyes full of a peace that seems out of place.

Muireall catches my attention, her brows knit together, her brown eyes softened by sorrow. She is at death's door again. Tears well up in her eyes. And behind the tears, regret.

"If Yvaine dies," Muireall says, "they will blame Caitrin. And they will punish her for it." She pinches her lips together, her familiar anger returning. "And I won't have another Raeburn die on my watch."

For the first time, she's not angry at me.

She's angry for me.

And we are all afraid of what might happen next.

THIRTY-NINE

Trusting that, despite his irritating personality, Knox would indeed fetch Dr. Kilpatrick, I escort Vaila home, where she and Yvaine live together, and take the opportunity to look for the talisman. Even if they don't want me to destroy it just yet, removing it from the cottage will ensure that Yvaine can return home without her condition getting worse.

And if I do find a talisman, then I'll know it's a curse, and perhaps I'll be able to help the others who have been infected.

The banntraichean's home is a more difficult walk than I expected. It is no wonder that Brodie picks them up for gleaning, and it's almost a miracle that Vaila made it as far as she did with Yvaine. I feel guilty for not offering to harness Ailbert to the wagon, but Vaila doesn't complain, even though her struggle is clear with each labored step.

Our journey takes us off the main road, cutting straight between a pasture and rows upon rows of a corn field. While the soil of the field is carefully maintained, perhaps even imported, the path we are on is littered with rocks.

"You live all the way out here with Yvaine? I would think you'd want to be closer to town," I say, more thinking out loud than expecting an answer.

Huffing to catch her breath, Vaila answers all the same.

"Well, my husband, when he was alive, managed the pastures up near the cliffs, pastures for the goats that Yvaine's family—the McDows—owned. Still own, in fact. Her granddaughter manages it mostly now, although she sold a large portion of the farm because, well, it's a lot of upkeep. They sold the farmhouse too, and her granddaughter lives in the old McDow cottage now."

Granddaughter? I shouldn't be so surprised that Vaila and Yvaine not only had husbands, but children, and grandchildren; I suppose I unconsciously picture them as being eternally as they are now. "I haven't heard you talk much about your families." I almost laugh, but it's more from nerves than amusement.

Vaila smiles, reaching for me to assist her as her legs grow more tired. We've passed the corn fields now, and the horizon has opened to nothing but blue sky and rock-ridden grass. The wind blows in strong gusts. I hold Vaila's arm to keep her steady as a little cottage in the distance comes into view.

"Well, not much to say for me. My husband and I never had any children," Vaila admits matter-of-factly.

I don't know quite how to respond, cautious not to reopen old wounds with questions.

Vaila pats my hand, a kind look in her eyes as she glances over at me. "But we took in a lad, Eoin, after his parents died in a house fire. He helped my husband with the goats till he was old enough to set out on his own."

"Where is he now?"

Vaila gestures out in front of us, where the edge of the cliffs has come into view, and the sparkling sea, barely visible beyond it. "Out there, somewhere. He found an apprenticeship sailing, delivering things to the mainland. He always came back, but he wrote a few years ago saying he'd settled down with a girl over there. Promised he would come and introduce her to me." She is still smiling, but her wrinkles speak of her pain. "Still waiting for that visit." She pats my hand again, then releases my arm as we near the cottage door. "Luckily, Yvaine keeps me company until then. She is my sister in all but blood."

Their home is larger than the garden cottage—two stories tall—but just as quaint with mismatched stone walls, a brown roof, and a stout chimney. A little bench is set just to the side under a lone, scrawny tree, facing the sea.

"Here we are!" Vaila sings as she opens the front door, the key already in the lock.

"Did you forget to lock up when you brought Yvaine to us?" I ask, concerned that her answer will not be forgetfulness.

Vaila swats a hand at me as she waits for her to enter. "Who would bother to come all the way out here and cause trouble?"

Clearly, some devious cairline would bother.

"Let me make you some tea before you head off then," Vaila says, going left into the kitchen. On the far right are stairs heading up to a second floor, but empty baskets, bonnets, and boots are stacked on the first few steps—their supplies for gleaning—and otherwise it looks like the stairs haven't been used in years. The entry room looks very comfortable with two sofa chairs, a cozy fireplace with glowing embers, and a hodgepodge of baskets containing various pastimes. One basket has yarn and knitting needles, while another holds books, a third contains tubes of paint and brushes, and a fourth is filled to the brim with marbles.

They certainly know how to keep themselves entertained.

"Do you mind if I look in Yvaine's room?"

"Go right ahead! It's the first one down the hall."

Following Vaila's directions, I go straight ahead and open the first door in the narrow corridor.

Yvaine's room is well kept, without the clutter of the living room. She has a simple four-poster bed, with a beautiful quilt, despite how the colors have faded. A little vanity with a clean mirror sits by a window with thin curtains. A chest sits at the foot of the bed. Besides a few other decorations and keepsakes, it's a small room and should be easy to search.

The bed is, of course, the logical place to hide a talisman. An unsuspecting victim would lie near it for hours without knowing. And the closer you are to the talisman, the more potent its magic is.

Going to my knees, I look under the bed, trying to spot anything out of the ordinary hiding there. Near the center of the bed, no doubt long-lost if only for it being out of reach, sits a single earring, three limp socks, and several light-colored marbles.

Flattening myself to the floor, I strain to thump each of the socks, making sure they are empty, then grab the earring, which may very well have the talisman set into it.

My fingers grasp the metal, and I sit back on my heels.

Just a normal, screw-on earring made of silver with a dangling, white pearl. Standing with a huff, I set the earring on the vanity and begin searching there amongst the old bottles, brushes, and jewelry for anything with a familiar black stone.

Nothing.

I turn back to the bed and pull aside the quilt—I'll make it good as new before I leave. Patting down the set of pillows and heaving up the mattress, reveal nothing out of the ordinary.

Nothing.

But it must be a curse.

I'm certain of it.

There is still one hiding place left in here.

I drop to my knees in front of the chest, undo the giant latch, and heave open the lid. It hits the frame of the bed with a *thunk*.

"What are you doin' in here?"

Spinning, I find a young woman standing above me, dressed just as she had been when I first met her, except with a loosely-knit shawl over her arms and the sleeves of her dress pushed up to her elbows.

Una.

Una McDow, I now recall.

"You can't just go through my grandmother's things without explainin' yourself."

She's trying to intimidate me, but I'm here to help. "I'm lookin' for a talisman." I turn back to the chest, searching through Yvaine's things with less care than I might have had if I wasn't determined to prove myself.

"A talisman?" Una nearly shouts, and it takes all my willpower not to turn and engage her anger. "How dare you—"

She grabs my shoulder but I wrench myself away from her.

"You think *I* gave it to her?"

Una frowns, staring down at me, her hands clenched in fists at her side, her shawl on the ground. Trailing around her wrists are white lines. She crosses her arms with a huff, hiding the markings. "Where else would she get one?"

"I don't know. I'm tryin' to figure that out," I say, returning to the chest. I squeeze every one of her blouses, skirts, and chemises, hoping to uncover the talisman hidden on one of them. Nothing. "She woke up with the Dhubd Blath this mornin', and I'm pretty sure it's a curse. If I can find the talisman…"

"Una! Thank Athair!" Vaila sighs with relief, placing a tea tray on the vanity and then embracing her. "Did Caitrin tell you?"

"Yes, she was just explainin'. I wish you'd come to me."

I move aside the items, trying to see the bottom of the chest clearly.

"Yvaine refused to be left in this house, and I wasn't about to take her further away from town. I was hoping to make it to Dr. Kilpatrick, but she couldn't go far on foot."

Nothing. My fingers trace the seams of the chest.

"But why go to the Raeburns? They aren't doctors." I can almost hear Una roll her eyes. "Are you sure *she* is the kind of help you want?"

Something pricks my finger. But there's nothing there.

"Una, I thought you of all people would understand," Vaila says, almost like she is scolding a child.

There it is again. Something sharp in the darkness.

"I *do* understand. That's why—"

Delicately, I pinch lightly on what feels like a ball of needles and lift it out of the chest. "I found it." The talisman is an orb covered in spikes and black as an abyss.

"So it is a curse." Una's voice is full of foreboding acceptance. I stand, still pinching the talisman, uncertain of what to do with it for the moment. Certainly, remove it from the cottage so Yvaine can come home, but it needs to be destroyed.

"That little thing did all this?" Vaila asks, shrinking behind Una, who stands tall and unafraid. She is no stranger to magic, even magic of the darkest kind.

"If we destroy it, Yvaine will—"

Una holds out her hand, palm up. "Give it to me."

"But you can't—"

"Give it to me!" Una demands. "I'll get rid of it."

"But you can't destroy it!"

Snatching the orb from my hand, she clenches her fist around it, breathing deeply through the stab of pain. "No, I can't. And glad about it. And I won't have you usin' my grandmother's blood to do so, either." She tucks it into her pocket as Vaila puts a hand on Una's arm.

They exchange a look that could have been a whole unspoken conversation, with how Vaila's eyes widen and Una's shoulders slump.

"If you would, tell Doctor Kilpatrick to help Yvaine home. I'll take care of her until she's well again," Una says, gesturing toward the front door.

I open my mouth to remind her that Yvaine would not get well without magic, but my eyes are drawn to the white lines like ribbons around Una's wrists again. Una shakes her head, a smile of pity on her lips.

"You aren't ready to hear my story, cairline. But when you want to know the truth about sgaoileaden, come and find me." A shudder runs through me at the word. Una waves her hand again, and I respect her wishes.

As I turn onto the main road, a quaint, boxy carriage passes by me. The man driving the coach nods to me politely enough, but there are curtains drawn over the windows. "Is that Dr. Kilpatrick?"

"Yes, miss. Best stay away," the driver says.

I feel utterly helpless. Yvaine is sick, cursed with an illness that will not improve without the intervention of magic, and yet everyone is preventing me from helping her.

Instead, I have to watch from a distance while she suffers.

Or find the cairline. If the cairline dies, all the talismans she has ever bartered will lose their power. But I don't have a single clue as to who it might be, and I haven't seen anyone else in town with the bonding bands of a cairline. Keres said it was a powerful cairline, so she would have more than red bands around her wrists; this cairline must have markings swirling up her arms.

Like my mother.

A shiver runs down my spine, and I shake free of it. Regardless of her power, I must find out who she is, where she is hiding, and then I will figure out how to stop her as well.

I absent-mindedly make my way back home, but I stop when Raeburn Manor comes into view. I can't endure Muireall right now. She will be nothing but a bundle of negativity. Of course, I can't blame her for being afraid, but if I'm going to help Yvaine, and clear my own name in the process, I can't be bogged down with her anxiety and pessimism.

What I need is to talk to Keres.

So I head into the thicket, and I start searching for something to barter with.

FORTY

FIVE KINGFISHER FEATHERS.

A broken stag antler.

Three small pieces of garnet gemstones. Or gem-pebbles, perhaps I should call them.

It's something to start with at least.

A drop of my blood falls from fingertip to flame. "Thig dhòmhsa."

The smoke swirls, twirls, and gathers into the form of Keres. The moon has begun to wane, and her darkness melts into the night. She takes her time appearing, no doubt making certain I am alone.

"Caitrin…" she hisses in greeting.

I lift my head with the shadow of a smile. "Keres. Did you miss me?"

Her short laugh echoes around me, like a tornado. "It's been over a week, and you haven't bartered with me even longer. Did that boy scare you away from me?"

I roll my eyes. "Of course not. But you certainly scared him away."

"Good." The word is barely a whisper.

But I have business to do, not games to play. "I need information about this cairline who is spreadin' curses like candy in Soarsa." I must choose my words carefully so that she doesn't take what I offer without giving me what I really need. "I want to know where I can find her."

"Little cairline, she would destroy you if—"

I change my request quickly, not wanting to waste any time with arguing. "Then tell me her motivation." I unfold a scrap of cloth to reveal my offering. "I have feathers, an antler, gemstones…and five fingers of blood."

Keres sways and swirls, considering my request. "Only five fingers?" With her wispy, black tendrils, she lifts the nine items from the scrap of cloth. They hover in the air. "Why not all ten?"

I shake my head at her silly suggestion. "Ten fingers would severely handicap me for the rest of the night. How would I change into my chemise with numb fingers?" I hold up my hands and wiggle my fingers. "And I know five is enough for such a simple dèiligidh."

"Simple? You think a dèidh seo dèiligidh is simple?"

"Dèidh seo…?" Did she misunderstand the deal I was trying to make? I am not asking to look into the future.

The smoke floats out, then pulls into a form that is almost like that of a human. Keres wraps what resembles an arm around my shoulders. "What you seek is not so simple as an answer, but a prophecy."

"A prophecy?"

"The cairline is obeying the will of the spirits, and while her methods are vile, she is trying to protect us. Protect you."

"From what?"

Keres goes silent, and I know what she is waiting for. "Five fingers," I say, unconvinced that this prophecy will be worth more than that.

With a sigh, she nods. Her fingers connect with my own, draining red and leaving my hand numb. I can't help but stand taller, having bargained her down successfully for the first time.

She takes the items and crushes them with the red smoke, tighter and tighter, until they explode like stardust. Wrapping a wisp around me, Keres gestures out toward the darkness of the thicket, where shadows and figures begin to form. Red sparkles taint the shapes, giving them movement and life.

The smoke plays out a story to accompany her words. The shadows look almost like spirits, hovering behind the human figures. A serpentine wisp moves around them, through them. "The bond between spirit and cairline is ancient, a power that the Croìthen god would have kept from us."

"Athair?" I ask, turning from the image to Keres. She hisses at the name.

The form of a large man stands in the center of the figures, spirits, and the serpent that slithers. "He has been scheming since the dawn of time to put magic back under lock and key so that all the power would belong to himself only, not shared with any cairline or spirit."

As interesting as her story is, it isn't giving me any answers. And I am starting to feel tricked. "Well, he hasn't succeeded yet so…"

"And he will not for a thousand years. Unless he claims you."

"Me?" My brow furrows with disbelief. Surely, she is making this up as she goes. "I'm hardly powerful enough to get the attention of some foreign god. Perhaps you mean Ma?"

"Well, it *could* be you," Keres says, correcting herself.

I cross my arms, growing tired of her riddles. "What is the prophecy exactly, Keres?"

The wisps of figures and spirits disappear as if blown away by the breeze, and in their place remains the figure of a girl. "That a cairline would be enslaved to a Croìthen prince." A man arises, shackling the girl, and then his figure becomes one with her own. "And she will be forced to create a corrupt bloodline from which the Sgaoileadh Rìgh would rise"—from the blob of combined figures rises a large man, wearing a crown, similar to the form she had made to resemble Athair— "who will reclaim every bond for himself, and thus all magic in the realm."

She breathes out, and it all disappears, leaving darkness in its wake. The only smoke remaining is Keres herself.

"So they are trying to kick me out of Soarsa, frame me by infecting the innocent, to ensure some prince doesn't come and arrest me?" I clarify, doubt laced in my words as I step away from her. "I would never allow myself to be enslaved."

Keres seems to watch me carefully, although there are no eyes in her darkened form as she floats to the other side of the candle, facing me. "It is impossible to know what will happen, but you must be careful, Caitrin. And you must strengthen your bond. No one would dare try to capture a powerful cairline. Only a weak one."

As she speaks, the skin of my arms begins to tingle. I look down to see my markings shift from a solid band, breaking away to twist and swirl up my forearm.

"Don't let them fool you, Caitrin. Once they see how strong you are, they will try to break our bond, get rid of your magic, your power, so that you will be weak once more."

Callen already has. But surely he doesn't know anything about this prophecy or the schemes of spirits. And I will never sell my bond. I have no reason to do such a reckless thing. "Don't worry, Keres. There is nothin' they could offer me that would convince me to give up my bond with you."

Her shadow dissipates and the reforms behind me. "What about love?"

A chill races down to my toes, but it's Callen's voice that echoes through my mind.

What do you want, Caitrin?

"Just remember, little cairline, it is forbidden for Croìthen to marry a bonded cairline. You will have to choose what you want more. One choice gives you freedom, while the other will leave you in bondage."

And then she is gone.

FORTY-ONE

I RECEIVE PLENTY OF FOUL looks when I make my way to town the next day, although I tell myself it's nothing out of the ordinary. Despite the fact that my arms are covered, everyone in Soarsa seems to know the truth of what I am.

When people cross to the other side of the street from me, or sneer with an insult under their breath as I pass, I want to feel a portion of pride. Though they may look down on me, they also fear me and my magic. *Fear is a tool, if wielded properly*, Ma had once said. But when people scurry from me, my heart pinches.

I don't have the talent for wielding fear as Ma does, so along with the pain of rejection, I shrink from the shame of weakness.

Shoving both away with a brave face, I do my best to ignore the scoffers all together. But when I arrive at Shona's shop, I find the truth of my situation is not something I will be able to ignore for long.

"Everyone is talking about Yvaine, so it's probably best if you take things home to work on them instead of being at the shop," Shona says as she folds three pairs of trousers and a bundle of fabric, placing them all in a brown paper bag. She keeps a wary eye on the closed door and large window behind me.

"I promise, Shona. I would never curse anyone. I would never use magic to hurt someone," I plead, clutching my hands to my chest in earnest.

"I believe you, I do, truly." Shona carefully places the necessary notions in the bag, then pauses to look at me. "But Dr. Kilpatrick has told everyone the Dhubd Blath is a curse and that *you* found a talisman in Yvaine's bedroom. They're looking for talismans at the Lennox's and the Irving's and Giles Wallas's, and if they find something, well, I don't know what they'll do but..." She sighs, knowing she doesn't need to explain the reasons my accusers have. "It's probably safest for you to stay close to home."

I take the bag and hold it close. "And not here where you'll have to guard me." With a nod, I try to give her a small smile, although my heart sinks at the thought of being alone in that big manor. "I understand, Shona. I don't want to cause trouble for you." Whether she views me as a friend or simply an employee, it is my furthest wish that my presence would negatively affect her.

"Thank you, Caitrin," Shona responds quietly, having the decency to not protest that I am 'no trouble at all'. Her gracious appreciation of my compliance gives me a bit of comfort.

But it also makes it clear that I'll need to prove my innocence in order to maintain my position at the shop. She is happy to send me home with hems and simple sewing projects now, but the longer the Dhubd Blath infects Soarsa, the more troublesome it will be for her to have me in her employment at all.

And what if the townspeople find out I've been touching their clothes? That is sure to cause Shona even more trouble. Trouble upon trouble, unless I can do something about it.

"I'll bring these things back as soon as I can," I tell her and hurry out so that watchful eyes will see me leaving rather than enjoying any friendly conversation.

And people are certainly watching. When I step onto the cobblestone street, those in the town square all pretend to avert their eyes or engage in idle chatter, but the air is thick with lingering gossip. I clutch the bag to my chest defiantly, and raise my chin, hoping to get out of town with at least my dignity intact.

I take three confident strides before my dignity is practically trampled.

A black horse comes out suddenly from the alley beside Hew's Textiles and Tailoring, nearly running right into me. It rears back on its hind legs, and I fall to the side, partially out of shock and partially in an attempt to get out of the way. Landing hard on the uneven ground, I first feel the sting of bone against stone, then the chill of water as mud splashes all over my side. I twist, hugging the bag against my chest and hoping the contents are protected enough by the paper packaging.

The horse whinnies in resistance and prances for a moment, attempting to calm down. Its rider is tall and broad, silhouetted by the sun so that he is all darkness and shadow

Lewis Baines.

With a scowl, I stand, ignoring the mud on my dress. "You should watch where you're goin'," I tell him, but I don't have the courage to say anything more when he smirks.

"I was. The horse just didn't comply."

Gawking with shock, I'm at a loss for words. Is he *admitting* to trying to injure me, or is he using the almost-accident to intimidate me? Either way, I snap out of my surprise. "Well, Mr. Baines, your horse seems to have better sense then his rider." I start on my way again, but Mr. Baines moves his horse to block my path, forcing me to retreat the steps I had taken.

I glare at him.

"Miss Caitrin Raeburn." He says my name mockingly, full of spite, as he stares down at me from his perch. "I wonder why you insist on covering up and pretending that you don't have the stains of a diabhal trailing across your arms. Knox told me all about them. And how they have grown."

I don't respond, not wanting to endure his tirade any longer than necessary, but neither do I look away.

"You do remember that magic is forbidden in Croìthe, don't you?"

"Magic is, but not simply having a bond," I correct him against my better judgement.

"Simply a bond, nothing more, of course." He narrows his eyes as if he is trying to read my mind. "Well, a bonded cairline cannot marry in Croìthe, you know that too?"

"What does that have to do with anythin'?"

A snicker escapes his lips as he pulls his gaze away. "Just remind that mother-in-law of yours that what's mine is mine. And at the first sign of trouble, I'll take everything left in the Raeburn name. Callen may think being Lord of Soarsa has some power, but that boy won't stop me from protecting my property."

"Consider us all well informed, Mr. Baines."

With a hiss, he kicks his heels into the horse and trots off into the town square.

I watch him go for a moment, wishing I had swiped something off of him for a dèiligidh. Nothing too harmful, just a trick perhaps to humble him.

But then I notice how many pairs of eyes are watching me, and I know that I'm in trouble whether I do magic or not.

They want a villain, and when they tire of the games, they'll make one out of me.

FORTY-TWO

GLEANING DAY ARRIVES, EXCEPT WHEN Brodie picks me up, neither Vaila nor Yvaine are with him, and his wagon is already filled with a few crates of produce, which he carries inside the manor. My entire body deflates, wondering if even Callen wants to distance himself from me and the accusations hounding me.

"Tell Callen thank you for me, I guess."

"Tell him yourself when we get to the Estate this morning!" Brodie calls back to me as he goes to set the crates down in the kitchen.

I skip after Brodie as my heart restarts with a spark, but the joy is dashed away as I remember my conversation with Keres two nights before. Is it wise to spend more time with Callen? While I enjoy my work in the shop and the companionship with Vaila, Yvaine, and Shona, just the thought of Callen floods me with giddy anticipation.

A future. That's what I see with Callen.

But surely it's a future that would require me to give up my bond, to be bought like cattle, and nothing is worth such a cost.

"You won't be gleaning today, Miss Caitrin," Brodie says with a wide smile as he heads back to the wagon.

A smile crosses my lips as I wonder what we'll be doing

instead. More dancing perhaps? While I'm still not a fan of Callen's gifts, I crave his company, and the chance to convince him that my bond isn't dangerous.

I lock the front door of the manor after I exit. While some hooligan could still climb through the broken glass of the windows if he was determined, it gives me some sense of pride to turn the key in the lock.

"We can't have you getting tired and dirty and sweaty just before tea." Brodie clicks his tongue and snaps the reins to get the two horses to start moving, pulling the wagon with them.

"Tea?"

"Tea with Lady Lockhart. She wishes to thank you for your, uh…" Brodie glances over at me, at my arms, where my bold, red markings swirl higher than ever, barely disguised by my fishnet gloves. "For your help in caring for her illness."

Tea with Callen's mother? I don't know if I trust Brodie's assessment that it will be to thank me. Perhaps she means to deter me from a relationship with her son, or chastise me for taking her blood to destroy the talisman. My stomach twists.

"*Just* Lady Lockhart?" If I'm lucky, Callen will at least be there as well. He may not like my magic, but he seems to like me well enough. And he tries to be respectful of my choices, even if he thoroughly disagrees with them.

"I believe so. Callen will be preparing for the big harvest this coming week."

I take a deep breath and resist the urge to tell Brodie to turn around and take me home. Lady Ardala seems so stoic and somber. I don't remember if I've ever really seen her smile. This tea will certainly be awkward, if not worse, and it is certainly not how I anticipated spending my morning.

When we reach the estate, Callen is talking with a farmhand, and my entire body melts upon seeing him. He spots us before the wagon comes to a stop, his face brightening when our eyes meet.

"Miss Raeburn." He reaches out his hand to help me from the wagon.

"Thank you, Lord Lockhart," I respond as genteelly as I can manage.

He feigns annoyance with a roll of his eyes, but a playful grin betrays him. "I'll escort you inside, then I must get back to work." He warps my hand around his arm, and his stare lingers for a moment on my markings. The change must be more noticeable than I thought. But he doesn't say anything about it.

"I spoke with Keres last night," I start as we enter the mansion. He stiffens slightly. "She said the cairline cursin' the town is tryin' to stop some prophecy."

"A prophecy?" That catches his attention, then he snorts, almost laughing. "About Soarsa?"

"About the 'sgaoileadh rìgh'," I say, and he goes quiet. "Have you heard of it?"

He shakes his head. "No. It must be ancient magic."

We turn into the parlor, where Lady Ardala is set before a canvas with a palette of paint and brushes next to her. But rather than the canvas facing the windows and the beautiful front garden, it faces the room so that the pure sunlight shines down over her like a halo.

"Mother," Callen calls out, announcing our presence.

Lady Ardala doesn't look up from the canvas, but she nods ever so slightly.

Callen squeezes my hand, and I turn to look at him. Our faces are inches away, and it makes my heart leap. I wish he wasn't leaving so soon. "You can't stay and have tea with us?"

"I have too much to do," he explains. "Don't worry. She's not as scary as she seems." He hesitates, smiles, then releases me and exits.

Even her own son finds her intimidating.

I take a deep breath, the scent of rose and citrus filling my lungs, and turn toward the room again, waiting to be acknowledged beyond the nod. It is elegantly furnished, with plush sofas framed in golden wood. There is a low table with a bouquet of fresh flowers, and several other potted plants arranged throughout the room. The large windows have long, flowing curtains hung over them, filtering the harsh sunlight. The whole room is gold and blue and white and light.

With another calming breath, I close my eyes, attempting to settle my nervous.

"Please, make yourself comfortable."

My eyes snap open. Her words are soft, but I nearly jump all the same. Lady Ardala still has not looked away from her canvas. With cautious steps, I go to one of the sofa chairs and sit down.

And the silence of the room settles in once more, accompanied by the quiet strokes of a brush against canvas.

Then a maid hurries in, wearing a blue dress with a white apron and bonnet, setting down a golden tray arrayed with all the essentials for tea on the table in front of me.

"Thank you," I mutter, but she barely glances my way. Moments later she is followed by a second maid, who places a tray with cookies and another with fruit, framing the tea set.

A full minute of silence later, Lady Ardala whips her brush from the canvas and wipes it on the cloth in her lap. "There…" she whispers, a light smile on her lips as she takes in her masterpiece. Then, finally, she glances over at me. "Thank you for your patience. You have to work quickly with this kind of paint."

"What kind?" I ask, eager to break the silence with easy conversation.

"Acrylics," Lady Ardala answers, setting her brush and cloth next to the palette on the little table beside her. Standing, she removes the sleeved apron, revealing a dazzling blue gown that brings out her eyes, the color of the sky on the clearest day. Without the canvas impeding my view of her, I notice her hair is carefully arranged in curls, pinned up away from her face and neck. Her fair skin warms pink.

"What were you paintin'?"

Her smile grows, and I see a hint of Callen's smirk on her face. "Oh nothing. Just a memory," she tells me coyly, and I wonder if she will display it when it's finished or if she will keep it secret forever.

She walks over and sits on the sofa adjacent to my chair. Without missing a beat, she begins to pour tea into a cup, places the cup on a saucer, and hands it to me. "Cream and sugar, if you'd like," she invites as she pours a cup for herself.

The silence has returned. Carefully, I pick up the tiny pitcher of cream and tip it so just a bit pours into my cup.

Without looking up, Lady Ardala hands me a tiny spoon to stir with.

Poised and elegant, she adds honey to her cup before sitting straight and taking a small sip. "Thank you for joining me. I wanted to have some time to talk with you," she says, looking over at me and holding my gaze. The eye contact is even more uncomfortable than the silence. "Surely you have heard about me. What have you heard?" She smiles sweetly, although she must know what I will say. Still, she is very good at pretending.

I summon my courage and answer truthfully. "That you used to be a prostitute on the mainland, and Callen's father brought you here and married you."

"And a handful of other rumors no doubt," she adds, her smile growing as if she is humored by the gossip. "No town is kind to a stranger with a sordid past. It takes a special kind of humility that not every person has necessarily learned to welcome someone who challenges you. To be patient, listen to their story, and offer compassion instead of condemnation."

I don't answer. I don't think I know how to have a conversation at all with her. She thinks and talks and moves in ways that are completely foreign to me.

"Shall I tell you what I have heard about you?" she asks.

My eyes go wide, but I restrain any further reaction. In an attempt to mirror her nonchalant attitude, I force a smile.

"Callen tells me that you are a hard worker, and very talented and kind, and not at all what he expected to find when I told him to go make sure our new cairline neighbor felt welcome." Her list is not the one I had expected to hear. But I know she disapproves of my bond, so I listen intently, waiting for her to acknowledge the truth. "You were married to Mrs. Raeburn's son, but he died, and you came to Soarsa with her, rather than stay in Cairlich."

"There was only my ma there."

Lady Ardala tilts her head to the side, her smile drooping. "You left your mother? Is she alone now?"

"She has her spirit," I say easily, wondering how Lady Ardala will respond to that.

"No spirit can replace a person." She reaches out to squeeze my hand. Not once has she glanced at my arms. "Especially not one's own child." She pulls away to take another sip of tea. Every movement is precise and fluid. "I'm sure she misses you."

It's not *me* she misses, if she thinks of me at all. "So how did you meet Callen's father? Unless…I'm sorry, that's probably a rude question." I blush and press my lips together, fiddling with my tiny spoon as lavender chamomile steam rises from the cup.

"Not at all! It's a wonderful story." Lady Ardala beams. Her excitement makes me even more uncomfortable. What kind of wonderful could there be in the story of a prostitute?

Still, I distract myself from looking too awkward by sipping my tea and listening politely, making sure I don't seem judgmental, or overly interested.

"I worked in a brothel owned by the temple on the mainland where they worshipped everything except Athair." She pauses, as if she expects I will ask a question. But I'm too respectful to inquire beyond what she will tell me on her own. "Croìthe was at war with the mainland, trying to reclaim the seaside villages and docks. Tuethal, Callen's father, was a close friend of the rìgh and a spy on one of the ships that laid siege to my city, which was built right up over the edge of the sea. That's where my little apartment was, built right into the wall on top of a dozen other homes.

"Tuethal snuck into the city, trying to find a weakness, but his little rowboat had been discovered and the alarm bells sounded through the city. I was saying my prayers for the night when—"

"Prayers? Who were you prayin' to?" The question came out of me without my permission, so captivated by the story that I forgot my manners.

"Athair." Lady Ardala smiles, knowing how curious her answer is. "Most on the mainland, and in my city, worshipped ideas and things of the flesh. But we heard the stories of the Croìthen god as well, of his power and how he protected his people in great trials, and…well, I had an easier time believing in him than in anything the temple offered."

"But you still…worked there?"

"I didn't have a choice." Lady Ardala sets her cup down on the table. "Maybe, once upon a time, I thought it was a choice, a position of honor that gave me financial freedom and power over others. Only when I tried to leave, did I understand I was enslaved. Sometimes, Caitrin"—she looks over at me, her expression gentle but somber—"our hearts lie to us." She shakes her head, releasing me from her gaze. "I was fortunate that my heart was freed from the lies, even if my body was still in bondage."

She starts to refill her cup as her story continues. "I was

saying my prayers when the bells rang out, and it must have been providence, for I threw open my front door and there stood Tuethal, dressed like a criminal and franticly searching for a place to hide. I took him up to the roof and hid him there until the patrols passed.

"If he was alive today, Tuethal would tell you it was love at first sight. For him. I was scared out of my mind. Scared that the patrols would find him and know I helped him—the enemy. Scared that he would kill me, because for all he knew, I was the enemy. Just scared. So I didn't waste any time and helped him escape the city through my window. Before he left, Tuethal had told me to hang a red scarf on my front door, a sign only the soldiers would understand. We tied together every bedsheet and towel and tablecloth I owned to make a rope that would reach the waters below. He had to swim all the way back to his ship."

She laughs at the thought, and despite her words, it is clearly a beloved memory. "When they invaded the city a few days later, not a single soldier attacked me. In fact, they rescued me, taking me out of the city while the battle raged. After the siege, he invited me to sail with him back to Croìthe." She nods sweetly, her eyes wandering the room. "It was on that ship, on those waves, that I finally felt safe enough to return his love."

I wonder if she will say more, hope that she will say more, but when she doesn't, I feel disappointed. It was clearly just the beginning of her story, not the end. "He didn't care about…" Perhaps that is another question I shouldn't ask, but she knows what I'm wondering all the same.

"There were times when my past was a struggle, for both

of us," she admits, her smile flattening once more. "But when I learned to let go of my past, to stop holding onto the lies my heart believed, that's when I began a new life. And there was a lot more joy than sorrow between us, and much more grace than condemnation. Tuethal never had anything in his heart for me except love and a clean slate."

A smile forms on my face, but it doesn't reach my eyes or my heart. Why do her words make me want to crawl out of my skin and run away?

I sip my tea.

"That's what Callen wants to give you, Caitrin."

I freeze as the cup leaves my lips, then swallow.

"I can see it when he looks at you, when he talks about you."

You will have to choose what you want more.

Whatever it is, Cait, I'll give it to you.

"I appreciate Callen—and your!—kindness greatly, but I'm not naive or helpless," I say, my smile becoming more of a chore. I drink the rest of my tea in one gulp. "And I don't need to be rescued." I look over at her, my chest burning with defiance.

She nods, looking away from me. Shame tries to replace my pride, but I refuse to let it to take hold. If she is offended, that is her own insecurity. Her pity for me makes more sense now, but her pity is misinformed.

Despite her assumptions, we have nothing in common beyond being foreigners. The similarities end there. But then, why do I feel a pinch of jealousy? An emptiness has settled into my bones.

"I should really go check on Muireall," I say, setting my cup and saucer down. I wince as they clatter carelessly on the table. "Sorry to leave so soon, but thank you so much for the invitation." I curtsy and head for the door.

"Caitrin!" Lady Ardala calls after me. I look over my shoulder at her, unwilling to turn fully least she summon me to return. "There is always an invitation for you in my home."

I smile and nod my thanks. But I don't respond. I don't know how to respond.

Don't let them trick you, Caitrin.

FORTY-THREE

"LEWIS STOPPED BY HERE LAST night too," Muireall tells me, musing over my story of my run in with Mr. Baines yesterday.

"What does he want? Why can't he just leave us alone?" I ask as I hang the last of my freshly cleaned dresses in my wardrobe. Muireall sits on my bed, a finger to her lips in thought.

Then she laughs to herself, quietly at first, then more boisterously. "He's probably afraid that you'll do some kind of spell to make him give us all that land back. And it wouldn't even really be a curse since the land does rightfully belong to the Raeburn family name."

"We'll be in real trouble, Muireall, if they catch me tryin' to steal some of his hair or toenail clippings to make a dèiligidh. They already have their suspicions; they just need proof."

Muireall sighs, looking away, bored of my ethics. "We'll be in real trouble, either way. Lewis isn't going to risk anything with how paranoid he is." She stands, crossing her arms and pacing in thought. I watch her, waiting patiently for her to continue. "I wouldn't be surprised if he just tried to..." Shaking her head, she stops.

"Tried to? What?"

Slowly, her gaze pulls up to mine, her eyes cold and dark.

"I don't know. Do something rash. Something violent."

"You think he would try to hurt us?"

"Everyone lost a lot during the famine, even the Baines family. I'm sure he doesn't want to lose again."

I nod in understanding. "We shouldn't underestimate him." Then an idea sparks. "And we should protect ourselves."

Muireall laughs at my suggestion. "Do you prefer a bow or a sword?"

With a smirk, I shake my head. "I prefer dèiligidh."

"Thig dhòmhsa."

Muireall has seen Ma's spirit but never Keres. I wish I had convinced her to stay at the manor, but with Lewis Baines on the prowl, she refused to stay anywhere alone. She said I needed a lookout if I was going to be doing any magic.

So in the dead of night, we trekked out into the thicket and found the darkest corner of the woods.

"Ah, the famous Meara Raeburn," Keres hisses, taunting Muireall. But I was clear: only I am speaking; regardless of what Keres says, Muireall promised to remain completely silent. She knows we can't waste time.

"We need a dèiligidh of protection." I get right to the point. "I don't want anyone uninvited to step a foot onto Raeburn land."

Keres sways and swirls, a giggle filling the air. I wish she would be quiet. "Oh, that is much too costly for you, little cairline."

I glance at Muireall, who is still as stone, her expression obscured by the smoke and shadow.

"Then just the manor. I don't have time to debate with you, Keres. We offer an arm each, and my weddin' band."

That catches Keres's attention. I hold out my hand and uncurl my fingers to reveal a simple gold ring. The gold might be fake for all I know, but it's the symbol of the thing that entertains Keres, as I knew it would. She picks up the ring, and it floats into the air.

"For *two* wedding rings, I'll throw in a conversation." Her offer seems to swirl around Muireall, and my chest tightens. Surely Muireall understands that Keres will require more blood as well.

I glance at my mother-in-law to see her left hand held in a tight fist, but her eyes reflect the starlight, wandering frantically. Then her gaze meets mine. "I thought you said you couldn't—"

"Oh, little Caitrin couldn't before."

I glare at Keres, wishing she wouldn't play games and tempt Muireall. Maybe I am strong enough to barter a conversation with the dead, but I won't pay the cost, and Muireall has nothing but her blood to offer. It's too dangerous.

"Do you accept my offer?" I say, cutting off the conversation. Muireall will have a flood of questions later.

Thankfully, Keres doesn't tempt Muireall further. "I accept."

Two numb arms later and Keres exchanges the single ring for four flat, black coin talismans. "One on each corner of the house, and I will make sure not a soul enters unless they have been invited."

It's not until we are sneaking back to the manor that Muireall mutters something about the dèidh seo dèiligidh.

"You would give her your wedding ring?" I ask her.

"My ring is a reminder of my husband. Why would I need a reminder of him if he was here?" Muireall argues, and I can see that no price will be too high for her. She trips, catching my arm to prevent her fall. "I'm just lightheaded from the loss of sleep."

But I know better. It is the loss of blood, though only taken from her arm, that affects her balance.

"If you plan on speakin' to your dead husband often, you should plan on being lightheaded more often as well," I warn her, and she releases my arm to stubbornly continue on her own.

FORTY-FOUR

WITH THE PROTECTION SPELL FIRMLY in place, Muireall decides to move into the manor, just in case, so I give her my bed for the night. We spend the next morning bringing not only her things but furniture as well from the cottage to the manor. Muireall says she despises climbing the stairs, so we set it all up in one of the downstairs bedrooms. I don't love the idea of living with her again, but since she has been complaining more about Lewis Baines than about me, I'm hopeful that we may be able to cohabitate better this time.

While we set up her room—I primarily move the furniture while she arranges her clothes in the dresser—we form a plan to clear my name once and for all.

For starters, I need to earn some trust from the town. Surely, references from the Lockharts, Brodie, Shona, and Yvaine and Vaila will help. And then, I need to prove I don't want to harm, I want to help. And while our plan is risky, it may also prove to be very effective.

While I bathe, brush my hair, and put on a nice dress, Muireall cooks up a savory vegetable broth. After the soup is done and sealed in a large jar, she rubs my shoulder with a nod of confidence. The small gesture takes me back months, to a time when Muireall was Meara and she didn't seem to mind quite so much that I was a cairline. Part of me thinks she will give me a hug for good luck, but instead she retires to her bedroom to rest.

I nestle the jar securely in a small bag, checking to make sure the lid is on straight and tight, then saddle up Ailbert and head for the Lennox's farm.

Past the Lockhart Estate, closer to the cliffs and far from town, I find the Lennox family home, which is no larger than the banntraichean's cottage. The salty sea air is tainted with manure and musk. Next to the quaint house is a small shed and a pig pen attached to a large barn. I guess the shed is where Stuart does the butchering. I swallow, hoping they don't try to butcher me.

Taking the jar of broth from the bag, I knock on the door, put on a friendly smile, and pray for the best.

Perhaps I should have made a dèiligidh to make myself more trustworthy.

The door opens cautiously.

"Hi! I'm Caitrin Raeburn, just here to bring you some soup my mother-in-law made for you. I heard Mr. Lennox is still sick…"

The door pulls open a little wider to reveal a small girl in a brown dress and knotted, curly red hair. Her eyes immediately go to the jar, then dull with disappointment. "Do you have any cookies too, maybe?"

"Bonnie! I told you not to—" A woman comes into view. She looks weary, not from age but from worry, as she scoops up the child in her arms. "You know we have the Blath here." She pulls away from the door, but she politely waits before closing it.

"Yes, ma'am. I brought some broth. And…I wanted to see if I could help your husband. May I come inside? I'm not afraid of the Blath."

After a moment of hesitation, the woman nods and moves aside so I can enter.

The sitting room is dreary and stale. While it doesn't lack character and comforts, it is clear that it hasn't been cared for as carefully as it once had been. I set the jar on a little table.

"How do you think you can help? Are you a medicine woman?"

I turn to face the mother and the child with a smile as she closes the door. My heart starts to race, pounding with the desire to both speak and run. I must do one or the other now. "Um…" I lick my lips and suck in a breath, but the words don't follow.

"What's on your arm?" Bonnie asks, pointing to my wrist where just a sliver of red can be seen.

With a gasp of shock, the woman falls back against the door, clutching Bonnie to her chest. "Oh, please don't hurt us! Please!" She starts to scream, and I hear a thud from upstairs as something heavy hits to the floor. Giant tears begin to fall down Mrs. Lennox's cheeks as Bonnie cries out in mere confusion of her mother's outburst.

"I won't! I won't! I swear! I want to help!" I say, trying to keep my voice calm and even, though I feel like I'm shouting just to be heard above all the clamor. "I can heal your husband! I promise I can, if you let me!"

"What?" Mrs. Lennox asks, shaking her head and straining

against the door, but she's too afraid to make any movement.

I take a breath and push up the sleeves of my dress, revealing my markings. "I am a cairline, but not the one who cursed your husband. And I can break the curse that infects him."

Mrs. Lennox is frozen at the offer, then the fear begins to drain away, leaving hopeful relief in its wake. She even almost smiles.

Knock! Knock! Knock!

Spinning, Mrs. Lennox curses under her breath. "Oh, sorry, Bonnie. Go check on your father, alright?" She sets the girl down, and Bonnie quickly obeys, sprinting up the stairs. "Who is that? Are they going to arrest us?"

"I don't know…"

"Caitrin?" A muffled voice calls out.

"That's Callen Lockhart," I tell Mrs. Lennox. How on the good green earth did he know I was here?

"Lord Lockhart? And he knows you?"

I nod, and she opens the door. Callen stands on the front stoop, his eyes wide as he breathes a sigh of relief at seeing me. Although, I don't know why he was so worried to begin with.

His gaze flickers to my exposed arms, and I pull down my sleeves.

"Just a moment, Mrs. Lennox," I say sweetly as I exit the house, leaving the door open behind me. Perhaps if she sees I don't have secrets and Lord Callen Lockhart trusts me, she will find accepting my offer easier.

"Callen?" His horse is beside Ailbert, and his cheeks are flushed from the wind. "Is everything all right?"

"You left yesterday without saying goodbye, and…" He scratches his forehead, then huffs and looks away. "Guess I was just worried."

My stomach flips, but he shouldn't be worried about me. I can take care of myself. "How did you know I was here?"

"Brodie saw you heading this way by horse, so I just…looked for the horse." He gestures back at Ailbert.

"Well, you don't need to be worried. I was just bringing some broth for the Lennox family. Since Stuart is still sick." I fold my arms over my chest and do my best not to look guilty.

Callen nods as if he believes me, but his eyes say otherwise, lacking their usual sparkle. "Have they found the talisman yet?"

My lips part in frustration, but I decide against lying. "I don't think so, but I will."

He takes my hands, shaking his head, but I don't let him speak.

"I want to help this family, Callen. Like I helped your mother."

He looks up at me, holding my gaze. I wish he would hold me forever.

I push away the thought, remembering the task at hand. "Mrs. Lennox needs her husband; Bonnie needs her father. I can give him back to them."

"But at what cost?"

"I promised you I wouldn't do magic on *you*, not that I wouldn't do magic ever. And I will certainly keep makin' dèiligeadh that help people. Would you really ask me not to help the Lennox family?"

"There are other ways to help."

I shake my head. "You won't win this fight, Callen." My words are harder than I meant for them to be.

Throwing a hand to the back of his neck, he takes a step backward, looking away from me.

"Did you say that *you* cured Lady Lockhart?" Mrs. Lennox says from the door.

Callen stills, unable to deny her the truth but just as unwilling to speak it, and drops his hands to his sides.

I can see the pleading in his eyes, the fear that I'll give Keres too much blood, that she'll hurt me. But I'm stronger now. And he doesn't need to be worried. I smile at him, hoping to encourage him, but his brow furrows with sorrow, and I can't bear to look at him any longer.

"Yes," I say confidently, turning my back to Callen. "And I can cure Stuart, too."

FORTY-FIVE

I FIND THE TALISMAN EASILY enough hidden between the bedframe and the mattress. The Lennox family certainly fears me, but their fear of the Dhubd Blath is stronger. I warn Mrs. Lennox that blood will need to be given, and she is all too eager to sacrifice to save her husband. It almost breaks my heart that she is so eager; would anyone be willing to do the same for me?

Back at the manor, Muireall is delighted by my success, asking over and over again why I seem so despondent. I tell her I'm focused, but really, I can't get that look in Callen's eyes out of my mind.

And when he shows up at the manor door at dusk, I realize he hasn't given up.

"Callen, you shouldn't be here," I say, pulling him away from the manor and Muireall's keen hearing. "You know what I have to do tonight."

"I know. That's why I'm here."

I slouch. "Callen, you've got it all wrong. I know Keres seems…it all seems…" Wrong. But I don't believe that. It may look that way to him, but I know better. "But what's the point of havin' this power if I don't use it to help people? You've seen what it can do!"

"Yes, I've seen!" he says, raising his voice, but he isn't

angry. He is desperate. "I've seen how she used you and harmed you—"

"Life from life, Callen!" I tell him, matching his volume. But the simple mantra has little effect on him.

"I've heard your arguments, Caitrin, but this is more dangerous than you understand."

"Of course I understand! Every time I prick my finger, it's *my* blood she takes!"

"And she took more than you bartered to cure my mother." Callen's voice is strong and clear.

My brow furrows and I step away from him. "She couldn't have. She has to honor the deal." I shake my head in disbelief. "You just don't understand what you saw." I'll admit I don't remember much about that night—I was so weak, weaker than I should have been—but Keres couldn't have taken more than we agreed. It's impossible. My pulse quickens. "And I gave my blood willingly that night to pay you back for everythin' you've done for me. And it cured her! How can you be upset with me for it?"

Callen frowns. "I'm not upset with you." I don't believe him. "I mean, I am upset but it's because I can't bear to stand by while you lose yourself to her lies. All I want, Cait…" He won't say it.

Now I know what favor he wanted from me all along.

"You want me to give up my magic? You want me to let Stuart Lennox and his family suffer? You want me to be useless?"

"I want to *love* you." Callen reaches for me, but I don't let him get close.

"Then *love* me," I retort coldly, angrily pushing up my sleeves to expose my markings. "Love me like this." I hold my arms out to him. My breathing grows shallow, hoping beyond hope that he will stop asking me to be something I'm not. Something I can never be.

"I do," Callen answers softly, so gently I wonder if his whisper is merely the wind. His fingers trace my markings down to my wrists, leaving goosebumps on my skin, then he takes my hands in his. "That's why I don't want to see you hurt. I want to see you healed."

The dagger twists in my gut. "If I'm broken, then it's beyond repair, Callen," I say as I rip my hands away from him. The words were meant to be harsh and strong, but my jaw quivers and my gaze blurs with the threat of tears.

Why am I crying?

I turn away from him, hugging myself tighter. "I have to do this. If I don't put an end to this curse, eventually they'll condemn me for it. And I'm not going to die for an evil I did not create." That gives me some more control, and I swallow back the shame.

Fingers brush against my shoulder, but I jerk away.

"I won't stop you," Callen says, resolve mixed with regret. "But I won't stay and watch, either."

I hold my breath and wait. Wait for his next argument, his next attack. Wait for him to wrap his arms around me and whisper that he doesn't care. That he understands. That he agrees. That I'm doing the right thing.

But it's silent. And he says nothing. Does nothing.

And for a moment, I wonder if I'm making a mistake.

Am I broken? Beyond repair?

When I look behind me, Callen is gone.

And the emptiness returns.

FORTY-SIX

ONCE NIGHT HAS FALLEN, I make the journey back up to the Lennox's home near the cliffs. While Stuart has gained some of his strength back, he is still too weak to travel to the thicket. I could summon Keres inside the house—although, like me, she prefers to be grounded by the earth and a ceiling of stars instead of caged indoors—but Mrs. Lennox refuses to do any magic in their home.

So, with my knife sheathed in my boot, and a candlestick and match box tucked in my pocket, I help Mrs. Lennox carry her husband to the nearby barn. I am tempted to try and persuade them to stay outside, in the dark of night, but we are all on edge. And even though Ailbert is tied up behind the barn, I still worry that someone will have followed me. Someone will find us. And better to barter with an irritable spirit than be caught in the open.

There is no sound except the whistle of the wind and Stuart's heavy breathing as he leans on his wife. The squeaking of the barn door on its hinges pierces the air, and the couple jumps in fright, glancing around, no doubt worried someone will come running.

"It's okay. Everyone else in Soarsa is soundly asleep." I gesture with a gentle smile for them to enter the darkness of the barn. The snorting of a few pigs, disturbed from their slumber, echoes into the air, almost like the whine of a babe. It makes my skin crawl.

Mrs. Lennox shares a look with her husband, but neither of them say a word. After a moment, Stuart nods, and Mrs. Lennox helps him into the barn.

The floor is hard dirt covered in a dusting of hay. Kneeling in the center of the space, I take out my knife, working quickly to dig a small hole in the ground and then wedge the candle in place. When I strike the match, Mrs. Lennox has settled Stuart against a post. They both have wide eyes, but Mrs. Lennox's skin is pale with distress, while her husband is covered in the black warts of the Dhubd Blath.

I take a deep breath, then light the candle.

"You promise this will cure him?" Mrs. Lennox asks, her voice barely louder than a whisper.

"Yes. He'll be in perfect health once it's over."

Stuart takes his wife's hand, his expression sober. "You healed Lady Lockhart?"

"I did. The very night she fell ill, in fact."

"Bonnie heard the story of her collapse from Elspeth when she brought us a pie the other day," Mrs. Lennox confirms quietly. I have to work hard not to react to the mention of Elspeth Kilpatrick and her meddling pies.

"Then we don't need to be afraid," Stuart says, nodding to reassure himself as well as his wife.

"No, you don't need to be afraid," I tell them, picking up my knife again. "It may be alarmin', but the spirit will only do what I command of her. And I won't let her harm you; I will command her to heal you." With a deep breath, I look at each of them for a long moment. "Do you remember the cost we agreed to offer her?"

Mrs. Lennox nods. "Both of my hands, and one of yours." But then passionate fear begins to take over as she stands. "But I would give anyth—"

"No!" I nearly shout, holding up my hands to silence her. If Keres is listening, she'll take everything Mrs. Lennox is willing to give. Worry knots in my stomach, and I suck in a breath to steady myself. I can't consider the possibility of Keres breaking a deal, but I don't trust her to barter fairly. "Just let me do the talkin'. No matter what, you must say silent."

I wait for them to nod in understanding, then I prick my finger.

"Thig dhòmhsa."

Mrs. Lennox falls to the ground as the flame flares and dies in a single breath, clutching Stuart's arm as they both watch with wide eyes, barely breathing. The smoke rises and fills the room, and I stand tall, resolute, determined. My markings are on full display, and I wonder if they will reach my elbows tonight. I think of my mother, covered from fingertip to shoulder.

I don't want to be like her.

But I'm not wasting my power on silly tricks to take advantage of grieving widows. I force myself to feel powerful, useful, in control. I'm nothing like Ma. I raise my head, breathing in Keres's smoke and letting it fill my lungs.

"Ah, bartering in a barn, how quaint!" Keres snickers, but she doesn't take form. Instead, her voice booms around us, frightening Mr. and Mrs. Lennox, and enjoying it.

"Yes. Things are not safe in Soarsa out in the open tonight, but that doesn't mean we don't have a bargain to strike," I say confidently. "He has the Blath, and we want a dèiligidh to break the curse and cure him. We offer three hands, a drop of blood from the victim, and the cursed talisman." I produce from my pocket the talisman I found under Stuart's bed. It is jet black, blacker than ink, crudely formed to look like a rock.

Keres's fingers reach out from the void and float the talisman out of my hand. Mrs. Lennox gasps at the sight of it, still clinging to Stuart, who seems to have forgotten to breathe. Finally, Keres takes an almost-form, shifting and swirling as she looks at the talisman. "This one is not as strong as the last," she muses, tendrils of smoke floating around her head like hair underwater. "I accept your offer."

I hum to myself as a smirk breaks out across my lips, and my gaze shifts to the Lennoxes. "Are you ready?"

"She will take my hands now?" Mrs. Lennox asks, her voice like that of a child, naive and eager.

"The blood from them, yes. They will feel numb, but you will regain your strength in them by morning. And you'll have your husband in good health to help you."

Stuart holds out his hand feebly toward me, and I step forward, ready to prick him for the drop due, but Keres takes my knife from my hand and I freeze. "Keres, stop it!" I hiss under my breath. Alarm shoots through my body as she floats the blade toward the couple, but I can't let them know my heart is racing.

"She cannot take more than agreed!" I shout, but Stuart's

entire hand is shaking, his eyes fixed on Keres, unblinking.

The knife lowers, teasing, and Keres glows with delight. Mrs. Lennox releases a whimper, and my heart shudders. My lungs fill with breath, ready to burst, wanting to shout for Keres to stop. Wishing I hadn't come at all. A chill races down my spine. I blink, and when I open my eyes, I don't see Keres the spirit; I see a diabhal, a demon born of darkness.

And then blazing orange light fills the room as the barn doors slam open, booming like thunder.

"Arrest her!" Knox shouts.

Keres shrieks, dropping the knife to the ground and filling the air with her darkness.

"Stuart? Stuart!" Mrs. Lennox begins to scream, but I can't see anything in the cloud of Keres's smoke.

The shouts of men—two, three, four? How many are there?—echo through the barn. How many just saw what was happening?

Keres's tendrils wrap around me, practically dragging me to the back barn window and throwing me through it. Ailbert is waiting for me, neighing impatiently as shouting continues to fill the barn.

"Fire! The hay caught fire!" Someone shouts.

"Stuart!" Mrs. Lennox continues to cry.

Ailbert whinnies loudly, rearing up on his hind legs, spooked either by the frightful sounds in the barn or by Keres herself, and races off into the night.

When I glance behind me, the smoke that had been Keres has been replaced with a blazing fire, quickly consuming the Lennox barn and anything, or anyone, trapped inside.

FORTY-SEVEN

WE RACE THROUGH THE THICKET, Ailbert huffing with each gallop. The air is cold, stinging my eyes, causing tears to be ripped from my cheeks. I don't know where to go except back to the manor, but I know Knox and the men can easily find me there if they come looking. I can only hope that the dèiligidh will hold. That Keres won't betray me once again.

Betrayed. No. She couldn't have. We are partners. She merely got out of hand. Everything would have been alright if Knox hadn't shown up. If I hadn't been caught.

She used you.

Did Keres know they were coming? She would have warned me. She wouldn't have shown up at all if she thought it would put me in danger.

Unless she wanted me to be caught. Anything to get me to leave Soarsa and go back to Cairlich. But she knows that I can't leave Muireall. If I do then…

My mind clears. Does Keres want me dead? But I am growing more powerful with every dèiligidh. What more could a spirit want from a cairline?

You are still not quite wicked enough for me, either.

My mind feels like mush. I don't know what to think or who to believe. Even my own heart feels untrustworthy.

When I learned to let go of my past, to stop holding onto the lies my heart believed, that's when I began a new life.

Lady Ardala's words cause a swell in my soul, a longing for that new life she had found. *Love and a clean slate.* But after tonight, there will be no fresh starts for me. And I don't even know how to discern the truth from the lies enough to stop believing them.

Ailbert slows as we near the manor. There is a light inside the foyer, the evening dew frosting the windows. Muireall must be waiting up for me. I don't know how I'll explain to her what a disaster I've caused. The panic begins to return with new vigor, and I lean down, wrapping my arms around Ailbert's neck. He snorts; I think he needed a hug too.

I've made a mess of everything. I can only hope that, for once, Muireall will help me clean it all up.

"They are going to take everything away!" Muireall cries, her voice echoing through the manor. The events of the evening were more than concerning, they were condemning, and it is only a matter of time before someone comes—

Knock knock knock!

"It's barely dawn!" Muireall's voice cracks as it drops to a whisper. She looks pointedly at the front door, then at me. "Get out of sight," she urges. "And pray those talismans do their job." I quickly tuck myself into the dark corridor that leads to the north wing of the manor.

Muireall clears her throat, shuffles forward, and opens the door.

"Lewis, what are you doing out here so early?" she mutters, stifling a faux yawn. "Can't you let an old banntrach sleep?"

"And where is Caitrin?" Lewis asks, his voice foreboding, echoing after me.

"How should I know? I never know where that girl is," Muireall answers coldly. "As far as I know, she hasn't been home in days."

"I must insist that I check her room——"

"You'll insist on nothing while on my property!" Muireall replies, adding a snort of amusement for good measure. "Now, whatever business——"

"Your daughter-in-law is a murderer." He speaks with authority and ice-cold rage. "I told her we'd be watching, but she was careless. Knox and a few other lads caught her summoning a demon at the Lennox farm, which she set ablaze with the flames of hell, and Stuart Lennox died."

Muireall is silent, and I hold my breath. Died? I didn't kill him, nor did I set the fire. It wasn't the flames of hell; most likely, Knox was scared out of his wits and dropped the torch he was carrying. Besides, Keres can't do anything without using me to conduct her power...can she? My heart stops, then sinks. Whether it was Knox or Keres, they were both there because of me.

Just before my head starts to spiral, I clench my jaw and force my thoughts to stay in the present. Gritting my teeth, I listen intently, Lewis' self-righteous rage fueling my own indignation.

"We should have kicked her out the moment she arrived with those red markings all over her!"

"Oh, Lewis. You realize how ridiculous you sound, don't you?"

"You're protecting a criminal, Muireall!"

"Better than a boggin feartie like you."

I hear the door start to squeak closed.

"What's this? Why can't I—" He must be trying to force his way inside, but Lewis Baines is no match for the talismans guarding the manor.

"Stay off my property, Lewis!" Muireall shouts, and the door slams shut.

We both stand in silence, breathing for a moment. Then, Muireall walks over to me, calm, collected, quiet.

"He's going to try to find a way in the house," she whispers. "Get upstairs. He won't be able to look through those windows. And keep quiet."

I obey without thought, dashing with quiet steps for the staircase and racing up to my bedroom. It's only when Muireall closes the door behind us that I realize how hard my heart is pounding.

"Murdered?" Muireall wants to shout, but she's afraid that Lewis will hear her. So instead, she stares at me with hard eyes.

"No! Of course not! I was just about to cure Stuart when Knox burst in, like I said," I explain, straining to keep my voice low and calm. "But Knox had a torch, and in all the confusion…who knows what happened. But I didn't kill anyone, and neither did Keres. I know that for certain."

Muireall huffs and leans back against the door. "I don't

know how you will ever prove such a thing if they are set on convicting you." She looks down at the floor, shaking her head. "And then what? Will they take the house, the land, all of it? Should you be fortunate enough to *only* be banished back to Cairlich, what about me? How am I to live in a town where my own daughter-in-law is a convicted murderer?"

Would she move from Soarsa, from the Raeburn legacy, if it meant saving me? I know the answer without asking. How could I ask her to leave because of my mistakes?

If this mionn is broken, cairline, I expect the payment you withheld from me tonight.

I shiver and push the memory away. It won't come to that. I won't let it.

"It will be fine, Muireall," I say, trying to balance out her barely-controlled hysteria. But I'm brimming with anxiety just as much as she is. Still, one of us needs to be rational. "They won't take anythin' away from you. It's me they'll take things from. Surely there is somethin' we can do. Some way to prove my innocence." I run my hands through my hair, pacing across my bedroom as my mind races for a solution. "Or maybe I can't prove my innocence, but they will have to prove my guilt, won't they?"

"You didn't curse anyone," Muireall says. "But you *did* create dèiligeadh. Lots of them." She sits on the vanity stool, defeated and deflated, her arms crossed tightly over her chest. "And your markings are proof enough. The judge won't need anything else to condemn you."

My heart skips a beat as hope tries to take hold. "The judge? I won't be convicted by....mob rule?" I almost laugh at the notion to keep from being completely despondent.

"Yes, a judge will decide your fate. Either by the town council. Or..." Muireall shifts, her eyes alight with inspiration. "Or the lord of the province."

And my heart stops beating all together. "You mean Callen."

"Yes, Lord Callen Lockhart has more than a title and wealth. He has the power to determine your fate." Muireall stands, the ghost of a smile on her lips. She nods, slowly at first, then more quickly as the idea takes hold. "Including declaring you innocent of all crimes accused."

After how we left things, I don't think he wants to see me again, especially once he hears what happened, what I've done. Besides, he knows the truth, he's seen me do magic with his own eyes. "He can't help me, Muireall. He won't lie for me." I wrap my arms around myself, my voice small as I speak.

"Just do to him whatever you did to Tate. Magic is the only way anyone falls in love with a cairline anyway."

I shrink at the statement as it sinks through my skin, into my bones. "What are you talkin' about?"

Muireall grimaces. "I found a talisman in my son's urn. He wasn't interested in marriage, not even when Ivor married, not until he laid eyes on you." Her gaze snaps to mine so sharply that I stumble backward a step. "It's true, isn't it?"

My blood runs cold and I want to run away, to deny it. But courage deep within me wants to be free, so I swallow back the tears and excuses. "I was too vague, and that was my first mistake. The way Keres interpreted my request was that...the next young bachelor to see me, would love me. I truly am sorry that he turned out to be your son. I didn't know what I was doin', Muireall, and that only made it more reckless. It was selfish."

She glances away, remaining as still as stone. How long has she known the truth?

I don't know what else to say. I don't know how to explain that I asked Keres to make a talisman that would make me feel loved instead of alone, not for her to enchant Tate. If anything, my actions prove how unworthy of love I truly am. Maybe she's right: magic is the only way anyone falls in love with a cairline.

"Recklessness seems to run in Raeburn blood," Muireall finally says, her words hard, holding in something more. "So just be reckless again. Maybe this time it will erase the consequences instead of multiplying them. You certainly know what you are doing now, so just make Callen helplessly in love with you."

"I'm not makin' a single dèiligidh until I know it's safe." But that's not the only reason. Callen will only love me without these bands, and if I force his feelings, that will be just as empty as my marriage was.

I'd rather be alone than create a world of lies to live in.

"Then blackmail him."

I look over to see Muireall standing tall, but her expression is as dark as her tone. "Blackmail him?"

"He may not love you, Caitrin, but even I've heard the rumors." Her fingers brush into my hair, tucking it behind my ear then drifting down to hold my chin firmly. "Given the right encouragement, you can get leverage over him and convince him to denounce these allegations."

"What are you talking about?" I want to push her away, but a desire to be near him again keeps me still as she whispers to me. I feel small, like a child, with Ma soothing me when I've awoken from a nightmare.

Don't be afraid of the nightmares, little Caitrin. Become the nightmare, and there will be nothing to fear ever again.

"Doesn't he have a big harvest coming up?"

"Yes, to send to Kaledon. It's sometime this week, I'm pretty sure." I shrug away from her. "But I don't know what difference that makes."

"So, in keeping with the tradition of farm owners, he will not only make sure everything is properly prepared, but he will personally guard and protect it until it is delivered. He'll probably have something to drink, a celebration of the harvest, and he'll sleep in the storage barns." Muireall guides me to the bed, and I sit down, listening attentively. Settling behind me, she strokes my hair, sending tingles from my head down my spine. "If you were to go to him in such a state, he wouldn't turn you away. He'd probably think you were a dream, and you would only need to do as he asks. Fulfill his dreams."

I frown and stiffen, hope slowly draining out of me as understanding takes hold.

"But he wouldn't want to ruin his reputation, and no doubt the threat of a child would motivate urgency on his part as well. With a little persuasion, you can convince him that it can all be kept secret, if he will help us deal with this little problem with Lewis Baines. And I bet you could even get him to throw in some gold, enough to buy back what is rightfully mine."

It's more than just blackmail. It's manipulation. It's

twisted. "I think I'd rather risk a dèiligidh to change his heart than do somethin' like that." And yet, I shudder at the thought of seeing Keres again. Panic seeps into my toes. I suck in a breath, trying to fill my lungs, but I only grow lightheaded.

"Darling, you said magic is too risky." Her hands still on my shoulders. "But really, it's all the same. And you really think you're not a villain?" She bends close to my ear. "You owe me at least this, cairline, after everything you've done."

There is slight pressure on my neck, and my hands start to shake.

What choice do I have now? There is no future for me in Soarsa, or in Croìthe, without Muireall. If she doesn't help me, allow me to stay with her, then Keres will take what I owe her.

She'll take every drop within an inch of my life.

And there will be no one to pick me up and heal my wounds.

It's either submit to Muireall or submit to my fate and finally give my life for Tate's.

FORTY-EIGHT

Muireall has never taken such gentle care of me in all the years I've known her, and, if I didn't know better, I would think maybe she actually views me as a daughter.

But I'm not fooled. This is her payback, her last ditch effort to right the wrongs done in Cairlich.

After I bathe, she brushes and styles my hair, pinning my ginger waves away from my face and letting them fall like silk down my back. She insists that I wear my blue dress, the one made with fabric from Callen that has buttons down the front, with only thin slippers and no jewelry. She uses her own cosmetics to enhance my features, applying a light blushing of rouge to my cheeks, with stronger color on my lips and kohl on my eyelashes.

And as she pampers me with her attention, she whispers little instructions, as if I am her prize pet or perhaps a young girl attending a coming out ball. And yet, there is a devious edge to her words that makes me feel empty and anxious.

"When you arrive, be careful not to be seen and go straight to the main barn. Take off your cloak and your slippers. Uncover his feet so the chill of the night air will wake him." Muireall takes a glass orb filled with perfume, squeezing the misting dispenser so that the aroma covers me: a stale floral smell that is decades old—Muireall's signature scent. "Then you are to do whatever he asks, Caitrin. Make sure he is happy and satisfied with you before he has time to realize his mistake."

His mistake. Perhaps making a dèiligidh would be a better idea.

No, either way, he will resent me. What is the point of pretending?

"Do you think you can do that?" Muireall asks. She moves to stand behind me and places a strong hand on my shoulder. In the vanity mirror, I meet her gaze.

I puff out my chest. "Of course I can," I say, almost too boastfully.

Her lips tug toward a grimace, but she has the restraint to keep her composure. Grabbing her cloak from the bed, she throws it around me, fastening the clasp. "The sun has gone down. If you leave now, he'll be fast asleep by the time you arrive. Remember, this is the only option we have to fix everything." The way she says 'everything' implies there is more than my mistakes on her mind.

I stand and start to exit the room. "No time to waste, then." I feel her eyes following me, and I can't wait to be out of this house and in the woods. We agreed I should take one of the trails through the thicket so that no one sees me on the main road.

If I'm caught, not only will I be arrested, but there will be no hope for Muireall's blackmailing scheme. And yet, the riskiest part of the plan is Muireall herself: can I truly trust her to have my back? Or will she turn me in just to clear her own name if things go awry?

"Caitrin," Muireall calls out as I start down the stairs into the foyer.

I slow, glancing back at her.

She blinks frantically, her brow furrowed, then turns away. "Pull up your hood, dear."

I obey, tugging up the hood, and then I hurry from the manor.

The sun has disappeared behind the horizon, the last colors of day lingering at the edges of the black sky, when I head for Callen's estate. With slow, deep breaths, I enter the thicket, trying not to rush as I navigate the narrow path that will take me to the far side of the apple orchid.

What if he doesn't think I'm a dream?

What if he thinks I'm a nightmare?

What if he isn't as drunk as Muireall hopes?

I try to focus on contingency plans for each worst-case scenario my imagination creates, determined to play my part. Perhaps our web of deception will bind Muireall and I together enough that she won't send me away.

Right now, staying alive is the most I can hope for.

Just as the thicket thins and the orchard lies beyond, my arms begin to burn. The pain is deep, searing straight to my bones, and I stumble, falling against a tree. I inhale sharply.

Why are you running away from me, little cairline?

Keres fills my mind as if she is present, and I shut my eyes closed, wanting to erase the memory of her in the barn.

You can't escape me, so let me help you.

Keres knows better. She knows I can't make a dèiligidh to change Callen's heart without something that belongs to him.

My fingers brush against the fabric of the dress, and the heat of my markings cool instantly. This dress belongs to him in some ways, doesn't it?

I could make him love me. No manipulation, no drunken tryst. I could make him love me, make him not care that I am bonded.

One little dèiligidh and I could free him from the restraint of his fears and ignorance.

A twig snaps behind me. I spin, peering into the darkness of the thicket, but my lantern doesn't reach far enough to illuminate any villains following me.

No. I won't do anything like that ever again. Especially not to Callen. It's the least I can do to keep my promise to him.

Blowing out the lantern, I leave it on the ground, moving quickly before I lose my resolve.

He'll never love you while you belong to me. You belong to the darkness, little cairline. You know there is no escaping it.

"I'm going to fix this my way, Keres!" I hiss at her, and she retreats…for now. The truth of her whisper lingers.

No cairline has the power to return from the darkness. Maybe that's why Ma never married. We cairlinen already belong to someone, and cairlinen can't serve two masters.

Steeling myself against emotion as my thoughts continue to race, I make my way through the pasture and around the mansion. The estate is quiet and still. Tiptoeing and keeping an eye on my surroundings, I sneak to the white storage barns.

There is a fading glow in one of the upper windows, and the barn door is slightly ajar. I don't give myself a moment to think about what I'm about to do, and I slip inside the barn.

FORTY-NINE

CALLEN IS SOUNDLY ASLEEP ATOP several linen bags stuffed with hay in the loft of the storage barn. The candle in the window blows out just as I step off the ladder, but he doesn't stir. In the light of the moon, I survey the loft, spotting a collection of dark bottles on the small wooden table. One is on its side, clearly empty with the cork discarded.

I let out a slow breath, expecting to feel more at ease, but I'm shaking all over.

Wine or spell, what difference does it make?

He is a good man, and he will do whatever I ask to keep his reputation pure.

I remove my cloak and lay it gently over a chair as I step out of my slippers.

He is a good man. A man who doesn't deserve to be tricked by a corrupted cairline. A man who only ever wanted to help.

My fingers linger on the cloak, and my gaze moves back to Callen.

His boots and socks are thrown to the side, with his suspenders hanging limp as his pants sit snuggly around his hips. The quilt that maybe had once covered him fully, barely clings to his legs, stretching over his feet. His shirt is soft, a few of the top buttons loosened to be more comfortable. His chest rises and falls steadily, his head tilted to the side, his eyelashes, nose, and lips catching the moonlight. The brown curls of his hair frame his head like a dark halo.

I could have loved him. Maybe we could have been truly happy.

But I wouldn't allow myself to love a man who despises everything I am. Who would want a man who condemns what cannot be changed?

Kneeling at his feet, I gently move aside the quilt, and it slumps to the floor. He stirs with a sigh, and I glance up at his face as he wets his lips and shifts, sparking the memory of his fingers caressing my cheek, holding my hand. His eyes lowering to my lips. Our almost kiss. He wanted me then, but my bond kept him at bay.

Now, if Muireall is right, nothing will stop him.

I grimace. Soon, I will prove him right. I am corrupt. I am a slave to the darkness, to my bond.

I am a slave. I'm not free. He was right.

A tear slips down my cheek.

I can't do this. I won't save myself by causing him harm.

Perhaps breaking the mionn would be better than becoming the very monster I always swore I wasn't.

I brush away the tear with the back of my hand, resolving to leave. Leave Muireall. Leave Soarsa. Leave Callen. Spare him this manipulation, this humiliation.

"Caitrin?"

My name fills the air like a wish, as Callen sits up. His brow is furrowed, confused, concerned. "Are you alright?" He scampers off the bags of hay and onto his knees in front of me.

Without hesitation, he grabs me by my shoulders. His eyes are soft, searching my own. "Why are you here?"

This is it. My opportunity. I could kiss him, so easily. Become a dream. Just like Muireall directed.

His thumb brushes against my cheek, wiping at a tear. My fingers wrap around his shirt sleeves, holding onto him like he is life itself. I know as soon as I speak, I'll break the spell.

But it is a spell that must be broken.

"I shouldn't have come." I move to my feet, but he stands with me, not releasing me.

"What is going on? Are you in trouble?"

I almost laugh just to hold back more tears. One wrong word, one wrong move, and I will break. "Of course, I am, Callen." I shrug off his hands and go to my shoes and cloak. "I *am* trouble. I'm sorry."

"Stop. Tell me, Cait." His pleading quickly twists into suspicion when he sees how wide my bonding bands have grown. "Why are you here? What have you done?"

"It's not what I've done, but what I'm doin'…" My throat closes up and more tears spill onto my cheeks, blurring my vision. I turn from him, bracing myself on the table. "I've made a mess of everythin'."

"Is it Baines?" Callen's voice is hard, raspy, and then he softens. "I heard…Brodie tried to tell me something happened but…but I wouldn't hear it. And even without knowing, all I could think was that it was my fault."

Whether or not I cursed anyone, it seems I have been nothing but a curse to every person I ever tried to love.

"No, Callen. I'm the only one to blame." I pick up the

cloak, hugging it against my chest. Taking a deep breath to find some stability, I face him. But I refuse to meet his gaze. "I'm going away, Callen." My arms burn, trying to light flame to my very veins. Keres is angry, regretting the price we agreed to. Unless she finds a way to save me, she'll lose her little cairline and have to find someone new to bond with. But what a far way off from Cairlich she is now. "I'm sorry for all the trouble I caused you."

"Cait…"

I shake my head. "I don't need your pity. You were right to be angry with me. You were right about me, Callen." Keres's rage becomes a small comfort as I grab my slippers and toss them down to the ground floor below. Perhaps I should have learned to hate myself a long time ago. It seems to be the most common emotion people have about me. Pity. Bitterness. Disappointment. Hatred.

"Caitrin, stop!" Callen grabs my hand, but his touch is gentle. And my heart breaks as he whispers, "stay."

Wrenching my hand free, I spin, embracing emptiness inside. "No, Callen! I won't. I can't! You'll hate me if I do. And I won't die knowin' you hate me."

He pulls me away from the ladder. His face is set and stern. "What are you talking about?" His nostrils flair as his eyes blink rapidly, trying desperately to understand.

"Lewis Baines is going to convict me of creatin' the Dhubd Blath, of killin' Stuart Lennox, of bein' a cairline. And I might as well be guilty of all of it because there's no way to prove I'm innocent. And they wouldn't care about my proof if I had any! And I'm not innocent, we both know that," I say, a declaration that there is nothing to be done. "The best I can hope for is to be exiled to Cairlich."

"I know you weren't behind the Blath or…did you say Stuart Lennox died?"

"Yes, right after I was caught tryin' to break the curse over him."

He frowns, his forehead wrinkling as he looks down. His grip on my arm, covering my bonding markings, doesn't loosen. He's worried I'll leave before he gets all the answers he wants. "Isn't there some way Muireall can help you?"

I look up at him, straight into his captivating green eyes. "She sent me to you. She wanted me to…trick you," I answer coldly. "But I couldn't…"

And then his hand slips from my arm. I can't bear to look at him, but I will give him all of the answers I can.

"She wanted to blackmail you, threaten to blemish your family's reputation, so that you would have no choice but to help us."

"No matter what Lewis Baines says…" His voice is filled with disbelief, uncertainty.

"You've seen me do magic. And so has Knox now, and plenty of others." I swallow. "You're a good man, Callen; I know you wouldn't lie, even to save me. And I'm not so sure I'm worth savin'. I'm already ruined beyond repair." I lift my arms, showing how my markings have grown, wild with swirls and dark magic. "Remember."

"Cait—"

"I've made up my mind." I throw the cloak over my shoulders, focusing on the clasp to keep from thinking about anything else. Callen's hands cover my own, and the cloak slips from my fingers to the floor. Grinding my teeth, I shove him away. "Pity can't change anything, even if it makes *you* feel better. I won't judge you for leavin' me to my own fate."

"I just want to help."

"You've helped enough. And I won't have you lie for me. I never deserved your charity before, and I certainly don't deserve it now. That's all it ever was for you: pity. But I'm still a cairline. I'm still bonded, corrupted, ruined. Your pity hasn't fixed me."

"I don't pity you," Callen says forcefully, but he doesn't try to stop me. His admission makes me frown. If not pity, then it's something worse he must feel for me now. Good. That makes this easier.

I bend to descend the ladder and get as far away from Soarsa as I can. As far as Keres allows before she takes her payment from me.

"Caitrin, I love you."

I hesitate, certain I misheard. Last time he said he *wanted* to love me, he was *trying* to love me, but he couldn't. Nothing has changed since then, at least, nothing that should make him love me. I don't even know what I would do, what I would feel if he actually meant those words. Could I believe them? I lower my feet to the first rung of the ladder.

"I love you, every inch of you."

I glance up at Callen. His eyes are earnest, desperate. His lips part slightly, waiting for a response. My silence and stillness seem answer enough.

He takes a step toward me carefully. "There is nothing so

ruined that it can't be restored, and no one so wretched that they can't be redeemed." He holds his hand out to me, offering me something that I don't think is even possible. "Please, I can help you."

And I can see in his eyes that he means every word he says.

Perhaps that can be enough.

As I take his hand, I'm certain that someone somewhere has cast a spell. But it is not Callen who is enchanted. This time, it's me.

I don't know if he's right, but I cling to one simple truth he has spoken: he loves me. Even with my bond. Even though I'm bound to darkness.

He helps me stand, and then takes both of my hands in his. He doesn't wait for me to say I love him back. Maybe he knows that I can't, that I don't know how to love him the way he loves me. And he doesn't deserve the corrupt kind of love I've learned.

"It will take more than words to silence the accusations and adhere to the law," Callen says, focused on the problem. "My title would protect you. Not to mention I would be able to buy back the Raeburn land by force." Callen's eyebrows bounce mischievously at the notion.

"Callen…" I whisper, focusing on his green eyes and pushing through the anthem of feelings erupting in my chest. "Wouldn't you have to…to marry me in order to do that?"

He smirks, his eyes staring straight into my soul. "Is that a proposal?"

"It's not possible," I say quickly, before my heart can get ahead of reality. I raise up my arm, reminding him of my bond.

"Cairlinen cannot legally marry in Cròithe."

He places his palm against my own, then entwines his fingers with mine. Twisting our hands, he kisses the soft skin at my wrist. "What do you want, Cait?"

The words leave my lips before I can stop them. "I want you."

"Then we must break your bond. It's the only way to prove you will no longer create dèiligeadh, and satisfy the law." His eyes flicker up to my own, the uncertainty returning.

"You mean sell my bond?" My eyes well with tears again at the words.

Callen's thumb brushes against my cheek, regaining my focus. "Surely there is a way for you to be free. Like Una."

Free.

Perhaps that's what Una was referring to when she mentioned her story. When she told me she knew the truth about sgaoileaden. Perhaps she has the answers.

I nod, my resolve growing. "I'll find a way." My voice is barely louder than a whisper, wondering if Keres is listening, fearing she will hear me.

"*We'll* find a way," Callen says with a soft smile on his lips. "Nothing will keep me from loving you." His fingers brush over my cheek, then into my hair, and he draws me closer. His nose brushes against mine, stirring butterflies in my stomach.

I press up on my bare toes to kiss him as a warm glow brushes over his features.

Morning.

"Master Callen!" Brodie shouts up from the threshing floor.

Callen spins us, moving me away from the railing quickly. "One moment, Brodie!" He shouts down, but he doesn't let me go.

"The boys from town we hired are here to help with..." The rest of Brodie's words fade as I pull back from Callen and stiffen. The shuffling and grumpy complaints of farmhands echoes up toward us. The excitement is replaced with urgency; we can't be caught together, like this.

I turn and grab a rope, unwinding it out through the window. It's not the most graceful way to escape, but the drop isn't far. I can climb down, and then I'll head for the cliffs, to Una's cottage, to answers.

"Have you taken to wearing women's slippers, Callen?" Brodie calls up, a teasing lilt in his voice.

Callen takes my hand, tugging me into his arms. The momentary alarm on his face has faded. Brushing my hair behind my ears, he tilts my chin up and kisses me softly, slowly, making this one kiss promise a lifetime. I feel his passion in how he holds back, both of us knowing this one kiss will leave us breathless and wanting more. He smiles against my lips, and he pulls away far too soon.

"I'll come find you as soon as I can," he whispers to me. Then he turns away. "I was just bored last night, I swear!" He turns to climb down the ladder, winking at me as he disappears from the hay loft.

My heart is fluttering so fast I can barely breathe. It gives me the courage to climb out of the window and the determination to find a way to break free.

FIFTY

THE SUN PEAKS OVER THE edge of the cliffs, casting brilliant pinks, oranges, and lavenders across the clouds. The air is heavier near the ocean, tasting of salt and blowing in strong gusts through my hair. The sound of the ocean waves lapping against the rocky cliffs echoes up into the sky, mixing with the wind that beats around me in gusts as strong as the waves themselves.

Even though I've never visited the McDow cottage, I remember Vaila said it was on the other side of the goat pasture from where she lived. My feet begin to feel sore not long into my journey, but I keep telling myself that I've bled for much less important tasks, so I can endure this pain as well.

And maybe Una will give me some shoes as well as the spell for breaking a bond.

I'm going to break my bond.

My arms haven't stopped stinging since I left Callen, even though night has ended and Keres wouldn't be able to come to me even if I did call for her.

She knows that I am not traveling away from the city with the intent of leaving Soarsa or even Muireall, or else she would have found a way to extract payment.

But there is nothing she can do to stop me from selling my

bond.

My heart seizes at the thought. Selling my bond. Selling myself. My soul. Is that really what I want?

I love you.

Callen's words continue to echo through my mind, like a hymn, or a dream. They are the one thing that press me forward, and keep me believing that breaking my bond will end everything—the pressure, the pain, this hold over my life, as if my life truly is enslaved to Keres. I am the conduit for her power, and while I may strike the bargain, it is she who decides the price.

The smoke from a chimney drifts into the sleepy, pastel sky, where a little brick cottage appears just above the fog that covers the pastures.

Una's cottage.

I pick up my pace, nearly running the rest of the distance to the house. I have to step lightly to keep from slipping on the dew-drenched ground and soft grass of the pasture beneath my feet. I swing open the little wooden gate just steps from the cottage door. There is the faintest light shining through thin curtains behind little glass windows.

It's still early. Hopefully she is awake and doesn't mind a surprise early visitor. With a deep breath, I raise my hand to knock on the door.

What if I'm making the wrong choice?

I hesitate as my gaze lands on my arm, covered in the markings from wrist nearly to elbow.

What if I am about to learn how to strip myself of the only power I have? I'll be weak, defenseless, and of no value to

Muireall for certain. Will I be of value to anyone?

I love you.

But my mother will be so ashamed of me, not only for leaving in the first place, but also for giving up my independence. I will certainly be a failure, never welcomed in the grove ever again.

I start to lower my hand, my feet moving backwards.

What am I doing? All of this for a man? Have I forgotten everything Ma taught me?

I turn from the door, shaking from an icy chill that brushes over my shoulders and down my back. But my wrists continue to burn, and what I had thought was pain, I start to wonder if it's a reminder of what I'd be giving up: power, security, independence. Yet I can no longer trust Keres, so is it all a lie?

"I knew you would come eventually," Una says.

I pause, lost in the sinking feeling of regret, failure, shame. And I don't know if it's because I am thinking about breaking my bond, or because I'm thinking about keeping it.

"Although, I suppose everyone needs some…*encouragement* to embrace change."

Looking over my shoulder, I see Una, a black shawl clutched around her shoulders, her hair wild and voluminous around her like a lion's mane. Her eyes are dark and curious, smirking as if she has been expecting me.

She steps aside, gesturing into the cottage. "Well, are you goin' to come in?"

Am I?

Suddenly, out from under Callen's spell, his comforting words and careful caresses, I am uncertain of what I want.

"Don't you at least want to hear my story?" Una asks, raising an eyebrow knowingly, dropping her arm back to her side. "Or just to warm up by the fire? You look like death has already taken you."

She turns from me and walks back inside. It's dark in the little cottage, only the faintest orange glow highlighting the shadows within.

I am freezing. I should have taken Muireall's cloak with me. And my shoes.

Muireall will be very upset if I don't get her cloak back.

I shake my head.

Forget Muireall for once. Forget about Callen even.

If I break my bond, it will be for me.

With a surge of confidence, I enter Una's cottage.

It's small and cozy, only one room and a door that leads to either a closet or washroom. Una is at a little stove shoved in the corner, pouring hot tea from a kettle into a pair of mismatched tea cups.

The warmth of the small fire covers me from head to toe, the wind of the cliffs nipping at my back. Una doesn't say anything, or even turn to face me, so I close the door behind me gently.

I rub my arms, helping the heat of the room to soak into my skin. Una approaches me, her smirk softened slightly. Handing a teacup to me, she gestures to the pair of upholstered chairs across from the fireplace. "What were you doin' runnin' across the Soarsa countryside with no coat and no shoes? And at dawn, no less?"

She takes a seat first. Following her example, I sit across

from her and take a sip of the tea, careful and slow, trying to figure out how to answer her question. I already knew I was acting recklessly, but now I feel just plain foolish. Surely, this could have waited long enough for me to return home and dress more appropriately.

"Then again, I suppose I probably looked much the same as you when I ran away, looking for an escape."

She did promise to tell me her story. Perhaps it'll be better to listen than try to explain myself. "Who were you tryin' to escape?"

Una nearly snorts as she sips her tea and then relaxes back in the chair, staring at the fire. "How to answer that... Everyone. Everything. My past. My bond. Myself." She crosses her legs, the fire reflecting, dancing in her brown eyes. "If I'd been smart, I would have run away a lot sooner, but I guess everythin' worked out as it was supposed to in the end."

She lifts her cup to drink, and the shawl slips from her arm, revealing something bright and light swirling on her brown arm where a red bonding brand would have been. Instead, the white markings, covering a third of her forearms, gleam in the firelight. Una doesn't look over at me to see my reaction, or cover herself back up with the shawl, content to let the fire warm her now. As if she doesn't even give a second though to exposing her arms.

"Were you a bonded cairline?" I ask, unable to look away from the white swirls that contrast her skin.

"Is there any other kind of cairline?" She laughs, shaking her head. "Of course I was bonded. Although my spirit was not very powerful, but I tried. Oh, did I try." She shifts so that she is angled more toward me than the fire.

I clutch my teacup in my hands to keep them from shaking, even though I'm no longer cold.

Una smiles, that strange, knowing, almost mocking smirk that she always gives me. Perhaps she doesn't mean for it to be so intimidating. "I grew up in Cairlich, like you. Raised by my ma—she was a cairline too—but my da was long gone by the time I was born. Ma said he wasn't interested in a baby, that he was a rotten man with a wife and family back in Croìthen. But she promised she would never leave me, although that promise ended up being one of control, not care. We lived just on the border, creating dèiligeadh for Croìthen. My bond might as well have been her own, because when she was tired or weak, my blood worked just as well. And my spirit didn't even stop her. Only when I left did I understand I'd been her fuilneadh—my blood instead of hers—but as a child...I thought we were partners."

Una scoffed at her past self, rolling her eyes dramatically, but a stab of compassion hits my heart. Compassion for not only her, but for my past self as well.

"Foolish little Una." She speaks the words casually, but I see the dimple of a grimace on her cheek. "And I made dèiligeadh. Oh, did I make them, to try and make my life better. Except everythin' comes at a cost. The spirits are cruel, twistin' even the most innocent of favors into somethin' you regret. They never make a deal that doesn't benefit them in some way, even if it's just makin' a little cairline more dependent on their power. They make us believe we are weak, that we are *nothing* without our bond. Isn't that how you feel now?"

Her question catches me off guard, striking me to the core. But she doesn't pressure me to answer. She doesn't need me to converse with her, only to listen.

"One day, a man came to our village, and Ma was set on cursing him. She sent me to steal from him at the little tavern inn, told me to be quiet and very careful not to wake him up. But he was awake when I snuck into his window. If he had been asleep, maybe I would still be there today. But he was awake. And he recognized me the moment he saw me. He wasn't married, no family; he *wanted* a family, with my ma. When she found out she was pregnant with his child, she disappeared. And he had finally found her, and me, after searchin' for years.

"When Da offered me a chance at a new life, I couldn't resist. I was tired and blood-dry, and my own spirit had no interest in helpin' me. I suppose the spirits all work together, don't they? Whisperin' and schemin' in the wind…" Una looks deep in the fire and takes a slow breath to refocus. "Ma would have taken me back if we stayed in Cairlich, so my da brought me here, to Croìthe, to Soarsa, and he hid me in this cottage.

"He didn't know what would happen if people found out I was a cairline—I was only fifteen, but I was still bonded—so he made sure I was safe and cared for, and he went back to Cairlich to find answers, to learn how to break my bond."

Una pauses to take another sip, tilting her head to look back at the fireplace, her expression softened with memory.

"My da was kinder than I deserved. Especially since he didn't even raise me. Especially since I had gone to him with the intention of doin' my mother's dirty work. But maybe I shouldn't be so surprised. Cairlinen are supposed to believe in the power of blood and the strength of the bond it creates. Except I didn't have to give any of my blood for him to offer me favor. In fact, he made sacrifices so that he could show me kindness. Da paid a price to show me love. Ever heard of a spirit doin' that for their cairline?" She laughs, looking over at me.

I can't bring myself to answer the way she wants, but I find myself needing to know how her story ends. "Then he found a way?"

"Surely you know. You lived in Cairlich longer than I did."

"A sgaoileadh." I frown, waiting for the twist in her story, the betrayal surely to come. "You became his slave?" Una spits out her tea, choking and holding in more laughter. My cheeks warm. What was so ridiculous?

"Yes, a sgaoileadh. And no, my da didn't *enslave* me." She takes a moment to get a hold of herself and calms again. Una wipes at her eyes. "Is that what they tell you a sgaoileadh is? Nothin' but a new master?" Una sets her teacup, still half-full, on the little table between us, but she doesn't relax back into her chair. She holds my gaze. "If he was my master, he was a kind master, and I wanted to obey him. If that's slavery, then I'm not ashamed of it. But he didn't buy my bond to make me his slave; he bought it to set me free."

Una holds up her arms, showing off the once-red swirls, white as snow against her brown skin. "That's the only way a bond is broken." She licks her lips, choosing her next words carefully. "Don't you know what sgaoileadh means?"

The meaning comes to my mind instinctively—as a

cairline, I know the old tongue well—but something inside me won't say the word.

"I can see in your eyes that you do. Your spirit won't let you say it, but you know. Just think about that."

I didn't know spirits could prevent a cairline from doing anything, and yet, even though I can't seem to force the word out of my lips, it is plain as day in my mind.

Redeemer.

"How is it done?" I ask urgently, worried that if Keres can prevent me from speaking, what are the limitations of her control over me? My heart begins to race.

"It is not easy, and it is not painless," Una says carefully, her expression falling sober and thoughtful, her dark eyes staring straight into my soul. "Do you remember the bondin' circle?"

"Yes," I answer quickly, recalling the circle drawn in dirt with a line straight through the middle.

"You'll need three candles: one for the cairline, one for the sgaoileadh, and one for the spirit. You and the sgaoileadh stand on opposite sides of the circle, with the candles on the center line. The sgaoileadh will make an offer to purchase the cairline from the spirit—there is no barterin'—and the spirit will either accept or decline the offer, so make sure it is good."

"What is a good offer?"

Una is quiet for a moment, looking down at her lap. "My da was my sgaoileadh, and he offered his lifeblood."

Lifeblood. Every drop. And there are no guarantees for survival. In fact, it is expected that if a spell requires lifeblood, the giver will not survive.

The payment you withheld from me.

She looks back up at me, and her eyes glisten with the threat of tears, but she won't let them fall. "He didn't want to risk being rejected by the spirit."

"So, he died," I whisper, needing to know the full truth.

Her eyebrows bounce up and then back down, uncomfortable. "We planned for the worst, but even with his lifeblood gone, he survived the night and recovered in time. And when death did come for him, it wasn't at the hands of a spirit." Clearing her throat, Una sips her tea, but she returns her gaze to the fireplace. "But my spirit was eager to be rid of me."

Could I really ask Callen to give his lifeblood to break my bond? He hadn't been willing to spill even a drop of his blood to save his own mother—why would he give every drop for me? And he made me promise to never use his blood to do magic again.

I promised.

"Didn't you move to Croìthe with your mother?"

"Mother-in-law," I correct her, but the difference seems insignificant when Una smiles with a shrug.

"Surely, a mother wouldn't want her daughter to dèiligeadh ris an diabhal."

I almost laugh, knowing that Muireall resents my bond just as must as she wishes I would use it in the ways she wants. "It's not a demon—"

"Isn't it?" Una cuts me off, her mouth in a firm, straight line, her eyebrows raised. "It might as well be, don't you think?"

I squirm in my seat and run a hand through my hair as the memory of Keres with a knife in the Lennox's barn flashes through my mind.

"It's a parent's duty to protect their children, Caitrin—"

"She's my mother-in-law."

"Even so. Who else do you have?"

Callen. But I know deep in my heart that when he said he would do whatever it took to break my bond, he didn't think it would mean giving his lifeblood. He hates magic, and I promised to never ask him to do it again.

So that leaves Muireall.

I've already failed her tonight in some ways, but perhaps I can prove to her that breaking my bond might give her all the things she has been wanting: wealth, the restoration of her land and home, the chance to get rid of me.

I can only hope Keres has grown tired enough of me, and of being in Croìthe, that she will accept whatever offering Muireall is willing to give to free me.

FIFTY-ONE

RETURNING TO MUIREALL FILLS ME with the dread of rejection rather than the hope of being free. My feet are blistering and sore from walking barefoot so far, but at least it gives me time to strategize how to best explain the situation to Muireall.

Or better yet, how to bribe her into understanding.

All she ever wanted upon returning to Soarsa was to fix up that rotten manor and reclaim her husband's lands. Callen can give those things to her. All she needs to give in return is a little bit of blood.

Or maybe a lot. I shudder, hoping beyond hope that Keres will be as eager to be rid of me as I am of her.

I open the front door and make my way through the manor until I find Muireall in the sunroom, basking in the morning light. Late morning. The sun is climbing higher by the second, and no doubt Muireall had expected me back much sooner.

"Caitrin! How did—goodness! You look like you walked ten miles in the marsh!" Muireall throws her shawl around my shoulders and ushers me to the creaky bench. I hug the shawl close, my heart pounding faster with each passing second.

Playing the dutiful mother, she sits next to me, rubbing my arm and then pouring me a cup of tea. I decline the gesture politely.

"What happened? How did it go?"

Unable to look at her, I take a deep breath to ground myself and recover from my morning trek across the countryside. She has no idea how far I've travelled in the past few hours.

"Good," I finally say, nodding to reassure myself. Better than good.

He loves me.

"Better than we planned," I add, looking over at her.

Muireall has changed and reset her hair, sitting tall and proper, her hands folded neatly on her lap. She is bright with anticipation, waiting for me to give her every detail of my evening with Callen.

I pray she isn't disappointed. If I'm lucky, she will see that this *is* better. I never wanted to trick anyone anyway.

"He wasn't drunk, but it was for the best—"

Muireall stiffens, concern coloring her expression, but at least she is patiently waiting for me to continue.

"I explained…and we talked, and everything is going to be alright."

Muireall tilts her head, blinking. "Is *talking* all you did?"

"I didn't do just as you asked, but the outcome is still the same." I break eye contact with her and resist the urge to slump. I can practically feel the frustration oozing out of her. "Fortunately, we have a plan better than blackmail now. He's going to help us and get your fields back." A shy smile slips onto my lips. "He wants to marry me, Muireall."

"Marry you?" Muireall gasps as if I am a child telling make-believe stories. She stands with a huff, busying herself by picking up the tea tray and standing. "Well, doesn't that sound nice."

"It's true!" I stand, and my feet almost crumple, remembering their sores. Muireall is flustered, hurrying with the tray out of the sunroom and to the kitchen. I hobble after her. "I didn't need to coerce him into helping us. I just had to be honest with him, and he…he said he loves me. That his title would protect me, both of us, Muireall." My tone is earnest, almost pleading for her to believe me.

"Did he forget that you're a cairline?" Muireall slams the tray down onto the kitchen counter, her words building in passion and volume with every word. "Did you put a spell on him so he *had* to propose to you, like you put a spell on my son?" Grabbing a tea cup, Muireall hurls it at the far wall, and it shatters into a hundred pieces. A ringing silence fills the dead air that follows.

I want to defend myself, to explain again that I regret what I did to Tate. But I can't change the past, I can only do something different the next time.

And this time, I did do something different.

"No, I didn't. It was his idea, actually." My voice is calm and steady, contrasting her outburst.

Muireall leans against the kitchen counter, facing away from me with her shoulders hunched high. "Well, he can't marry you. Not legally. Croìthen can't marry cairlinen, so whatever he promised you"—her shoulders sink—"he was lying."

"He didn't lie, Muireall." I step gingerly toward her, wishing there was a plush rug under my feet instead of hardwood boards. "We both know the law. But we can break my bond, and that will not only vindicate me, but allow Callen and I to marry."

Muireall snaps straight at my words, as if lightning struck her. "Break your bond?" She thinks I'm delusional again.

"I went to see Una. She used to be a cairline too."

Muireall slowly turns to face me. Her brow is furrowed, her lips pinched, her eyes glassy and cold. "What good are you to me without your bond?"

I force myself to stand taller. "I'm not going to create dèiligeadh for you, Muireall, especially not one that disrupts the dead—if you are even speaking to the dead! That dark form the spirit says is your husband could very well be a puppet of her own creation."

Muireall opens her mouth to debate my theory, but I can't let her respond until she fully understands.

"I'm not my mother; I don't ever want to be her." I drop the shawl to the floor, urgency rising in me, and take two steps toward her, exposing the swirling bands around my arms. "These are shackles, binding me to a darkness that I want to be free of. And without this bond—which has done nothin' but harm both of us and those we love—without it, we can *both* be free. You can have the life you came here to find."

"What life?" Muireall scoffs, crossing her arms over her chest. "I came here to die, Caitrin. But the good Athair denies giving me even that grace!" she shouts up at the ceiling, as if her god is on the roof.

"Then if all you desire is death, you can have it, if you give me my life." My heart feels heavy as I stare at my arms, the red marks like briars piercing my skin. I drop to my knees, my arms extended out to her, my head bowed. "Please, Muireall. I've never asked anything of you until now; only you can free me."

I look up at her, hoping to find compassion in her eyes, or pity on her lips.

But her expression is as heartless as ever. Maybe more so. She stares down at me like a judge, ready to condemn.

"Maybe if I could forgive you for bewitching my son and taking him from me, I would be able to show you some sort of kindness," Muireall says, standing tall and still, her eyes unwavering. My vision blurs, but I hold her gaze, praying for her to have a change of heart, or even just a change of mind. "But as I see it, your bond is your punishment. Your demon can have you and keep you." She takes a step toward me, looking down her nose at me. A tear slips down her cheek and her expression hardens into stone. "Now get off my land, and don't you dare come back."

FIFTY-TWO

My FEET SEEM TO HAVE a mind of their own. I stumble out of the cottage and find myself wandering on the edge of the cliffs and as far away from Muireall and town as I can get.

Muireall won't help me break the bond. She wants me to be alone, to suffer.

And Callen can't marry me, can't save me if I'm still bonded.

Promise that you will never use my blood for magic ever again.

Even if I could plead with him, I'm not able to change course. Keres is calling me somewhere. She knows what must be done.

Muireall has sent me away, for good. And so the only way to obey her is to betray my vow. To break the mionn.

My mind feels blank, like I'm in a dream and my body is not my own. My breath echoes in my ears, and the light of the sun is shrouded by fog. It could almost be night with how dark the world feels.

My foot catches on a rock that juts out of the ground, and I trip forward. How long have I been walking? My feet are numb, the pain of stones and twigs barely registering. Or maybe that pain is the only thing I feel.

I'm numb all over.

Lost.

My gaze focuses, but I can't place myself. There is not a tree or cottage in sight. Lifting my eyes, I see the edge of the cliffs just a little ways away, and the air fills with the crash of waves.

Then a drop of water hits my cheek, and I look straight up.

The sun is gone, blocked out by the blackest of storm clouds. Too black even for rain.

A shiver runs through my limbs, and my breathing gets heavier as the clouds above me swirl toward the earth like a tornado.

The wind begins to rip around me in rage, but I hold still, focusing on breathing. Possibly my last breaths.

I broke the mionn.

The swirling tornado touches the ground feet from me just as thunder booms and lightning strikes. I fall onto my side, landing hard on the ground.

But it's not a tornado.

It's Keres.

Did she summon the darkness to punish me? Could she not wait until nightfall?

"Little cairline…" Keres's voice echoes around me, and the tornado shifts, gaining the slightly human form of my spirit. "Wee hen…"

My wrists begin to sting. And then they are pulled up against my will, as if tied together with rope, and I'm tugged forward, hands first, and thrown to my knees by the wind. I bend in front of Keres, my hands extended to her, palms up, weak.

"It appears you will not be able to keep your oath after all," Keres says, her voice dark and as booming as the thunder. Maybe she is the thunder, the lightning, the darkness, the rain that is now falling steadily over me.

No one can save me now. This is the consequence of my actions.

"You wanted your bond broken, and so it will be," Keres whispers. One of her wispy tendrils brushes against my chin, beckoning me to look up at her. I raise my head slowly, shaking. Red orbs like eyes are bright in the spirit's form, and the world around is darkened by her tornado of tendrils.

Another clap of thunder echoes around me. "Don't be fooled by your friend, Una. She lied." My eyes flash at the name, and a deep despair sinks into my heart. "No one survives a lifeblood offering."

Something stings my chest, and I twist under the sharp pain as my arms are thrown apart. As if hanging by a loose thread, my body floats up from the ground. Ribbons of red, as wispy as Keres herself, begin to flow from my heart and into the darkness.

FIFTY-THREE

THE WORLD IS A BLUR, flipped upside down and gray, every spot of color washed away. I am floating in a storm, powerless to stop it. I just want it to end.

Keres will take every drop. I don't know what she will do with it, with no cairline to conduct her power. But she will take every drop nonetheless, as was our deal.

My head goes fuzzy, and the world shifts.

Then she drops me, and I land hard on a wooden stool, my elbows cushioned by a bed.

I sit at Tate's bedside, his final breaths coming slowly and laboriously. I have to come to terms with my own feelings about what is happening, and my part in the events surrounding it.

I take his hand as I pull at my shawl to keep it from falling off my shoulders. A single lantern burns, lighting the tiny cottage room. A quaint window is covered by a floral curtain I made myself. The fabric is so thin that moonbeams break through, lining Tate's pale face with a silvery glow.

When he squeezes my fingers, I wince. I should have given him my other hand. While the prick had been sealed moments after being made, a benefit of my bond, it feels like it is still bleeding, soaking my skin, Tate's hand, the bedsheets.

"Where is Ivor?" he asks, his voice raspy and weak. It's the same question he has asked on and off all night as the delirium truly set in. Soon, just like Ivor, he will get a rush of adrenaline and then nothing.

"You'll see your brother soon, Tate," I tell him, slipping my hand from his to remove the damp cloth at his brow. He was always warm, but tonight his entire body is like a furnace. The skin under his stubble and up his arms began peeling away, burning from the inside out, three days ago.

That's when we all knew the worst was to come.

Tate opens his eyes, dreary, looking over at me. I want to smile for him, give him some courage, but my lips feel as tight as the knot in my stomach. I keep the tears at bay, knowing they wouldn't be for him, but for myself. Tears of guilt. Of regret. "Keep resting," I whisper, urging him to pass on quickly and end the pain.

"Where is my mother?"

Instead of being at the bedsides of two dying sons, his mother has spent more money than ever to speak with her husband—her dead husband—as if he would have any answers to change their fate.

"Orla and I have kept her away so that she'll stay healthy," I lie. In my heart, I hope she is only in denial, but her increasing visits to my mother make me question whether or not she might actually be going insane.

Speaking to the dead tends to fracture one's grip on reality.

"You must take care of her," Tate says, struggling to sit up. I lean forward, off my stool, to move the pillow behind his back and keep him comfortable. He slouches back down as soon as he settles and grabs my hand tightly.

His eyes seem brighter. My heart pulses furiously, wondering if he knows. I haven't made a single dèiligidh since we were married four months ago.

He turns over my hand, and his fingers graze the thin, dark red ribbon of skin that wraps around my wrist. "Promise me that you will."

"Of course, I will," I say, but I don't even know what such a promise will mean. What if Meara returns to Croìthe, to her homeland? Surely, he doesn't expect me, a cairline, to follow her.

"No, *really* promise me," he says, clutching my hand in both of his. He shakes from head to toe, sweat dripping down his temples—his hair is damp with it—and his eyes light up with the fire within. Stubborn and sincere, he holds my gaze. "The kind of promise that cairlinen make with one another."

I try to pull my hand away, to calm him, but his grip is too strong. "You don't know what you're sayin'."

He leans forward, moving one hand to my shoulder, then my cheek. The fire in his eyes swells and hot tears begin to build. There is pain there, pain that sinks deep into his heart. I put my hand against his as my shawl slips from my shoulder. In the chill of the night, his burning skin is almost soothing.

"Please, Caitrin," he whispers. "She has already lost everything, and now she's losing me too. I know you will be good to her, because you've been good to me."

I have to look down at his words. *Good to him*. The talisman that hangs around my neck, close to my heart, swings between us. If only he knew what its purpose was. His affections for me didn't begin naturally, and I had been too naive to know how to make a clear bargain.

It was supposed to be a simple spell. But nothing is simple with spirits.

"She wouldn't like it if she knew you were doin' blood magic on your death bed." I laugh nervously as the word *death* slips through my lips.

He coughs a chuckle in response, leaning back. "I have always been curious how it is done," Tate says, and, for a moment, his beautiful, carefree boyish grin appears on his face with a mischievous glint in his dark eyes.

I think I could have loved him, if I hadn't made him love me first.

How can I deny my dying husband's last wish? I've tried to be a good wife, but as I sit here with him dying and no heir to keep his memory alive, I wonder if I ever really tried that hard. Or maybe I was too young to know how to try to begin with.

"Alright, if you're sure." I go to my sewing box and pull out a sharp straight pin. From the basket on the small table, I grab my box of matches and candle. The wax is still soft from earlier that night. But he won't be able to tell. I set the candle down, knowing it would be better to be outside. Then again, if Keres ignores me, maybe that is for the best.

Tate watches me with baited attention, staying focused on the distraction from the heat and the pain. I strike the match and light the candle. Then, with a prick of the pin, I let a drop of blood fall into the flame. "Thig dhòmhsa," I whisper. The flame dances, flickers, then the candle and lantern are snuffed out.

The light of the moon tints red, but Keres doesn't appear.

Did you change your mind?

I stiffen at the question, searching the shadows for her darkened, wispy figure. But Tate's gaze is fixed on the flame. He didn't hear her.

Thank the moon and stars.

"Why…" Keres's voice fills the room, echoing softly over us, and Tate jerks in his bed, his hands clutching the sheets. "Do you call for me to come to you again, cairline?"

"I wish to make a mionn, between myself and my husband," I say, trying to imitate the strong voice with which my mother always speaks to her spirit. But I know Keres can sense the pounding of my heart. She reigns supreme in our bartering. She always has.

I take the talisman from around my neck. It's fitting that I should use it again. "It's a dyin' man's wish."

She laughs, and the sound snakes through my hair and into my ears. *What would his living wish have been, do you think, cairline?*

I clutch the talisman in my hands, hardening myself against her taunts. "For this favor, we will offer our blood as one, one finger each. I know you have done more for less."

Tate shifts, watching me. His face is pale, and I don't know if it is the illness or the chill that Keres brings with her wherever she goes.

"Unless you've changed your mind," I ask him, trying to be gentle as my voice cracks and my hands grow clammy.

"Are you sure you want to use *that* talisman, cairline? It may break your spell over him…"

Tate frowns. "Caitrin, what does she mean?"

"She's just teasin'," I reassure him, but I wonder if Keres speaks the truth. "Keres, we don't have time for your games. Do you accept my terms?"

"And what is the mionn you wish to make?"

"An oath, that I will care for Tate's mother, Meara Raeburn, and stay at her side, until she joins her husband and sons in the after."

Keres hisses, and she doesn't respond for a long time. She is considering not only my offering but also my request.

"She has no one left, spirit," Tate adds, his voice pleading, speaking to the empty corners of the room.

If this mionn is broken, cairline…

My hair slips off my shoulder and down my back. It's as if she is whispering directly into my ear. A chill runs down my spine.

I expect the payment you withheld from me tonight.

I swallow hard.

"We have a deal then," Keres says, her voice filling the room. I am eager for her to leave, for fear that she may spill more of my secrets, and I would spare Tate the pain of the truth for one more night at least. His last night should have more peace than the truth would offer him.

"Hold up your hand, Tate." He shakes as he lifts his arm, and I weave our fingers together to give him strength. A darkness swirls, lifting the talisman into the air. Tate and I lean toward each other, our hands clutched together, as Keres's wispy, black tendrils brush over our fingers and then pull away red.

Tate slumps against his pillow.

Something slams into my heart, burning, branding.

And I fall through the ground into the earth.

FIFTY-FOUR

I STAND BEFORE KERES, MY fingertip bleeding, a pearl necklace clutched in my hand.

"You think I can create a dèiligidh that will cure your husband from only a cheap piece of jewelry?" Keres scoffs.

"It's not cheap!" I argue. I can't let Tate die. Somehow, it's my fault he caught the sickness at all, I just know it. If I hadn't enchanted him with my spell, caused his family to settle with our sudden marriage, he might have moved away and married a girl who wouldn't curse him into loving her. "What about my hair?" I offer without thinking. It feels so rash, silly even. Truly the necklace is worth more to Keres.

"Would he love you without your hair?" Keres taunts, swirling around me. Then she is whispering in my ear, the words echoing through my head. "You know only lifeblood can save him now."

"Lifeblood? *My* lifeblood?" My toes curl into the dirt.

"I don't see anyone else bargaining for him to be saved?"

I drop the necklace to the ground, backing away. *My lifeblood.* She wants me to *die* for him. But I don't even know if I love him. I certainly have wanted to love him, felt love for him, but a deep enough love to give my life for him?

"Without a powerful dèiligidh, you know he will die."

"He may be dead already," I say, my gaze hardening as I stare her down. Why make a dèiligidh if he has already passed on? Ivor went so quickly, and, while I had only been gone half-an-hour, Tate could have easily gotten much worse in such a short amount of time.

My stomach twists and revolts as if it has more of a conscience that I do.

Keres merely laughs. "On second thought, his life may be worth far more than your own, little cairline. Perhaps even your lifeblood isn't enough to save him now."

I stumble backward, through the swirling tendrils and wisps of Keres. Something catches against my heel, and I fall, straight through the earth, sinking into an abyss.

FIFTY-FIVE

"CAIT…"

Everything is black and dark. If I am still on earth, it feels far away, muddled and muffled.

But also warm.

Weak.

Am I dead?

"Caitrin, wake up…"

Has it all been a dream?

I'm on the ground—the hard, wet ground—but someone has wrapped me in a thick, flannel jacket. My head is cradled on their lap, gentle fingers brushing over my cheek and caressing my jaw, leaving a tingling sensation in their wake. I lean into the hand.

"Caitrin?"

The thunderous sound of wind drowns out the voice.

My eyes flutter open. A spike of lightning illuminates the world around me, and the crack that follows booms into my bones. Am I dead? My head feels faint, and I press my palms to my temples. I can't keep my eyes open. Arms wrap around me, pulling me against a firm chest, and I relax back.

"She is mine…"

Keres.

My heart restarts and begins racing. The tornado rages around me. Keres has been taking my lifeblood. Is it all gone? Is this all that remains? I feel so weak. How long until I pass out again? Or pass away.

"I've come to buy her bond!" A strong voice shouts out above the storm.

A shriek fills my ears, and I twist in pain.

"Caitrin belongs to us!" Keres retorts, her voice surrounding me, consuming me, as if it is coming from inside of me.

"No!" Whoever is behind me stands, cradling me up in their arms. Strong arms. His arms.

My fingers grab at his shirt, pulling my head up to see Callen carrying me, with his curls blown wild in the wind, his green eyes fierce and determined.

"Callen?" He doesn't know what he is asking. He should leave me to my fate.

"Cait?" Callen looks down at me, his expression brightening momentarily. He pulls me close, pressing his cheek to the top of my head. "It's going to be okay."

"You can't do this," I tell him weakly, forcing strength into my bones and dropping from his arms. I nearly crumble to the ground when my feet hit the earth. He keeps a hand on my back, steadying me. I find my footing against the hammering of Keres's tornado. "Finish it, Keres!" I demand, my hand still clinging to Callen.

"Gladly…" Keres hisses.

"No, Caitrin!" Callen pulls me back to himself, holding me fast, gazing down at me as the rain drenches us, drowns us.

"I'm here to break your bond. Una told me how…she said she told you too…" His voice cracks. "Why didn't you come find me?" The whisper of his words hits harder than the wind and the rain, louder than the thunder.

I shake my head, dropping my gaze from his and hoping the rain disguises my tears. "It's blood magic, Callen. To break my bond, you'd have to…"

His fingers tighten on my arms. "I love you. I'll do whatever it takes."

"She owes me a debt, Lockhart!" Keres shouts, screams, like a banshee in the night.

"I will pay her debt! And buy her bond!" Callen shouts back at her, full of stubborn passion.

"Callen…"

He breaks away from me, taking a knife from his boot and drawing a circle in the mud, then slicing it in two. Keres shrieks, and the rain falls harder, the wind whipping faster, trying to erase the mark. But the circle stays steady, impervious to the elements.

However, that doesn't mean any fire could hold in this rain. Even to contact a spirit for a simple dèiligidh requires a clear night. It's hopeless. And yet, Callen places the three candles and produces a matchbook, which is soaked through already. He strikes a match against the box, and it doesn't take. Of course it doesn't.

"Callen, please…" I beg. Please don't make me suffer another failure. "Just forget about me."

Callen strikes another match. Nothing.

"Give up, boy. She belongs to us…" Keres says from the

wisps that surround us, swallowing us. She laughs at his wasted efforts. "The Sgaoileadh Rìgh will not come." Lightning crackles, then breaks into thunder as Keres's maniacal laughter fills the storm.

Then fire, bright and bold in the wind and rain, sparks to life.

Keres's laughter is cut short with a gasp that summons another strong gust of wind, pushing me to my knees behind Callen. I grab his leg to ground myself, so Keres's storm won't carry me away.

Firm, as if he is a tree planted in the ground, Callen bends and lights the other two candles: one for me, and one for him.

The spirit cannot deny...

The tendrils of wisps pull together into Keres's shadowy form. The rain ceases, but the wind remains, as furious as ever. Callen takes my hand and helps me to stand. His hold on me is firm, comforting, resolved.

"So, Lockhart." Keres's red eyes flash to life and she snickers. "What offer will you make to free her? There is only one offer I'll accept."

"Take everything," Callen says quickly. "Every drop."

I grab Callen's arm, pulling him to look at me, shaking my head. "No, no, don't give anything to her." My heart aches, pinching with guilt. "You don't deserve...you don't owe her anything! Not like me..." I shudder, the tears streaming more freely now, and accept my fate. I brush my fingers over the stubble on his cheek. "You said you would never do blood magic again, and I won't let it kill you now. Not just to save me."

"Just to save you?" Callen takes my hand. "You say that like you are worthless."

"I am certainly not worth your life."

Callen smiles, his forehead wrinkled in concern. Bending low, his lips brush against mine, like a gentle caress. Like a goodbye. "Beloved, you are worth more than all the stars in the sky and all the blood in my veins. Every drop." I close my eyes, yearning for his words to be true. "And it is only my love and my life that can free you."

There is a stillness. Acceptance.

"Deal!" Keres hisses.

Something wrenches me from Callen and slams me onto the ground. When I look up, Callen is bent back, unnaturally, as if an invisible hand holds his limp form, the toes of his boots barely brushing against the ground, his arms hanging at his sides.

Keres grows as large as the storm itself, and dozens of smokey fingers strike Callen's chest all at once. As they drink his lifeblood, the entire storm taints red.

"Callen!" I shout, standing, wanting to rush to him, to pull him away, to save him. A tangle of wisps pushes me onto my stomach and into the ground, imprisoning me. My fingers claw into the mud and grass, trying to escape. But it's useless.

Callen's skin has grown pale as the warmth is taken from him. He almost looks like a ghost, his body as white as his shirt. Keres laughs and hisses as her dark cloudy form grows more and more red, filling with his lifeblood.

It should have been mine.

And yet, my strength is returning, blood filling my veins.

And I feel hot, like I'm on fire.

Keres's wisps push me further into the mud, but my eyes catch sight of one of my arms, outstretched beside me. The markings that swirl up from my wrist are glowingly bright, like white hot metal. I turn my head to see my other arm, which is lit up like lightning dancing across my skin.

Keres's laughter begins to scratch and crack. Another clap of thunder rings across the sky.

Then she shrieks so loud it makes my ears ring.

And my markings have grown so bright it's blinding.

No, the light isn't coming from me. I push against the wisps to look up and see Callen, still floating in the air. His entire body is light, growing brighter with every moment. Brighter than the darkness around us, consuming the darkness.

Keres cries out in pain, an earth-shattering sound that is cut short when the light forces its way through her form, breaking apart the wisps that hold me down and the tendrils piercing Callen.

She disappears in an instant.

And Callen falls to the ground, the sound hard and hollow. Dead.

FIFTY-SIX

I SCRAMBLE TO MY FEET and rush to Callen. He is lying on his side, his back facing me. And he isn't moving.

While Keres and her storm are gone, a fog remains, filtering the light of the sun. I drop to my knees beside Callen and turn him onto his back. His head slumps over, face toward the sky. I watch him for a second, praying for his eyes to flutter open, or his chest to rise and fall.

But he is perfectly still, his face pale, drained of color.

"Callen…" I whimper, leaning over him, placing my hand on his chest, waiting for the faint thumping of a heartbeat. I notice my skin for the first time. Gone are the red markings of a cairline bond, replaced with stark white swirls. But underneath my palm I feel nothing.

Even if I still had my magic, no cairline has the power to bring anyone back from the dead. Once the great darkness has taken someone, there is nothing we can do to bring them to the light again.

And Callen was my light. Without him, the world is darkness.

The breeze brushes over us again, bringing the chill of death with it.

"I love you, Callen," I whisper. "I don't want my life

without you."

A love like Callen gave me can't be bought, it can only be given. And now I won't ever have the chance to give it back to him, not as a debt to be paid or a favor returned, but as a priceless gift, a piece of my very being that would have been the heartbeat of every kiss shared, every word spoken, every step taken.

My love pours of out me, but there is no one to give it to.

My fingers curl around his shirt as I bend over him, pressing my forehead against his shoulder. My tears mix with Keres's rainwater, which soak his clothing, and my body shakes with a pain deeper than any cut with a knife.

Another breeze, this one gentler and stirring, like a ray of sunshine. I sink against Callen, holding him.

Now I truly have nothing left in this world. I may be freed from my bond, but my mother-in-law despises me, sent me away, and the only person who truly loved me lies cold, drained of his lifeblood. Dead.

The breeze sweeps over me, with a warmth that I'm sure is the sun breaking through the clouds, although I don't open my eyes to see. I'm overcome with the emptiness, the longing. I don't care if the sun is shining. It changes nothing.

The breeze lifts me slightly, attempting to give me wings. But I'm not ready to rise and face the future. I don't know how I will face it alone.

And right now, I feel more alone than ever.

The breeze comes again, trying harder to lift me off Callen, but I won't let go. I wrap my arms around his torso, hugging him close. I swallow my tears to focus on staying close to him.

The distant sound of thunder echoes over me.

My breathing calms as warmth pools over me, breaking through the mud and dirt on my skin and soaking into my bones. And my breaths find a rhythm with the thunder, rising when the wind comes and falling when it disappears.

The wind groans, softly, as if calling another storm. The sound is comforting and close.

Then I catch my breath as the breeze comes again, and my eyes snap open.

He's breathing.

His heart is beating.

"Callen!" I gasp, sitting up and leaning over his face.

His head tilts, waking. His eyes move behind eyelids, as if he has forgotten how to open them.

"Wake up." Bending over, I gently kiss his forehead. My hand slips around his head, and I wait. His chest is rising and falling; it's shallow but sure. "Callen, it's over."

He groans again, and his lips twitch, finding life again. His color is returning too. The sun has peeked through the clouds, falling over him and brightening his sun-kissed skin. I place my palm on his chest, feeling the steady thumping of his heartbeat. I smile weakly, brushing away the tear-stains on my cheeks.

Then his eyes pull open, slowly, wincing against the bright sunlight that streams over us. "Caitrin…" Callen's lips tug at a grin, but even that takes too much effort. I take his hand in mine, not wanting to rush him as a new flood of tears springs from my eyes.

His gaze drops from my face to my hands. "I'm not bonded to her anymore." I lift one of my arms, showing him my new markings, white as snow. "Now I belong to you."

Then he smiles fully, vibrantly. Using all his energy, he lifts himself up and throws his arms around me. "We belong to each other," he whispers, pulling me close.

I return his embrace, holding him up against me. His hands smooth over my hair, and he kisses my shoulder. I pull back from him, keeping my hands on his arms, although he seems able to sit up on his own now.

Callen laughs as he runs a hand over my cheek, or more accurately, the dirt on my cheek. "I'm a mess," I say, brushing away the tears and hoping the dirt goes with them.

He leans close, his breath on my lips, his bright green eyes filling my vision. "No, you're beautiful." And then he kisses me, a kiss full of life and love and a future. A kiss of belonging. This is where I belong. With him. To him. And him to me.

We break apart, Callen taking deep breaths as he rests his forehead against mine. "How is this possible?" I whisper.

"I'm not sure. Ancient magic?" Callen pulls back, memorizing every inch of my face with a curious smile, as if remembering a dream. "There was a voice…"

"Keres?"

His brow furrows. "No. I think…I think it was Athair. Is that crazy?"

I laugh, kissing his cheek and running my fingers through his curls. "Nothing seems impossible right now. What did he say?"

"'Lifeblood given out of pure love cannot be corrupted.'" Callen falls back against the ground. "I love you, Caitrin."

I lean down over him, my hands braced on either side of

his head, my hair falling like a copper curtain to the side. "I love you, too." Our lips meet again, and I think I could stay here like this with him for all of eternity.

"Master Callen!" The words echo on the wind, breaking us apart.

Turning toward the forest, Brodie appears on horseback, with Una on a horse beside him. My brow furrows as I remember there is more trouble than just my bond.

There is the Dhubd Blath. There is Baines. There is the accusation of murder that hangs over my head. There is another cairline somewhere in Soarsa.

Callen and I stand as one, our hands clutched together as Brodie and Una gallop to us.

"Brodie! How did you find us?" Callen asks.

"Probably the same way you found Caitrin. The storm," Brodie says, his breathing labored with worry. Then his eyes shift to me, hope brightening his face. "Did it—" His eyes land on my wrists.

"It's done," Callen says, holding our hands up to show off my new markings better.

"So you're no longer bonded to a spirit?" Una asks, a smile of pride breaking out over her face. I've never seen her smile like that before, carefree and sparkling, and it makes her much less intimidating.

I nod and swallow, almost just as shocked myself. I am no longer bonded. And the burst of joy is threatened by doubt. I'm powerless.

"She is free," Callen says, pulling my hand to his chest, his gaze full of understanding and reassurance. I am safe. "And now I can truly protect Caitrin if they bring her to trial."

"They may not wait for a trial," Brodie says soberly. "Baines is set on burning down the Raeburn manor. He thinks you are hiding there—they know you put some kind of enchantment over the place—and that if he destroys you, it will destroy the disease as well."

Una shakes her head with a long sigh. "He's gathered a mob and they are marching to the Raeburn estate. When Callen came to me looking for you, and with that storm brewing…I knew something bad was about to happen, so I sent him to search along the cliffs, and I went to the Raeburn manor and spoke with Muireall. She told me that she…" Una's gaze dips from mine. "I left to keep searching. That's when I saw the mob—"

"And when I saw Una," Brodie interjects. "And we both came to find you two."

My mouth opens to respond, but it is nonsensical. "But I've told them: the only way to stop the disease is to destroy the talismans infecting each person."

"Which, we no longer have the magic to do," Callen adds.

The realization makes my heart pound faster. "Or to kill the cairline who has made them."

"How many are infected now?"

"Over a dozen," Brodie answers. "The ones Dr. Kilpatrick thought were improving are no better off, and with Stuart's death…" He doesn't need to explain. We all understand what is at stake.

"And whatever this cairline's goal is, she will no doubt keep infecting people until she gets what she wants," Callen says.

"What does she want?" Brodie asks.

"Lewis Baines is probably just trying to keep his property, the Raeburn fields, that is. He's afraid of the teasairginn, that Muireall will find a way to take it from him."

But I know the truth. A shiver runs down my spine. "Baines is just a pawn," I say. "Keres told me the spirits want me to leave Soarsa, that this cairline is obeying their wishes, and she may even be working with Baines to do so."

"What? Why?" Callen's question is more one of anger than anything else. He grips my hand tightly as if that alone will keep me safe.

"To stop the Sgaoileadh Rìgh from comin'. There's a prophecy that through the bloodline of a cairline and a prince will come a man, the Sgaoileadh Rìgh, who will destroy magic for good."

"And the spirits think you're that cairline." Una chuckles, amused as she dismounts her horse. "And that makes *you* her prince." She hands her horse's reins to Callen.

"Either way, we need to get to the manor before it's burned to the ground, and Mrs. Raeburn with it." Brodie pulls Una up onto the horse behind him.

But I hold back. Do I want to save Muireall?

Callen snatches up his knife from the ground—it is still glowing ever so faintly of whatever ancient magic saved him. "Cait, what is it?" Callen asks as he prepares to mount, his foot in the stirrup.

I look up at him, wrapping my arms around myself, remembering how disheveled I am. Muireall certainly doesn't deserve to have me save her. After all, she wouldn't even consider helping me in my most dire hour. In fact, she basically cursed me to die.

"Caitrin…" Callen holds out his hand to me, and I look up at him.

I didn't deserve for Callen to save me, to love me, to die for me. My life is barely even my own anymore. Callen, my sgaoileadh, my redeemer, has paid for me to be free. Perhaps I can be Muireall's sgaoileadh. Perhaps I can give her what she doesn't deserve but I know she needs, what I have in my possession: the priceless gift of a love given freely.

FIFTY-SEVEN

I SLIP OFF THE HORSE to the ground below. The side of the manor is just barely in sight through the thicket. In the front courtyard, Baines and his mob have gathered with torches and oil, ready to set the crumbling structure ablaze. Callen has the best shot at stopping them if I'm not there to fuel Mr. Baines' rage. An angry mob won't believe a word I say, regardless of the change in my markings, but the word of the Lord of Soarsa might carry some weight.

At least, that's what we're hoping.

"I'll be right back," Callen tells me with a wink, his hand lingering on mine for a moment. He hisses, kicking his heels into his steed and busting out of the woods into the clearing with Brodie and Una just behind him.

Mr. Baines turns toward him, and I crouch down behind the bushes to watch.

"The Sealg Dorcha has long ended, Mr. Baines! You know this is not the way things are done anymore," Callen calls out to him, his voice full of confidence and authority.

"We have no choice, Callen! We should have never let that cairline into our town to begin with!" Baines retorts, and a cheer rises up from the mob. They've been driven into a frenzy long before we arrived. I pray their fury doesn't turn on my friends.

Peeking around the shrubs, I watch as Callen marches his horse straight through the crowd, blocking the front door. "I will judge Caitrin Raeburn fairly, not with fire, if that is what the town demands. But this solves nothing." Callen's steed paces nervously.

"You'd have to catch her to put her on trial!" Mr. Baines shouts, then his eyes turn toward the thicket, and I hide again. "Or perhaps you already have. You certainly look like you've been through hell…" His voice is coming closer.

"Baines!" Callen shouts after him.

Stepping as lightly as I can, I move further into the thicket, staying low and hoping the mud on my dress disguises me.

I can't even see the manor anymore, and soon I won't be able to hear what is happening there, either. Hopefully that means I'm safe. Callen shouts something else, but his words are drowned out by the wind rustling the leaves. The faint scent of blackberries and copper fill my nose.

"There you are, wee hen."

I stiffen as a wave of fear ripples through me.

No, I must be hallucinating.

"Caitrin? Aren't you happy to see your ma?"

I turn slowly, dread soaking me from head to toe, drenching every fiber and vein.

Nessa Malloch, my mother, stands as still as a tree, mere feet from me, tall and poised and full of power. She is dressed in one of her tight black dresses, a dark fur draped over her shoulders and clasped with a chain that has a silver spider on the end. Her flaming red hair hangs loose and full around her pale features. She is just like I remember, and yet she is also more terrifying. Because now…

Her eyes flinch to my sides, and I almost start to hide my arms behind my back, but it's too late. Her eyebrow twitches, and she raises her head, looking down her nose at me. Her taunting smile disappears. "So, it is true. What a shame."

A shout echoes out toward us. Callen.

Nessa glances toward the manor, then shifts her weight, like a snake, one vertebra at a time. "And he lived? How interestin'…"

"Why are you here, Ma?" I ask, trying my best to be brave, but the fact that she seems to know so much is startling.

She walks toward me, plastering a fake smile on her lips, but her eyes are hungry. It's the same expression she gives a customer who is eager to see a future she knows will be terrible. "To check on you, wee hen." Nessa looks at my wrists again, this time with disappointment instead of mere shock. "You've been causin' so much trouble, haven't you?"

A cairline in Soarsa. "How long have you been here?" I step backward, needing more distance between us.

"Don't be afraid, Caitrin. Don't you know I love you?"

I grimace, knowing whatever she feels for me, it's not love.

She snickers at my reaction and pulls something from her pocket. "I have a gift for you." I hesitate, a far off and foolish hope seizing me. She opens her hand, palm up, to reveal a large black talisman, formed into the bulbous shape of a spider like the brooch on her fur. I half expect it to come to life, but then with a flash, I realize what it is: a mallachd dèiligidh.

"And who is that meant to curse, Ma?" I ask, still slowly

drawing away from her and toward the manor.

"I didn't want to make it, but you left me no choice."

I shake my head, speaking the truth even if she won't hear it. "There is always a choice."

Nessa's expression takes on a dark grimace, her brown eyes growing black, without a glimmer of light in them. "The spirits cannot have both you and that boy alive."

"Why can't you just leave us alone?"

Nessa snorts, a smirk twitching on her lips in amusement. "I thought Keres could keep you under control, keep you happy, but you are so reckless. The Sgaoileadh Rìgh won't come for perhaps a hundred generations, but he will come, unless I stop it."

My mind whirls with the scheming, and my heart burns with the realization at how I have been manipulated and used. I clutch my chest, hot tears falling down my cheeks as my mouth hangs open, wordless.

"I always knew you were too weak for the gift you had been given," she growls, her anger growing. Soon, it will be too late, and I don't know what will happen if she gets that talisman any closer to me. Already, I feel my heart beating faster, as if racing to its death.

But I've survived death once this day already.

"And I won't let you take my power away!" Nessa snarls and lunges for me.

Ready for her attack, I spin and sprint for the manor. I hear her fall on the ground behind me, but she will quickly be back up on her feet, and I don't know how many talismans she might have on her, giving her supernatural abilities.

The shouts of the mob fill the air as I break out of the forest and into the clearing.

What if they see me?

I glance behind me, every muscle in my body tense, to see Nessa running, flying, through the forest behind me.

Rushing forward, I jump through a broken window of the manor and race for the foyer. Now that my bond has been broken, the power of my talismans will have faded as well.

"No, stop!" Callen orders.

The marble tiles beneath my feet are slick. Oil. Shattered bottles litter on the foyer floor, leaking the fluid.

"Burn it to the ground!" Baines shouts, and, in a matter of seconds, fire slips under the door and consumes the walls around me.

FIFTY-EIGHT

THE FIRE CLIMBS UP THE columns of the foyer, snaking into the dining room and blocking my escape.

"Wee hen!" Nessa calls out for me, her voice echoing throughout the manor as if she could come from anywhere at any moment.

"Callen!" I shout at the doors as the fire crackles and consumes the wood.

"There you are, little cairline," Nessa hisses, and her voice sounds eerily like Keres.

"Callen!" I call out one more time—hoping he hears me, hoping he will come and save me once more—and then I race for the stairs, taking them two at a time. I don't turn around, but I can feel Nessa right at my heels.

And yet there is no escape upstairs, unless I'm willing to jump out of a window. Perhaps that is the only way out now.

Racing across the balcony, I make for one of the unused rooms. The fire is climbing up higher, hungrily consuming the old, brittle contents of the house. It catches quickly on the dry rug that is spread across the balcony floor, and I halt, making a sharp turn. The door is wedged, and I have to throw my weight against it to get it open.

Nessa's hands brush against me as I crash against the door.

It rips from its hinges, falling against the floor, and bringing me with it.

Dust explodes into the air, and I scamper to my feet.

The room is empty, stripped of whatever valuable items had been stored here. The windows are cracked but not shattered. I will have to either pry them open or…

A hand grabs my wrist, spinning me around.

I raise my fist, ready to strike, but something cold—colder than ice, colder than death—is pressed against my collarbone and it sinks its talons into my skin. With a blast of power, I am knocked backward onto the ground. Nessa stands over me.

"I'm your daughter!" I cry out, but something swallows up my voice.

"*Were* my daughter," she corrects me calmly, backlit by the flames. "I don't know what you are now. Well…" She snorts, a grimace on her face, her eyes nothing but black. "I guess you're nothin' now."

I grab at the talisman, and it hisses, vibrating with life and power.

"Wee hen…foolish cairline…" Keres's voice fills my mind, and I twist, a deep agony seizing my heart.

I didn't escape death once today only to be killed now.

Wrapping my fingers firmly around the talisman, I strain every muscle trying to pull it from my skin. My eyes close, and I clench my teeth together, refusing to give up although it doesn't budge.

But my strength is waning.

"She may not be your daughter—"

I open my eyes, Muireall standing in the midst of the

flames, a skillet clenched in her hands.

"—but she is a Raeburn." Nessa barely has time to register her presence. "And Raeburn women don't waste time on dafty woppers."

Muireall swings, landing a hard hit against the side of Nessa's head. The cairline spins from the attack, her red hair fanning out around her as she falls to the floor with a groan. Muireall glances at me but doesn't rush to my aid, keeping a wary eye on Nessa.

With revived strength, I clench the talisman tighter and tug. A sensation like a thick thorn being pried from my skin floods my chest.

"You can't stop it, Caitrin!" Nessa hisses. "You've betrayed your family, your people; accept your punishment."

"No," Muireall says, looking over at me as she raises the iron pan for another strike. There is something new in her eyes, an awareness, truth. "It was her family who betrayed her." And I know it's not just of Nessa that she speaks.

As Nessa starts to stand, Muireall swings. The skillet hits Nessa's head hard, and she slumps to the ground.

My arms seem to glow, ever so faintly, as I give one last tug and the talisman comes free. Blood drips from the spider's legs where it had buried into my flesh. I stare at it for a moment.

"Caitrin! The fire!" Muireall shouts, dropping the pan and turning to the balcony, searching for the exit.

Standing, I hold the talisman for a second, unable to look over at my mother. She cursed the town. To punish me. To keep me enslaved.

I throw the curse into the fire.

"This way, Muireall! Out the window and onto the ledge," I tell her, rushing to the window and pulling at the latch. It snaps free, and I push the window open, gesturing for Muireall to hurry.

"Caitrin…I—" Muireall takes my hand, not knowing what to say.

But now isn't the time for apologies.

"Go, go!" I lean out the window. "Callen! Brodie!" Holding her hand, I help her out of the window and onto the small ledge.

Glancing back at the gathering flames, something scurries out of the fire and into the darkened corner of the room.

"Mrs. Raeburn! Down here!" Brodie shouts. Keeping a hand on Muireall, I make sure she is steady on the ledge and spot Brodie holding his arms out below us. "Jump! I'll catch you!"

Nessa groans, and just as Muireall prepares to jump, I look over my shoulder to see her twisted form standing.

But it isn't my mother.

Her eyes are no longer black with power; they are red with possession.

"Muireall! Jump!"

As she falls, the wall explodes, blasting me backward onto the floor.

Not wanting to be caught unaware again, I rush to my feet, facing Nessa. Her fur has fallen away, and the talisman has crawled onto her chest, sinking into her skin, filling her veins with black death that stretches to her fingertips. The red bond markings that swirl up her arms shift, covering every inch of her exposed skin, burning as red as the flames.

I don't have any power to stop her.

All I can do is run.

I race for where the outer wall used to be, but now it is just open space, and jump. I may break a few bones, but it's the only escape.

But instead of falling down, a strong gust of wind picks me up and sucks me back into the belly of the house. I'm thrown through the flames and dropped onto the foyer floor.

My back lands hard on the marble tiles. I groan from the pain that shoots up my spine, but when my eyes open, I see the fire climbing on the ceiling.

And then it comes crumbling down.

I roll, barely making it out of the way as the rafters crash onto the floor. The heat surrounds me, reminding me that now there is truly no escape.

And Nessa, or whatever she is now, is coming for me.

Then I won't run. I don't know what power I have left to fight her with, but I will stand my ground. Looking up, I steel my resolve and move to my feet.

Nessa floats over the railing, her hair spread out around her as if she is underwater, and she descends down to me. "Time to finish what we started," Keres's voice comes out of Nessa. The spider talisman glows, clawing into her chest.

I glare at her, balling my hands into fists.

"Wee hen…foolish cairline…"

"I'm not a cairline anymore," I remind her firmly. "And I won't give you any more of my blood."

She snickers, and it echoes through the building, becoming

one with the crackling fire. "Then I'll have to take it from you." I brace myself for her attack, determined to fight back until my last breath.

Just as she starts for me, the glass behind the staircase shatters, and Callen soars through the window.

Keres spins sharply as Callen lands on the ground. In his hand, he grips the knife with its faint glow. She hisses, and another rafter from the ceiling falls, smashing the stairs and splintering into flames.

Embers fill the air.

"How fortunate. I'll get to kill both of you. Again." Keres throws out her arms, and tendrils of black smoke spill out of her.

But Callen catches my gaze, a spark of confidence in his eyes, despite the heat, despite the demon that stands between us. If we are to die, I will do it at his side.

At the same time, we rush forward, resolved to reach each other, despite the demon floating in our way. She twists, shocked by the attack, then she starts to laugh, claiming her victory.

Callen tosses the knife in the air, the blade glinting in the light of the flames. By some miracle, I catch the hilt, just as her tendrils sink into my back, paralyzing my muscles.

Keres's head arches toward the ceiling, basking in her power. It was a power I never controlled; it was always I who was the slave.

"Caitrin…" Callen whispers, pulling my focus back to him. He's too far away; Keres is keeping us apart. Sweat drips down his forehead. His eyes dip toward my hand.

I see the glow. Faint but alive, my white markings gleam like the sun through a storm. I tighten my fingers around the knife, and, with one burst of energy, one flash of light, I drive the blade into Keres's chest.

It sinks into the talisman, shattering the black stone into a million pieces of dust, and then the blade buries itself in flesh. A shriek explodes from Keres, fading into Nessa's own voice screaming and crying out in pain.

Leaving the knife in her chest, I release the hilt and Nessa collapses to the ground.

Another rafter falls, and Callen tackles me out of the way. The flames blur Nessa's face, but her eyes have regained their normal color. And I see the grimace of fear mark her features as the flames rise higher around her.

"Hold tight," Callen says in my ear.

"I won't let go," I answer him as we turn to face the disintegrating front doors.

Together, we sprint forward and jump.

FIFTY-NINE

THE AIR IS FRESH AND cool, still wet from the rain.

We land hard on the dirt. Seconds later, the flames devour the building whole, and the manor crumbles into ash. Callen's hand still holds firmly to mine. He lays on the ground next to me, looking weary and battle-worn, but he is smiling. Laughing.

We're alive.

I join in his laughter, and for a moment, that is all that exists. Us and the joy of being alive.

"Well, you did what you came here to do, you ruffians!" Muireall shouts, and for the first time, the sound is comforting.

Callen and I both move to our feet, and he puts an arm around my shoulders, keeping me close as the mob surrounds us, eyes wide and staring blankly at the manor. Mr. Baines looks equally terrified, melting in with the crowd instead of standing out from them as their leader.

Muireall stands tall with her hands on her hips, like a teacher scolding her pupils, gray ashes and dirt smudges covering her black mourning gown. "Well, are you happy?"

Mr. Baines steps out from the crowd, his hands clenched in fists at his sides. "But…the cairline… If she is alive, then the curse still has a hold on this town."

Do they think I was Keres? That I was that monster they heard inside the manor?

"I'm not bonded anymore," I say, showing them my arms. The mob stirs with gasps and whispers. "And the cairline who has cursed this town"—I catch Mr. Baines' gaze. He swallows, trying to gain back his confidence as he stares at me. But then his courage fails and he looks away—"is dead. You'll find anyone who was infected has been cured."

A few take off from the crowd, racing for the main road, no doubt to see if my claims are true. Or eager and optimistic that their loved ones have been saved from the brink of death. I smile at the thought and raise my head with pride.

"And I am marrying Caitrin."

Mr. Baines' gaze shoots up to glare at Callen. His face burns red, but he knows he can't stop us now.

"And I will evoke the teasairginn, taking the name of Raeburn and reclaiming the lands of her former husband."

"You can't do that!" Knox says, bursting forth from the back of the mob where he had been hiding. "Those lands rightfully belong to us!"

"According to tradition, they can be bought back. Reclaimed by any man willing to give up his own name for a lost bloodline. Like the Raeburns." Callen smirks, his eyes narrowing in challenge. "Unless you would like to oppose me, Mr. Baines. Take the honor for yourself?"

Baines snorts, his nose wrinkling up at the idea, but he shrinks back against the crowd.

"Pa, he can't—!"

"Just stop jabbering, Knox!"

Callen takes my hand in his, beaming as he stands taller. "Now, perhaps you all would like to stop terrorizing poor banntrach Muireall Raeburn, whose home now lays in ash and fire, thanks to your kind efforts." Rather than dripping with sarcasm, there is an air of amusement in his voice. "For far too long the people of Soarsa have neglected to care for each other."

"Yes, water! Get water from the pond!" Brodie shouts, rallying the mob to more constructive work.

"And someone get some fresh clothes for these women," Una says with her usual spite and confidence as she looks pointedly at Paisley. Paisley's face is pale, her brows furrowed in confusion and shaking free of the frenzy. "Go on!" Paisley twitches and rushes down the pathway, although I have no idea if she is running away from Una or running to fulfill the command.

I turn toward Callen. "You saved me twice in one day. Are you tired of all the trouble I cause yet?"

He brushes hair out of my face and behind my ear. "No, my love. I'd save you a thousand times from a thousand evils and I would never tire of rescuing you." Callen presses his lips against my forehead. I wrap my arms around his waist and sink into his embrace. I feel safe. And in his arms, I feel strong.

"Caitrin..." Muireall's voice is careful, almost hesitant. I open my eyes to see her staring at me, her jaw quivering and her eyes wet with tears. She presses her lips together to stop her shaking.

Pulling away from Callen, I reach out to her, and she takes my hand. "I know, Muireall. I'm sorry, too."

SIXTY

"IT'S OFFICIAL."

Callen holds up the letter as the wagon pulls up to the mansion. A new wooden sign has been anchored into the flowerbeds under the front windows, and a woman sits in front of it, a palette of paints beside her. A wide-brim white hat covers her head and shoulders.

Muireall pulls Ailbert to a halt with a sigh and glances behind her into the wagon. There are no bags or belongings. Nothing survived the fire. Instead, there is a lone crate with three urns that had been left in the cottage.

"What's official?" I ask as I hop down from the wagon. Callen takes my hand and threads our fingers together.

"I'm officially a Raeburn."

"Good green earth, I think I've finally lost my mind!" Muireall says as she climbs down from the wagon and hobbles over grumpily to stand beside me. She barely agreed to accept Callen's invitation for us to stay at the Lockhart Estate until the cottage was properly fixed up. Even she couldn't argue that it was a little disconcerting to stay on the Raeburn property, especially since, even after a few days, the embers of Raeburn Manor are still hot.

There is a lot she still can't say, but I've noticed the small changes. The squeeze at my elbow. The hint of a smile. A kindness behind her eyes. One day, she'll be able to say more.

"Let me see that."

Callen jumps when Muireall snatches the paper from him, reading every word critically.

Her rapt attention gives us the illusion of privacy, and Callen leans close to me, nuzzling my ear with his nose. "And I have another gift for you."

I roll my eyes as a laugh escapes me. "Will you ever run out of gifts for me, Callen?" I look up at him just as he pecks me on the lips. I lean toward him, the kiss far too brief.

"Everything I have is yours." He leans toward me.

"This is…" Muireall gasps. Callen's smile grows wider, winking at me before turning his attention back to Muireall. "So this is…" She looks up at the mansion, then spinning to take in the fields.

"It all belongs to the Raeburn family." Ardala rises from in front of the sign, moving to reveal the swirling, artful words she has painted: *Raeburn Estate*. "Our home is your home now." Her light blue gown swishes inches from the paint palette, a soft smile on her lips. She is a direct contrast to Muireall, who is dressed in her usual black mourning clothes.

"Lewis Baines didn't even put up a fight for the fields. It's the least he could do, and he knows it," Callen adds. "Which makes me Lord *Raeburn*, now. Well, after we're formally wed."

"There will be enough time for that later." Muireall waves a hand in the air. While this was *almost* exactly what she hoped would happen, I think she still feels a bit uncomfortable having to accept so much help. "Which room is mine?"

"Right this way, Muireall," Ardala says, her voice a bit unsettled.

"Meara," Muireall says, a declaration, but her voice cracks. "I think I'll go by Meara again now." The widows share a glance, and I don't know what goes unsaid between them when Ardala simply nods and leads Muireall…Meara into the house.

"And that's when I rode up on a horse, like a true hero in those storybooks, and I said, 'you stop terrorizing these banntraichean!'"

Brodie comes out from around the corner of the mansion, surrounded by women. On one arm is Yvaine, a basket filled with carrots in her hands. On the other arm is Shona, wearing a dress I made of light pink. And just behind them, Una helps her grandmother, Vaila, who is still recovering.

I lean my head against Callen's shoulder, watching them. Content. Safe.

"That is *not* what happened," Una says with a snort.

"Well, it's pretty close! And I did catch Mrs. Raeburn when she jumped from the window."

"Did Meara really jump?" Yvaine asks, gasping at the outrageousness of the notion.

"Are your baskets plenty full?" Callen asks, pulling them from the story.

Una lifts Vaila's basket as high as she can manage. "A little too full if you ask me. They're just two old banntraichean! What do you do with all this food every week?"

"We eat it!" Vaila says, grabbing the basket from Una forcefully.

Brodie releases Yvaine from his arm, lazily walking over with Shona to Callen and I. "Fine morning to you both," he says with a cheesy grin.

"I don't suppose I'll be seeing you in my workshop again, now that all this belongs to you." Shona smiles politely, looking up at the mansion. "I was just getting used to your company."

My mouth opens but words escape me. Do I want to keep working? I certainly want to keep sewing.

Now that all this belongs to you.

I hadn't thought of it that way. Just Callen. That was all I wanted. I never even considered his estate or his money.

I'm not some potato-digger, after all.

"Would you want to keep working at the shop?" Callen asks, and I look up at him, an amused grin on his lips.

"Shona needs more friends," Brodie whispers harshly, and Shona blushes. "She's been talking to the buttons!"

"Now you shush," Shona says, nudging him as hard as she can. Which is barely hard enough to knock over a piece of paper. "The help was greatly appreciated, but I understand if you don't care to do such tedious work."

I shake my head as warmth fills my heart and spills out in a smile on my face. "As much as I love makin' things for myself, makin' clothing for friends is much more rewardin'. And I'd probably run out of closet space eventually!"

"I don't know about that…" Brodie says. "Have you seen some of the closets in there?"

"Not one!" I exclaim with a laugh. The others join in, perhaps out of politeness or maybe the joy, more than the joke, is contagious.

"Well, I think a grand tour is in order!" Brodie loops his arm back around Shona's and marches through the open front door. "This is the grand foyer. That statue is actually of Callen's great-great-great…"

I start after him, but Callen grabs my hand, pulling me back to him. "I have a better idea," he whispers, nodding to the apple orchid. With a playful kiss on my nose, he leads me toward the trees under the clear, blue sky.

EPILOGUE

Green and yellow streamers hang over the orchard, swaying in the breeze, leftover from the celebration. White petals lay scattered in the grass and caught up into the leaves of the trees. The apples have long fallen away and new green leaves fill the branches, warmed by the sunlight.

A flower crown sits on my head, white hyacinth and rosebuds woven together with ribbons that tie and trail down over my hair. The light cream fabric of my dress flutters around my body, and though the last chill of winter lingers in the air, my arms are bare, proudly displaying the white markings, boasting of my redemption.

I wrap my arms around Callen's neck, pulling him close. His hands settle on my waist as our foreheads press together.

"I never get tired of looking into those green eyes of yours."

Callen laughs, pulling back. "Never?" He scrunches up his nose with an incredulous glare. "What about now?"

Playfully rolling my eyes, I kiss his nose, instantly restoring his expression to one of pure joy. "Even then."

"Well, I will never grow tired of you," he whispers, brushing my hair behind my ear and giving me a peck on the lips. But it's not enough—it never is—and I lean into him for a more passionate kiss.

"There they are!" Meara shouts, her voice full of life like I've never known. In fact, the women in town sometimes gossip that Meara must have had a spell done to reverse her age years back. But it is no magic that has given Meara the will to live again. It is love.

Callen leans forward for another kiss, but I playfully give him my cheek, turning my attention to my mother-in-law and her shadow.

"Did you have a good birthday picnic, Gilly?" I call out, bending low and spreading out my arms.

My son crashes into my embrace. Barely three years old, he is as rolly-polly as ever. I hug him and lift him up into the air. He giggles, falling against me with a hug that uses every ounce of his strength, and then I settle him on my hip.

"Oh yes, Gildas ate almost all of the pie and cookies I baked for him. And we fed the rest to the ducks in the pond," Meara answers, proud of her spoils. Even though Meara and Gilly aren't biologically related, their bond is stronger than blood. No one would ever doubt that Meara was truly his grandmother if they didn't know better.

Callen kisses Gilly's temple, and the boy squirms and twists, reaching for his father. "Oh, I see who's your favorite!" I say, handing my son off. "He's my favorite too," I whisper before letting go. Callen tosses Gilly into the air, and our son erupts in absurd laughter at the rush.

"Again! Higher!" Gildas demands, and Callen is happy to indulge. After a few throws, Callen begins spinning so that Gilly's limbs stick straight out, and the child screams with delight.

Meara places a hand on my arm, smiling, eyes bright. Changed.

Running from Callen playfully, Gilly runs straight into Meara's pink skirts, wrapping his arms around her legs and giggling as he tries to hide in the folds.

Breathing deep to recover from the burst of spent energy, Callen comes to my side once more and puts an arm around my waist. "And the cottage is holding up just fine?" Callen asks Meara, raising an eyebrow.

Meara waves away his comment. "Yes, of course! Plenty room for me, and a wee one now and then," she says, swooping Gildas up into her arms. Callen has adamantly offered more than once to rebuild the Raeburn manor, but Meara has always rejected the idea.

Even though she had finally begun to accept the death of her husband and sons after the manor burned to the ground, it wasn't until Gilly came that she let go of the bitterness as well. And the letting go made room for love in her heart again, for our relationship to not only heal, but grow.

And we both had more than our fair share of apologies to make.

Bruised by my broken relationship with Nessa, I had heaped expectations upon Meara that she could never fulfill, especially while she was still grieving so much loss. I thought if I loved Meara well, she owed me love in return. But I don't think either of us really knew how to love in the beginning.

People aren't born knowing how to love right. In fact, I think people are born knowing only how to love wrong. I knew only how to love conditionally, selfishly, so eager to take my love back when it wasn't returned as I desired.

The kind of love that is forever, complete and perfect, is a love that must be learned, felt, experienced. A love given when I was undeserving. A love that sacrificed everything to be shown. And when I finally learned love, I was able to live love.

My legacy will not be one of bricks and briars, but of love learned and lived.

Knowing that you were ransomed from the futile ways
inherited from your forefathers, not with perishable things such
as silver or gold, but with the precious blood of Christ, like
that of a lamb without blemish or spot.

1 PETER 1:18-19

For those still searching to be fully loved
there is nothing you need to do
except receive the free gift—
Love has a name;
His name is Jesus.

DISCUSSION QUESTIONS

1. Read the book of Ruth in the Bible. Comparing the original story of Ruth to *A Bond of Briars*, identify corresponding characters or plot points and note the differences. Read Matthew 1:1-6 to identify Ardala.

2. Which character in *A Bond of Briars* did you relate to the most and why?

3. What does Caitrin think of her bond and Keres at the start of the story, and how does her opinion change by the end? What characters or experiences helped shift her perspective?

4. When Caitrin arrives in Soarsa, people tend to react to her with fear, hatred, curiosity, or compassion, because she is a bonded cairline. If you were a citizen of Soarsa, how would you have treated Caitrin? When you meet people with sordid pasts, how do you usually react?

5. Caitrin has only known conditional love from her mother and Meara/Muireall until she meets Callen. Read 1 Corinthians 13. What do you think are the differences between conditional love and unconditional love? Who is someone who loves you unconditionally?

6. When Caitrin feels like she isn't being shown kindness in return, she stops caring for Meara/Muireall. Do you find it difficult to love and serve those who don't reciprocate? What do you think are healthy boundaries to have when loving someone difficult?

7. Meara/Muireall asks, "Is it gossip if it's the truth?" and Caitrin responds, "Yes, most certainly, if its main goal is selfish superiority or some other twisted purpose." Do you agree with Caitrin's response? What advice would you have given Caitrin in this situation?

8. The "threshing floor" scene between Ruth & Boaz is highly debated, especially concerning the intentions of Naomi's instructions for Ruth (as explored in this book). Have you ever been asked to do something that felt wrong by a person you trusted? What did you do in that situation? What advice would you have given Caitrin?

9. The last line in *A Bond of Briars* is "My legacy will not be one of bricks and briars, but of love learned and lived." What do you think this means? What kind of legacy do you want to be remembered for?

10. This book ends with 1 Peter 1:18-19. How you do you think verse relate to Caitrin and Callen's story?

ACKNOWLEDGEMENTS

As you have just turned the last page, so have I, and it is with tears in my eyes that I say thank you for trusting me enough to open this book. Ruth is a beloved Bible story, one full of romance and sacrifice, and, while I certainly put my own twist on it, I hope you see yourself in these pages. Whatever is in your past, whoever you have hurt or who has hurt you, you are not unlovable.

Thank you, always, to my husband, Jeremy. Truly, I am no romance writer but even after ten years of marriage, he continues to demonstrate daily true unconditionally love for me.

Thank you to my family—Miskiewiczs, Phillips, Lawlers, and Cotnoirs. It is no small blessing to be surrounded by a family of believers on both sides, and I am forever grateful for your support.

Thank you especially to Andrea "Millie" Phillips, who is not only a fantastic mother-in-law (you can rest assured, Meara/Muireall is a stark contrast to my Millie!) but also my wonderful copyeditor who always makes my words shine.

A huge thank you to Alissa Zavalianos, my kindred spirit, soul sister, dear friend who also proofread this story! Thank you for being there for every struggle and celebration, as well as your endorsement of this story.

A special thank you to my endorsers— —who have given me such courage with this story, and especially to Caroline George, for your check-ins and encouragements, helping me to believe in myself and reminding me to rest in Christ.

Thank you to my amazing alpha readers—Robin Degan and Anna Augustine—who were the first to take this story for a spin when it was barely held together with duct tape and gum. You saw the potential in this story and gave me so much direction and encouragement from the beginning.

Thank you for my lovely beta readers, who helped me find all the plot holes and missing pieces and polish this story up into something beautiful: Tiffany Goldman, Kayla Jones, Allison Dininger, Valerie Cotnoir—my wonderful cousin and writing buddy—and extra love for Renae Powers, who became my beautiful sounding board in the final edits to let me know that the changes were working!

Huge Shout out to my Crownlings! You all are an unparalleled force and such an enormous encouragement to me in the months leading up to release day. Thank you for your prayers and support in helping me get the word out about this book!

And at the end of it all, there is only one that I can never say enough about and yet words fall short every time—Thank you to Jesus, my savior, my Sgaoileadh, my redeemer, for giving every drop of your blood on the cross so that my sins could be made white as snow.

And He did it for you too.

ABOUT THE AUTHOR

Erin Phillips believes that story teaches our hearts to believe, and tries to fill every second with stories, whether it's an audiobook while cleaning, a movie with her hubs, or just snuggling up with a good book. She is not afraid of a dark story, as long as there is also hope.

Besides writing novels, Erin also writes and publishes Christian musicals with her husband at The Faithful Troubadour Publications. She graduated from the University of North Carolina School of the Arts with a B.F.A. in Costume Design & Technology, and lives in North Carolina with her husband, Jeremy, and their happy corgis, Parker and Fable.

If you enjoyed this book, please do this indie author a favor and leave a review on Goodreads.com or Amazon! For more info about Erin Phillips, visit erin-phillips.com, or follow her on Instagram @erinphillipsauthor.

Made in United States
Troutdale, OR
06/07/2024

20402142R00246